SEANAN McGUIRE

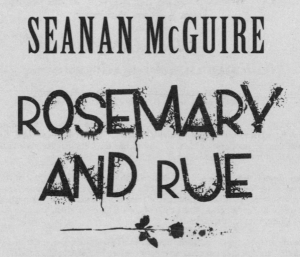

ROSEMARY AND RUE

AN OCTOBER DAYE NOVEL

DAW BOOKS, INC.

DONALD A. WOLLHEIM, FOUNDER

375 Hudson Street, New York, NY 10014

ELIZABETH R. WOLLHEIM
SHEILA E. GILBERT
PUBLISHERS

www.dawbooks.com

First Printing, September 2009
8   9

"Make sure they don't win."

"October? October, are you there? October, this is Evening." There was a long pause. I heard her take a wavering, unsteady breath. "Oh, root and branch . . . October, please pick up your phone. I need you to answer your phone *right now*." It was like she thought she could order me to be home. There was no telling how much time had passed between messages, but it had been enough for the worry to stop hiding and come out to the surface of her voice, obvious and raw. The only other time I'd heard that much emotion in her voice was when her sister died. This wasn't sorrow. This was sheer and simple terror.

"Please, please, October, pick up the phone, please, I'm running out of time . . ." The message cut off abruptly, but not abruptly enough to hide the sound of her crying.

"Oak and yarrow, Eve," I whispered. "What did you get yourself into?"

I thought I wanted an answer. And I was wrong, because the last message answered me more completely than I could have dreamed.

The speakers crackled, once, before her voice began to speak for the final time.

"October Daye, I wish to hire you." The fear was still there, but the command and power that was her nature shone clearly through it, brilliant and terrible. She was looking at the end of everything, and it was enough to remind her of who she really was. "By my word and at my command, you will investigate a murder, and you will force justice back into this kingdom. You *will* do this thing." There was a long pause. I was starting to think the message had ended when she continued, softly, "Find out who did it, Toby, please. Make sure they don't win. If you were ever my friend, Toby, please. . . "

**DAW Books presents the finest in urban fantasy
from Seanan McGuire:**

InCryptid Novels:

DISCOUNT ARMAGEDDON

MIDNIGHT BLUE-LIGHT SPECIAL

HALF-OFF RAGNAROK

POCKET APOCALYPSE*

SPARROW HILL ROAD

October Daye Novels:

ROSEMARY AND RUE

A LOCAL HABITATION

AN ARTIFICIAL NIGHT

LATE ECLIPSES

ONE SALT SEA

ASHES OF HONOR

CHIMES AT MIDNIGHT

THE WINTER LONG

*Coming soon from DAW Books

For my mother, Mary Mickaleen McGuire,
who never made me stop reading.

ACKNOWLEDGMENTS

There were a lot of people involved in making this book come together. Huge, huge thanks to my crack team of machete-wielding proofreaders, whose tireless efforts took care of a lot of bad grammar and more than a few misplaced commas; without them, I would make a lot less sense. My agent, Diana Fox, knew exactly what to ask for, and my editor, Sheila Gilbert, knew exactly how to make me answer. Here at home, Chris Mangum and Tara O'Shea organized my Web site, while Kate Secor and Michelle Dockrey organized everything else.

Finally, thanks to Rebecca Newman and Amanda Weinstein for logging countless telephone hours dealing with the details, and to Tanya Huff, for assistance above and beyond the call of duty. The errors in this book are mine. There would be a lot more of them without all the people who helped me get it done.

PRONUNCIATION GUIDE

Bannick: *ban-nick*. Plural is Bannicks.

Banshee: *ban-shee*. Plural is Banshees.

Cait Sidhe: *kay-th shee*. Plural is Cait Sidhe.

Candela: *can-dee-la*. Plural is Candela.

Coblynau: *cob-lee-now*. Plural is Coblynau.

Daoine Sidhe: *doon-ya shee*. Plural is Daoine Sidhe, diminutive is Daoine.

Djinn: *jin*. Plural is Djinn.

Glastig: *glass-tig*. Plural is Glastigs.

Gwragen: *guh-war-a-gen*. Plural is Gwargen.

Kelpie: *kel-pee*. Plural is Kelpies.

Kitsune: *kit-soon*. Plural is Kitsune.

Lamia: *lay-me-a*. Plural is Lamia.

The Luidaeg: *the lou-sha-k*. No plural exists.

Manticore: *man-tee-core*. Plural is Manticores.

Nixie: *nix-ee*. Plural is Nixen.

Peri: *pear-ee*. Plural is Peri.

Piskie: *piss-key*. Plural is Piskies.

Pixie: *pix-ee*. Plural is Pixies.

Puca: *puh-ca*. Plural is Pucas.

Roane: *ro-an*. Plural is Roane.

Selkie: *sell-key*. Plural is Selkies.

Silene: *sigh-lean*. Plural is Silene.

Tuatha de Dannan: *tootha day danan*. Plural is Tuatha de Dannan, diminutive is Tuatha.

Tylwyth Teg: *till-with teeg*. Plural is Tylwyth Teg, diminutive is Tylwyth.

Undine: *un-deen*. Plural is Undine.

Will o' Wisp: *will-oh wisp*. Plural is Will o' Wisps.

PROLOGUE

June 9, 1995

THE PHONE WAS RINGING. Again.

I turned my attention from the rearview mirror and glared at the cellular phone that lay jangling in my passenger seat next to a bag of Fritos and one of Gilly's coloring books. It had been less than ten minutes since the last time it rang, and since there were only three people who had the number, I was pretty sure I knew who it was. I'd only had the damn thing for a month, and it was already complicating my life.

"These things will never catch on," I muttered, hitting the flashing call button. "Toby Daye Investigations, Toby Daye speaking, what is it now, Cliff?"

There was a long, embarrassed pause before my live-in fiancé asked, "How did you know it was me?"

"Because the only other people who use this number are Uncle Sylvester and Ms. Winters, and they know I'm on a stakeout, which means they're not calling." I've never been good at being mad at Cliff; the words might be irritated, but the tone was purely affectionate. Call me a sucker for a man with a great ass who knows how to bake a macaroni casserole and can tolerate six hours of *Sesame Street* a day. Shifting the phone to my left hand, I reached up and adjusted the mirror to keep the front of the restaurant in view. "What is it this time?"

"Gilly wanted me to call and tell you she loves you and hopes you'll be home in time for dinner, and that you should bring back ice cream. Chocolate would be best."

I suppressed a smile. "She's watching you make the call, isn't she?"

"You better believe it. If she wasn't, I would've just called Information. But you know how she gets. She's got ears like a rabbit." Cliff chuckled. Our affection for each other didn't come close to our love for that little girl. "That's from your side of the family, you know."

"Most good things are, but yes, she gets her hearing from me," I said, fiddling with the mirror. Was that a figure or a fingerprint? I couldn't tell. The man I was following was so far out of my league that he could be strolling naked down an otherwise empty street and still keep me from seeing him.

Abandoning my efforts to make the mirror behave, I pulled a spray bottle full of greenish water out of the glove compartment and liberally misted the glass. Call it experience or call it intuition, but I know a good don't-look-here spell when I fail to see it. A very good don't-look-here spell, if I had to break it with a marsh water charm. That's the sort of trick the purebloods disdain as being practically beneath the *humans*.

Beggars can't be choosers, and it didn't matter if the charm was cheap, because it worked; as soon as the water hit the mirror, the reflection of a tall redheaded man snapped into focus, standing just in front of the restaurant I'd been staking out for the last six hours. A valet pulled up in a sleek-lined sports car painted that particular shade of red peculiar to expensive vehicles and hookers' lipstick.

The valet could see him, yet I hadn't been able to: he was only blocking himself against fae eyes. He knew he was being trailed.

"Damn," I whispered and dropped the bottle. "Cliff, the guy I'm after just came out of the restaurant. I gotta go. Tell Gilly I love her, and that I promise I'll stop for ice cream on my way home."

"You don't love me?" he asked, mock wounded.

"I love you more than fairy tales," I said—a ritual phrase that had long since replaced "good-bye" for us— and hung up the phone, throwing it into the backseat. It was time to get to work.

The man tipped the valet, got into the car, and pulled away from the curb, merging into passing traffic. His snazzy red sports car stood out among the more worka-day vehicles like a cardinal in a flock of pigeons ... at least until he took the first corner and disappeared, leav-ing the reek of smoke and rotten oranges in his wake. The smell of magic can cut across almost anything else, and since every caster has their own magical "taste," it also serves as a signature of sorts. The scent confirmed that I was following Simon Torquill and not some paid double. Which was good to know, except for the part where I'd lost the man.

Swearing, I grabbed the pot of faerie ointment off the seat beside me and smeared it around my eyes until it started running down my cheeks. The car reappeared ahead of me in a hazy outline, like I was seeing it through water. "Won't be losing you again, you asshole," I mut-tered and pressed down on the gas.

Don't-look-here spells are trickier than true invisibility;

Simon's car was still there, and the drivers around him avoided it automatically, making him safer from traffic accidents than he would have been without the enchantment. People—mortal people—saw him; they just didn't acknowledge it. At the same time, anyone with a drop of fae blood couldn't see him without outside assistance. It was a nice piece of work. I might have admired it, if it hadn't been interfering with my job.

It was almost unfair. My own abilities barely extend to a few charms and parlor tricks, while the man in front of me was causing an entire city of humans to act like he wasn't even there. That's Faerie's genetic lottery for you. If you're a pureblood, you get it all, but if you're a changeling, well, I hope you have good luck with that.

Simon turned the wrong way down a one-way street, taking advantage of the semi-invisibility I didn't share. Swearing again, I hauled my own car into a hard left, beginning a pacing maneuver along the next block. As long as I didn't hit any traffic lights, I'd be able to catch him at the other end. I wasn't going to let my liege down. Not today, not ever. I'm not that girl.

Luck was with me, along with a working knowledge of the San Francisco streets. Simon's car shot back into view a quarter block up ahead. I eased off the gas, dropping back several cars to keep from rousing his suspicions. I needed Simon as relaxed as possible. There might be lives riding on it. Two lives, to be specific: the wife and the daughter of my liege lord, Duke Sylvester Torquill, twin brother of the man I was following. They had vanished without a trace three days ago, from the middle of Sylvester's lands, where the security was so tight that nothing could have touched them. But something had, and all signs pointed to Simon.

Even if Sylvester hadn't been my liege, I would've taken the case because of the people involved. Duchess

Luna was one of the sweetest, most egalitarian women I'd ever known. And then there was their daughter: Rayseline Acantha Torquill, also known as Raysel. As the presumptive heir to one of the largest Duchies in the Kingdom of the Mists, she could easily have grown up more spoiled than any human princess. Instead, she grew into the sort of little girl who's always up a tree or down a hole, a magnet for mud, queen of worms and frogs and crawling things. She laughed like she'd just invented laughter. She had her father's signal-fire red hair. And damn it, she had the right to grow up.

Simon sped up. I did the same.

As far as Cliff knew, I was working a standard abduction case, just another deadbeat dad who took off with the kid when he got the wrong end of the stick during divorce proceedings. My work for the Courts had been dwindling since Gilly was born, but it was still there, and I'd had a lot of practice hiding it. Maintaining a business as a private investigator made it easier. I could explain almost anything by saying that I had to work, and a lot of the time, it was the truth. It's just that sometimes my cases were more Brothers Grimm than *Magnum PI*.

You don't get knighted for nothing; it's a title you earn, either through long service or by having a set of skills that someone really wants to have at their disposal. I've always had a talent for finding what I need to know, and when that came to Sylvester's attention, he grabbed me, saying there were worse things than having a detective on the payroll. I go out, I find out what's going on, and I let the knights who earned their titles in battle take over. I'm not stupid; I don't engage. What I am is good at what I do.

One trace turned into two turned into two dozen, all pointing straight to Simon Torquill. He was renting a room in downtown San Francisco, paying cash on a daily basis. It was located on the Queen's land, even, with no local regent or fiefdom to confuse the issue. Maybe that should have been a sign that something was wrong; after all, Simon was supposed to be a big mover and shaker in the local fae underworld. He should have known how to cover his tracks. I didn't even think about it. I was too fixated on bringing Luna and Rayseline home.

Simon's car switched lanes, moving toward Golden Gate Park. I followed. I'd been tailing Simon for three days, and if I hadn't known better, I would've thought I was chasing a dead end. But a woman and a little girl were missing, and we didn't have any other leads.

Finding a parking place in Golden Gate Park is never easy, but luck still seemed to be with me, because Simon pulled into a handicapped spot—the first actual crime I'd seen him commit—and I managed to snake in behind a departing minivan, cutting off three families that had probably been circling for an hour. I kept my eyes on Simon, ignoring the rude gestures being directed toward me.

The don't-look-here dissolved when Simon emerged from his car, brushing imagined dirt off his pristine suit. Giving the area a disinterested glance, he started toward the Botanical Gardens. I stayed in my car long enough to give him a reasonable head start, then followed.

Simon strolled through the gardens like a man with nothing to hide, even going so far as to pause and admire the ornamental lake, watching the swans that floated on the water like merchant ships on a quiet sea. Just when I was ready to back off to better cover, he started to move again, heading out of the garden and across the plaza. I followed to the end of the path, waiting to see what his destination would be.

He was heading for the Japanese Tea Gardens. I hesitated.

Golden Gate Park is carved into dozens of tiny fiefdoms—some no bigger than a single tree—and their boundaries are rigidly enforced. The Tea Gardens are held by an old friend of the family, an Undine named Lily. I could count on her for backup if I needed it, and there's never been any love lost between her and the nobility. Maybe more important, there's only one exit. Simon could get in, but he couldn't get out.

That was the problem. Simon Torquill had always struck me as an arrogant jerk, and a lot of people were willing to say that he was evil, but he'd never seemed particularly stupid. He had to know Sylvester suspected him of kidnapping Luna and Rayseline and what would happen to him if his brother's suspicions proved to be true. So why was he walking into a dead end?

If this were any normal case, this was the point where I'd have backed off. I'm not an idiot, and I don't have a death wish. But this wasn't a normal case. My friend and liege was crying alone in his hollow hill over a woman I'd known and respected my entire life, and a little girl who braided dandelions in her hair was missing. There was no way I could walk away, not when this might be my only shot at finding them.

I backed into the shadows of the bushes, kneeling to run my fingers through the damp grass. My own magic rose around me, the taste of copper and cut grass hanging in the air until the spell caught hold with an almost audible click. A bolt of pain shot through my temples. Changeling magic has limits, and those limits make themselves clear when you try to go too far. I'd mixed a marsh water charm, spun a human disguise, and now I was casting a don't-look-here on myself. Put it all together, and it spelled "too far."

The pain was worth it for the safety of going unseen. I reminded myself of that as I straightened, wincing, wiped my fingers on the leg of my jeans, and followed Simon into the Tea Gardens.

The spell worked well enough that the girl at the fare booth looked right through me as I passed. The tourists aiming cameras at the bonsai and traditional Japanese sculpture did the same. I suppressed a shiver. I had stepped out of the human world entirely, and unless I took the spell down, they'd never know I'd been there.

The paths inside the Tea Gardens were narrow enough that keeping Simon in sight meant following more closely. I shortened the gap between us, trusting my elementary illusions to hide me. The more powerful someone is, the less time they spend looking for small magic. Changeling games are the most primitive of all. I was betting Simon would overlook me completely, because my illusions were too small to be a threat.

Simon walked on for a good twenty minutes before stopping at the base of the arched moon bridge that was the gateway to the fae side of Lily's domain. I fell back, stepping behind a stunted Japanese maple. I couldn't risk moving any closer; that would be pushing it, illusions or no. I'd just have to wait. He seemed to be waiting, too, hands in his pockets as he gazed across the water, the perfect picture of a tourist admiring our city. I forced myself to stay alert, waiting for him to act.

"Simon!" called a laughing female voice. He turned, suddenly smiling. I mirrored the gesture, looking toward the source of the voice, and froze.

She looked like just another teenage girl, dressed in skintight clothes, black hair unbound and hanging past her hips. I knew better. I knew her name. Oleander de Merelands: nine hundred years of nasty wrapped up in a pretty little package that could pass for sixteen in any mortal setting. She's half Tuatha de Dannan, half Peri, and entirely hazardous to your health. The Peri have always been a race that enjoys causing pain, but they aren't social—avoid them and they'll avoid you. The Tuatha, on the other hand, enjoy the company of others. Oleander got her fondness for hurting people from the Peri side of the family, and her willingness to seek them out from the Tuatha. Rumor puts her at the sites of half the assassinations in the last hundred years and there are rewards on her head in half the kingdoms I can name. The other half just haven't gotten around to it yet.

"It's wonderful to see you, my dear." Simon folded her into his arms and delivered a kiss that made several passing tourists blush and look away, embarrassed by what they perceived as a pervert with his jailbait girlfriend. If only they knew. The Torquill brothers are barely five hundred years old; if anyone was cradle robbing, it wasn't Simon. I put a hand over my mouth, appalled for reasons that had nothing to do with anyone's age. There had always been rumors, but no one had ever been able to prove a direct connection between Simon and the fae underworld. Seeing him with Oleander changed everything.

I had to get to Sylvester. I had to tell him. I started backing up, getting ready to run.

"This is getting dull, darling," Oleander informed Simon, pouting in a way that would have been pretty if it hadn't been for the malice behind it. "Finish it?"

"Of course, sweetheart." He raised his head, looking past the tree I was crouching behind and right into my eyes. "You can come out now. We're ready."

"Oh, oak and ash," I hissed, and scrambled backward—or tried to. That was the order I gave to my legs, which were suddenly not obeying my commands. I staggered into the open, dropping to my knees. I tried to stand. I couldn't. I couldn't do anything but wait.

Lily, where are *you?* I thought desperately. She was the Lady of the Tea Gardens; this was her fiefdom and her domain. She should have been there by now, rallying her handmaids and running to my rescue, but she was nowhere to be seen. There weren't even any pixies in the trees. The mortal tourists looked at us the way they would have looked at air. I had never in my life been so afraid, or so alone.

Simon's smile was almost warm as he knelt, placing one hand beneath my chin and raising it until our eyes were level. I tried to struggle, to find some way to look away from him, but couldn't force myself to move.

"Hello, my dear," he said. "Did you enjoy our little walk?"

"Go . . . to . . . hell," I managed through gritted teeth.

Oleander laughed. "Oh, she's a sassy one." Her expression darkened, mood shifting in a heartbeat. "Make her pay for that."

"Of course." Leaning forward, Simon pressed a kiss against my forehead and whispered, "I'll make sure someone finds your car in a week or two, once they're ready to give up hope. Wouldn't do to make your family wait for you too long, now, would it?"

If I could have, I would have screamed. All I could do was snarl behind clenched teeth, breath coming hard and fast as panic gripped me. I had to get out of there. Cliff and Gilly were waiting for me, and I had to get away. I just couldn't see how. I couldn't even drop the don't-look-here that was guaranteeing no one would see what was happening. I was bound too tightly.

Simon stood, putting his hand on top of my head and shoving downward, whispering and moving his free hand in a gesture I couldn't quite see. I made one

last wrenching attempt to pull away. Oleander laughed
again, the sound cold and somehow distant, like it was
being filtered through a wall of ice. Without any warning
or fanfare, I forgot how to breathe.

All magic hurts. Transformation hurts more than
anything else in the world. I gasped for breath, trying
to break out of Simon's enchantment. My own meager
powers were giving way, and I felt myself warping and
changing, melting like a candle left too long in the sun.
His binding relaxed as the change entered its final stages,
and I flopped against the path, gills straining for another
breath, for anything to keep me alive for just a few more
seconds. My eyes were burning so that I could barely
focus, but I could still see Simon, right at the edge of my
vision. He was smiling, and Oleander was laughing. They
were proud of what they were doing to me. Oberon help
me, they were *proud*.

"Hey!" shouted a voice. "What are you people doing?"
Then there were strong hands underneath me, boosting
me off the wood, down into the water. I dove, driving
myself deep into the water, away from the air, from the
fear, from my own existence. The instincts of my new
body took me into the cool darkness under the reeds
while I was still trying to make my head stop spinning. All of the other koi watched with disinterest, and
promptly forgot that I hadn't always been there. Fish are
like that.

All fish are like that, and thanks to Simon, I was one
of them. I managed to force myself back to the surface once, frantically looking for help, and not finding
it. Simon and Oleander were gone. I was disposed of,
as good as dead, and they didn't need to worry about
me anymore. The fish I had become was taking me over,
like ink spreading through paper, and as it pulled me
down, nothing really mattered. Not Sylvester and Luna,

not Cliff, waiting forever for me to come home. Not my name, or my face, or who I really was. Not even my little girl. There was only the water, and the blessed darkness that was my home now, the only one I'd know for four-teen years.

ONE

December 23, 2009: fourteen years, six months later

There's fennel for you, and columbines;
There's rue for you, and here's some for me. . . .
You must wear your rue with a difference.
—William Shakespeare, *Hamlet*

DECEMBER HAD COME to San Francisco in fits and starts, like a visitor who wasn't sure he wanted to stay. The skies were blue one minute and overcast the next; tourists overheated or shivered in their prepacked wardrobes, while residents traded sweaters for tank tops and back in a single afternoon. That's normal around here. The Bay Area exists in a state of nearly constant spring, where the color of the hills—brown with a strong chance of brushfire in the summer, green and suffering from chronic mudslides in winter—is the only real difference between the seasons.

It was half past six in the morning, and the Safeway grocery store on Mission Street—never much of a happening nightspot, no matter how you wanted to slice it—was virtually deserted. The usual rush of drunks and club kiddies had passed through several hours before, and now all we had was an assortment of early risers, grave-shift workers, and homeless people looking for a warm place to spend the tail end of the night. By silent, mutual agreement, the homeless and I ignored each other. As long as I didn't admit I could see them, I wouldn't need to ask them to leave, and we both got to avoid the hassle.

I'm getting good at ignoring things I don't want to see. Call it an acquired skill. It's definitely one I've been working on.

"Paper or plastic, ma'am?" I asked, not bothering to conceal the weariness in my tone. Half an hour and my shift would be over, leaving me with just enough time to get home before the sun came up.

"Plastic's fine, honey," said the woman occupying my lane. Running a hand through oily black curls, she gestured toward my name tag. "Is that really the name your parents gave you?"

Plastering a smile across my face, I began bagging her groceries with the automated ease that comes with long practice. "It is." She was buying six pints of gourmet ice cream and a twelve-pack of Diet Coke. I've seen stranger.

"Hippies, huh?"

No; a faerie woman and her Irish accountant husband. But that was impossible to explain, and so I simply nodded. "Got it in one. That'll be eighteen fifty-three."

She swiped her Visa with a grunt, barely waiting for the machine to catch up before she was grabbing her groceries and heading for the door. "You have a good night, honey."

"You, too, ma'am," I called. Grabbing her receipt off the register, I held it up. "You forgot your—"

Too late; she was gone. I crumpled the receipt and dropped it into my trash can, leaning against the divider separating my lane from the next. She could come in later and complain to my manager about not getting a receipt, if she felt like it. With my luck, she'd feel like it, and I'd wind up with another black mark on my record. Exactly what I didn't need. This was my third job since I won free of the pond; the first two were abject failures, largely thanks to my limited working hours, general lack of cultural awareness, and incomplete understanding of modern technology. Who would've believed that it could take so much computer know-how to be the night clerk at a 7-Eleven? Not me, that's for sure, until my inability to reboot the register got me fired. Checking groceries on the graveyard shift might not have been my last chance, but it sure felt like it. At least at Safeway, there was a manager to fix things when they broke.

My fellow employees were nowhere to be seen. Probably hiding in the stockroom again, smoking Juan's reportedly excellent marijuana and trusting me to hold the front of the store. I didn't mind. I didn't take a job as a check-out girl because I wanted to make friends; I did it because I wanted to be left alone.

A flock of pixies was circling the display produce near the side door, flitting in wide circles as their sentries watched for signs of danger. Dressed in scraps of cloth and bits of discarded paper and armed with toothpicks and sandwich-spears, they looked ready to go to war over a few grapes and an overripe pear. I braced my elbows on the conveyor belt and dropped my chin into my hands, watching them. I don't care much for pixies as a rule. They're pretty but savage, and they'll attack if you provoke them. Maybe that doesn't sound like much of a threat, considering that the average pixie is about four inches tall and weighs three ounces soaking wet.

They're like mice with wings and thumbs, except for the part where mice don't usually come armed with knives carved from broken beer bottles and homemade spears that may have been dipped in equally homemade poisons. At the same time, I had to admire the way they'd adapted. They had an entire community thriving inside this downtown grocery store, and nobody knew about it but me.

Me, and the members of San Francisco's fae community who chose to shop here. I'd chosen this store specifically because it was so far away from the likely haunts of the people I'd known in my other life. I hadn't considered the fact that some of them might come looking for me.

"Is this lane open?"

The voice was gruff, familiar, and more than enough to shake me out of my reverie. I jerked back, one arm going out to the side abruptly enough to knock my chin against the conveyor. Vainly trying to recover a shred of my dignity, I forbade myself to rub it as I straightened up, pasted on a smile, and turned toward the source of the voice, replying, "Yes, sir. Just put your groceries on the belt."

The man at the end of my lane stared at me, concern evident in his expression. "Root and branch, Toby, didn't that hurt?"

I forced my smile to stay in place. It wasn't easy. Through my teeth, I said, "I'll put some ice on it later. Can I have your groceries, sir?"

The man sighed, beginning to unload his cart. "Are we still doing this? I really hoped we'd be done by now. You sure you don't want to be done? I can wait around. You can come home with me after your shift. I'm off for the night, and Stacy would love to see you. She'd even make pancakes if I called and told her you were coming . . ."

I didn't answer him, busying myself instead with running his groceries across the scanner. I'd been doing the job long enough that it didn't require any concentration to take care of such a simple task. That was a good thing, because he didn't take my lack of answer as a reason to shut up; he kept rambling, trying to catch my interest as I focused on ringing and bagging his groceries.

Once upon a time—not my favorite phrase by a long shot—I let myself admit that the man now standing in front of my register had a name. Mitch Brown. We were kids together in the Summerlands, the last of the fae countries, the place that exists on the other side of every mirror and beyond every unpierced veil of mist. We were both changelings, mixing human blood with stranger things; Nixie and Hob in his case, Daoine Sidhe in mine. We were about the same age, and both of us were struggling to figure out who we could be, living in a world that was nothing like the one we'd started out in. It was natural that we'd latch onto one another, and to the other changelings who came our way—Kerry, half Hob, half airhead; Julie, half Cait Sidhe, all trouble; and Stacy, weak-blooded Stacy, my best friend and his eventual wife.

"That'll be twenty-six fifteen," I said, looking up.

Mitch sighed, brushing colorless blond hair back from his forehead. "Toby . . ."

"Cash or charge, sir?"

Mitch paused before sighing again and pulling out his wallet. "You can't do this forever, you know," he said, as he handed the money across to me.

"Three eighty-five is your change," I replied, putting it down on the divider between us. "Thank you for shopping at Safeway."

"You have the number," he said, taking the change

and shoving it into his pocket without looking. "Call when you're ready. Please. Call us."

Then he was gone, walking toward the exit with broad shoulders clenched tight and grocery bags dwarfed by the size of his hands. Hobs are usually tiny people, but in Mitch's case, his human heritage won out: he could give your average Bridge Troll a complex. Stacy's barely five foot three. I've never understood how the two of them worked things out, but they must have done it somehow, because they had one kid before I vanished and four more while I was gone. I didn't want to know that. Mitch told me, just like he insisted on telling me everything else I didn't want to know. He was trying to pull me back into my life while all I wanted to do was run away from it.

Their eldest, Cassandra, is almost the same age as Gillian.

That thought was enough to send my mood crashing even further down. I closed out my register with quick, automatic gestures, counting out the cash drawer and locking it down before anyone else could try to get through my lane. Not that there was much to worry about—the front of the store was deserted except for me and the pixies—but I didn't care. I needed out.

Three of my fellow employees were in the break room, settled around the coffeepot like vultures around a dying steer. They barely looked up when I came storming in, yanking my apron off over my head and throwing it over the hook with my name on it. Retail: where everybody makes fun of your name.

"Something wrong, October?" That was Pete, the night manager. He always tried to sound compassionate and caring when he was talking to his underlings; mostly, he just managed to sound bored.

"Female troubles," I said, turning around to face him.

He took an automatic step backward. "I know my shift doesn't end for fifteen minutes, but tomorrow's my day off, and I didn't take a break tonight. Can I—"

"Go home. I'll clock you out." His gruffness barely concealed his dismay. He was clearly afraid that if I stuck around, I'd start giving him details.

It's best not to question good fortune. I kicked off my uniform shoes and shoved them into my locker before grabbing out my coat and sneakers, pulling them roughly on, and taking off for the door without giving Pete a chance to change his mind. Three long steps past my disinterested coworkers and I was free, charging out into the freezing cold of the alley behind the store. The door slammed shut behind me, and everything was reduced to a pale, watery gray lit by the distant glow of streetlights.

The fog had rolled in since my shift started, making it impossible to see more than a few feet in any direction. I shoved my hands into my pockets, shivering. When it decides to get cold in San Francisco, it doesn't mess around. As a little added bonus, I could feel the moisture already beading on my hair and skin. My shoes and the cuffs of my pants would be soaked through long before I made it home.

"Whee," I muttered, and turned to start for the mouth of the alley. Once I was on the street, I could begin the long, mostly uphill walk home. If I'd stayed to the end of my shift, I would've taken the bus, but the encounter with Mitch had left me shaken, and the walk would do me good.

The chill dropped away as I began climbing the first hill between me and my destination, exertion providing the warmth I so desperately needed. I glanced at my watch. If the almanac at the supermarket was correct, we were about thirty-three minutes to dawn. It was enough time, if I didn't slow down, stop, trip, or do anything but walk. The dawn destroys small enchantments, and that includes everything I'm strong enough to cast—like the illusion that allows me to pass for human. Worse, it's incapacitating, at least temporarily. If I was in the open when the sun came up, I could find myself with a starring role in a tabloid before noon. Still, there was time, as long as nothing got in the way.

The street curved as it moved up the hill, taking me through the slowly paling morning. I kept my hands in my pockets and kept walking, trying to focus on getting home, trying not to think about Mitch going home to his family, or about much of anything else. All thinking did was make me remember what I'd already lost.

Everything was quiet, save for the distant rumble of traffic on the freeway. Shivering, I walked a little faster, heading down a side street into a neighborhood that smelled like rotten fruit and sweet decay. A black horse stood by the curb in the deepest part of the shadow, the smell of debris masking its characteristic blood-and-seaweed scent. Its eyes were red, and the look it gave me was inviting, promising wild adventures and fantastic delights if I'd just get onto its back. I waved it off with one hand, walking on. Only an idiot would trust a Kelpie this close to the water. Getting on its back with the scent of the sea in the air would be a fast, painful means of committing suicide, and I'm not a fan of pain.

The Kelpie took a few steps forward, eyes glowing. Hard as I'd been trying to deny the existence of Faerie, ignoring the threat wouldn't make it go away. I sighed and stopped, folding my arms. "Are you sure you want to do this?"

It continued to advance.

Right. A more direct approach was needed. Unfolding my arms, I shoved my hair back and dropped the illusion hiding the shape of my ears. Careful to keep the exhaustion out of my voice, I asked, "*Really* sure?"

Kelpies are smarter than horses, and they recognize a threat when they see one. I'm just a changeling, sure, but I was apparently willing to face down a Kelpie, alone, on a foggy night, within spitting distance of the water. It couldn't count on my willingness being based on bravado. It took a step backward, baring an impressive array of fangs.

"Just keep going," I said. That seemed to be the last straw. The Kelpie snorted, as if to say that there was bound to be easier prey somewhere else in the city, and took another step back, outline fading into the fog until it might as well not have existed. Camouflage is the hunter's first and best defense. I stood there for several minutes, waiting for it to reappear, before slipping my hands back into my pockets and starting to walk again, a little faster now. Maybe the Kelpie was gone, but there was nothing stopping it from coming back with friends. More than one would be more than I could bluff.

Seeing Kelpies on the streets of San Francisco is annoying and a little unnerving, but it's nothing to worry about. They have illusions to hide them when they need to be hidden, and even I can handle a Kelpie—they bite if you get too close, but they're not that dangerous if you just refuse to ride them. There's nothing wrong with having a few monsters in the shadows. They keep me remembering what it is that I'm walking away from.

My name does the same thing, and that's why I've never changed it to something more normal. My mother was what she was, and I am what she made me, and she thought "October" was a perfectly normal name for a little girl, even one born in 1952 at the height of human conservatism. If that little girl's last name happened to be "Daye," well, that was all the better! She was a loon, even then, and I miss her.

The sky was getting lighter; my encounter with the Kelpie had slowed me down enough to take me into dangerous territory. I started to walk a little faster. Getting caught outside at dawn won't kill me—sunrise is painful, not fatal—but dawn also means a massive increase in the human population, and the last thing I needed was someone deciding I needed medical aid while my illusions were off. I look closer to human than a lot of changelings do, but "close" doesn't cut it on the streets of a human city.

The streetlights above me flickered and went out, giving a final warning of morning's approach. Time was up. Hiking up the collar of my coat for a little more cover, I started to run. Not that it was going to do much good; I was still blocks from my apartment, and the light was moving a lot faster than I was. There was no way I was going to make it.

A narrow alley stretched between two buildings about half a block ahead. Forcing one last burst of speed, I raced to the alley's mouth and ducked inside, moving as far back as I could before the growing pressure of the dawn forced me to stop and slump against the wall. I could feel it spread across the city, ripping down all the small illusions and minor enchantments of the night. Then the light hit the alley, turning my slump into a collapse, and I stopped thinking about anything more complicated than taking my next breath.

There's nothing kind about the way sunrise affects the fae. Just to make it even less fair, it's harder on changelings than it is on purebloods, because we have fewer defenses. The light didn't quite burn, but it came close, filling the air around me with the ashy taint of dying magic. I kept my eyes closed, forcing myself to take slow, measured breaths as I counted down the moments between the dawn and the day.

When the pressure of the dawn passed enough to let me move again, I straightened, taking a shaky breath, and moved deeper into the alley. The aftereffects of sunrise last for five minutes—ten at the most—but most spells just won't take during that time. That's part of why it's so dangerous to be outside at dawn. The threat of discovery is always there, and it's not a good idea to take chances.

It helps that humans don't believe in faeries anymore. Not even the people who say that they do. Oh, sure, they may believe in cartoon sprites and sexless fantasy creatures, but they don't believe in the real thing. There are reasons for that, and some of them are even good ones, but there are also the reasons they believed in the first place. Dawn is one of those reasons. It pulls down our illusions, making us too easy to see and too hard to deny; after all, even the most stubborn humans will usually believe their own eyes. All it takes is one moment of carelessness on the part of the faerie world, just one, and after that . . .

After that comes the iron and the silver and the rowan wood, and the mass graves on both sides, and the burning. In the end, it always comes down to the burning, and that's a risk I've never been willing to take. I may be playing at being human, but that doesn't make me stupid.

People were starting to pass on the sidewalk outside the alley. Humans have always preferred to live their lives by daylight. I used to think it was because human beings have crappy night vision, and it wasn't until I got older and more cynical that I realized it was because they have less to be afraid of during the day. Illusions don't last as long in broad daylight. The monsters can't find as many places to hide, and all Faerie's lies get easier to catch and define. You can be human and still be safe, during the day.

Something rustled behind me, and I tensed. I wasn't alone.

"Great."

First I got caught outside at dawn, and now I was sharing an alley with somebody who could see me for what I really was. If this day got any better, I was going to scream.

I turned, hiking my coat up around my chin. Anyone who looked closely would be able to see that something wasn't right, but the alley was dark and narrow, and frankly, the sort of person you meet in dark alleyways at dawn is looking for things besides pointed ears. "Hello?" I peered into the shadows.

Two green circles flashed in the dark. I yelped, jumping backward and pressing myself against the wall.

"And may I wish a very good morning to you, too, October." The voice was amused, underscored by a chuckle like thick cream. "What happened? Did the prettiest little princess miss her carriage home?"

"Tybalt," I said, surprise dissolving into disgust. I straightened. "Don't sneak up on me like that."

The shadows parted, flowing around the man who stepped through them into the alley. They slid together again once he was through, closing seamlessly. I've always wished I could do that—but then, Tybalt's pure-blooded Cait Sidhe, and he can do a lot of things I can't. He smirked. I glared.

I'm not short, but Tybalt's about six inches taller, giving him just enough height to look down on me when the fancy takes him. He's got the sort of sleek, muscled build that only comes from a few specific types of exercise programs. For most men, that would mean yoga or running. In Tybalt's case, it means bloody control of the local Court of Cats. He became their King by right of blood; he's held the position by beating the crap out of anyone who tries to take it away. The Cait Sidhe take a more direct and violent approach to succession than most of Faerie.

Even in the dim light of the alley, I could pick out the darker bands of brown that streaked his short-cropped, slightly tousled hair, mimicking a tabby's coat. His eyes were narrowed, but I knew that if I could see them, they'd be green, split by cat-slit pupils. Add all that to skin like ivory and the sort of face that winds up on magazine covers, and it's no wonder that Tybalt's looks get him a long way with a lot of people. Not with me. That doesn't mean I haven't noticed them—the man is basically walking sex appeal—but I'm not dumb enough to do anything more than look. Even when I was inter-acting with Faerie of my own free will, I only looked when I was sure he couldn't see me. Some games are too dangerous to play.

"But you're so *easy* to sneak up on." He crossed his arms, leaning back against the wall. "You should be hon-ored that I bother, since there's no challenge to it."

"Right," I said, dryly.

Tybalt has never made a secret of his contempt for changelings in general and me in particular. Not even the fourteen years I spent missing and presumed dead could change that. If anything, it made things worse, because when I came back, I promptly removed myself from all the places he was accustomed to finding me. Hating me suddenly took effort—an effort he's proved annoyingly glad to make. On the other hand, it's actu-ally been something of a relief, because it's something I can count on. Dawn comes, the moon wanes, and Tybalt hates me.

His smile broadened, displaying the tips of oversized canines. "Maybe I should make it a hobby. That might give you something to look forward to."

"You could get yourself hurt that way."

If the threat bothered him, he didn't show it. He just smirked. "Is that so?"

His words were mild, but there was a warning underneath them, telling me that if I pressed things further, it was at my own peril. It's moments like these when I think he's not the King of Cats just because he's so tied to his subjects, but also because of the way he plays with people. And I, of course, had put myself into the perfect position to be a plaything, since I couldn't exactly claim the protection of my liege lord while I was denying all of Faerie.

"Probably not," I admitted, as calmly as I could. I didn't need to get myself hurt just because I was being jumpy. "I just don't like it when people sneak up on me." Past experience told me he could smell my fear; it also told me that the anger accompanying it would pretty much cover the scent. It's good to know how to compensate for your own weaknesses.

"I do adore the costume. What are you these days, a maidservant? A charwoman in one of these glass towers?" Tybalt tilted his head to the side, studying me. "The trousers fail to flatter, but the blouse is sufficiently gauzy."

"Ha, ha," I said, pulling my coat closed and folding my arms over my chest. I was blushing, much as I didn't want to be. Bastard.

"Really, if you'd just do something with your hair, perhaps you could take a few steps up the social ladder. I understand that there are things called 'scissors' these days, very advanced, they allow you to—please don't be alarmed, I promise it's painless—*shorten* and even out the strands. It's far more flattering."

I reddened further. "Did I miss the announcement that today was 'mock Toby' day?"

"Don't be silly. That's every day. But if you'd like a new topic, we can talk about something else. For example, what brings you out at such an unpleasant hour? Did you feel the need for a little company and come to watch the sunrise from the privacy of my alley, hoping I'd show up?" He put a subtle stress on the possessive, watching me with a territorial air that was more intimate than I liked. He didn't like me, and he never had, but that didn't mean he couldn't take a certain perverse glee in watching me squirm.

"I got caught out, Tybalt. I'm only here until I can hide myself and go home." I had every right to be where I was, and he knew it. Rules are rules, and this one came straight from Oberon: it doesn't matter whose territory you're in, you can hide from the dawn. "And this isn't your alley any more than it's mine. You should be in the park." The Court of Cats is hard to find or pin down, so officially it's part of the myriad fiefdoms of Golden Gate Park. That was probably part of why he was taunting me—I'd caught him out just as much as he'd caught me.

Tybalt's answering smile was thin. He wasn't happy that I'd called him on that one. I spared a moment to consider the wisdom of pissing him off while we were stuck together in an alley and shrugged. It was too late to take it back. "I go where the urge takes me, October; you should know that by now. All places are alike to me, and today I wanted to check on my little fish. To see where she was . . . *swimming*."

The last word was almost a whisper, all smooth edges and insinuation. I stiffened, hands clenching as fury cut through my fear like turpentine through oil paint. "That was uncalled for."

"If you can't take the heat, maybe you should go

back to the pond." His tone was triumphant. He knew he'd managed to get to me, and at that point, I didn't really care. All I cared about was shutting him up and forcing the memories back into the hole where they belonged.

"Tybalt," I said, and paused to choose my words with care. The sunrise lull was ending: I could feel the potential for magic creeping back into my blood, almost unwillingly. "I'm going to pretend you didn't say that, and I'm going to leave now. You're not going to follow me. Understand?"

"Running away already?"

"I'm walking away before I do something we'd both regret." Reaching out, I grabbed a handful of shadows from the alley wall, molding them between my hands as I ordered them to hide me. Illusions have always come easier when I'm angry—I don't know why, because nothing else works that way. Still, sometimes it seems like I can only craft a really good disguise when I'm so mad I can't see straight.

Tybalt didn't bother to look away as I blunted the tips of my ears and glossed over my eyes with a veneer of human blue. My hair and skin could be left alone, which was a good thing; there are too many steps involved in a stable disguise, and none of them are simple ones. Thanks to my father's blood, I look almost entirely human. Someone seeing me with my masks off might think I had an unusually fine bone structure, or that there was something wrong with my eyes, but they'd be unlikely to think "fairy-tale creature walking the streets of San Francisco." Thanks to my mother's conditioning, I'm basically incapable of taking the risk.

It was a good five minutes before I shook the clinging shadows from my hands and let them drop, resisting the near uncontrollable urge to pant. The smell of copper hung heavy in the air.

"Good job!" said Tybalt, applauding. I glared. He grinned, displaying his fangs. "I could almost believe that you were really a trained monkey and not just the worse half of one."

"Stick a cork in it, Tybalt. I'm out of here." The traffic outside was getting more urgent as the city woke. "You should do the same."

"Should I? Good-bye, then; open roads, kind fires, and all winds to guide you." He laughed, seeming to fold inward. There was a popping noise as a rush of warm air that smelled of musk and fresh pennyroyal blew over me, leaving a brown tabby-patterned tomcat where Tybalt had been. If I hadn't known better, I'd have said he was smiling.

All Cait Sidhe are drama queens and jerks as far as I'm concerned. Tybalt's never seemed interested in proving me wrong.

"Good idea," I said. "You go your way, and I'll go mine."

The cat winked and stood, slinking over to rub up against my ankles. I lashed out with one foot, aiming a kick at his middle, but he dodged effortlessly and bounded away, tail held high. Shaking my head, I watched him blend into the shadows at the rear of the alley. "Damn cat," I muttered, and left the alleyway for the street and the rest of my long walk home.

TWO

THE FOG HAD BURNED away with the dawn, and I walked the rest of the way through a city with no illusions at all. There weren't any fairy tales in the streets around me. If there was ever a Cinderella, her glass slippers shattered under her weight and she limped home bleeding from the ball.

My apartment isn't in the best neighborhood, but it suits my needs. The roof doesn't leak, the managers aren't nosy, and my rent includes a spot in the attached parking garage, where my car languishes day in and day out, thanks to the lack of employee parking at the Safeway. I punched in my code at the side gate, unlocking it, before following the narrow outdoor path to my building. I'm in one of the ground-floor units that actually has an outside door. There are neighbors above and to my left, but there's nothing to my right but walkway and grass. I like having at least the illusion of privacy.

That illusion didn't last either. There was a teenage boy slouching in my doorframe, hands jammed into his pockets, every inch of him radiating discontent. The shimmer of magic around him was visible even half-way down the path, tagging him as fae. The air tasted like steel and heather; the illusion that made him seem human had been cast recently, and on my doorstep. He'd been there since before dawn.

I hesitated. I could ignore him and hope he'd let me into my apartment without a scene. I could go to the Starbucks down the street, nurse a coffee, and hope he'd go away. Or I could get rid of him.

Never let it be said that I'd chosen the easy way out or shown a fondness for uninvited visitors. Narrowing my eyes, I stalked down the path toward him. "Can I help you?"

He jumped, turning toward me. "I . . . what?"

"Help you. Can I help you? Because you're between me and my apartment, and I was hoping to get some sleep today." I folded my arms, scowling.

He squirmed. Judging by body language alone, he was actually the age he appeared to be, putting him somewhere in his mid-teens. His hair was dandelion-fluff blond, and his eyes were very blue. He'd probably have been beating the girls off with a stick if he hadn't been dressed like he was about to ask me if I'd accepted Jesus Christ as my personal savior. Any kid dressed that formally and standing on my porch at dawn had to be on some sort of official business, and that just made me scowl deeper. I prefer to avoid official business. All it ever does is get people hurt.

"I . . ." he stammered. Then he seemed to remember himself and straightened, puffing out his chest in the self-important manner that seems to be endemic to pages everywhere. "Do I have the privilege of addressing the Lady Daye?" He had a very faint accent. Whoever he answered to now, he'd started life somewhere in or near Toronto.

"No," I snapped, pushing past him to the door. The red threads that store my warding charms were still taped above the doorframe, almost invisible in the early morning light. Dawn damages wards, but it usually takes three or four days to destroy them completely. I dug for my keys. "You have the 'privilege' of annoying the crap out of Toby Daye, who isn't interested in your titles, or whatever it is you're selling. Go away, kid, you're bothering me."

"So you *are* the Lady Daye?"

Eyes on the door, I said, "It was Sir Daye, when it was anything at all."

"I'm here on behalf of Duke Sylvester Torquill of Shadowed Hills, protector of—"

I turned to cut him off before he could launch into a full recitation of Sylvester's titles and protectorates. Holding up my hand, I hissed, "This is a human neighborhood! I don't know what you think you're doing here, and frankly, I don't care. You can take your message and your on-behalf-of back to Shadowed Hills, and tell Sylvester I'm still not interested. All right?"

The kid blinked, looking like he had no idea what he was supposed to say. My reactions didn't fit inside his courtier's view of the world. I had a title, one that had clearly been awarded to me for merit, rather than out of courtesy, if I was insisting on the use of "sir" over "lady." Changelings with titles are rare enough to be conversation pieces, and changelings with titles they actually earned are even rarer; as far as I know, I'm the only changeling to be knighted in the last hundred years. I had a liege, and not an inconsequential or powerless one at that. So why was I refusing a message from him? I should have been turning cartwheels of joy just to be remembered, not blowing off a Duke.

"Perhaps you misunderstand . . ." he began, with the

sort of exaggerated care that implied he was speaking to a child or a crazy person. "I have a message from Duke Torquill, which he has tasked me to—"

"Sweet Lady Maeve protect me from idiots," I muttered, turning back to the door and jamming my key into the lock. The wards glared an angry red. "I know who your message is from. I just don't care. Tell Sylvester . . . tell him anything you want. I got out of that life, I quit that game, and I'm not listening to anymore messages."

I waved my free hand and the glare died, replaced by the grass-and-copper smell of my magic. Good. No one had broken in. Someone who didn't have the key could open the door without breaking the wards, but not without voiding the spell woven into them, and even a master couldn't replicate the flavor of my magic that exactly. I couldn't mistake one of Tybalt's spells for one of Sylvester's anymore than I could mistake sunset for dawn. That's the true value in wards; not keeping things out, but telling you if something's managed to get *in*.

"But—"

"But nothing. Go home. There's nothing for you here." I shoved the door open and stepped inside.

"The Duke—"

"Won't blame you for failing to deliver this message. Trust me on this one." I paused, suddenly tired, and turned in the doorway to face him. He looked very lost. It was almost enough to make me feel sorry for him. "How long have you been with Sylvester's court?"

"Almost a year," he said, confusion shifting into sudden wariness. I couldn't blame him for that. I hadn't been exactly pleasant.

"Almost a year," I echoed. "Right. That explains why you drew the short straw. Look: I *am* a knight in the service of His Grace. That's true. I can't make him release my fealty. But unless he gives me a direct order, I don't have to listen. Did he send you here with a direct order?" The kid shook his head, silent. "That's what I thought. Tell him I appreciate him thinking of me, and I'd appreciate it even more if he'd stop." Almost gently, I shut the door in his face.

The knocking started less than a minute later. I groaned. "Root and *branch,* don't some people know how to take a hint? I'm not interested!" The knocking continued.

Swearing under my breath, I shrugged out of my coat and threw it over the back of my battered, Goodwill-issue couch. It's the little touches that can make a house a home, right?

The knocking wasn't stopping. I glared at the door, considering telling him to go the hell away before I shook my head and moved farther into the apartment instead. Sylvester has a knack for inspiring loyalty. If he told the kid to deliver a message, the kid was going to do his damnedest to deliver it. It might have been easier to just open the door and let him say whatever it was Sylvester felt needed to be said, but the thing was I didn't want him to. As long as I didn't hear it, I didn't have to run the risk that I might care.

Sylvester started trying to contact me as soon as someone told him I was back. First it was with letters delivered by pixies and rose goblins. Then it was messages passed through mutual acquaintances. If he'd moved up to sending pages, he must be getting desperate, but I still didn't want to hear it. What did he have to say to me? "I'm sorry you screwed up this simple little thing I asked you to do and got yourself turned into a fish while I kept suffering alone?" "Maybe you didn't find my family, but hey, you lost yours, so I guess it all evened out?" Thanks, but no thanks. I can wallow in guilt just fine without any help from my titular liege lord.

One day, Sylvester's going to move up to ordering me to answer him, or worse, to come to Shadowed Hills and see him in person. When that happens, I won't be able to disobey—even if I'm trying to deny Faerie, he's my liege, and his word is law. Until then, I'm free to disregard his messengers as often as I like, and as often as I like is always. Let the kid hammer on my door until someone called security. I was going to get some sleep.

The cats were puddled on the couch in a tumbled heap of cream and chocolate. I walked past them, heading for the narrow hallway that connects the living room and kitchen to the back of the apartment where the bedrooms are. The hall lights have been burned out since I moved in, but that's not a problem; fae are essentially nocturnal, and even changelings see well in the dark. I left my shoes by the kitchen door and my shirt on the floor outside the extra bedroom. Keeping up a human disguise for the duration of a night's work was exhausting, and I needed to sleep.

My battered secondhand answering machine was on a low table just outside my bedroom door, dingy red display light flashing. I winced. It was probably another message from Stacy, inviting me to come over for dinner with the family, or out to coffee with her, or anywhere, just as long as I was willing to see her and let her make it better. I couldn't deal with it. Not after Mitch and his concerned looks, and Tybalt in the alley, and Sylvester sending a page to hammer on my door until I let him yell at me. Stacy could wait. Hell, if I was lucky, maybe the machine would malfunction again and wipe the tape before I got around to listening to it.

Silencing the phone's ringer with a flick of my finger, I walked into my bedroom and left the answering machine to flash at an empty hall. Almost as an afterthought, I closed the door.

I kicked off my jeans, taking my well-thumbed copy of the works of Shakespeare from the bedside table before crawling, otherwise dressed, into bed. My bookmark was set in the middle of *Hamlet*. The text was familiar enough to be soothing, and I fell asleep without noticing, sliding straight down into dreaming.

The dreams always start in the same place, and they always start so kindly, with a sunny kitchen in a little house in Oakland, California, and a smiling woman with white-blond hair baking cookies like a Donna Reed fantasy come true. My mother. Amandine.

I always knew she wasn't human; that's not the sort of thing you can hide from a kid. It took me longer to understand that I wasn't human either. They've called my mother's side of the family the Kindly Ones, guardians of the garden path, stealers of children . . . or in her case, before she met my father, assistant clerk at the local five-and-dime. Playing human teenager amused her, and I guess when you plan on living forever, you do whatever it takes to make the days pass. The arcane mechanisms of modern retail served well enough to keep her entertained for a while.

That was in 1950. They say the mortal world was simpler then, but it was complicated enough for her.

Daddy wasn't like her, and that drew Mother to him like a moth to a flame. She played faerie bride better than I did; she could weave an illusion in an instant, hiding pointed ears and colorless eyes behind a human smile before the people around her had time to blink. She never got caught out by the dawn or wound up shouting excuses from the bathroom while she tried to shove her "face" back into place. The fae are liars, every one of us, and she was the best. They met in 1951, married three months later, and had me in '52, in the month I was named after.

In the dream, she puts the cookies on the table and takes me in her lap, and we eat cookie dough while we watch the house clean itself, feather duster and broom and mop moving as smoothly as anything animated by Disney. Amandine was really my mother then; she grinned a chocolate smile as she held me, happy as anything with her weird little version of reality. She'd never played faerie bride before. The game enchanted her, and she followed its rules with the scrupulousness that was her hallmark. They were happy. We were happy. That's something I try to hang on to. We were happy once. She held me in her lap and brushed my hair; she taught me to love Shakespeare. We were a family. Nothing can change that.

My blood meant it was inevitably going to end.

Every changeling is different. Some, like me, are relatively weak. Others get a full measure of faerie magic—sometimes more than their pureblood parents—and they can't handle it. Those are the ones that get whispered about in the pureblood Courts, the ones no one names once the fires have been extinguished and the damages have been tallied. I learned the stories when I was little, first from Mom as she tucked me into bed, and later, after things changed, from the ones who came to get me. I don't know who was more relieved when we found out how weak my powers are—my mother or me.

Even weak changelings can be dangerous. They're allowed to stay with their human parents while they're young enough to keep their masks up instinctively, but that early control fades as they get older, and choices must be made. Some changelings have to make the Changeling's Choice as early as three; others hold out until their late teens. That was the only time in my life that I've been on the precocious end of the curve, because I was seven years old when my baby magic started to fail.

I don't know how they knew, and I don't know how they found us. I was in my room conducting a tea party for my stuffed animals, and they were suddenly there, stepping through a hole in my wall, beautiful and terrible and impossible to turn away from. Looking at them was like looking into the sun, but I did it anyway, until I thought I would go blind from looking.

One of them—a man with hair the color of fox fur and a long, friendly face—knelt in front of me, taking my hands. "Hello there," he said. "My name is Sylvester Torquill. I'm an old friend of your mother's."

"Hello," I said, as politely as I could through a mouthful of awe. "I'm October."

He laughed, unsteadily, and said, "October, is it? Well, October, I have a question for you. It's a *very* important question, so I need you to think hard before you answer. Can you do that for me?"

"I can try," I said, frowning. "Will you tell me if I answer wrong?"

"There are no wrong answers, October. Only right ones." The door—the real door—opened, and my mother stepped into the room. She froze when she saw Sylvester kneeling in front of me, holding my hands, but she didn't say a word. Tears started rolling down her cheeks. I'd never seen her cry before.

"Mommy!" I shouted, trying to pull my hands free, to run to her and stop those tears.

Sylvester tightened his grip. "October." I kept tugging. "October, look at me. You can go to your mother when you answer me." Sniffling and sullen, I stopped pulling and turned to face him. "Good girl. Now. Are you a human girl, October? Or are you fae?"

"I'm like Mommy, I'm just like Mommy," I said, and he let me go, and I ran to her. She put her arms around me, still crying, and she never said a word. Not when

Sylvester stepped up to kiss her cheek and whisper, "Amandine, I'm sorry," not when the ones who had accompanied him grabbed her by the shoulders and pulled her, and me, through the hole in the wall. It closed behind us, but not before I saw my bedroom burst into flames, wiping away the traces of our passing.

My human life was over the moment they found us; the only real question was whether I went to live with the fae, or whether I learned firsthand how cold immortal "kindness" can be. Changelings don't grow up in the human world. It simply isn't done. If I'd chosen to stay human, there would have been an accident, something simple, and my grieving mother could have stayed with her husband in the mortal world. Instead, I chose Faerie and condemned her to the Summerlands. That's when she stopped being the mother I knew: I couldn't fill the hole my father left in her heart, and so she never let me try.

Sometimes I wonder if the ones who choose to die aren't making the right decision. No one told me "changeling" could be an insult, or that it would mean living trapped between worlds, watching half your family die while the other half lived forever, leaving you behind. I had to find that out on my own.

I tried to fight free of the dreams, surfacing just far enough from the unsettling memory of my Changeling's Choice to actually believe I might be able to wake myself up. I could handle collapsing at work, I could go and talk to Sylvester's page, anything, I would have taken almost anything over the dreams of my childhood and the choice I didn't mean to make. Almost anything . . . except for what I got. I slid back into those golden-tinted dreams . . .

. . . and back into the pond.

I dream the fourteen years I lost to Simon's spell often, although there aren't many specifics; my memory of that time is a long blur of ripples through the water, and that's probably a mercy. A few things stand out, but not many: the first light of day coloring the water; humans walking by on narrow wooden pathways; frantically circling at the surface of the water twice a year, on the Moving Days, even though I didn't know why. I never saw any pixies on Moving Day, but I didn't understand what their absence meant. I didn't understand much of anything.

Even as a fish, dawn burned. I rose to the surface every morning, letting the light hit my scales, and for a moment, things would almost start to make sense. Part of me knew, however dimly, that something was wrong, and that part understood that dawn could free me, if I was patient. If I hadn't been able to hold onto the knowledge that something about that place, that world, that ... everything ... wasn't right, I might have stayed in the pond until I died. Maybe the sunrise helped, peeling the spell away one slow layer at a time until it broke. Maybe not. The odds are good I'll never know.

What I do know is that Simon's spell gave way just before dawn on June 11, 2009, exactly fourteen years and two days after it was cast. There was no warning. The spell didn't compel me to rise to the surface or lift me out of the water like some modern Venus on the half shell. It just let go, and I started to drown. I shoved myself away from the water, sobbing in helpless confusion and gasping for air. The spell had released my body but still held my mind, and I couldn't understand what was happening. The world was wrong. There were colors that shouldn't exist and everything I saw loomed straight ahead of me instead of being tucked properly to the sides. Acting on disoriented instinct, I stood, and promptly fell backward as my already shaky grasp on reality refused to admit that I had legs.

The sky paled while I huddled in the water. The cold eventually drove me to the land, and I somehow managed to stand without killing myself. I don't remember how I did it. I just found myself walking down the paths on half-frozen feet, totally alone. None of the normal denizens of the Tea Gardens were there—no pixies, no Will o' Wisps, nothing—but I was too confused for their absence to seem strange. That would come later, when I started understanding what had happened. A lot of things would come later. For the moment, I wandered at random, occasionally stumbling or stopping to cough up more water. I didn't know my name, or where I was, or what I was. I just knew that the pond had rejected me, and I had nowhere else to go. I couldn't remember any other life. What would happen to me now that I couldn't go home?

I was in a state of utter panic by the time I reached the gates, ready to bolt at the slightest provocation. And then the mirror that hangs next to the ticket booth caught my eyes by glittering, and held them with the image it contained.

It was a tired face, with the tips of dully pointed ears barely managing to poke through its frame of wet, shaggy brown hair. Her skin was pale from over a decade without sun, and her features were too sharp to be beautiful, although people called them "interesting" when they were being charitable. Her eyebrows were arched high, making her look perpetually surprised, and her eyes were a colorless foggy gray. I stared. I knew that face. I'd always known that face, because it was my own.

I stood there, still staring, as the sun finished rising and the dawn slammed into me, bringing the truth about who and what I was crashing down, along with the inevitable comprehension of what had happened. It was too much. I did the only thing I could to make the pain stop: I passed out.

Lily didn't appear during my slow stagger through her domain, but she must have been there, because when the maintenance man found me sprawled naked in front of the ticket booth with no identification or reason to be there, he saw nothing but a human woman who had been the victim of some brutal attack. He called the police, and they came, collected me, and carried me off to the station for questioning. I didn't fight them. Shock is a beautiful thing.

The police station looked pretty much like every other station I've ever seen: a little sad, a little overused, and seriously in need of a good steam cleaning. I didn't notice the computers on the desks or the dates on the calendars; I still wasn't used to being bipedal, and most of my attention was fixed on staying upright. The attending officer, a brisk, no-nonsense man named Paul Underwood, called for someone to clean the scrapes on my elbows, hands, and knees, and had them bring me some clothes. They were kind enough to let me dress alone in the bathroom; I guess having no possessions or pockets makes you seem less likely to be a dangerous criminal, and the various small injuries I'd picked up during my trek through the garden made them more inclined to believe me when I claimed to have been assaulted and left for dead. Being in a state of shock helped me ramble convincingly.

Now that I was starting to understand what Simon had done, I couldn't get past the fact that he'd actually turned me into a fish. My thoughts were chasing their tails like puppies, caught between fear and fury. I thought the worst was over. I had no idea that the worst was still to come, or just how bad that could be.

Officer Underwood fed me coffee and stale donuts

until I started making sense, and then he gave me papers to fill out—name, social security number, residence, place of employment—all the standard questions. He took them away when I was finished, presumably to be filed. Still standard procedure . . . at least until he came back ten minutes later with murder in his eyes.

"Just what are you trying to pull, lady?"

It was my name that did it. He knew it because he'd been assigned to the case when I disappeared; he spent a year turning over rocks, questioning witnesses, even dredging the big lake in Golden Gate Park looking for my body and finding nothing, and he didn't think it was very clever, or very funny, for me to be posing as a dead woman. He handed me a clean set of papers, ordering me to fill them out correctly, without any stupid jokes. I think that's when I started understanding just how much trouble I was in. Numbly, I turned the papers over, starting to fill them out, and the first correction came before I even got to my name.

"You've got the date wrong. It's June eleventh, two thousand and nine, not nineteen ninety-five. Christ, lady, pay attention."

My fingers tightened, snapping the pencil in half as I stared at the attending officer, eyes wide and uncomprehending. "How long?" I whispered.

"What?"

"How long did he leave me . . . oh, no. Oh, oak and ash, *no*." I closed my eyes, letting myself go limp as the enormity of it all struggled to sink in. Fourteen years. I'd been afraid the spell might have lasted weeks, maybe even months, but fourteen *years?* It was too much to wrap my mind around. But I didn't have a choice, and it just got worse from there.

Everything was gone. Every single thing I'd built or worked for in the mortal world . . . all gone. Cliff sold my business to cover my debts after my investigator's license expired; after *I* expired, since seven years on the missing list is the limit of a human existence. I've always found that slightly ironic—after all, seven years is also the traditional period of confinement for those humans who manage to find their way into the hollow hills. October Daye, rest in peace.

Thank Oberon for Evening Winterrose, known as Evelyn Winters in the mortal world. She was the only person I knew whose telephone number wouldn't have changed in the intervening years. I used my one phone call to beg her to come and get me. I expected her to yell, but she didn't. She just came to the station, confirmed that I was who I was claiming to be, and somehow convinced them to release me into her custody. Then she took me to a motel where I could get my head on straight. We both knew that taking me to her place wouldn't have helped, and so neither of us suggested it; I wasn't up for entering someone else's domain.

She stayed with me all day. She ordered pizza for dinner and scolded me into eating it; she hid the telephone book so I couldn't try to find Cliff; she summoned pages and sent them to notify the other local nobles of my return. And when the sun went down and I finally started crying, she took me in her arms, and she held me. I'll always remember that. Evening was never a nice person, but she held me as long as I needed her to, and she never said a word about my tears staining her silk blouse, or about the way I'd thrown her world into disarray. When push came to shove, she did what needed to be done, and she didn't refuse her own.

Things got a little better after that. The purebloods of the city were willing to help as much as they could, and the changelings were willing to help even more. My refusal to have much to do with them tied their hands a bit, but they did their best before they left me to my own devices. Evening offered to have my P.I. license reinstated. I refused. I've been down that road before, and it didn't do me a damn bit of good.

I think they told Mother I was back, but I'm not sure she understood. She doesn't understand much these days. She spends her time wandering the Summerlands, humming songs no one recognizes and rattling at doors no one else sees. In her own way, she's lost more time than I have.

Evening said not to contact Cliff until I was ready. I held out longer than I thought I could: I made it almost three days before I called him. I couldn't tell him where I'd been or what had happened—there's no real way to say "I was turned into a fish" to a man who thinks you're as human as he is—so I fell back on old clichés, saying I had amnesia due to being attacked by the man I'd been tailing, saying I didn't know what had happened. Our relationship was based on lies, and he must have known that, deep down. Maybe I shouldn't have been surprised when he hung up the phone, or when Gilly didn't want anything to do with me. They'd gone on without me, creating a life that had no room for a deadbeat who left them grieving for fourteen years. I couldn't explain why I went away, and so all we had was a silence that didn't allow for love. I keep calling. They keep refusing to talk to me.

That was June. I've done what I could to reassemble the trappings of a life, but nothing can bring back the years. The summers, the winters, the last hours with my mother before she slipped completely into her own private world, every precious minute with my little girl, they're gone for good, and I'll never get them back. Maybe that's why it was so easy to turn my back on Faerie. It's taken me away from the mortal world twice now. It doesn't get a third try.

Six months passed in a blur of despair, self-pity, and isolation. I didn't understand the world; I was as much an alien as my mother on the day she left the Summerlands for the first time. I called it my penance, I called it what I deserved, and I just kept going. The world was falling down around me, and I didn't care anymore.

That's where the dreams end: with the realization that it doesn't matter where I am, whether I think I'm a woman or a fish or something in-between. I've never really left the pond. I still can't breathe.

THREE

I WOKE UP JUST AFTER SUNDOWN with a pound-ing head and the vague, nagging feeling that something was wrong. Cagney and Lacey had somehow managed to open the bedroom door while I was sleeping and had migrated from the couch to the warmer and hence more desirable bed. They started to wail as soon as they real-ized I was awake, Siamese voices vibrating in my skull like buzz saws. I groaned, clapping my hands over my ears. "Can't you two be *quiet?*" They didn't oblige me. Cats never listen. They're dependable that way; when Rome burned, the emperor's cats still expected to be fed on time.

The fae have always lived with cats. They're the only mortal animals that can stand to have us around, and that holds true for all of us, even half-breeds like me. Dogs bark and horses shy away, but cats can look at Kings, and a lot of the time, they do. Cats put up with us, and in exchange, we treat them with respect, and we feed them. We're related in a way, and I don't just mean through the Cait Sidhe. We both tend toward pointed ears, stealing cream, and getting burned alive when the wind changes. It was only natural that we'd form an alliance where both sides said, "I don't need you," and both answered, "You'll still stay."

"All right, you win. I'll feed you. Happy?" I pushed Cagney off my chest. She jumped off the bed, joining Lacey on the floor, where the two of them continued to yowl as they made it clear that no, they wouldn't be happy until the food was *in* the dish. I rolled out of bed, retrieving my robe from the floor. The cats twined around my ankles, doing their best to trip me, and I pushed them ineffectively out of the way with my bare feet, heading for the door.

I got the cats so I wouldn't be so lonely. I was starting to reconsider that idea. Maybe lonely was a good thing. Lonely certainly got more sleep. In my blackest moods, I tried to tell myself the increased sleep was the one good thing about losing my mortal family; living with Cliff and Gilly forced me to pretend to be diurnal and left me with a coffee addiction that verges on the epic. I don't know how much caffeine it takes to kill a changeling, but I may someday find out.

The cats fell back once I reached the hallway, letting me walk unencumbered to the kitchen, where I filled their bowl with kibble. As they descended on their feast, I put a pot of coffee on to brew and made myself a quick nighttime breakfast of toast and scrambled eggs. Protein, carbohydrates, and best of all, cheap as hell. Combine minimum wage with the San Francisco housing market, and that sort of thing becomes an issue.

My food was still cooking when the cats finished theirs. Cagney wandered out into the living room while Lacey sat down in the middle of the kitchen floor and started to wash her paws, purring loudly.

"Laugh it up, brat," I said, eyeing the level of the still-brewing coffee as I waited none too patiently. "We'll see how much cat food you get after we've been kicked out for not paying the rent." None of my magic was strong enough to make the landlord believe I'd paid him. I'd be out on my ass if I gave him the slightest excuse, and he'd be fitting a new happy couple into my previously rent-controlled apartment before I had a chance to find myself a cardboard box to live in. Evening wouldn't solve my housing situation twice.

The fog in my head cleared as I ate, and I almost felt like myself by the time I'd finished my second egg on toast and third cup of coffee. I tossed the dishes into the sink, rumpling my hair with one hand as I walked back toward the bedroom. The answering machine light was still flashing. I paused.

"It's probably Stacy, but it could be work," I mused. "If it's work, it probably means coming in on my night off. But it also means there might be money left after I pay the rent. Guys? Opinions?"

The cats didn't answer. Cats are good that way. Their lack of answer saved me from needing to explain my secret, lingering fantasy, the one that woke every time the answering machine flashed: the hope that Gillian might have found my phone number forgotten on her father's desk somewhere and decided to reach out for the mother she hadn't seen in fourteen years. It was never going to happen, but it was a wonderful dream.

What the hell. I needed the money, and it wasn't like my creditors could threaten me with anything I hadn't heard before. If it was Stacy, I could just delete the message. I leaned back against the wall, sipping my coffee, and pressed the button marked "play."

The speakers crackled, intoning, "You have three new messages," in a bland mechanical voice that cut off with a strident beep. I winced and reached for the volume control, intending to turn it down. I was still reaching when the playback began, and I forgot about everything but the message.

"October, this is Evening. I believe I may have a problem. In fact, I'm nearly sure of it." Her tone was clipped, tight with some unacknowledged worry. She always sounded repressed, but this was new; I'd never heard her sound scared. It takes a lot to scare most purebloods. It takes a lot more to scare someone as naturally scary as Evening herself.

"Evening?" I straightened.

Evening wasn't just someone I called to fish me out of jail cells: she was Countess of one of San Francisco's smaller fiefdoms, and sometimes, she was even a friend. I say sometimes because she and I had very different ideas about what social standing meant. She thought it meant she got to order me around because she was pureblooded and I wasn't. I disagreed. So we hated each other about half the time, but we spent the other half helping each other survive. I found the man who killed her sister and I cleared her name when she was accused of plotting the destruction of the Queen's Court; she bailed me out when I got a little too enthusiastic following the Duchess of Dreamer's Glass. If there was a pureblood other than Sylvester that I'd trust with my life, it was her.

Damn her anyway, for making me care.

"If you're there, please, *please* answer your phone. It's truly essential that I speak to you immediately. Call me as soon as you can. And October . . ." She paused. "Never mind. Just hurry." She hung up the phone, but before she did, I could have sworn I heard her crying.

The second message started immediately, before I had a chance to move, or even breathe. It was Evening again, sounding even more harried than before.

"October? October, are you there? October, this is
Evening." There was a long pause. I heard her take a
wavering, unsteady breath. "Oh, root and branch ...
October, please pick up your phone. I need you to answer your phone *right now*." It was like she thought she
could order me to be home. My machine was too old
to have a date and time feature so there was no telling how much time had passed between messages, but
it had been enough for the worry to stop hiding and
come out to the surface of her voice, obvious and raw.
The only other time I'd heard that much emotion in
her voice was when her sister died, and while Dawn's
death had broken the shell of her calm, even that hadn't
lasted long. This wasn't sorrow. This was sheer and simple terror.

"Please, please, October, pick up the phone, please,
I'm running out of time ..." The message cut off abruptly,
but not abruptly enough to hide the sound of her
crying.

"Oak and yarrow, Eve," I whispered. "What did you
get yourself into?"

I thought I wanted an answer. And I was wrong, because the last message answered me more completely
than I could have dreamed.

The speakers crackled, once, before her voice began
to speak for the final time.

"October Daye, I wish to hire you." The fear was still
there, but the command and power that was her nature
shone clearly through it, brilliant and terrible. She was
looking at the end of everything, and it was enough to
remind her of who she really was. "By my word and at
my command, you will investigate a murder, and you
will force justice back into this kingdom. You *will* do
this thing." There was a long pause. I was starting to
think the message had ended when she continued, softly,

"Find out who did it, Toby, please. Make sure they don't win. I need you to do this, for me, and for Goldengreen. If you were ever my friend, Toby, please . . ."

She'd never called me Toby before. We'd known each other for more than twenty years, and I'd never been anything but October to her. I knew then what had happened to her, even though I didn't want to. I knew as soon as she started speaking, and I still wouldn't let it be true. I couldn't let it be true. Not moving, not breathing, I listened in stunned silence as she brought down what little remained of my world.

There was another long pause before she whispered, "Toby, there isn't much time. Please, pick up. I can't leave, and you're the only one I trust enough to call, so damn it, please! Answer your goddamn phone!" I'd never heard her curse before. The night was full of firsts, and I wasn't even out of my bathrobe yet. "I know you're there! Dammit, I am *not* going to let your laziness get me killed! Toby, damn you . . ."

She took a breath then, before continuing in a firm cadence. By the time I realized what she was doing, it was too late; I'd heard the binding begin, and I would listen until the end.

"By my blood and my bones, I bind you. By the oak and the ash, the rowan and the thorn, I bind you. By the word of your fealty, by my mother's will, by your name, I bind you. For the favors I have done you in the past, you promised that I could ask anything of you; this is my anything. Find the answers, find the reasons and find the one who caused me this harm, October Daye, daughter of Amandine, or find only your own death. By all that I am and all that I was and all the mercies of our missing Lord and Ladies, I bind you . . ."

I felt the curse catch hold, sinking thorny talons into my skin as the bittersweet smell of dying roses flooded my nose and mouth. I dropped my coffee cup and staggered backward retching, clapping a hand over my mouth as I tried not to throw up. Promises bind our kind as surely as iron chains or ropes of human hair, and Evening had bound me with the old forms, the ones anyone with a trace of fae blood can use. No one uses the old bindings anymore, not unless things are so bleak that even our missing King and his Hunt couldn't mend them. They're too strong, and too deadly.

The fae never swear by anything we don't believe in. We don't ask for thanks and we don't offer them; no promises, no regrets, no chains. No lies. If Evening said failure would kill me, it would kill me. I just hoped she had a good reason, or I was going to have to kill her myself.

"Oh, Toby, I'm sorry," she said, and put the phone down, not quite in the cradle. The connection continued. I don't know whether that was an accident or not, but I don't think it was. She wanted me to hear. She knew that if I heard what came next, I wouldn't even try to break the binding she had thrown over me.

It doesn't matter. I'm still never going to forgive her.

The story the message told next was one I'd never wanted to hear, not on the worst of all my bad days. A door, slamming open; the sound of footsteps. Evening shouting something I couldn't quite make out . . . and a gun going off. Her voice rose in a soaring scream, only to be silenced by another gunshot.

I jumped to my feet, bile rising in my throat as I shouted an involuntary "No!" at the phone. Evening screamed again. The gun fired a third time, and the message ended, the machine hissing on for several seconds before it stopped with a small, final click.

Somehow, that was what made it all seem real. I stared at the machine for a moment, breath hitching in my throat, then turned and bolted for the bathroom. I was fast enough, barely; I got to the sink before I threw up.

Time never runs backward when I need it to. Not for me, and not for anyone else.

FOUR

I THREW UP THREE times before I could leave the bathroom. I splashed water on my face before heading for my room, numbly starting the answering machine's playback over again as I passed. There wasn't time to shower, and I wasn't sure I could work the taps without scalding myself. Even getting dressed was almost more than I could manage. Evening's words were no kinder the second time, begging me to pick up the phone, to answer her, to do anything—anything at all—to save her. When did the last call come? Oak and ash, when did it *come?*

I was pulling on my coat, accompanied by Evening's recorded screams, when realization hit me: she got what she wanted. Sure, I'd turned my back on Faerie, I'd refused to let her have my license reinstated ... but I was on the case now, and I'd stay on it until I had the answers I needed.

Evening was my worst friend and my best enemy, and she never really knew me, because even in the end, she didn't understand that I would've done it without the curse. All she had to do was tell me the stakes were as high as they'd apparently gotten. She was my friend. I would have done it.

The reality of the situation still hadn't fully sunk in as I reset the wards and walked down the concrete path to the garage. Evening *couldn't* be dead. She was the frigid, ruthlessly efficient Countess of Goldengreen, she was the woman who yelled until they let Sylvester knight me, she was pureblooded Daoine Sidhe, and she was going to live forever. That's what people like her *do*.

You never think of death in terms of yourself or your friends until it gets too close to ignore. When did the last call come? Was I already home? If I hadn't been such a selfish brat, if I'd listened to my messages, could I have saved her?

My car started easily despite the lingering December cold. That's part of why I like the original Volkswagen bugs: they break down constantly, the parts are impossible to find, and the mileage sucks, but they always seem to start when you need them to. I pulled out of the garage without checking for traffic and barely avoided a collision with a group of teenagers packed into Daddy's Lexus. We traded expletives across a narrow strip of asphalt before heading in opposite directions—them toward downtown and me toward the South City, where you can find some of the most expensive residential neighborhoods in San Francisco.

Most purebloods Evening's age live full-time in the Summerlands rather than dealing with the daily stresses of mortal living. Even Sylvester, the most "human" pureblood I've ever known, lived entirely on the other side of the hill. Evening was stubborn. She saw San Francisco built around her, watching it grow from a little dock town into a thriving city. Somewhere along the way, it became her home, and after that, she simply refused to leave.

I asked her about it once. "I prefer San Francisco," she said. "The lies are different here. When you've lived as long as I have, you start appreciating new approaches to dishonesty."

I don't remember how I found my way to her apartment. When I try to think about the drive, all I can think is that I must have had my eyes closed the whole time, because I was praying so damn hard. The fae aren't big on gods, but I prayed anyway—prayed that my ears had lied to me, that this was some sort of cruel wake-up call on Evening's part, or that maybe, just this once, the universe would see that it had made a mistake and would take it all back.

The neighborhoods had been getting more upscale as I drove, the buildings taking on an elegant, cookie-cutter uniformity. Evening's choice of residence was nothing unique among the purebloods who live on this side of the hills. Not only do they tend to have bank accounts going back centuries, but the electronic age has broadened the horizons of magical fraud to an astonishing degree. Faerie gold can be used for more than just party tricks; it works pretty well on the stock market, for example, where money's an illusion anyway. The only purebloods who live poor anymore are the ones whose magic is too weak or whose morals are too strong to let them lie on that sort of scale.

Evening never had those kinds of problems. Unfortunately for me, it doesn't work like that for changelings. Sustaining illusions that strong for the amount of time required would kill me, assuming I could cast them in the first place. So the purebloods live on veal and candied moonbeams, while I've become a connoisseur of macaroni and cheese.

Oh, well. Pasta's probably better for you anyway.

Police cars lined the street in front of Evening's

building, lights spinning in an endless flashing dance of red-blue-red and shattering the illusion of wealthy, untouchable serenity that the neighborhood worked so hard to project. Those lights made it impossible to pretend that everything was perfect or that this was the mythic San Francisco the pop songs promised; this was too real for that. The people walking by looked nervously at the police cars, like they were afraid whatever crimes or tragedies their imaginations had conjured would rub off on them. Humanity has always had a flair for guilt by association. What was Evening guilty of—dying?

I found a parking place at the end of the block, where I wedged my car into the space between a news van and a battered Studebaker. My fender dinged the news van, and I felt a flare of satisfaction. They'd never pick out the dent in the colony already established on my car, and they deserved it. They shouldn't have been rushing after the sound of the sirens like vultures after road kill.

The way I retreat into trivial concerns when I'm scared amazes me. All I have to do is get to the point where I'm so panicked I can't see straight, and suddenly the expiration date on the milk is all that matters. I guess that's how my mind protects itself.

It took twenty minutes to walk the half block to Evening's building. I stopped to read flyers tacked to telephone poles and watch cats sitting on windowsills, doing everything I could to make the trip just a little longer. I didn't want to get where I was going. Not that it mattered; all too soon, I was looking up at the elegant building that had been the home of the Countess Evening Winterrose for the last forty years. I didn't want to go in. It wasn't real until I went inside: it wasn't a fact, just a possible plot twist, like a cat stuffed into a closed box. If I turned around and went home, I could wait until Evening called to gloat over how gullible I'd been. We'd laugh and laugh . . . if I didn't go inside. The police would turn off their sirens and go back downtown. I'd be able to forget her binding me; I'd forget the cloying taste of roses and the stench of burning rowan.

I'd forget that it was my fault.

I turned up the steps to the door.

A policeman was standing by the buzzer, a clipboard in his hands. I paused. He was clearly checking off people as they came and went—an entirely logical thing for him to be doing at the door of a private complex where someone had just been killed, but one that was more than a little bit inconvenient for me. Straightening my shoulders, I dug a crumpled receipt out of my pocket, holding it up as he turned toward me.

"The Queen of Hearts, she made some tarts, all on a summer's day," I said, thinking *I am authorized to be here* in his direction. The smell of copper and cut grass swirled around me as his eyes glazed over. I lowered the receipt. "I trust everything is in order?"

"Yes, ma'am," he said, and smiled, waving me inside. "Third floor."

"Got it." Whoever he thought he saw was allowed to enter the crime scene; beyond that, I didn't care who he thought I was.

The hall was carpeted in a shade of gray that complemented the cream walls and the dark teak of the decorative end tables, tastefully elegant without being ostentatious. Of course it was tasteful—a month's rent could probably have fed me for a year. I revised my estimate upward by at least six months when the elevator doors opened to reveal five police officers and an honest-to-Oberon elevator operator.

The police filed out into the hall and I slipped past them, nodding to the operator as I said, "Third floor." He returned the nod, pressing the button, and the doors slid closed. The elevator started to move, so smoothly that I could barely feel it. I tensed. I hate it when I can't tell which way I'm actually going.

I hadn't visited Evening's building since 1987. From what I could see, it hadn't changed a bit—the place stank of elegance and the sort of timelessness that only money can buy. Stasis is one of the benefits of being very, very rich. Nothing ever changes unless you let it.

The operator glanced at me nervously. I tried to smile at him like I meant it. Your first murder is always the hardest. Not that they ever get easy. We stopped on the third floor, and I stepped out, letting him retreat back to the ground floor.

There were police everywhere, bustling back and forth, murmuring in the barely audible whisper used only by cops and children. There are more similarities between the two than you might think, starting with whether or not you'd want them waiting for you in a dark alley with a gun. I've worked with the police, and I've even liked some of them, but that doesn't mean I have to like them as a breed. Power brings out the worst in almost everyone.

Most of the doors in the hall were closed, but Evening's was ajar, propped open just far enough to let the police slip in and out without revealing anything to anyone who might manage to get past security. I paused in front of the door, taking a deep breath. This was it: last chance to turn around and walk away.

Pushing the door the rest of the way open was almost impossible. After that, stepping inside was somehow anticlimactic. That didn't make it easier.

There was an officer just inside. I whipped out my receipt before he could finish turning, chanting, "The Knave of Hearts, he stole those tarts, and took them clean away." The officer froze, expression taking on the same faintly baffled air as his colleague. A bolt of pain lanced through my forehead; I'd pushed too hard, and the headache was coming on. I did my best to ignore it, lowering the receipt and saying, "May I proceed?"

"Yes, proceed," he said, still looking stunned as I brushed past him.

The apartment was decorated in pinks, ranging from a deep shade bordering on red to a pale, near-white cream. Her blood probably fit right in until it started drying to an ugly shade of brown. I couldn't see the body, but I could see the blood, just a few drops of it staining the carpet near the door. It seemed like half the room was already tucked into neatly labeled plastic bags, and what hadn't been bagged looked small and gaudy in the artificial light. Murder strips everyone's illusions away, no matter how carefully they were created.

There were officers everywhere, milling like ants while they gathered evidence and studied blood splatters. I glanced at the bags as I moved across the room, checking to be sure they'd found no sign of Evening's true nature. I didn't need to worry. Evening was old, and she was careful, and they'd find nothing to show that she was anything more than a rich businesswoman named Evelyn Winters who somehow managed to get herself killed.

Almost against my will, I was moving toward the body, the weight of Evening's binding seeming tight and heavy in my chest. I flashed my increasingly crumpled receipt at every officer I passed. None of them tried to stop me from approaching the body—or what was passing for it, anyway. If the police were already this ensconced, the night-haunts would have long since been and gone. I'd have to be content with what they'd left behind.

Fae flesh doesn't decay. It makes sense; the fae don't age past the point of physical maturity, so why should they rot? But it means something has to be done about the bodies, and that's where the night-haunts come in. They come when we die, take our dead for their tables, and leave replicas behind. Their toys do everything the natural dead do. They bleed, stink, and decay with a perfection that says a lot about their makers. Really, there's just one thing that differentiates the night-haunts' mannequins from our real dead: they're human. Their ears are round, their eyes are normal, their skins are white or brown or tan, but never blue or green. There's nothing about them that can give us away.

The night-haunts devour our true dead, and they leave pretty fictions in their place for the mortal world to mourn. I don't know when we made that bargain with them, but there's no breaking it now, and disgusting as it is, it has its purpose.

Knowing that what I was dealing with wasn't really Evening's body didn't make it any easier. The night-haunts only mimic what they see.

The replica was sprawled by the couch, open eyes staring at the ceiling. I fought the urge to turn and run, perversely glad that I'd already thrown up breakfast. Part of me was still able to marvel at the detail the night-haunts had worked into their creation. Every inch of her human disguise was flawlessly replicated, even down to the obvious violence of her death.

I knelt beside the body, letting the analytical part of my mind click on as I scanned the area around it. There were bloody footprints on the near-white carpet, but those were unavoidable; there was nowhere to step that wasn't covered in blood. A few of the officers had plastic bags tied over their shoes and if the killers were smart, they'd done something similar; none of the prints I could see had a distinctive enough tread to let me pick them out of a crowd. If the murder weapon was left behind, the police tagged and bagged it before I got there. Back when I was a P.I., I sometimes lamented not working directly with the cops—my job would have been a lot easier if I had access to hard evidence. Unfortunately, I hate the sight of blood and I can't work mornings, so a career with the force isn't really in my future.

I caught myself with a jolt, realizing where my thoughts were going. No. This was a one-time thing; it was about necessity, not about my future. I gave up that life. I wasn't going back.

There was one way to distract myself from thinking too hard about police procedure, or much of anything beyond why I never wanted to do this again. Steeling my nerves, I turned my attention to what was left of Evening.

Her bathrobe had been white when she put it on; now it was a dark brownish-red, except for a few spots on the sleeves. The body holds an amazing amount of blood. There were two obvious gunshot wounds, one in the shoulder and one in the stomach, but neither should have killed her. They would have hurt like hell, but she would have lived.

Everything considered, she probably died when they slashed her throat.

Her arms were straight at her sides, but her legs and hips were twisted—she was kicking right up until the end. Someone pinned her down while her throat was cut, then held on until she stopped struggling. That meant there were at least two killers, maybe more. I had to give her one thing: she hadn't been taken by surprise. The look on her face was pure anger, almost hiding the underlying foundation of fear. She died kicking, yes, but she also died pissed off.

The blood wasn't the worst part. Neither was the second mouth beneath her chin. That title went to her round-eared, blunt-featured face, framed by black hair shot with veins of gray and matted down with blood. The Evening Winterrose I knew had features that looked like the last, perfect work of a dying sculptor, ears that tapered to sharp points and eyes the impossible dark blue of midnight; she had hair that wavered between black and purple, with highlights of pink, orange, and blue, like an aurora. She was wild and terrible and strange, one of the Daoine Sidhe, the fairest of the fae, and she was never, ever human. What the night-haunts left would never be anything else. Death wouldn't even let her keep her true face.

Something wasn't right about the body. I leaned in for a better look at her wounds, already knowing that they wouldn't tell me anything. Maybe there are forensics experts that can look at a knife slash and tell you everything there is to know about whoever made it, but I'm not one of them. All I know is what I've learned through experience, and my experience was telling me that something was wrong.

There are two kinds of problems in my world: human and fae. Back when I was doing private investigation on a professional basis, most human problems could be solved with a camera and a well-placed microphone, and when a human problem looked like it was getting deadly, I gave it back to the humans. They can handle their own trash.

Fae problems are another matter, because my loyalty is to Sylvester, even now, and my actions reflect on him. I'm his knight, and that means that no matter how bad the fae problems get, I have to see them through. This was a fae problem. Whether I liked it or not, it needed a fae solution.

Some of the blood in the carpet was still wet enough that it was soaking through the knees of my jeans. I ran a finger across one of the deeper stains, forcing fresh blood to well up through the fiber.

My mother is Daoine Sidhe. That means I am, too, debased as I may be. There are ways of talking to the dead that are almost exclusively ours—or, if not talking to them, at least coming to a better understanding. Evening's blood could let me taste her death. The body was gone, but the blood would remember. Blood always remembers.

I raised my finger to my lips.

Blood magic is dangerous, because it skips the brain and goes straight for the gut. When you're talking about someone as weak as I am, you're lucky if nobody winds up trying to fly off the top of a ten-story building. Out of all Titania's descendants, only the Daoine Sidhe can measure another's death by the taste of their blood; everyone else with that capacity descends from Maeve and the darker paths of Faerie. Evening was my fifth time. It doesn't get any better with practice.

The world twisted until I was looking at the apartment through a red-tinted fog. The police and the body were gone; this was what the world looked like through Evening's eyes just before the end. It was disorienting but not painful, like trying to walk after three beers. The knowledge that coming down from this would be worse than a hangover hovered on the edge of my awareness, but I pushed it away, forcing myself deeper into the red.

The room snapped into focus, clean, perfect, and unmarred by any signs of a struggle. A warm wave of satisfaction flowed over me. Everything was where it belonged.

Especially the key.

Pulling myself back from the veil of Evening's memories, I dragged my fingers across the bloody carpet again.

Key? What key? Her blood was bitter and sweet at the same time, and my eyes unfocused, sending me crashing back into the moments before Evening's death.

The door slams open, but it doesn't matter; they're too late. I know that as I turn to face them, phone in my hand. It's too late. October knows, and she'll come to chase her answers to ground. They're too late, too late to take the key, and she'll find what's been left for her to find, she'll end this mockery at last . . .

A flash of memory that wasn't mine cut across the images the blood was feeding me:

I was handing a key to a small winged figure—a sprite? Where did the sprite come from?—and it took a gift of blood from my palm, running a hand along the shallow cut I had opened there, and then it flew away, leaping out of my window with the key in its arms. And then I made a final phone call, summoned October, who would never understand, who would end this at last, and the door slammed open, and I screamed, and then . . .

Then the pain came.

Riding the memories of the dead is unpleasant at the best of times. Whatever they felt, you feel, and there's always the risk you'll hold on too long. Following them into death is like riding a roller coaster into hell: if you're lucky you might come back, but you shouldn't bet on it. I ripped myself out of her memories after the shots were fired, after her throat was slit, and just before her heart stopped.

I staggered to my feet and out of the apartment, shoving my way past the police. I made it halfway down the hall before my knees buckled. I grabbed the rim of the nearest decorative pot as I fell, retching. No amount of gagging was going to get the foul taste out of my mind. You ride the blood and you pay the price, and part of that is remembering whatever you set out to remember.

You get to keep it and treasure knowing what death feels like for however long you live.

I'd ridden deaths before, and come through shaken but stable. But Evening . . . oh, rowan and ash, what they did to Evening.

There are a lot of ways to kill the fae. Most of the things that kill humans will kill us—I've yet to meet anyone short of a Manticore that could survive being hit by a train or wouldn't be bothered by losing their head. Even so, there are ways of killing us that would make decapitation seem like a picnic, and the worst is death by iron. It kills the magic, then the mind, and finally the body. It's the great leveler, the one thing that can kill anyone. Death by iron is slow, painful, and all too often inevitable.

And the bastards killed her with it. It wasn't enough that they'd invaded her privacy and ended her life: they had to make a show of it. What could she possibly have done to deserve that?

A cop walked by, heading for the apartment, and muttered, "Rookie," as he passed. I'd obviously hit him before, and he was still seeing me as whatever he wanted to see; good. The last thing I needed was questions about why I was kneeling outside a murder scene covered in blood when my head was still spinning.

Even inside Evening's memory, I hadn't seen her killers. They'd somehow managed to keep themselves out of sight, or had erased themselves from the blood before they went. I didn't know if that was possible, but I couldn't discount it. These people were dangerous, and this was bigger than murder: someone used iron to end a life. Not just any life, either. The purebloods might have looked the other way if it had been a changeling, called it a "reprehensible affair" and left it alone . . . but Evening was one of them, born under the hills when mankind still thought fire was a neat new idea. The purebloods have their failings, but they look out for their own.

If I didn't move quickly, things were going to explode.

FIVE

GOING BACK INTO THAT apartment took all the self-control I had, but I did it; I had to. I had heard three shots fired, and there were only two gunshot wounds on the "body." That meant one of the bullets might still be somewhere in the room. If I wanted to be certain of the way that Evening died, I needed to find it.

Iron bullets are heavy and uneven. That changes their ballistics; they can't fly smoothly. Even if the police knew about the third bullet, they would've been starting their search from the shooter's position with an incorrect idea of how far the bullet could have gone. I found it buried in the wainscoting of the wall across from the balcony, a small, uneven sphere that told me everything I needed and didn't want to know.

It was iron, pure enough to sting even from several feet away. I left it where it was and left the apartment for the last time. Physical evidence wasn't required, and you can't work sympathetic magic with iron. I'd just needed to *know*.

The news van was still on the street as I walked back

to my car, got inside, and pulled away, but the camera crew was nowhere in sight. That was good. My misdirection spells aren't strong enough to stand up on film, and I didn't want them recording me with blood caked on my hands and jeans.

The iron told me two things: first, that Evening's killers were fae, since no human would have used that particular weapon, and second, that I wasn't dealing with any of the usual suspects. My own wounded sensibilities wanted to jump straight to the assumption that Simon and Oleander were involved, but they depended too much on magic to carry that much iron. They don't have many scruples. That doesn't mean they'd be willing to deaden their own magic for weeks, maybe even months, by having that much contact with iron. All that would do was get them caught, and they're just too smart for that.

Evening's blood had its own share of information to impart, although it was a bit more nebulous in its usefulness. She didn't call anyone else before she died; I was the only one who knew she was gone, other than the night-haunts—and her killers. Somehow I doubted the people who killed her would be spreading the news that they'd broken Oberon's first law—the prohibition against killing purebloods except in formally declared war—and the night-haunts aren't big conversationalists. I don't even know anyone who's actually seen them. I was on my own, and I was on a time limit, because I had to find her killers before I found myself drowning in her curse instead of pond water.

And all that would have to wait, because I had more immediate duties to fulfill. There were rites to be observed, words that needed to be said, for the sake of the ones who hadn't died. The purebloods don't take death easily. Something has to cushion the blow. Beyond that,

there was the simple fact that a woman had been bru-
tally murdered by someone who clearly knew her nature. Humans don't carry cold iron knives—they're
heavy, clumsy things, and modern technology is so far
beyond them that they only appear in fae hands. Whoever killed Evening made sure her death would be as
painful as possible. That made this a matter for her liege,
and that meant I had to go someplace I really didn't
want anything to do with: the Court of the Queen of the
Mists, monarch of Northern California.

The current Queen of the Mists didn't take the throne
under the world's most auspicious circumstances; she
became Queen in 1906, when the great San Francisco
earthquake took out half the fae in the city, including
her father, King Gilad. She'd been raised somewhere
outside the Court, and no one ever knew her mother, but
Evening—who was already Countess of Goldengreen—
supported her claim, and no one really wanted to argue.
She's been in charge ever since, first from her Court
in North Beach, and, after her first hollow hill was destroyed, from her Court by the Bay. No one knows her
name, or where she grew up, or much of anything about
her, really, beyond the fact that she's the Queen, and her
word is law.

She and I have never gotten along. Sylvester and
Evening were the ones who insisted he be allowed to
knight me for services to the Crown when her original
Court was destroyed; the Queen was all for throwing me
out with the rest of the changeling rabble. Maybe it's the
fact that she's a mixed-blood—her heritage is a strange
blend of Siren, Sea Wight, and Banshee—or maybe she's
just a snob, but the woman has never liked changelings,
and titling me went against all her sensibilities. She did
it anyway, because the services I'd performed were too
large to be ignored, and because Evening was pushing

for it. I don't think the Queen has ever forgiven me. I've made it a rule to stay out of her presence as much as possible, just to avoid reminding her that she's unhappy.

It doesn't help that changelings form the lowest rung of fae society; we're too mortal to belong and too fae to be sent back to our human parents with a pat on the head and a "have a nice life"—assuming our human parents are still alive after we've been in the Summerlands long enough to realize how raw the deal there can be, which is by no means guaranteed. Most of us wind up spending the centuries as hangers-on in the various Courts of Faerie, following our immortal relatives and begging for crumbs like puppies until our own mortality catches up with us and we crawl off to die. That's the way the game is supposed to work. Only I've always refused to play by those rules, and it hasn't exactly endeared me to the higher echelons of the nobility.

It was late enough that there were few cars heading for the bay. Some places are too cold to take a date on a December night, even in a city whose fame is based around an icy ocean and constant fog. Since freezing to death isn't conducive to having a good time, the tourists had set their sights farther inland, leaving me with a clear shot at my destination: a little cluster of streets and crumbling businesses about six miles down the coast from Fisherman's Wharf. The beach I was aiming for wasn't part of any nature preserve, coast trail, or tourist attraction. It was just a small, stony stretch of ground on the inside curve of the coastal wall, isolated enough to be forgotten and important as all hell from the faerie point of view.

There were no street vendors or tourist traps where I was headed: just the smell of the sea and the natural decay of any seaside city. In most of the city, parking is at a premium because of the tourists. Near the Queen's knowe, it's hard to find because there just isn't very much of it. Warehouses and aging industrial buildings don't exactly inspire the construction of parking lots. It took fifteen minutes of circling before I found a space without a meter tucked halfway down a side street that was more like an alley. I shoved my purse into the glove compartment before getting out. Maybe it was an invitation to theft, but I don't like to carry anything unnecessary when I'm visiting the Queen. There's too much of a chance that I'll need to run.

The taste of roses flooded my mouth as I got out of the car. I staggered, the image of a sprite with tattered oak-leaf wings flashing across my mind. *The key . . .*

Whatever it was, it was important, but it was something I'd find when I was through telling the Queen what had happened. I forced the image down, along with the thorny arms of Evening's entangling curse. I had a job to do. Hiking my coat up around my chin, I started down the alley, moving toward the sea.

Almost all fae Courts are tucked in hidden places called "knowes," little pockets of reality balanced between the mortal world and the Summerlands. Some of them are easy to get to while others require everything up to and including blood sacrifice just to get inside. It depends on who built them, and who controls the doors.

I've seen doors tucked away in carnival photo booths, gas station restrooms, and old cardboard boxes, as well as in the more traditional grass rings and stone gateways. The Queen of the Mists opened her own doors, which means that her knowe is well-hidden and not easy to reach; getting inside means walking a quarter mile of largely uninhabited beach, scrambling over damp rocks coated in seagull shit and old seaweed and trying not to fall into the Pacific Ocean on the way. An after-dark hike across a slippery beach isn't exactly the ideal follow-up to a murder scene unless you're a masochist, which I'm not. Fortunately, the tide was out. Unfortunately, the moon wasn't providing much light, and even changeling vision is no help when the fog is rolling in.

Sneakers aren't really made for wet sand and slippery stone, but I somehow managed not to fall into San Francisco Bay before I reached the cave that marked the entrance to the Queen's Court. It was narrow, dank, and dark, almost hidden behind a seemingly random fall of rocks. Altogether, it managed to project the impression that the whole thing might come crashing down at any moment, and of course that meant it was the only way in.

I stepped off the rocks and winced as my socks were immediately soaked through with seawater. The night just kept getting better. Now I had bad news to deliver to a powerful woman who didn't like me, a terrible crime to avenge, and wet socks. Grumbling, I walked into the darkness.

The water in the cave got deeper as I moved farther in, reaching to the middle of my calves and soaking my jeans to the thigh. I shivered, keeping one hand against the damp wall for guidance. Someday, I hope Her Majesty discovers central heating and basic drainage systems. Until then, visiting her is a matter of stumbling around in the dark and hoping that there's nothing nasty waiting there to jump out and shout "surprise."

The stone began to glow a pale, luminescent white about twenty feet from the entrance. I kept walking, ignoring the feeling of phantom hands plucking at my clothing and hair. The ground abruptly leveled out, water disappearing as the rough stone was replaced with polished marble. I walked on, my wet shoes slapping against the marble with every step, and after another ten feet, the walls opened up, and I was suddenly walking through a vast ballroom with ice-white marble floors and fluted columns holding up the distant ceiling. Courtiers thronged like exotic birds, pointing and whispering behind their hands as they took note of my untidy appearance. I pressed on.

The trouble with the Queen of the Mists is that she's so far above normal protocol that she feels no need to live by it, save when it suits her, even as she forces it on everyone around her. If I broke the slightest rule, I could find myself in more trouble than I'd ever get out of. She, on the other hand, could do whatever she wanted, and all I could do was curtsy. That meant I needed to head for the throne room, because propriety says that visits begin with a formal presentation. If I was lucky, she'd be there.

I'm so rarely lucky. There was a shimmer in the air, and the taste of frozen salt assaulted my tongue. The sound of wet shoes hitting the floor stopped as my sneakers were replaced by low-slung heels to go with the floor-length blue silk gown that had taken the place of my clothes. I only know one woman rude enough to do something like that without my consent, and technically, it wasn't rude when she did it. Rank hath its privileges.

Burying my hands in the skirt, I dropped into a deep, low curtsy, bowing my head. "Your Majesty, it's an honor."

"October." The voice was light and airy, like a half-forgotten dream. There was no surprise in her tone; she sounded mildly pleased, like I came traipsing through every day. I guess ennui is a good thing when you're facing an eternity in politics. "How very delightful it is to see you."

From the sound of her voice, she was somewhere off to my left. Good. If I could just avoid looking at her, this might not go too badly. "The delight is mine, Your Majesty," I said, and straightened, keeping my eyes turned straight ahead.

The Queen was standing right in front of me.

I didn't expect it, and I didn't have time to look away without giving offense. Forcing myself to swallow the urge to recoil, I looked into her face. She smiled slightly, expression saying she knew what she was doing, and didn't care. It was, after all, her right.

A lot of Faerie's children are beautiful, but the Queen takes it past beauty, to the point where beautiful and terrible collide. It's hard to look at her and stay focused on anything but continuing to look at her, making her happy, making her smile for you. It's part of the reason I don't come near her when I can avoid it. I hate being forced into things.

She was wearing a snow-colored velvet gown that brought out the pink undertones of her skin, saving her from looking like she'd been carved from ivory. Her silver-white hair fell to the floor in an unbroken line, trailing almost a foot behind her. I've always assumed that her hair is at least part of the reason she never leaves the knowe—give her five minutes in the mortal world and her shampoo bills would be astronomical. A thin band of silver sat atop her head, but it was really just for show. There was no question of who the monarch here was. I stayed standing, fighting the urge to drop to one knee.

She stepped toward me, her dress rippling like water. Only a pureblood would accessorize with the ocean itself.

"What are you doing here, October? You avoid my court when you can. That seems to be most times, these days. I was beginning to think you had, perhaps, forgotten the way."

Never lie to anyone who can have you locked up for looking at them funny. It's just a good survival strategy. Still, I could try to skirt the issue. "I've been keeping to myself, my lady."

"First your mother stops attending us, then you vanish into your own little world. One might begin to think your bloodline has lost its love for us." Her eyes narrowed as she studied me, daring me to argue.

"I'm afraid I don't care much for your Court, my lady." The crowd whispered around us, expressing quiet disapproval. Candor may be wise, but excessive bluntness isn't one of the socially accepted arts in Faerie.

"Do we bore you?" asked the Queen, still smiling.

"You scare me."

"Is that better or worse?"

"I don't know." I shook my head. "I'm here on business."

"Business?" Now she grinned, openly amused. "What sort of ... business ... brings you here, when you've been avoiding us so long? Have you brought another fish story to tell us?"

I winced. Between Tybalt and the Queen, it's a wonder I don't need therapy. "I wish that were the case, Your Majesty. I'm here because of the Countess Winterrose."

"Because of the Winterrose? What, are you here to claim some offense against her?" Her grin remained, and the Court around us buzzed with speculation. Changelings rarely claim offense against purebloods. The battles when we do are invariably a lot of fun to watch, full of blood and glory, and almost always fatal for the changeling.

"No, Your Majesty." This is the society that created Evening, and my mother, and every time I have to deal with it, I'm happier that it's not the only thing that created me. "I'm here because she's gone."

"What?" Her smile faded into surprise, wiping away the smooth curl of her disdain.

For once, the overstylized formality of Faerie was a blessing, because it meant I didn't need to figure out what to say on my own. "When the Root and Branch were young, when the Rose still grew unplucked upon the tree; when all our lands were new and green and we danced without care, then, we were immortal. Then, we lived forever." I looked down and away, not wanting to see the look on the Queen's face. It didn't matter: I could hear what I didn't see in the sudden stillness of the Court. There's only one reason for the death chants.

It was too late to stop. It was too late when the gun went off. I pressed on. "We left those lands for the world where time dwells, dancing, that we might see the passage of the sun and the growing of the world. Here we may die, and here we can fall, and here my Lady Evening Winterrose, Countess of the fief of Goldengreen, has stopped her dancing."

I left my head bowed until the quiet was too much to bear. The Queen had gone so still that she might as well have been a statue, somehow carved from mist and sea foam. I couldn't blame her: I'll live a long time, if I'm careful, but the most I can expect is a few centuries. That's a lot in human terms. It's nothing compared to what the purebloods get. The reminder that they can die is sometimes more than they can take.

"Your Majesty . . ." She raised her hand, pale fingers shaking as she warded my words away. I quieted, waiting for her to compose herself before I continued, saying, "Your Majesty, she charged me to find the cause of her death. May I ask . . ."

"No."

I stopped, surprised. I'd expected a lot of things. I hadn't expected her to refuse me. "Your Majesty?"

"No, October Daye, daughter of Amandine." The Queen lifted her head, jaw set. "I will not help you, and we will speak of this no more. What's done is done; when the moon is high, we will dance for her, and until that day, no one here will speak the name of the Winterrose, and after that day, no one will speak her name again. I will not help you . . . and you will not ask me to."

"But . . ."

"No. Amandine's daughter or no, I will not give you what you would ask me for. I would refuse you and be damned before I did such a thing." She shook her head. "I have done enough for you down the years; there are no debts between us, and I will not help you now."

Not even being slapped would have surprised me more. "But, my lady, Evening was murdered, with iron—"

"Don't tell me how she died!" I rocked back on my heels, clapping my hands over my ears in a vain attempt to block out the voice of the Queen. Maybe time had diluted the blood of her Banshee and Siren ancestors enough that her scream wasn't fatal, but I've never been much for roulette. "Don't *tell* me!"

The Court was buzzing again, but this time, their whispers were directed at the Queen. She was shaking where she stood, eyes gone moonstruck-mad with fury. Her rage might have been impressive if it was focused on something else, but it was focused on me, and that made it terrifying. Humanity has instincts that kick in around the fae, forcing them to be good and humble. Changelings don't get the full brunt, but we get some of it, until sometimes even our own parents can scare us away. I backed up several steps, dropping a hasty curtsy. "Your Majesty, if we're done, I . . ."

"Get out!" She snapped her head from side to side, an unearthly wail seeping into her voice. *"Now!"*

I didn't need another invitation. Whirling, I ran toward the far wall, and through it, back into the darkness of the cave on the other side. My shoes were made for dancing, not running over seawater-slippery rocks. After the third time I nearly fell, I pulled them off, carrying them in the hand that wasn't being used to keep my skirt as far out of the water as possible. Bruising my feet was a small price to pay if it meant I could get away from the queen before she decided to shut me up herself, or worse, forbid me to involve myself in Evening's murder.

The air outside the cave was so cold that running into the open was like being slapped. It didn't matter; I didn't stop. I ran across the beach, stopping only when I hit the pavement, and there only long enough to put my shoes back on. My original clothes hadn't come back, and I doubted they would—the Queen is strong enough that a transformation of the inanimate was likely to be forever. I didn't care. I kept running.

SIX

MY CAR HADN'T BEEN DISTURBED. I dug the spare key from under the bumper and fumbled with the lock until I managed to stop the shaking in my fingers and get the door open. I climbed into the driver's seat, nearly slamming the trailing hem of my dress in the door as I closed it and started the engine. Evening's liege wouldn't help me. This wasn't a mortal problem. Mortal tools wouldn't solve it, and my camera wasn't going to save my ass this time. The police could study Evening's "body" forever if they wanted to, but a lot of the fae don't leave fingerprints. They'd never find anything, and that meant there wouldn't be anything I could steal from them.

Slamming my human disguise back into place, so that I just looked like a hard-used brunette in a party gown, I slumped in the driver's seat and scowled. I needed to look at things from a different direction. Maybe I couldn't do anything as an investigator, but as a knight ... there are resources in Faerie that don't exist in the human world, and this was a faerie crime. I could solve it, if I found the right spells and called in the right favors. But still . . . I'm just a changeling. Evening was ten times more powerful than I'll ever be. Whatever took her down wasn't just lucky; it had to have been strong, too, or it wouldn't have scared her that way. That meant I needed some power of my own, or I wouldn't stand a chance.

Asking the Queen for help after she'd all but thrown me out of her knowe might be rude enough to get me killed. Dying wasn't part of my plan for solving the case—it was bad enough that it might be the price of failure—and that meant our Lady of the Mists was actu-ally a hindrance, because if I got in her way, I wouldn't have time to run. There were other Courts and nobles I could go to, but only a few had the resources I'd need, and of the choices I had, only two didn't leave me cold. I wanted to get out alive, and that ruled out both Blind Michael and the Tarans of the Berkeley Hills. I consid-ered the Luidaeg, but cast that thought aside as quickly as it had come. Some things are worse than dying.

I couldn't go to Lily. I just couldn't. That wasn't as self-involved as it sounds; Lily's an Undine, and she's tied to her knowe. Unless Evening's killers sat in the Tea Gardens discussing what they were about to do, she wouldn't be able to help me anyway.

Sylvester would help me if I went to him. Sylvester would *insist* on being the one to help me, and I couldn't take it. I'd have to go to him eventually—he'd have to know that Evening was gone, and he was my liege; it was my duty to make sure he knew—but I couldn't go until I was going to be able to say, "It's all right, I have help, I don't need you." I could stand a lot of things, but I wasn't ready for the idea of him being able to make me come back.

If I couldn't trust the Queen, and I couldn't turn to Sylvester, there was really only one place left that I could go. Devin. Devin, and Home.

Lips thinned with new resolve, I pulled out of the alley, heading away from the water and into the part of the city that smart people do their best to avoid after the sun goes down. I try to be smart when I can, and careful when I can't, but at the moment, neither of those was going to work for me, because I was doing something I'd sworn I'd never do. Oberon help me, I was going Home.

A lot of changelings have fled the Summerlands over the centuries, building an entire society on the border between Faerie and the mortal world. The purebloods know—of course they do—but they don't know what to do with their precious half-blood children when they turn into angry adults, and so they've never done anything to stop it. It's a vicious, cutthroat place, where the strong feed on the weak, and it's where changeling runaways always seem to end up.

I was twenty-five when I ran away from my mother's household. I could barely pass for a young sixteen. I starved in alleyways, fled from Kelpies, and ran from the human police, and was on the verge of giving up and going back when I found what looked like an answer. Devin.

He took me in, fed me, and said I'd never have to go back there if I didn't want to. I believed him. Maeve help me, I believed him. Even when I realized what he was doing—what the "little favors" and the increasingly bigger assignments would lead up to, even when he came to my room at night and said I was beautiful, that my eyes were just like my mother's—I still believed him. He was all I had. I knew I couldn't trust him, that he'd use me, and that he'd break me if I let him. I also knew he wouldn't turn me away, because his place was Home, and Home was where everyone stopped. Home was where they didn't care what color your eyes were, or that you cried when the sun came up, or that your hair was brown like your father's when the Daoine Sidhe are supposed to be brightly colored and fair. Home was willing to have me, and I knew I could earn myself a life there, if I was fast, clever, and heartless. I could earn my own way.

If Devin had just wanted me for my body, he would have used me up and thrown me away, and no one would have been able to stop him. I've seen changelings better than me get destroyed by the border world. Mortal drugs don't have anything on their fae equivalents, and Faerie offers a lot of ways for the innocent to get themselves killed. I was lucky; Devin wanted me for the cachet of having me. My mother wasn't nobility, but she was a celebrity of sorts, the strongest blood-worker in the Kingdom, a friend to Dukes and more. No one ever thought she would bear a changeling. And Devin was the one who took me away from her.

I was his lover and his pet and his favorite toy, and he let me have my temperamental little ways, because it was all paid for when he got to walk into a pureblood party he'd bartered an invitation to attend with me on his arm. He gave me what I needed to survive on the outskirts of the mortal world; a birth certificate, lessons in mortal manners, a place to stay. I paid my keep with the shame I let him bring to the people who loved me, and I tried to tell myself it was worth it.

Maybe I was addicted to him; to the way he looked at me, and the way he touched me, and the way he made me feel like I was something more than just another half-breed. He hurt me, but everything I knew told me I deserved it. I never told him no. I never wanted to. Everything I let him do, everything I did, was of my own free will.

When Sylvester got me knighted, leaving Home was part of the price. I agreed without hesitation, and I only saw Devin twice after that. Once on the day I told him I was leaving, and once . . .

I yanked my attention back to the road. The streets were getting worse as I drove, squalor giving way to decay. My destination was at the heart of the rot, in a place where only the people with nowhere else to go ever went. It wasn't a place for children—it was never a place for children—and maybe that's why we flocked there, gathering in a dying Neverland ruled by a man who was more Captain Hook than Peter Pan. "You'll be back," Devin said on the day I left him, with my wrists still scraped and my lips stinging, and he was right, because here I was. Coming Home.

The building I parked in front of looked abandoned, but was probably home to twenty people after the sun went down. The air seemed even colder now that I was inland. I gathered my damp skirts around myself, shivering as I locked the car door. Nothing had really changed. The wrappers in the gutter had different logos and the music thumping in the background had a different tone, but the eyes of the people who watched from doorways and windows, taking my measure as I passed, were just what they'd always been: hungry, angry, and hopeful. They all needed something, and every one of them was hoping I'd be the one to provide it.

Catcalls and insults followed me down the block to a tiny, nondescript storefront wedged between a crumbling motel and an all-night massage parlor. I paused, feeling like I was falling backward through time. It was all exactly the same, even down to the old miasma of pleasure, pain, and promises, as falsely alluring as a call girl's perfume. There were no tricks required to get inside, because Devin wanted you to come in. It was getting out that would be the hard part.

The big front window was blocked off with graffiti-covered plywood, and a simple brass sign was mounted over the door. HOME: WHERE YOU STOP. That sign never tarnished or got dirty, and it served as the focus for a misdirection spell so powerful that I'd never seen a human glance toward the building, much less the door. Devin said he bought it from a Coblynau pureblood, trading the sign and its enchantment for nothing but an hour in his arms. I called him a liar the first time he told me that. Coblynau are ugly, lonely people who love metal more than they love air, and the promises you have to make to get a blade or bracelet of their crafting are dear enough that I couldn't see him winning so much as a ring.

It didn't take long for me to realize he hadn't been lying. Casually turning someone else's needs to his own advantage was exactly the sort of thing Devin did best. He stole whatever he wanted, sharing his ill-gotten gains with his children, the empty-eyed girls and damp-palmed boys who came to him praying he'd have the answers. Now here I was again, praying for the same thing.

I opened the door and stepped inside.

The main room at Home was large and square, littered with ancient furniture and lit by a scavenged electrical generator that powered two refrigerators and an antique jukebox as well as the overhead lights. Heavy metal blared from the jukebox at a volume high enough to almost vibrate the floor. The air smelled like smoke, vomit, stale beer, and yesterday's desires; all the things I left behind when I went off to live in a different, cleaner world.

A handful of teens lounged around the otherwise deserted room like the casual ornamentation they were. I didn't know any of them, but I recognized them on sight because they were Devin's kids, and so was I. Our fellowship went deeper than our faces. It went all the way down to our bones.

ROSEMARY AND RUE   87

How many of you is he fucking? I wondered, and was immediately ashamed. Front room duty was always the hardest. You had to stay alert without seeming to pay attention, and no matter how long you had to sit there, you didn't dare fall asleep. I hated it. You were a visible challenge to anyone who felt like calling Devin out for some real or imagined sin, but you couldn't say no and you couldn't leave once you'd been told to stay.

These new kids could so easily have been the ones I remembered, only changed by updates in teenage fashion. They were all changelings, and not one of them was wearing even the most basic human disguise. There was a calculated reason for that; seeing them as soon as you entered told you that when you were Home, you came as you were. It made the edges of my own illusion itch, like a coat that didn't quite fit. I wouldn't take it off yet, though. Not until I'd seen Devin.

Four kids were in view, which meant there were at least three more I hadn't spotted. A boy and girl who looked too alike to be anything but siblings sat near the jukebox, their sharply pointed ears and glossy gold hair marking them as descendants of the Tylwyth Teg. A half-Candela girl with pale green eyes leaned against the wall by the door, juggling globes of dim light, and a boy with hedgehog spines instead of hair squatted in the corner, a clove cigarette dangling from his lips.

All four had turned to watch as I entered, an inquiring band of Lost Children studying the grown-up who had wandered into their territory. Maybe I used to be one of them, but they didn't know me. For once, this proof of my escape didn't make me feel any better.

"Nice dress," said the Candela. The room erupted in snickering. I stayed where I was, waiting for it to die down.

Knowing Devin's kids, they were all armed and ready

to jump me at the first sign of trouble. That was fine. I hadn't come to Home looking for a fight, but starting a small one would get me to Devin faster. Protocol said I should be polite: introduce myself, make nice, put up with whatever crap they handed me, and ask if I could see Devin before the end of the night. Maybe they'd even let me, if I was nice enough. But I was tired and Evening was dead, and I didn't have the time or the patience to play at pleasantries.

The brother of the paired changelings looked like he was the oldest one in the room, if only by a year or two. That made him the point man. I walked toward the pair, and they looked back at me, expressions not betraying any interest in who I was or what I was doing there. Never be the first one to show that you care; that kind of weakness can get you killed.

"I need to see Devin," I said. Now that I was closer, I could see that their eyes were the glaring neon green of pippin apples. Faerie is anything but stinting in the colors it uses.

The brother blinked, obviously expecting something subtler. Good. If he was off balance, he was more likely to give me what I wanted. Unfortunately, it was his sister who spoke, flicking her bangs out of her eyes as she announced, "That's not gonna happen."

Her accent was a mixture of inner-city Spanish and downtown punk so thick it verged on parody and a perfect complement to her overdone makeup, rat's nest hair, and seemingly permanent sneer. She could have been pretty, if she'd been willing to gain twenty pounds and stop trying so hard, but as it was, she looked like a cross between Twiggy's younger sister and every downtown whore I'd ever seen. There was no way she was more than fourteen.

Of course, that was looking at her from a mortal perspective. I looked sixteen when I came to Devin, and I always did my best to look even younger when I had to do bar duty. It helped if they underestimated you. So she might have been older than she looked . . . but I saw her as fourteen, and the way she held herself told me I was pretty close to right.

"Sorry, lady, but you can go home now," she continued. "He's busy."

I sighed inwardly. I hadn't been underestimating her; she was as young as she looked, and she had no idea what she was messing with. I narrowed my eyes, glaring, and she licked her lips, fixing me with what was probably meant to be a languid sneer. I managed not to laugh. Instead, I shook my head, and repeated, "I need to see Devin. Now, please."

"So why do you need to see the boss-man?" she drawled. Her accent was starting to get on my nerves. "I don't think he's expecting you. I think you're trying to sneak in while he's not looking."

Well, she was smart enough to guess my motives. Not that it was going to do her much good, since I wasn't planning to let her stop me. "Does it matter?" I replied. "I need one of you—I don't care which—to tell Devin that Toby's here, and she needs to talk to him right away."

The girl smirked, obviously thinking I would back down. "I think you should go sit down for a while."

Was I ever that young or that stupid? That young. Maybe. "I think you should go tell Devin that I'm here."

"Really? Because I'm thinking . . . no. I think you're gonna sit, and he'll see you in an hour. Two, maybe. It's really no difference to him, lady." She started to turn away. I grabbed her arm, twisting it up behind her back. She yelped, trying to wrench herself free. "Hey! Crazy bitch!"

Her brother tensed, but didn't move to help her. Clever boy. "That's right, I am a crazy bitch," I said, tightening my grip. "Maybe we should start over. My name's October Daye. Does that ring any bells?"

Her eyes widened. "Uh . . ." she said, in a voice that was suddenly much softer, and almost devoid of an accent. "Daye? Like the fish lady?"

"Yes, very much like the 'fish lady.' Exactly like the 'fish lady,' actually. Do you know what happens when you mess with someone who's known your boss as long as I have? I worked for him before you were born. Do you think he'll like hearing how much trouble I had getting in?" She paled, trying to yank away. I almost felt sorry for her—almost—but when you've just been dragged back into fae politics against your will, been cursed, and lost a friend all in one night, "sorry" isn't high on your list of priorities. "I don't think you'd enjoy his reaction. What's your name?"

"Dare, ma'am, my name's Dare," she said, stumbling over her own words. She looked like she'd just stepped outside to find Godzilla on the lawn. I wasn't sure which worried me more—that I'd made her look that way, or that I was enjoying it.

"Well, Dare, I have an idea," I said, and released her arm. She backed out of reach. "You go tell Devin that I'm here, and I'll forget about this little chat. Do you like that idea?" She nodded rapidly. I smiled. "Good. Run along, then. Shoo."

She turned and ran for the back of the room, leaving a trail of glitter in the air behind her. It dissolved as it drifted toward the ground. I raised my eyebrows. Pixie-sweat. Some of Devin's new flunkies had one of the pixie breeds in the woodpile; that was interesting. The Small Folk don't interbreed much with humans, and their blood tends to run thin when they do. When you combined that with the Tylwyth Teg blood indicated by their hair and eyes, well, somebody in the family tree sure got around.

I breathed in quickly, "tasting" the wake of her departure against the innate knowledge of the fae races that I inherited from my mother. She tasted of Piskie. That made more sense; they were size-changers, after all, as well as being natural thieves, which would naturally have drawn their descendants to a place like Devin's.

The brother was watching me, expression caught somewhere between awe and terror. I quirked a brow. "Yes?"

He flinched. I found that strangely satisfying. I guess having people die doesn't bring out the best in me. "You're October Daye," he said. His voice was more lightly accented than his sister's, reinforcing the idea that she was exaggerating for effect.

"Yes," I said, resisting the urge to add anything else. Considering the look he was giving me, he might turn and run. That would upset Devin, and I didn't need Devin mad when I was already in his domain uninvited, looking for favors.

"You knew the Winterrose," the boy said, in an almost mournful tone.

I paused, reappraising him. He was taller than I was, with that thin, lanky teenage build that always seems to fill out while you aren't watching. Overall, he looked like a movie producer's idea of a street thug—too clean, with unnaturally golden hair bundled into a rough ponytail and his too-green eyes softened by an almost puppy dog expression. Only the pointed ears broke the image, making it seem more like he'd escaped from a game of Dungeons & Dragons than from the set of the latest teen drama. I wouldn't have put him at more than sixteen, maybe seventeen, if you stretched the truth and squinted. "What's your name, kid?"

He blushed under my scrutiny, but managed not to squirm as he said, "Manuel."

"Is Dare your sister?"

"Yeah," he said, looking embarrassed. Almost against my will, I found myself warming to him. "I'm sorry about how she talked to you. Sometimes she doesn't do too well with people who aren't . . . who aren't from around here."

"People who aren't family" was what he meant, but I could tell he wouldn't say it to my face. I upgraded my opinion of his intelligence a few notches, saying, "It's not a big deal; I used to live here, and I've had more punks talk down to me than I can count." He colored again, trying not to glare. The kid got points for that: even if your sister's a brat, you should stand up for her. "Relax, okay? I said I wouldn't tell Devin, and I meant it. She doesn't deserve that sort of trouble just for mouthing off."

Manuel smiled, and I smiled back automatically. He was going to be a heartbreaker when he finished growing up. "Th–that's very kind, Ms. Daye." Oh, he was young: I could hear the hastily avoided "thank you" in his stutter. It takes a while for certain rules to become instinctive, especially for changelings. We're not born to them, and our mortal parents tend to drill basic manners into us long before the Choice rolls around.

I shrugged. "It's not a problem. I screwed up, too, when I was her age, and if folks hadn't been willing to give me a break once in a while, I'd be long gone." I paused, choosing my words carefully before I continued. "You said that I 'knew the Winterrose' . . . who did you mean?" Silently, I added, *And how did you know she was dead, kid?*

"Countess Winterrose." He brushed his hair out of his eyes with the back of one hand. "You've heard, right?" He sounded nervous again: he didn't want to be the one who told me I'd just lost a friend. Or maybe he just didn't want me to keep asking him questions.

"Yes. I've heard." How did this kid know Evening? She would never have come this far into the changeling slums fourteen years ago. Then again, even purebloods can change. It just takes them time; maybe a decade and a half was long enough.

"I'm sorry."

"Join the club. How did you find out she was dead?" The words were out, cold and flat between us.

To his credit, he met my eyes as he said, "News travels fast. A Glastig that lives in her building told us—Bucer O'Malley? He saw the police going into her apartment. He listened long enough to find out what was going on and he came here and told us."

"Bucer lived in her building? How the hell did he afford—never mind. It's not important." I remembered Bucer. He was never one of Devin's kids, but he'd done piecework for Devin from time to time. If he thought there was a profit in it, he would've carried the news of Evening's death Home as fast as he could. "Do you know where he was going from here?"

"To the Queen's Court, he said. To tell her."

I grimaced. "Lovely." That was one lead down: after he'd spoken to the Queen, there was no way Bucer would speak to me.

Manuel frowned. "If you haven't seen Bucer, how did you . . . ?"

"I just know. All right?" I knew it all: every little detail, from the way it felt when the blood started filling her lungs to the bite of iron against her skin. I knew everything except for who did it, and that was the thing I needed to know more than anything else.

"I'm sorry," said Manuel. "I should've known you'd

know. They always know up there." *Up there.* So they were still using that charming euphemism for the pure-blood holdings in the city, were they? I hadn't liked it when I was living in the changeling slums, and now that I was doing my best to abandon fae society altogether, I still didn't like it. It's not hard to marginalize people when they've already done it to themselves.

I came back from pondering that reminder of my roots just in time to hear him finish, ". . . but she was good to us, and we'll miss her. We'll always miss her."

My dislike of his language slipped into my tone, making me sound harsher than I intended when I said, "We're talking about the same Evening here, right? Daoine Sidhe, dark hair, didn't give a damn about anything she didn't own?"

That seemed to galvanize him. He straightened, eyes narrowing to slits. Insulting Evening was apparently worse than insulting his sister, and I once again found myself doing some rapid rethinking about someone I thought I knew. What could Evening have done to inspire that reaction in a back-street changeling kid who probably hadn't seen the inside of a school since he was eight?

"The Winterrose was a friend of the boss. She did many things for us here . . . ma'am." He used "ma'am" like it was a dirty word. Only the barest of margins saved it from being an insult, and that gap was shrinking.

"Cool it, Manuel," I said, raising my hands. "I didn't mean to piss you off. Evening and I were friends for a long time, even if we didn't always act like it. I'm going to find out who killed her, and they're going to pay."

The anger in his eyes faded, soothed by the promise of revenge. "I just wish we'd known sooner. If someone had told us . . . we could've saved her." He sounded so sure of himself, secure in his misplaced faith. Part of me wanted to shake him, but the rest of me wanted to swaddle him in cotton and hide him somewhere where the world would never take that faith away from him. The world isn't a nice place—ask anyone.

Ask Evening.

"It wouldn't have done any good," I said. I hated myself for the words, but I wasn't willing to lie to him, not even by omission. Not about this. "We couldn't have saved her."

"We could have kept her alive, gotten her to someone . . ."

"She was killed with iron."

He froze. "Iron?"

"Yes, iron. We couldn't have saved her." The sound of the door opening saved me from his response, and I turned, painfully glad for the distraction. Maybe he was going to grow up someday; that didn't mean I needed to watch.

Dare stood in the doorframe, trying to look cocky and unconcerned. She was failing. Maybe it was the red welt on her cheek that spoiled the effect, already darkening around the edges toward the bruise it would become. "The boss-man says he'll see you now, but you better hurry if you want him to keep on waiting." There was a panicky look in her eyes: those were Devin's words, not hers, and she expected to be the one that got punished for them. The old bastard never changed.

Maybe that's why I loved him for so long.

"Great," I said, and stood, pushing past her into the back hall. The door swung shut behind me, but not fast enough to keep me from hearing Manuel start to cry. Damn it.

He would have found out eventually: if he had been Evening's pawn, someone else was bound to grab him and keep using him in the great chess game of faerie society. Any piece, however small, is too valuable to be allowed to just walk away. Hope isn't always an easy thing in Faerie, but I wished him what hope I could—that he would find his feet before the world found him, and that his new master would be as kind as his old one. Evening was a lot of things, but she was never cruel, not even to her puppets. Her hands were always gentle on my strings.

SEVEN

THE HALL WAS THICK WITH stale cigarette smoke, and the walls were lined with tattered concert posters. The irregularly-spaced lights didn't so much dispel the darkness as displace it, forcing it back into the corners. The dim light and low ceiling combined to keep even fae eyes from seeing what was really underfoot. I stepped on something that squished under the heel of my shoe and grimaced. Maybe the limited visibility was a good thing.

Only one of the hall's four doors was labeled. The doors on the left led to the bathrooms, while the first door on the right led to the broom closet. The three were identical in everything but position, and it was always fun to watch a new kid trying to figure out which he needed. Some of them always got it wrong, but that's the way life works; you grab a door at random and hope it's the one you want, especially if your business won't wait.

There was a sign on the fourth door, marking it for the sake of folks who didn't feel quite as adventurous, or

maybe for the ones who wanted to play a more dangerous game. It was just a piece of tattered cardboard, with
the word "Manager" scrawled in black marker. Someone
had written "is a serious bastard" underneath, in crayon.
Both statements were accurate, in their own ways: Devin
was in charge, yes, and he was also someone you didn't
want pissed off at you. His temper was legendary, and he
rarely gave second chances. He was also the first man I'd
ever loved, and now that I was Home, I was starting to
realize how much I'd missed him, even after everything
we did to each other. I should have come to see him
before there was blood between us to force my hand.
Maybe we would both have been happier if I had. My
eyes on the sign, I raised my hand and knocked.

"Come in," called Devin, in the sort of rich, melodi-
ous tenor that makes teenage girls preen and swoon. I'd
heard it before, of course, but that didn't stop the hairs
on the back of my neck from standing on end as I turned
the knob and stepped through.

Devin's office was lit by a dozen lamps that threw
the grimy walls and aging furnishings into sharp relief. It
wasn't flattering, but it also wasn't an illusion—he showed
you what you were getting, right up front. I had to respect
him for that, even as it worried me a little. Most purebloods are obsessed with light, immortal moths chasing
mortal flames. They can see perfectly well without it, unlike humans or changelings; they want it anyway. Maybe
the attraction is in the uselessness. Devin wasn't a pureblood, but that didn't stop him from following the light.
I'd never been able to figure out why.

Devin himself was behind the desk, half reclining in
his chair. I stopped in the doorway, just looking at him,
trying to breathe.

You'd never guess by looking at us that Devin had
more than a hundred years on me; he was a change-

ling, but his blood was stronger than mine, and the years had been more than kind. Everyone's born to fill a certain role in life. Devin was born to rule his own private Neverland, and he came almost supernaturally well-prepared for the part. His hair was a dark, wavy gold that made my fingers ache to run through it, and his face would have been better suited to a Greek god. Only his eyes betrayed his inhumanity—dark purple crossed with white starburst patterns, like flower petals. You could fall into the crossed and counter-crossed flower-petal darkness of his eyes if you looked into them for too long, finding out what he really was even as you lost track of yourself.

No matter how hard I tried to taste the balance of his blood, I never figured it out, and he never told me. I always suspected that there was Lamia somewhere in his background; the serpent-women have been known to slow their dances long enough to love human men and it's not impossible that there could be children. Stranger things have happened in Faerie. It would have explained the way he sometimes seemed to look deeper with those eyes of his than anyone had any right to look.

He raised his head, a smile lighting his features as he met my eyes. With a small pang, I realized that he was genuinely glad to see me. "Toby!" he said. "You finally decided to come home. I was starting to worry. I didn't think you'd stay away this long." He paused, and smirked before adding, "Nice dress."

"I was a little busy being enchanted and abandoned . . . and please, for Oberon's sake, don't mention the dress." I dropped myself into the chair in front of his desk. It groaned under my weight. Keeping my eyes on his face, I asked the most neutral question I could. "How are you?"

Devin sobered, frowning. "Better than you, from

what I hear. Toby, what happened? Why didn't you come back? I would have let you come back. You're always welcome here."

"You know why I couldn't," I said, glancing down. "Do we really have to go over this again?"

"Maybe if we do, we'll finally get past it."

I took a deep breath, words catching in my throat. Twice. I saw Devin twice after I left Home for Sylvester's Court. The first time was cold and bitter, but it was a natural end; he knew better than to challenge Sylvester's claim on me. The second was the day I came looking for Julie and found him in the front room, waiting for me. He grabbed my arm and asked if the rumors were true—if I was really pregnant with my human lover's child. And I told him I was.

That was the beginning of the biggest fight we ever had. I'm sure the kids still talk about it in the hushed tones usually reserved for natural disasters. We screamed, we ranted, we threw things at one another's heads, and in the end, he let me go, but not without extracting one last promise in payment for the favors he'd done for me: I wouldn't marry Cliff until Gillian was thirteen years old. She was only a quarter-blood, and if she hadn't been forced to make the Changeling's Choice by then, she probably wouldn't have to. Until then, for her sake, he wanted me to be ready to walk away. I laughed in his face and told him I'd send him a wedding invitation. I'm sure he wasn't surprised when it never came.

Finally, head still bowed, I whispered, "I didn't even get to see her thirteenth birthday."

"But that's not why you're here today."

"No." He was backing off, showing mercy. For once, I decided to take it. "It's not."

Raising my head, I looked around the room. All the same furniture was there, although the old brown couch had a larger dip in the middle now, and the same stains were on the wallpaper; even the dent by the door was still there, marking the spot where Julie tried to shove Mitch through the wall for making a crack about her latest boyfriend. I cleared my throat. "The place hasn't changed."

"I didn't want it to."

I looked at him, arching one eyebrow. "I thought change was your hobby."

"Not here. Never here." He shrugged, and for a moment I could see how old he really was. All the years were in his eyes. "Why didn't you come before now? We were thrilled when we found out that you weren't dead. We could have helped. *I* could have helped. I've been waiting for you."

"Why? So you could remind me how stupid I was to leave? How you always knew the purebloods would just use me? I'm sorry, but I've never been real fond of paying for my abuse. Most people are willing to hurt me for nothing." I was lashing out. I knew it, and I didn't care. Evening was dead, the life I'd worked so hard to build was gone, and Home . . . Home was still where I stopped, and all the old ghosts were waiting. It wasn't fair.

His expression didn't change. That just made it worse. "We missed you."

"I missed me, too." I sighed, trying to keep my temper under control. I'm not usually that touchy, but Devin always brought out the worst in me. "I'm sorry. It's been a hard night."

"We heard about the Winterrose. I'm sorry, Toby." There was genuine sorrow in his voice. I frowned. Devin always hated Evening. Hearing him say he was sorry for her death was almost unbelievable.

"What was she to you?" I asked. Real tactful there, Toby.

He stared at me. When he spoke again, the warmth was gone, replaced by a bitter chill. "She kept this place alive after you disappeared. You know the purebloods would love to shut us down. All they need is an excuse—any excuse—and you seemed like a great start.

"You're the one that went out and played the brave knight, Toby; you're the one that started here and went on to something more. You made the Queen leave us alone, because she couldn't rise against your home fiefdom without insulting your liege. That offended the hell out of her, and once you weren't standing between her and us anymore, she stopped backing down."

That was news to me. "She was going to move against you?"

"She almost *did,* until the Winterrose stopped her, in your name. Evening never approved of us, but she protected us anyway, and she did it for you. Did Sylvester try that hard to keep your memory alive?" He paused, expression challenging. I looked away. There were no words that could say what I needed to say to him; I wasn't even willing to try.

There was a long pause, and when he continued, he sounded almost impossibly tired. When did the world get so old? "At first she was doing it for you, but I like to think that maybe, toward the end, she was doing it for herself. That she finally understood why we were here."

"I didn't know."

"No," he said, "you didn't *want* to know. You pigeonholed her the way you've pigeonholed everybody else, and you ignored her when she tried to step out of the role you'd given her. You've done that for as long as I've known you, Toby, and I think I've known you longer than just about anyone else in this world."

"I didn't think—"

"That's not much of a surprise." He stopped and

took a deep breath before flashing me a smile that managed to show all of his teeth at once. "But enough about you—let's talk about me. Did you come here to sleep with me?"

I forced a smile, back on familiar ground. I could ignore the way his words stung until the job was over. "Sorry, Devin. Not this time."

"Afraid that you can't walk away from me twice?"

"Maybe." I relaxed, my smile becoming real. "I really did miss you."

"And we really did miss you, too," he said. "I kept the kids looking for you for ten years, you know. We didn't want to give up."

"I'm glad of that," I said. "Sometimes I think the whole world gave up on me while I was gone."

"I think a lot of the world did, but I was never part of the crowd," he said, and smiled. There wasn't any phony sex in that smile; just old friendship and genuine welcome. I'd forgotten how good that could feel. "Most of the folks you knew aren't here anymore: Jimmy's dead, Julie's working for Lily, John and Little Mike are both down south in Angels. As for the new generation, well . . ." He shrugged.

"The new generation needs to be kept on a leash. Starting with that little blonde bimbo-in-training you have doing front duty. I know everyone stands sentry, Devin, but you should teach her some manners before you let her out in public."

"What, Dare? Did she give you any trouble?" He sounded affronted, but I could tell he was pleased. He wanted his kids to have a certain amount of spirit, as long as they did as they were told.

"Plenty of it, until I told her who I was. Could you have possibly found a kid with a worse attitude problem?"

"No, Toby, you were one of a kind."

"Hey!"

Devin leaned forward, putting his hands on the desk. "She was worse when she got here. The kid couldn't say two civil words to anyone, and now, well, she's just a little mouthy. She's a handful, but she does her share. They all do."

"There are always more kids, aren't there?" I said, looking at the wall behind his desk. He kept a giant bulletin board there, plastered with snapshots of every lost boy or girl that had ever come Home. I was in there somewhere, just another gawky teenager with badly cut hair, a bad attitude, and no common sense to speak of. It was comforting to realize that no matter what happened to me, my picture would always be buried in the collage behind Devin's desk.

"Yes," he said, voice softening. "There are always more kids." How many had he seen die, or vanish, or just fade away? I left Home for Sylvester's Court, thinking it was better: Devin lost me, but at least he knew where I'd gone. How many of his kids just left and never came back at all?

And at the same time, how many of his kids did he bury in unmarked graves after the night-haunts had been and gone? So many changelings are like me, the stolen survivors of supposed childhood deaths. No one would miss them. No one would go looking. If I called one of the Courts in the Kingdom of Angels, and asked about a changeling Silene named John or a half Gremlin called Little Mike, would anyone know who I was talking about? I knew what Devin was. I'd always known. I needed to make sure I didn't forget it.

I knotted my fingers in my skirt, trying to banish that line of thought. This wasn't the time to dwell on it. Later. I could cry about it later, when Devin wouldn't see me.

"We should probably get around to business. I'm sure you have other people that you need to see."

"What do you need?" he asked. I looked up, startled. He wasn't planning to barter: he was just going to give me whatever I asked for. That was what coming back from the dead had earned me. I'd belonged to him, and he'd given up on me, and then I came back to him—how could he refuse me?

It took me a moment to get my bearings. Finally, I said, "I need to know who killed Evening."

"Why?"

"So I can return the favor."

"If I knew who killed her, I'd kill them myself."

"It's not your job, Devin."

"So what makes it yours?"

I took a deep breath, and felt phantom thorns scrape against my skin. "Evening called me before she died. She knew what was coming; she knew they were coming to kill her."

He froze, flower-petal eyes narrowing. "She knew?"

"Yeah, she knew. I don't know why she didn't run."

"Maybe she didn't have time . . ." he said. "Did she tell you who she thought was coming for her? Or why they were coming?"

"No. If she knew, she didn't tell me. But she hired me to find them." It was technically the truth. He didn't need to know that she'd bound me, or how tightly the binding held. No one needed to know. "I'm on a case, Devin, and I can't quit when the person that hired me is dead."

"You can't get paid, either."

"I don't care." Money wasn't the issue anymore; survival was. "She was my friend, and I'm going to do this for her."

"Are you intending to follow her?" His tone was cold.

Fine: if that was how he wanted to play, that was how we'd play. It was his call. Manuel hadn't known the details, and I was betting Devin didn't know them either. "No," I said, curtly. "If I wanted to die, I wouldn't commit suicide by handing myself over to anyone that would slit a woman's throat with an iron blade."

Devin hesitated. "What?"

"Iron." It took a lot of effort to keep my tone level. "They shot her so she wouldn't run, and then they slit her throat." I swallowed the sudden taste of roses, forcing back the sensory memories of Evening's death. Ah, the glorious aftereffects of blood magic.

"How do you know . . ."

"I'm Amandine's daughter, remember?" I waved a hand, not needing to feign the irony in my voice as I said, "Just doing what comes naturally."

"Then you know who killed her," he said, leaning back in his seat.

"No, I don't. They hid it from me somehow, and I need to know. I'm not as familiar with this world as I used to be. It's been too long, and I need help."

"So why are you here? Why aren't you at the Queen's Court, going through all your precious pureblood contacts?" His voice was bitter. I frowned. He didn't approve when I "moved uptown," but this seemed more raw than it should have been. I'd left a long time ago. How long was he planning to resent me for it?

"I went to the Queen before I came here," I said, and held up a fold of water-stained silk, shaking it for emphasis. "Where did you think I got this fabulous dress? It used to be my second-best jeans. I had to announce the death."

"And you came here anyway? What, are you hedging your bets now?"

"No. She refused to help me." Devin frowned, motioning for me to continue. I sighed. "She threw me out, Devin. She wouldn't even let me tell her how Evening died."

"She threw you out? What did you say?"

"Just that Evening was gone. I recited the proper death announcements and everything—I didn't miss a step, but she flipped out." My frustration was spilling over into my voice. "I don't know what's going on there. Her reaction wasn't entirely sane."

"Do you think she did it?"

I paused, considering this for a long moment before I said, "No. It's not like I could touch her if she had, and she freaked out way too much for it to be purely guilt. It could have been someone close to her, I guess, but I don't think so. I think she's just . . . I think there's something wrong with her."

"So there's no help from that quarter. Where else can you go?"

"Shadowed Hills. I can beg Sylvester—but you know he hasn't got any real power in this city." I was buttering him up. He probably knew it, and I didn't care. If putting Sylvester down made him more likely to help me, I'd do it. I'd hate it, but I'd do it.

He sagged in his chair, shaking his head. "You need my help."

"Yes. I need your help. There isn't anyone else."

"I can't give you this one for free, Toby. If there's someone out there that's desperate enough to use iron . . ."

"I never asked for a freebie, remember? You offered." So he was taking it back? Somehow, I wasn't surprised. This was more than a favor to a friend: this was a matter of life or death—most likely death—and that sort of thing is too expensive to just give away.

"It'll cost you."

"I can pay."

He looked at me steadily. I looked back, starting to realize just how much of a difference the last fourteen years had made in him. You can only fight the good fight for so long. Devin gave up a long time ago. "Are you sure?" he said. For a moment, I couldn't find an answer.

Then I remembered Evening sprawled on the floor of her apartment, with a second mouth where her throat should have been. "I'm sure."

After a pause that felt longer than those missing years, he nodded. "Done. I'll send some kids to your place in the morning to check in and make sure you remember your part in the deal."

Oh, I remembered. How could I ever forget? I'd dealt with this devil before; he had my signature under lock and key in his personal files. I didn't sign in blood—he would never have been so gauche—but he trusted the power of my given word to bind me. He trusted, and he was right. I'd pay for any information he brought me, I'd pay for anything his kids did for me, and if he helped me find what I was looking for, I'd pay double. He liked me. I knew enough about what happened to people he didn't like when their bills came due to hope he'd never stop liking me.

"Tomorrow morning doesn't work," I said. "I have to go to Shadowed Hills and talk to Sylvester. Tomorrow night's the soonest I'll be ready for them."

"At least let me have someone escort you home."

I rubbed my forehead with one hand. "Devin, I'm exhausted, and exhausted means I can't deal with your kids right now. I need to get some sleep, or I'm not even going to be able to handle Sylvester."

"If he has no power, why are you going to see him?"

"Because," I replied, looking down at my silk-clad

legs so that I wouldn't have to see his expression. "He's still my liege, and I'm embarking on a murder investigation. I don't have to ask for his help, but I have to tell him before I endanger myself."

I could feel Devin watching me. "You can break your fealty. He's done you no favors."

"Please. Don't ask me for that." I glanced up again. "Not yet." Oath breaking is almost expected from a changeling. That's why I've never done it. Sylvester would release me if I asked him, and I never will, because it would just prove all the things that have ever been said about my kind. I might regret my promises, but I keep them.

Devin looked at me for a moment, expression flat, before he sighed. "Have it your way—I know better than to argue with you." He opened the top drawer of his desk, pulling out something the size of a deck of cards and shoving it toward me. "Take this."

"What is it?" I asked, picking it up.

"Cell phone. I keep spares on hand for just this sort of thing." Devin's nod was small, but satisfied. Purebloods respond to change slowly, if at all. Flexibility and adaptation were changeling traits. If he still had them, he was doing just fine.

After the night I'd had, I would have said there was nothing left that could shake me. I definitely wouldn't have placed my bets on a little plastic box that weighed no more than a few ounces, keys hidden by a flip-down front that made it look like something out of *Star Trek*. Suddenly numb, I lifted my head and stared at Devin.

Fourteen years is no time at all in Faerie. It's the blink of an eye, it's the turning of a single tide. There have been balls that lasted longer than that, waltzes and banquets that stretched on for decades. The mortal world, though . . . the mortal world doesn't work that way. The phone I used to talk to Cliff for the last time before I vanished weighed almost a pound. It was ugly and clunky and almost impossible to lose. This was a sleek, streamlined accessory, the sort of thing every person on the street would carry. It was the future, condensed into something solid. I'd been able to handle it when it was just the humans carrying the things; I could pretend that Faerie, at least, had stayed the same. But it hadn't. Nothing had.

Devin saw the confusion in my eyes, because he smiled a small, hurtful smile, saying, "It wouldn't have happened if you'd stayed here," before he turned to press the button for the intercom. The equivalent button in the main room was set in the wall, under glass. I'd only seen the intercom from the main room used twice. Once it was a prank, and the kid that did it wound up beaten within an inch of his life by half a dozen of the bigger kids. The other time it was because Julie had been hurt so badly that we didn't know how to put her together again, and even then we hesitated, afraid of the consequences. No one bothered Devin without good reason.

"Dare, I need you to come back here and escort Ms. Daye to her car. Now," he said. If Dare was in the bar, she'd come. If she wasn't, someone else would come in her place, and she'd be in a world of trouble.

Lucky for her, she hadn't stepped out for a cigarette. The door opened a few minutes later, revealing a very nervous Dare and her slightly more relaxed older brother. Neither looked happy. That was my fault, but I was still too stunned to really care. I hadn't known what Evening had meant to these people. I would never have guessed—I would never even have dreamed—and I should have known. What happened to the world while I was gone? How much needed to change before the most arrogant pureblood I'd ever known could come to a place like Home and earn that much respect?

"Sir," said Dare, bending in what looked like a six-year-old's approximation of a curtsy, "you need me to take Ms. Daye to her car?" Her accent was substantially lighter when she was speaking to Devin. The bruise on her cheek was flowering now, turning purple and gold.

Devin narrowed his eyes. I used to try guessing how much of The Look was real and how much was an act before I realized it wasn't important. It worked. That was what mattered. Devin might lie to you, but he always got results. "That was why I called you, Dare. You can hear, can't you?"

She cringed. Manuel turned to me, pleading with his eyes. I just shrugged. Devin used the same look and the same lines on me, once; I wasn't foolish enough to try undermining his authority with someone who still believed they meant something. Dare gave him all the power he had over her. Once she grew up enough to figure out that Devin could only control her as long as she let him, she'd be fine, and if she never grew up that much, she belonged at Home, where someone else would take care of the real world and she could take care of the chores.

"Yes, sir," Dare said, straightening. "I can hear, sir. I'll take her to her car right away, it's just outside, and then I'll come back and wait, just like I'm supposed to."

Devin settled back in his chair with a nod. I'd have been scared of him if I hadn't known him so well—and knowing him like I did, I was terrified. He was putting on this little show for my benefit, reminding me that he was in charge and his word was law. He was always putting on the show for someone's benefit, even when no one else was there. Playing mind games with Devin was like playing with dynamite: someone always got hurt in the end. I was hoping like hell that it wouldn't be me.

"Good girl, Dare," he said. She preened under the praise. I think all kids are hungry for a kind word, not just the lost ones that wind up drifting into places like Home. They all react the same way when they're given the validation they need, locking fear and love together so tightly that they never even notice the moment when they grow up.

Dare turned to me, apple-green eyes wide, and said, "I'll show you to your car now, Ms. Daye. You'll follow me?" Manuel watched from behind her. It was hard to face both sets of eyes at once: the color was too bright, too needy.

"Yeah," I said finally, giving in to the unspoken plea in Manuel's eyes. "I'll follow you."

She smiled—the first honest expression I'd seen on her face—and led me away. I could hear Devin making a soft, almost smothered sound as the door swung shut behind us, but I couldn't tell whether he was laughing or crying. For all I knew, all I still know, he may have been doing both.

EIGHT

THE REST OF DEVIN'S KIDS WERE still at the front of the bar. They watched warily as Dare and Manuel escorted me out. I didn't say anything, and neither did they; we didn't have anything to say. I'd been in their position, and I'd gotten out. From my perspective, they were being used, and from their perspective, I was just a sellout. I think we were all glad when I got into my car and pulled away, leaving Home, and the two golden-haired figures on the curb, to dwindle in the distance. Maybe there's something to Devin's little sign after all: every time I think I'm free of that place, it finds a way to pull me back in.

The sky was still dark; dawn was hours away. I'd been awake less than half the night, and I was so tired I could barely see straight. Multiple confusion spells, a major act of blood magic, an encounter with an angry monarch, and a trip Home all inside of six hours will do that to me.

Once I was far enough from Home to feel like I could stop the car without Devin's kids coming knocking at the window, I pulled over to the side of the road and threw the cell phone onto the passenger seat. It landed without a sound. Putting my forehead down against the wheel, I closed my eyes. I only needed a few seconds. Just long enough for me to collect my thoughts and swallow the taste of roses before it could rise up and overwhelm me. Then I could start moving again.

Something knocked on the window.

I raised my head. Either the fog had rolled in with phenomenal speed or there was something strange going on; the world outside the windshield was solid gray, making it an interesting but useless watercolor study. The knocking came again as I scanned for signs of movement. This time it was coming from the back of the car. I whipped around, catching a blurred glimpse of something roughly the size of my cats before it vanished again. Great. I was cold, exhausted, and cursed, and now I was being harassed by something that moved too fast to see. That's always how I like to spend my time.

Moving slowly to keep from startling whatever it was, I opened the door and slid out of the car. Almost immediately, I wished the queen hadn't seen fit to turn my coat into a thin silk ball gown, and that I hadn't abandoned the habit of keeping an emergency change of clothes in the trunk when I decided to retire from my previous line of work. Shivering, I scanned the area. There was no one there. The dim streetlights barely made a dent in the fog.

"Hello?" The air caught my voice, echoing it back to me. That was strange. Most street corners don't have the sort of acoustics that echo. "Hello?" I called again. The echo was stronger this time—something was bouncing my voice back at me. Oh, that was *so* not what I needed. The mist was too thick to be natural. A lot of Faerie's creatures of the night have started taking their special-effects tips from horror movies during the last few decades, and that meant I could be dealing with something nasty.

Of course, it could also be something that just really liked fog. Either way, it wasn't the only one that could use the stuff. Reaching out with both hands, I dug my fingers into the gray, pulling it toward me. I've never been good at shadow-weaving or fire-work, but give me a thick veil of water vapor and I can manage the basics. This time my aim was clarity: water's excellent for scrying, and fog is just water that's forgotten its beginnings.

My head started to pound as I yanked, gathering fog between my hands until I had a sphere the size of a basketball. That was a good sign. If my headache was getting worse, the spell was probably working. I pressed the sphere into a disk, muttering, "Please do not adjust the horizontal. Please do not adjust the vertical. We have control of what you see . . ." The air on the other side of my captive fog began to clear, until I was holding what had effectively become a portable window through the gray. My headache flared before dimming to a slow, grinding ache. It wasn't comfortable, but I'd had worse. I could deal.

Holding the disk at arm's length, I began turning in a slow circle. I spotted my quarry on the second turn: a creature the size and shape of a small cat crouching on the roof of my car, covered in short, soft-looking pink and gray thorns. Shorter thorns ran down its ears and muzzle, making it look like the bastard child of a housecat and a rosebush. It looked small, harmless, and completely out of place. Rose goblin. Not one of Faerie's bigger or badder inhabitants. You don't usually see them in an urban setting.

It rattled its thorns as it saw me looking at it, and it whined in the back of its throat; a grating, almost subsonic sound. The fog swirling around it smelled like dust and cobwebs. That was another oddity. Rose goblins normally smell like peat moss and roses, and while they have a few parlor tricks, fog-throwing isn't one of them. Whatever spell had created this fog was attached to the goblin, but the goblin wasn't casting it.

"What are *you* doing here?" I asked, trying to keep my voice level and soothing. Someone must have wrapped this goblin in magical fog and sent it after me, and that meant whoever it was, they were either clever enough to bind the goblin into following through or really desperate. Rose goblins don't make good messengers for anyone who doesn't have a solid way of controlling them. They're about as intelligent as the cats that they resemble, but they're related to the Dryads, and they share the Dryad flightiness. If you send a rose goblin on an errand, you'd better have something following to make sure it remembers to come *back*.

"Hey, little guy," I said, letting go of the disk of fog and stepping toward the car. The goblin wouldn't be able to disappear as long as I didn't take my eyes off it. Rose goblins are purebloods, but they're not strong ones, and even a changeling has a good chance of keeping hold of them. It whined again, flattening itself against my car until it was basically a doormat made of spines. I stopped, raising my hands. "I won't hurt you. I'm a friend of Luna's. You know Luna, don't you? Of course you know Luna, all the roses know her . . ."

The rose goblin stopped whining, watching me with wide, gleaming eyes. Good. Some flower spirits are more closely tied to their origins than others, and rose goblins tend to cling to the plants that birth them. I meant what I said: I've never met a rose that didn't know Luna Torquill. Being a legend to the flowers must be interesting. It certainly keeps her busy during pruning season. I took another step forward. "Are you okay?"

The goblin sat up, whining in the back of its throat again. Rose goblins can't talk. That makes getting information out of them an adventure all its own.

"You don't look hurt." I leaned forward, offering my hand. The whining stopped, replaced by something like a purr as it arched its back against my fingers. Rose goblins are built like porcupines—if you rub them the right way, you don't have to worry about the spines. They're sort of like people in that regard, too. "Aren't you a friendly little guy?" It was kind of cute, really.

Opening its mouth, it displayed a fine set of needle-sharp teeth. "Nice." It hissed. "Not so nice. What's up?" It crouched away from my hand, rattling its spines, and arched its neck. Something red was wound around its throat. "Hey—what've you got there?"

Purring again, it tilted its head to show me the red velvet ribbon tied around its neck. Something silver was hanging from it. I reached down and twisted the ribbon carefully free, slipping it over the rose goblin's head. The goblin stayed still, purring encouragingly the whole time, but even with this token assistance I pricked myself five times before I pulled away, clutching the ribbon in my hand.

I knew the key before I saw it: my hand remembered the weight of it, even though I'd never held it before. The image of a sprite with wings like autumn leaves darting out of Evening's window, paid for its service in blood, flashed across my mind. I hadn't been there, but I remembered. Blood has power in Faerie, and that power is greater when the blood is given freely. Only the Daoine Sidhe can ride its memories, but other races can use it in other ways—everyone needs a little bit of death. That sprite would have been able to mimic Evening's magic for at least a night, and maybe longer. Long enough to make some smaller bargains of its own.

Faerie's smaller citizens have their own culture and their own customs. Most of us are almost human one way or another: almost human-sized and almost human-minded. The smaller folks never acquired that "almost" and they scorn and resent the rest of us for having it. They don't wear suits, get mortgages, or attend PTA meetings. They haunt the garden pathways, living in the space between what the eye sees and what it chooses to ignore, and they never pretend to be anything that they aren't. I guess that makes it harder to forget what they really are, and what they are is inhuman . . . and greedy. I had no trouble believing that the sprite Evening paid would have commandeered a goblin to finish the deal without endangering itself.

The rose goblin started grooming itself as I pulled my hand away, washing the space between its front claws like a cat. I spent a moment watching it before looking down at the key. It was carved silver, covered in so many rings of ivy and roses that it was barely recognizable as a key, but it knew its nature: it knew what it was meant to do. The roses on the shaft never neared the teeth. They wouldn't interfere. It was warm and heavy in my palm, and it gave off a pale light that colored the mist around it. I got the feeling that there were very few doors it couldn't open. I just hoped it could handle the ones ahead.

The taste of roses was suddenly cloying on my tongue, surging back in tandem with the prickle of phantom thorns. If logic hadn't already told me the key was important, the sudden strength of Evening's curse would have. It was a clue, and her final gift to me. She gave me a job to do, one that might still involve the dubious privilege of dying in her service. She might also have given me the key to my own salvation.

"So where do we go now?" I asked, looking back to the car.

The rose goblin was gone, and the fog it brought with it was already thinning. I bit back a curse and bit my tongue at the same time, hissing to keep myself from shouting. The goblin was my one potential link to the lock that fit the key, and I'd been dumb enough to take my eyes off it. It was probably gone the second I looked away. Just great. Leaning against the car, I closed my eyes. The metal was freezing on my back and shoulders, but at least it stood a shot at easing my headache. I hoped so, anyway.

The key was the last piece I needed to make the situation perfectly frustrating: a murder without a motive, a curse without a cure, and now a key without a lock. If I could fit them together somehow, I would be in business. Fighting to focus past my headache, I opened my eyes and climbed back into the car, where the dome light would let me see the key more clearly and the heater would keep me from freezing.

There seemed to be no logic to the twisted brambles making up the key's head and handle; they were tangled like real vines, and looked like they'd keep on growing if left alone. For all I knew, they would. I narrowed my eyes, looking for the place where the briars began. There were differences in the lines of metalwork if I looked closely enough. Some of the tangles were picked out in darker metals—copper, bronze, or gold—while others blended back into the silver handle. I chose a vine outlined in gold, following it through an overhang of carved ivy and rose branches until it faded behind a triple-twist of interlocked thorns. Jackpot.

Threes are sacred in Faerie. We have three Courts and three rulers, the absent King and Queens that parented our myriad races. Most of our legends say there are three roads to any destination: the hard way, the easy way, and the long way. Evening was a traditionalist. Even when she played human, part of her wasn't willing to fully hide what she was, and so her human name was Evelyn Winters, and the name of her human business was Third Road Enterprises. She brokered her faerie gold and natural skills through the doors of Third Road, and no one ever looked twice, even though the name announced what she was hiding.

Third Road Enterprises, whose offices were coincidentally just a short drive from where I was studying the key she'd been so anxious to protect. I don't believe in coincidence. Everything happens for a reason in this world. I had a destination again. Now . . . well, now I just needed a lock to go with my key.

NINE

THIRD ROAD ENTERPRISES WAS DARK when I arrived. According to the clock on the dashboard, it was a little less than an hour to dawn, when the janitorial staff would probably start to arrive. The rest of the staff wouldn't show up for a few hours after that, if they came to work at all. It was two days before Christmas, after all. If there was any time when I'd be reasonably able to get in and out undetected, it was now.

Despite my best efforts, I found myself wondering how many of the people who worked there would spend the next few days feigning sorrow before suddenly finding work a lot more pleasant. Evening was even worse with people than I am; she froze them out, while I just let them pass me by. Most folks would forget me if I disappeared again, but they'd remember Evening. They always remembered Evening: she was too wild and strange and fair to forget.

The people in that building would never have believed in Evening's true face. They thought they knew her, but they were wrong. They knew a woman as human as they were, and I was willing to bet none of them ever looked for anything deeper. They'd never needed to, because in their world, you put Faerie away when you turned off the nursery lights. There's no place for us in the human world these days, and still we can't let go.

And when the hell did it go back to being "we"?

I walked toward the building, grateful for the lack of security guards. Considering my stained and increasingly grimy gown, no one was going to believe I had a good reason to be entering an upscale office building in the middle of the night. There's pushing the bounds of credibility, and then there's just getting silly.

The taste of roses faded as I walked. It was like playing a game of Hot or Cold with the rules reversed: the closer I got to my goal, the harder it got to know where I was going. If I caught Evening's killer, the curse would snap and the roses would fade altogether, leaving me free to live or die as I chose. My fingers continued tracing the outline of the key cupped in my palm, trying to puzzle out its secrets. Evening had been more worried about it than she was about her own life. Why? Borrowed memories moved in the back of my mind, hissing, *The key will open the way in Goldengreen,* in her voice. I stopped where I was, almost stumbling.

Riding the blood isn't an exact art: bits and pieces of the person you travel with can linger for days afterward, their secrets shaking loose like sand through a sieve. I hadn't thought of the key in conjunction with Goldengreen before. It made perfect sense. I didn't want it to.

Goldengreen was Evening's knowe, and the gateway to her small holdings in the Summerlands. It was locked and sealed to her desires, and the idea of going in didn't appeal. Once I set foot inside the boundaries of Goldengreen, the odds of being caught would go through the roof. I hadn't considered that. What would someone who'd been able to kill Evening do to me? Probably nothing I'd enjoy. Not that I had any choice—not with Evening's curse egging me on. If the key unlocked something in Goldengreen, Goldengreen was my next destination.

The front door wasn't locked, despite the lateness of the hour. I hesitated with my hand on the handle, then walked inside and crossed to the elevator. There were no security guards. I still didn't relax until the elevator doors closed between me and the lobby, and I was headed upward, toward the administrative offices on the ninth floor. The last thing I wanted was to be questioned about what I was doing there, but my luck was holding.

It couldn't last. The door from the elevator lobby on the ninth floor was locked. Worse, it was one of those new keycard locks, which meant I couldn't even try picking it. I rattled the handle a few times before I gave up, scowling. "Great," I said, "now what am I supposed to do?"

Sometimes reality stops being subtle in favor of smacking you upside the head. Standing in front of a locked door with a magic key in your hand probably counts. I lifted the key. Somehow, not even the dimly flickering safety lights could make it look like the tacky stage prop it should have been.

"Will you let me in?" Hoping that I wasn't completely insane, I pressed it against the lock, and said, "I'm here by leave of the Countess of Goldengreen."

Nothing happened. I hit the door with the heel of my hand, saying, "Open sesame, damn it."

The key flared, and the door swung open.

I gaped. Then, recovering my senses, I stepped through the door before it could change its mind. It made sense, in a twisted sort of way: most people would assume that Evening had her locks set to the more florid formal patterns. She could keep almost everyone out just by keeping things simple.

The office was almost totally dark. I pulled the door shut behind me, easing it closed, and stayed where I was, giving my eyes a chance to adjust. I hadn't seen any guards or tripped any alarms that I was aware of, but that didn't mean turning on the lights would be a good idea—and I, prepared as always, had left my flashlight in the trunk. Finding a path through the office would've been a cakewalk for Evening or my mother, but I knew the limits of my changeling's eyes. If I didn't take time to adjust, I was going to smash my shins against someone's desk.

Unfortunately, my eyes weren't adjusting. My head hurt, and thanks to the expensively tinted windows, there was almost no ambient light in the office. "Next time I bring the flashlight," I muttered. The key in my hand suddenly blazed a brilliant white. I jerked my face away with a small, incoherent cry.

It took a moment for the afterimages to fade. When I was sure I hadn't been blinded for life, I turned back toward the key, which was glowing with a rich, rosy light. I stared at it for a moment before shaking my head, muttering, "Lovely," under my breath. Holding the key in front of me like a strange art nouveau torch, I began picking my way through the maze of desks.

The work spaces were almost all decorated with some small, personal touch—a photograph, a selection of small toys, a child's drawing. One of the desks was practically a shrine to Tinker Bell, decorated with a half dozen ceramic representations of the world's most famous pixie. I paused, looking at a figurine of the little blonde bitch posed coyly atop a thimble. Every changeling in the world would love to shove her into a microwave, but Disney, alas, is more powerful than most of us could ever hope to be. Shaking my head, I moved along.

Most of the desks were in cubicles, open to anyone that passed by, but there were a few more enclosed offices along the back wall, their doors closed and locked. The one I wanted was tucked into the far corner, where the view of the city would be at its best. A plain faux-brass nameplate was mounted on the front, engraved with the name "Evelyn Winters." Oh, Evening. We hated each other so well and loved each other so badly . . . and I had no idea what I was going to do without her.

I lifted the key higher, and whispered, "Evening, I'm sorry." There was a click as the lock came undone, and the door swung open.

Some people live where they work. Others just visit. Third Road Enterprises was just a diversion to Evening, and her office was practically empty, reflecting her lack of true dedication. A mortal lifetime was small change for her: by the standards of faerie time, spending thirty years building a company was just another game. There was nothing on the desk or the walls to indicate who worked there, or whether that person was coming back.

Morbidly, I muttered, "At least they won't have to do much cleaning." I had no idea what I was looking for, or what it would look like. Evening's illusions were some of the strongest I'd ever seen, remarkable even for one of the Daoine Sidhe. If she'd concealed whatever it was, it would probably be under a spell I couldn't see, much less break.

After a few minutes of scanning the room, I started turning in a slow circle, holding the key in front of me like a dowsing rod. It made a strange sort of sense, really: the key got me in. It was probably connected to whatever I was trying to find. I made two full turns before the key started to vibrate, nearly jerking itself out of my hands as it was pulled toward the filing cabinet by the window. Lowering it, I moved to kneel and continue my search.

Three of the four drawers opened easily. The second from the top was stuck fast, and when I touched the handle, it felt unnaturally cold; a signature sign of Evening's magic. "It's okay, Evening," I said, touching the key against the drawer. "I got here first."

The binding spell released with a gust of snow-cold air and the smell of roses, and the drawer slid open easily when I tried again. The key's light went out at the same time, leaving me blinking in the sudden darkness. "Crap."

I've done worse things than navigating my way out of an office building by feel. I tucked the key into the front of my bodice, where it would hopefully recharge—that sort of magic item usually does if you give it enough time—before I reached into the drawer. The thought of booby traps crossed my mind, and I quashed it as firmly as I could. Still, doubt lingered, and it was a relief when my questing fingers hit only hanging files.

I let my hands slide past the folders, guiding myself by feel. There was something hard at the back of the drawer, half buried under a pile of loose papers. Brushing the papers aside, I felt for the edges of the object. It felt like a box, a wooden box, about the size of a thick paperback book. My fingers tingled as they brushed against it, and the tingling became a burn, spreading up my arms as I lifted the box and removed it from the drawer. The burning wasn't painful. It was almost pleasant in a way, like rubbing hot oil on sore muscles.

My eyes must have adjusted while I was fumbling in the file cabinet, because I could clearly see what I was holding. I stared, the steadily increasing burning in my arms forgotten.

It was a hope chest.

A real, genuine, hope chest, carved by Oberon's own hand from the four sacred woods of Faerie—oak and ash for bracing and balance, rowan and thorn for pattern and protection. I knew what it was. Any child of Faerie, no matter how thin their blood, would have known what it was. And it couldn't be what I knew it to be, because it was an impossible thing, a bedtime story. It didn't exist. And I was holding it, and it was the reason Evening had been killed. There was nothing else that it could be.

The stories say there are twelve hope chests, that Oberon made them when mankind was still nothing but an interesting diversion. Some people say the chests hold secrets, or stars, or nothing at all; that the Heart of Faerie is hidden in one and the others are decoys, or that they hold a map that would lead us to our missing King and Queens. Some say the chests hold the keys to the deeper lands of Faerie, the places on the other side of the Summerlands. And behind closed doors, they say the hope chests hold a different sort of key: the key to immortality. That they can change the balance of a changeling's blood, making them pureblooded ... or human.

If anyone had asked me whether the hope chests were real, I would have laughed. But at that moment, with the weight of the wood solid against my fingers and the burning spreading through me, I believed, and I understood why Evening chose to protect the key before she protected herself. There's not a pureblood in Faerie who wouldn't die to keep a hope chest safe.

My hands pulled the box to my chest without consulting my brain, thumbs caressing the lid. For the first time since I woke up, Evening's death was the furthest thing from my mind. There was nothing in the world but the hope chest and me. I almost thought I heard it whispering to me, offering the world if I'd lift the lid and see what the stories didn't tell us. I could play Pandora, if I wanted to. I could remake the world.

Pandora was an idiot. I dropped the box, shuddering from cold as much as from temptation; as soon as the hope chest left my fingers, the burning died. Whatever it was selling, I wasn't in the market. I had enough to deal with without being pushed around by magical items that shouldn't exist.

There were plastic trash bags in the office kitchen. I grabbed one, wrapping it around my hands before I picked the hope chest up again, and then wrapped the rest of the bag around the box. It didn't help. I could still feel it. I hadn't seen anything that powerful since I left the Summerlands—maybe not even then—and honestly, I'd never wanted to. Magic that strong never causes anything but trouble. I wanted it away from me as quickly as possible.

Tucking the bag under my arm, I made my way back to the elevator. Time was running short, and there was maybe half an hour left before dawn. I felt horribly conspicuous, like someone was going to jump out of the shadows and accuse me of theft at any second. No one did. I made it back to my car and climbed inside, putting the black plastic bundle of trash bag and hope chest down in the foot well on the passenger's side. It looked so small, wrapped up and set aside like that. It certainly didn't look like anything worth killing for. Unfortunately, somebody thought it was, and that meant I needed to hide it, and fast.

But where? It had to be someplace no one would look. My apartment was at the top of the list of places they would look first. Home and the Queen's Court weren't far below it. I hadn't exactly been subtle. And even finding a hiding place wouldn't be enough; nothing's really safe unless there's someone there to guard it. One way or another, I was going to have to trust somebody, and when it comes to finding someone you can trust with something no one can know exists, you always turn to the ones you hate.

TEN

"TYBALT? TYBALT, IT'S TOBY. Are you here?" I stepped cautiously into the alleyway, holding my skirt away from the ground with one hand. The plastic-swaddled hope chest was under my other arm. It felt more visible than it was, and I kept glancing behind me, waiting for someone to lunge out of the darkness and attack me. Thus far, no one had. I didn't trust my luck to hold. "Come on, Tybalt. We don't have much time. The sun's coming up, and I'm supposed to work tonight."

Oberon only knew what I was going to do about *that*. My nerves were shot. I'd spent most of the drive to the alley where I'd seen Tybalt most recently trying to pretend that what I had riding in my passenger seat was no big deal. It had worked about as well as the time when I was nine and tried to convince myself I could walk through walls. At least this was leaving fewer external bruises.

Maybe more important, I *couldn't* lie to myself about the hope chest. My fingers were still tingling from having held it, and my headache was gone. Wherever it came from, it was the real deal. That made it vital that I get it out of changeling hands. Tybalt isn't the nicest person I've ever met, or even the nicest Cait Sidhe, but he's a pureblood. He wouldn't have a changeling's longing for the hope chest—and no matter how much of a bastard he is or how little he likes me, he keeps his promises. Honesty's not a virtue among the fae, but when a pureblood makes a promise, he keeps it. All I had to do was make him swear.

Not that it was going to matter if I couldn't find him. "Why are you always here when I *don't* want you?" I muttered, moving toward the back of the alley. He'd been haunting me for most of my adult life. I was never sure whether he hated me because I was a changeling or because of something more personal, and I didn't care. Hate was hate, and ours was mutual.

Dawn was close, but the sky was still dark, and the fog was thick enough to reduce my range of vision to practically nothing. I'd tried waving the key around in the hopes that it would do its firefly impression again, but it just hung there like so much ornately carved metal. Getting the flashlight out of my trunk was out of the question—I wanted to attract Tybalt, not blind him. That meant standing alone, effectively blind, in a place he'd claimed as his own, when no one knew where I was or how to find me.

Ever have one of those epiphanies that just screams you're a complete moron? I'd been having one since I got out of the car.

I stood there until my toes were numb and I was shivering so hard that I was running the risk of dropping the hope chest. The sky was starting to get lighter overhead. I had time to make it home, but barely. "Fine, Tybalt," I said. "You win." I turned to go.

He was standing behind me.

I squawked in surprise, barely managing to stop myself before I walked straight into his chest. He crossed his arms, one corner of his mouth slanting upward in a smile.

"Really?" he said. "What's my prize? And why, my dear October, are you gowned so fetchingly? You don't need to make yourself beautiful for me, you know; you'll never win my heart. Although you're welcome to keep trying, if you insist. Next time? Try wearing a corset."

He kept smiling as I fought to get my breath back, and grinned when I snapped, "Oberon's fucking balls, Tybalt, give me some *warning* next time!"

"Why? It's more fun this way."

I blinked, the urge to slap the smile off his face fading. He wouldn't be teasing me if he wasn't interested in what I was doing there, and as long as he stayed interested, he'd listen. Cats are like that. "Well, hello to you, too. Took you long enough to get here."

"I was busy." He frowned, mood turning on a dime. "What are you doing here? The sun's about to be up, you know. I didn't think we were going to be making this a habit."

"Actually I was looking for you."

"You were looking for me?" Now he looked outright disbelieving. "Have you finally lost your mind, or is this some sort of joke that I'm simply not getting?"

"Neither," I said. "I need to ask you for a favor."

"A favor? You're not serious." He took another look at my expression, and his eyes widened, pupils contracting. "You *are* serious. When did you start deciding to ask me for favors? Have I missed something?"

"You want to know why?"

"Since I don't generally ask questions I don't want to have answered, yes, that would be pleasant."

I opened my mouth to reply, and stopped, almost stumbling into him as the pressure of the sun increased, signaling the final approach of dawn. He sighed.

"Ah, the pleasure of your company at dawn. How could I ever have wished to forgo it?" We were already so close together that he didn't have to move to put his arms around my waist; he just did it, advising mildly, "You may want to hold your breath."

"Wha—" I asked, too surprised to pull away.

"Suit yourself," he said, and fell backward, dragging me with him into the shadows still lingering at the mouth of the alley.

It had been cold before, but that was a natural cold, the chill of the early morning in a coastal city. This was freezing, the sort of cold that runs all the way down into your bones. My eyes were open, and all I could see was blackness, the sort of endless dark that children swear waits for them beneath the bed and in the closet. I gasped, and felt the back of my throat burn as the cold seared it.

At first, the only source of warmth was Tybalt, who had me tight against him, arms still locked around my waist. Then I felt the hope chest again, heating my skin through the plastic I had wrapped around it. I didn't throw the warmth away this time; I clung to it, struggling against the urge to take another breath. I had no idea what was going on, but I knew that fighting Tybalt wouldn't get me out of the darkness. It would strand me there.

Just as I was sure I'd die if I didn't breathe, Tybalt moved, pushing me forward, away from him, back into the blazing brightness of the morning. I stumbled, going down on one knee on the damp pavement of the alley as I took in huge, blessedly warm gasps of air. Once I was sure I wasn't dead, I raised my head and stared at him, feeling ice crystals melting in my hair.

"What the hell . . . ?"

"You can talk," he said, expression radiating utter calm. "Your illusions are intact. You aren't panicking or in pain. Can you really say that was worse than standing through the dawn?"

I hesitated, actually looking around me. The sun was up. I could taste the ashes of the previous night's magic in the air . . . and Tybalt was right. My own magic, small as it was, was still entirely intact. I was chilled, but that had been, in its strange and alien way, easier than the sunrise. I stood carefully, testing my balance as I watched him.

"You could have asked me."

"What would you have said?" I hesitated, and he smiled, looking satisfied. "You see? You would be uselessly gasping for air, and not only would I still not know why you came here, but I would have missed the amusement of watching your expression when I pulled you into the shadows. Now. Since I've spared you the dawn, you can honor me with an answer to my question. Why are you here?"

There was no nice way to say what needed to be said. I didn't even try. "Evening Winterrose is dead." Tybalt recoiled, eyes going wide. I continued, "You knew Evening. You know what she could do. She used the old forms when she died, and she bound me. She wrapped me in a chain so tight that it's choking me, and you're the only person that can help me."

Tybalt's eyes remained wide as he frowned. "Me? Why me?" His expression was pained. He and Evening were never friends—they never even cared enough to be enemies—but they'd been in the same city a long, long time. Some ties run deeper than friendship. The news of her death had him off-kilter.

"Because I'm still in her service, and that means I

have to keep going, even if it kills me. I need somebody
to back me up if things . . . if things don't go as well as
they might."

He flinched, and demanded, "Why in the hell would
she choose *you?* You couldn't even find a living woman.
How are you planning to avenge a dead one?"

For once, the reminder didn't sting. Yes, I'd failed, but
that didn't mean I'd fail again. Not this time. "Please,
Tybalt. I need you." I bowed my head in a calculated
gesture of submission. A lot of purebloods still say we
owe that sort of thing to our "betters." The world has
changed, but they don't care; time can't get much of a
foothold in fealty. "My skills have limits." I was laying it
on pretty thick. I didn't think he'd object.

"What do you want from me?" His voice was flat. I
glanced up to find him standing at attention, shoulders
tense, glaring. I'd handed him a full measure of grief and
then asked for favors; if I was lucky, he'd let me finish
talking before he ripped me open and left me for the
night-haunts.

"I want you to guard this." I pulled the garbage bag
off the hope chest, holding it up for him to see. The touch
of the wood against my skin set my hands tingling again,
sending bolts of heat up my arms.

Tybalt froze, confusion washing across his face. "Is
that . . . ?"

"Yes."

"But they don't exist."

"Guess we were wrong about that, huh? It's real.
Evening had it. She hid a clue with the autumn sprites
and told them to bring it to me." I paused before saying the words I'd been hoping to avoid: "I think she got
killed for it."

"I don't understand. They're not . . . the hope chests
aren't *real.*"

I shook my head. "I know that. I also know that at least one of them exists, and this is it, because I can feel it, Tybalt, I can feel it singing to me. I don't know how true the stories about hope chests and changelings are, but I know enough to know that I can't trust myself with it. I can't trust any changeling with it. It has to be in pureblood hands, at least until I find out who killed Evening." *Please,* I added silently. *I don't know how long I can hold out.*

The burning was getting strong again, faster than it had before. The hope chest knew who I was now, and whatever it had been designed to do, it was eager to get to work.

Tybalt glanced away. "The Queen . . ."

"She won't help me. She's already refused."

"Why?" He looked back, suddenly frowning. "What does she know?"

"If I knew that, I'd feel safe asking someone at Shadowed Hills to guard it. But I don't know why, and that means, for everyone's sake, that it needs to stay with someone she doesn't control." The Courts of Faerie have no control over the Cait Sidhe, by Oberon's own decree. The Queen couldn't touch Tybalt. Maybe she wasn't a murderess, but our brief encounter had left me with the sinking suspicion that she was going insane, and if that was the case, I really didn't want to deal with her while I was cursed and looking for a murderer.

Tybalt's eyes narrowed. "Why not just take it Home? I've heard you'd still be welcome there. Surely your ban on changelings can't extend so far as that."

"Devin's got enough trouble with the Queen. I don't need to cause him more." I studied Tybalt's expression, and frowned. I didn't know of any bad blood between him and Home. Fourteen years is plenty of time to start a feud.

"The Tea Gardens, then."

"That's the first place anybody who's trying to find it would look. If they know I can't hide it with Sylvester ..."

"They'll assume you've taken it to the Lily-maid."

"Exactly." I cocked my head, watching him. "So you'll do it?"

"You still haven't said why you're coming to me. I'm not the only cat in this city."

"Because you hate me." Seeing his confusion, I clarified: "There's never been any love lost between us, and there probably never will be, but you keep your word, and I know that if you say you'll do this for me, you'll do it. Your honor might survive betraying a friend, because the friend would forgive you. I wouldn't."

His expression hardened. "What's in it for me?"

"The chance to get me in your debt." I allowed myself a thin smile. "That's worth enough that I know you'd keep your word."

He was silent for a long moment; long enough that I started to worry that I'd gone too far. Finally, voice hushed, he said, "So you'll trust me because you don't trust me?"

I swallowed. "Yes," I said.

"You'll owe me for this. You may never pay this debt; I may never let you. I could hold it over you for centuries. I could decide to never let you go." There was an odd warning note in his voice, like he wanted me to reconsider.

"That's my problem, isn't it?" I raised my head a little further and met his eyes.

· He blinked, apparently surprised by my boldness. Then he shrugged, saying, "Very well," and reached for the box, trying to tug it from my hands.

I kept my grip on the hope chest. "No," I said, sharply. "Promise first."

He glared at me; I glared back. "You know the rules. You want me in your debt, fine, I'm going willingly. But I'm going by the rules. Now promise."

"If you insist," he said, and straightened, squaring his shoulders before chanting, "By root and branch, by leaf and vine, on rowan and oak and ash and thorn I swear that what is given to my keeping shall remain in my keeping and shall be given over only to the one who holds my bond. My blood to the defense of the task I am set, my heart to the keeping of the promise to which I am bound." The air grew thick with the taste of penny-royal and musk as his magic crackled around us, drowning out the taste of roses.

"Broken promises are the road to our damnation," I said, the copper and cut grass smell of my own magic undercutting his. "Promises kept are the meeting of all our myriad roads."

"And such a meeting will my promise be." The magic shattered around us as the formalities ended and he pulled the hope chest away. This time I let it go, my fingers aching as they pulled away from the wood. How badly did I want it? I didn't know. I didn't want to.

"Thank you, Tybalt," I said, lingering on the forbidden words. Thanks implies fealty. As long as Tybalt held that chest, he was in mine. It was rude beyond belief for me to point it out that way. I wasn't sure exactly why I did it; chalk it up to stress.

He tucked the chest under his arm, glaring, before he turned and stalked away. He turned back as the shadows parted like curtains in front of him, saying, "There will be a reckoning, October," before he stepped through them and was gone.

Shivering, I wrapped my arms around myself and walked back down the alley, heading for my car. There was no time to linger; I needed to go to Shadowed Hills, and I was exhausted. I needed to get some sleep. Evening's curse wasn't crippling me yet, but it would start eventually, and once that happened, it wouldn't matter how tired I was. Somehow, time had become a limited commodity.

I stopped beside my car, looking back into the darkness of the alleyway. "Yes, Tybalt," I said to the empty air. "I know."

ELEVEN

IT WAS ALMOST SEVEN by the time I staggered back into my apartment, stumbling over the hem of my stained silk gown and garnering curious looks from the cats, who weren't used to me coming in smelling of smoke and the sea. The sky outside the window was turning slowly from rosy gold to a clear, crystalline blue as the sun finished its climb above the buildings. That's one thing you've got to give San Francisco: there are too many people, the rent is hell and the politics are worse, but we have beautiful mornings. Somehow, in the koi pond and everything that came after, I'd forgotten that part.

I shut the door and leaned against the wall, letting my human disguise waft away into the faint, distant taste of copper. Lowering the spell left me feeling oddly refreshed and clean despite the layers of grime I'd acquired during the night. The cats twined around my ankles, complaining. I vaguely remember spooning food into their dish before collapsing facedown on the bed, too tired to bother shutting the curtains, and falling into my dreams.

For the first time in weeks, I didn't dream of the pond. I don't remember what I dreamed, but whatever it was, it didn't stay with me long enough to be remembered. I woke up stiff, aching, and still dressed in the blue silk gown that used to be my second-favorite pair of jeans. I sat up, pressing a hand against the side of my head, and paused. The headache I expected wasn't there, and it only took me a moment to remember why. I touched the hope chest. I touched the hope chest, and my headache went away. Had it changed me in just that brief, accidental contact? Root and branch, how powerful was that thing?

My memories of the previous night were jumbled but clear enough to understand, from Evening's last frantic phone call to being ordered away by the Queen of the Mists, the discovery of the hope chest, and my bargain with Tybalt. It was the Queen's reaction that puzzled me the most. Evening's death was a mystery and a tragedy, but there was an answer waiting somewhere for me to find it; the existence of the hope chest told me that, if nothing else. The Queen's response to her death was another matter. I could have understood shock, sorrow, or even anger at the messenger. What I didn't understand was her panic at the very concept of Evening's death. Why had she reacted that way? Where did Evening get the hope chest in the first place, and who knew she had it? Too much of this wasn't making sense, and I didn't like that one bit.

The lack of a headache was more worrisome than anything else. I'd done more magic than was good for me the day before. On a good day I can maintain my illusions without any slips and still reset my wards. That's on a good day. Add several small misdirection spells, fog-scrying, and an adventure in blood magic to the mix and I should have found myself one exit past pain and approaching the highway to agony. Magic-burn hurts more than anything physical, digging down until it finds nerves you didn't even know existed. What, exactly, did the hope chest do to keep all that from happening?

Lacey jumped onto the bed, strolling up to butt her head against my chin. At least someone was having a good day. Of course, the cats would have a good time in nuclear winter, as long as somebody was left to feed them. I scratched her behind the ears and sighed. If the cats could get up, so could I.

Pushing the cat off my chest, I levered myself out of bed. "I already fed you, Lacey, stop pretending I didn't. I need a shower before . . ."

The sentence died as phantom rose branches slapped me across the face and throat, driving invisible thorns deep into my skin. I bent double, too surprised to stop myself from screaming.

Sylvester warned me once about how badly a binding curse could hurt you if you didn't do what it demanded. That didn't mean I really understood him until now. Every breath hurt. It felt like my skin was being peeled away, and the world was drowning in the cloying stench of roses. I struggled not to fall over, gagging on the scent. Inaction wasn't an option: not with the knives of Evening's command digging into me.

Squeezing my eyes closed, I said, "I know. I'm doing it. Please? Wait." The stinging receded, although I could still feel thorns brushing my skin. That didn't matter—I could think and move again. That was all I needed.

Getting out of the grimy ball gown was a challenge. Forcing myself through the process of showering and getting dressed was harder. I kept stumbling, catching myself against the walls as I tried to remember how things like pants worked. The cats milled around my ankles throughout the process, but I didn't pay them any attention; my thoughts were far away, reviewing Evening's death over and over again. I hadn't dreamed of her. I'd thought that was a mercy, but it turned out the dreams were just waiting until I was awake. Lucky me.

After half an hour of tripping over my own feet, I was finally dressed, wearing clean jeans, a plain white shirt, and a loosely knit gray sweater for warmth. The sky outside was gray with clouds, making me really start to miss my coat. Unfortunately, I didn't think going to the Queen's Court to ask for it back would be a good idea. After a moment's hesitation, I shoved the key I'd taken from the rose goblin into the pocket of my jeans.

The cats were crying to be fed. "I still say I fed you already," I said, as I filled their dish before making myself a peanut butter and marshmallow fluff sandwich, acting under the sadly reasonable assumption that I wouldn't get another chance to eat. To my surprise, the food went down easy, and I made myself a second sandwich before heading into the bathroom to fit my human disguise into place.

Maybe being cursed is good for me, because the spell came together the first time I tried it, blunting the too-sharp angles of my ears and cheeks into something more realistically human. I left my hair loose, blunting those angles still further.

"I can do this," I said to my reflection. It didn't contradict me.

The cats were on the couch when I left the bathroom and watched impassively as I strode through the apartment and out the door, grabbing my keys off the counter as I passed. Resetting the wards took a matter of seconds, the magic coming, again, with surprising and unsettling ease. There were wild mushrooms growing on the narrow strip of grass beside the door. I paused to pick a few, tucking them into my pocket. You never know what you're going to need.

There was no one in sight as I walked to my car. It was too close to Christmas. Everyone was either at work, shopping, or with their families, not hanging around the parking garage, and that was fine with me. I was already planning to see enough unfriendly faces. Evening's curse relaxed when I started moving; there was no need for it to hurt me when I was actually getting things done.

Taking one last breath to steady myself, I climbed into the car, put the key into the ignition, and started for the freeway.

Shadowed Hills is the largest Duchy in the Bay Area, consisting of the area around Mt. Diablo. That mountain defines their boundaries; if you can see Mt. Diablo, odds are good you're in the Duchy. It's one of the largest political entities in the Kingdom of the Mists, but it makes up for it by having several semi-autonomous Counties and no political aspirations whatsoever.

Still, it's big enough to support some pretty spectacular architecture. Maybe that's why, as if to spite the expectations of anyone who might come to visit, the Torquill knowe is located in a park called Paso Nogal in the sleepy suburb of Pleasant Hill, about twenty miles outside the boundaries of the Mt. Diablo State Park. It would take a little less than an hour to get there, driving counter-commute. Getting into the knowe might add another twenty minutes. They're big on security, and I couldn't blame them; not after what happened to Luna and Rayseline.

I pulled into the parking lot at Paso Nogal and got out of the car, actually somewhat grateful for the cold. From the look of the grass, it had been raining, and that had driven off the bored teenagers that might otherwise have been spending their Christmas vacation hanging around in the park. Silently blessing the weather, I began the trek up the side of the nearest hill.

The Torquills believe in taking precautions: entering their knowe requires jumping through a series of metaphorical hoops that range from silly to annoying. I stopped to catch my breath after walking up the largest hill in the park, crawling under a cluster of hawthorn bushes, and running six times counterclockwise around an oak tree. The ground was slick and muddy, but at least the rain had stopped. My one and only trip to Shadowed Hills in the rain convinced me years ago that there was nothing that pressing.

Once I was sure I wouldn't collapse, I turned, knocking on the surface of a nearby stump. The sound echoed like it was rolling through a vast hall, and a door swung open in the hollow oak nearby. Smoothing my shirt and brushing my hair away from my face in a gesture that was half anxiety, half courtesy, I stepped through into the knowe of Shadowed Hills.

Whoever built the knowe had very firm ideas about how space was meant to be used—lavishly and without limits. The knowe meets and exceeds the physical limitations of the hill that supposedly contains it; there are rooms that haven't known footsteps in more than a decade, places only children remember, hidden passages and gardens that haven't been tended since we lost our Lord and Ladies. It wasn't opened in Paso Nogal, I know that much. Sylvester shifted the doors there at some point in the last two hundred years, connecting otherwise unrelated locations in the mortal world and the Summerlands.

Evening told me Sylvester took my disappearance as a dark omen and sealed the knowe, swearing not to step outside until his family came home. I can't blame him. He and Luna were a perfect match, and losing her might have killed him. Instead, it just drove him insane. His seneschal ran the Duchy in his place, and Shadowed Hills fell into despair. Among the fae, the King is the land, and in Shadowed Hills, the King was mad.

That madness broke when Luna came home. Of all the news Evening relayed while she explained the things I'd missed, that was the only part that made me smile. Walking through Shadowed Hills for the first time since I'd come home, it was like there'd never been anything broken there at all. It was the same now as it had ever been. Everywhere I looked there was too much gilt, too much velvet, and generally too much of everything. Even the windows were ringed with garlands of silver and pale blue roses. The smell made me cringe, but you can't have Shadowed Hills without roses—not with Luna there. She's the Lady of the Roses, and the Duchy reflects her as much as it reflects Sylvester.

People bustled past in all directions, purebloods and changelings alike, displaying the frantic activity needed to keep a Ducal Court running. None of them knew me, and so none of them stopped to ask why I was there. I stopped and opened a door at random, looking into a small room with dust piled several inches thick on the floor. A donkey-tailed maid brushed by me with a reproachful look, beginning to sweep up. I smiled wanly, moving on.

Evening didn't tell me where Luna and Rayseline had been, and I hadn't pressed; I got the impression from the things she wasn't willing to say that they still didn't quite know what had happened. Luna and her daughter were gone, and then they weren't. Sometimes that's how it works. It's one of the downsides of living in a land that sometimes seems like it's based on a children's story.

A footman met me at the end of the hall, sneering at my clothes. I sneered at him in return, although I had to admit that he was probably more justified. He was dressed in the blue-and-gold livery of Shadowed Hills, ready to receive anyone up to Oberon himself, and here I was, in jeans. Not exactly Ducal Court material.

"Would my lady care to state her business?" he asked.

"Your lady is here to see the Duke. How would you like her to go about doing that?"

He gave me another, even more disdainful look. "Perhaps my lady would care to change first."

"Certainly," I said. There are ways of following form that need to be obeyed. Changing for Court when asked to do so is one of them.

The footman waved toward a door off to the right. Offering a shallow bow, I walked over and opened it.

The room on the other side was larger than it had any right to be, walls mirrored and reflecting an infinity of weary-eyed women draped in the thin flicker of a hastily-spun illusion. A table at the center of the room was heaped with leaves, feathers, flower petals, and carded spools of spider-silk. The implication was plain, by fae standards: if you couldn't make a workable glamour from what was offered there, your business probably wasn't that important. It's a subtle sort of pureblood prejudice, and one of the few that still hangs on in Shadowed Hills. I took a deep breath, letting my disguise wisp away until an equally-weary changeling blinked at me from all those myriad reflections, ears pointing through uncombed brown hair. Time to make myself presentable for the nobility.

After studying the table's contents, I selected a handful of leaves and a spool of spider-silk. Artistry in dresses takes seamstresses and the resources to hire them. Most changelings aren't that well off, and so we wind up using an endless stream of disposable illusions and short-term transformations, crafting couture from whatever raw materials the various Courts are willing to provide. As long as we don't come out looking like kitchen help, we do okay.

I closed my eyes and crumpled the leaves in my hands, mixing them with spider-silk until they formed a gummy paste that stuck my hands together. Once the mess stopped crackling as I squeezed it, I ran my hands down the sides of my torso and hips, picturing a simple cotton dress in golden brown—I've always looked good in that color—with matching slippers sensible enough to run in. One night in heels was enough to hold me for a while. The scent of copper and cut grass grew thick around me, almost banishing the taste of roses as the spell took shape.

The gummy feeling on my hands faded, replaced by the swish of heavy skirts around my suddenly bare legs, and the absence of hair brushing against the back of my neck. With a final burst of copper, the spell snapped closed, sending me reeling. Even as fresh as I was, casting a spell that complex was enough of a strain that it took a moment of leaning heavily against the laden table before I could get my eyes to focus on the mirrors. Once they did, I studied myself, and sighed.

The dress was wrong.

I'd been aiming for cotton, and I wound up with velvet; the neckline was substantially lower than I'd intended, and the bodice was embroidered with climbing ivy, making it look even more like I'd been trying to draw attention to something other than my eyes. The slippers were practical, thankfully, but they were embroidered to match the dress. Even my hair was wrong, pinned up in an elegant series of layers that made it almost look like it was something other than stick-straight. I glared at my reflection. It didn't change.

It wasn't what I'd intended, but it was a decent dress, and I didn't feel like crafting a new one. It would have to do. Turning, I left the room.

Despite exiting through the door I'd entered by, I stepped out into a different hallway altogether. The footman who had ushered me in was gone, replaced by a page standing at rigid attention in front of the audience chamber doors. His starched tunic and breeches were probably real, unlike my dress: this kid was definitely upholding the dignity of his office. Ah, well; he'd probably loosen up as he got older.

His expression hardened when he saw me, eyes settling on the dull points of my ears. Not just young; young enough to think changelings had no business at Court. Interesting.

Sometimes the best way to deal with prejudice is to ignore it. "Morning," I said. "Here to see Sylvester."

"And you are?" he said, giving me the sort of look usually reserved for people with contagious diseases and unpaid bills. There was something familiar about him. He had the blond hair and blue eyes common in young Daoine Sidhe, and looked like he was maybe fourteen years old.

"Sir October Daye of the Kingdom of the Mists, once of the Fiefdom of Home, Knight of Lost Words, sworn to Sylvester Torquill, daughter of Amandine of Faerie and Jonathan Daye of the mortal world," I said. My full title takes far too long to say, and I'm just a knight. When the real nobles get going, it can take hours. "Also an old friend of the Duke and Duchess, so are you going to let me by, or should I sneak in through the kitchens?"

The page blinked, once, eyes narrowing. "Oh," he said. "It's *you*."

I blinked. "Have we met?"

"In only the strictest sense of the word," he said. He spoke with a very faint Canadian accent.

It was the tone, even more than the accent, that tipped me off. "Oh," I said. "Uh. Hello. You look much better this way. The whole human thing didn't suit you."

"I'm sure His Grace is waiting," said the page frostily.

Sylvester absolutely wasn't waiting; Sylvester didn't know I was coming. Given that, I was tempted to stay in the hall and talk to the page a little longer, take the time to try to change his mind . . . but time wasn't exactly something I had in abundance. Evening's curse would move me if I didn't move myself.

Reunions don't get any easier when you delay them. Offering a last, formal bow of my head, I moved past the page and into the audience chamber.

The room was deserted when I entered, save for four figures sitting on the dais at the far end. Most of Shadowed Hills is built a little larger than it needs to be, and no single room defines that aesthetic better than the audience chamber, which could be used to host an indoor carnival, should Sylvester ever feel the urge. He hasn't, as far as I know, but some of the parties he and Luna have thrown were large enough to become the stuff of legend. The knowe's designer probably intended the room to seem majestic and to create an atmosphere of awe in the petitioner. All it's ever done for me is create the urge to get a pair of roller skates and cut my travel time in half.

My steps echoed against the marble floor. I was halfway across the room before I could see any details of the figures on the dais; two men and two women, one man and the younger of the women with that characteristic fox-red Torquill hair, the other woman more literally foxlike, with silver-furred ears and three tails curled beside her on her velvet cushion. The younger man looked awkward and almost out of place alongside the other three, his hair an untidy mop of gray-brown curls, his concession to the Ducal colors a pair of blue jeans and a yellow tunic.

I must have seemed like just another member of the Court for most of my trek across the audience chamber, a brown-haired woman in a brown velvet dress with nothing unusual about her. Luna was the first to realize who I was. She straightened in her seat, ears going flat against her head, tails uncurling and starting to twitch. Her sudden attention alerted Sylvester, who turned toward me, frowning. I could see the confusion on his face, growing more pronounced as I continued to approach.

Then the confusion faded, replaced by something I hadn't expected. I thought I was prepared for almost anything. I wasn't prepared for this.

"Toby!" he cried, sheer joy transforming his features as he rose, almost knocking over his chair in his hurry to descend from the dais. I froze, stunned. Sylvester crossed the space between us at something close to a run, catching me by the waist and swinging me up into the air before I had time to remember how to move. He was laughing now, joy fading enough to show the emotion behind it: relief. Pure, unadulterated relief.

I'd been hiding from Shadowed Hills because I didn't want to face him; I didn't want to see the look in his eyes when I came creeping back and admitted that I'd failed. But all I saw when I looked at him now was the joy of a friend who's finally seen something they'd thought was lost come home.

Finding something to say seemed impossible. Luna saved me from the need, stepping up and putting a hand on Sylvester's arm as she said, "Dear, you might want to put her down before she gets motion sickness. I'd really rather not have to explain to the Hobs why they need to mop the floor before tonight's Court."

Still laughing, Sylvester swung me back down to my feet, saying, "Yes, yes, of course," before pulling me into a hug. He smelled, as always, of daffodils and dogwood flowers, and the solid, reassuring scent of him was enough to make it difficult not to cry. I sniffled, pulling away to wipe my eyes. Sylvester hesitated, and then let me go.

I stumbled back a few steps, taking refuge in formality as I bowed, holding myself at the low point of the arc. I can say one thing for the nobles: they probably have the combined thigh strength to take on every synchronized swimming team in the world. Holding a formal bow hurts, and it's always good incentive toward doing heavy stretches before I have to do it again.

"Toby?" said Sylvester quizzically.

"I don't think she's going to stop doing that until you acknowledge her, dear," said Luna.

"I picked her up. Doesn't that acknowledge her presence?"

"I meant a little more formally."

"Oh." Sylvester cleared his throat. "Yes, October, I see you. Can you stop that, please? Where have you *been?* Well, I know where you've been, that was a silly question, forget I asked it, but we've all been worried sick about you, you know. We only found out you were back when Evening called out of courtesy." He sounded faintly hurt now. "I've sent messages. Didn't you get them?"

"Yes, Your Grace, I did," I said, straightening. "I just . . . I wasn't ready to answer them."

"But why?" Sylvester asked, looking at me like a kid who's just been told that Christmas has been canceled.

"I think I know the answer to that one," said Luna, putting her hand on his arm and offering me a warm, if slightly sorrowful, smile. "Hello, Toby. You're looking well."

"As are you, Your Grace," I said, smiling back. I couldn't help it. It's hard to look at Luna without smiling.

Short, slender, compact; you could describe the Duchess of Shadowed Hills in those words, if they wouldn't make her sound so fragile. Luna was a small woman, but she was anything but breakable, with arms strengthened by hours of gardening and all the magical defenses her Kitsune blood implied. Their strength is advertised by the number of their tails, and she had three to call her own, silver-furred and sleek. Her waist-length brown hair was plaited back, and she was dressed for gardening, ignoring the formality of her surroundings. Luna has never been much of one for standing needlessly on ceremony.

"You should have come before this," she chided lightly. "We've missed you."

"I've missed you, too," I admitted, and turned to face Sylvester. "Your Grace . . ."

"We looked for you," he said. There was an urgency to his words, like there was nothing in the world I needed to hear more than I needed to hear what he had to tell me. "We looked for you everywhere. You have to believe me. When you vanished, I set Etienne to scouring the city, I sent half my knights with him, I did everything I could, and you were just . . . you were just gone, Toby. I'm so sorry."

Sorry? He was admitting that he'd taken resources away from the search for his wife and daughter—admitting it while his wife was standing right next to him, no less—and he was telling me he was *sorry?* I gaped at him, not sure what I could say.

Rayseline saved me from answering by stepping up on her father's other side, sliding her hands around his arm and looking at me. Her eyes were the same gold as her father's, but while on him the color was warm and welcoming, on her it seemed almost reptilian, the gaze of a predator.

"Oh, look," she said. "She's finally deigned to come and see the consequences of her failure. Hello, failure. How've you been?"

"Hello, Rayseline," I said, keeping my tone measured. Whatever relief I might have felt at her interruption died at her words.

We don't know what happened to Luna and Raysel during the twelve years that they spent missing—twelve years that corresponded with the first twelve years of my own missing time. But while for me, those years were lost, whatever they went through, they lived it. The few people I'd spoken to said that Luna came back a little sadder, a little stranger, but Raysel . . . Raysel came back wrong. Growing up the way she did broke something inside of her, and looking at her now, I began to realize why the whispers said it might never be repaired.

"I wondered when you'd come sniffing around here," she said. "Looking for something else that you can't do? I'm sure Daddy has plenty of unsolvable puzzles and quests that can't succeed. Go do some of those."

"Raysel, that's enough," said Sylvester, sharply. "I'm her liege. October is always welcome here."

"She wants something," said Raysel. "I can smell it on her."

"Rayseline, that's quite enough," said Luna. The normal calm of her tone was gone, washed in worry and barely concealed irritation. Raysel's unpleasantness wasn't just an act for my benefit, then.

"She's right," I said. Sylvester and Luna both turned toward me. Raysel smirked, looking triumphant. "I'm afraid I am here because I want something. Or, well. Because I need to tell you something, and I need to ask for a favor."

"Anything," Sylvester said. "You know that."

"I'm not so certain about that," I said, glancing from him to Luna and back again. "Have you heard the news?" *Please say yes,* I prayed. *Don't make me be the one that tells you.* If the Queen were reacting at all sanely, her heralds would already have been and gone ... but everyone seemed much too calm for that, and the Queen had said no one would even speak Evening's name. That would make it sort of hard for her to send out notices.

If Sylvester didn't know, it was my duty to tell him. And I desperately didn't want to.

"We heard there was going to be an end of winter ball at the Queen's knowe in two weeks," offered Connor, finally abandoning the dais and moving to stand next to Rayseline—next to his wife. Smirking at me, she transferred her hold from Sylvester's arm to his. "Please tell me you didn't finally decide to come visit cause you thought we'd missed the latest exciting issue of the Kingdom newsletter. Hey, Toby."

"Hey, Connor," I said, smiling despite the grimness of the news I was about to share. It's hard not to smile when looking at Connor.

Take your standard California beach bum, give him spiky brown hair streaked with seal's-fur gray, brown eyes so dark they verge on black, slightly webbed fingers and a baked-in tan, and you've got Connor O'Dell. He was the Undersea emissary to Sylvester's Court when I was serving there. We were ... friends. Good friends. We might have been more than just good friends, if his family hadn't objected to the idea of him being involved with a changeling before Connor and I could move beyond a few sweet, fumbling encounters in the gardens that dotted the knowe. He said he was sorry; so did I. And then I let myself get swept off my feet by a human man who would never say he couldn't love me because my blood wasn't pure enough.

I never blamed Connor for the way things happened. That's just the way it goes for a changeling in a pureblood's world. Coming home to hear that he was married to Rayseline Torquill was a shock, but it didn't decrease my fondness for the man. Just the likelihood that I was going to let his wife catch me checking out his ass.

Sylvester, meanwhile, was simply looking puzzled. "No," he said. "There's been no news—at least, not anything big enough to bring you back to us. What's going on, Toby? It's not that I'm not thrilled to see you, but . . . why are you here?"

I swallowed. "So you haven't heard anything about the Countess of Goldengreen?"

Sylvester's look of puzzlement increased. "Evening? No, nothing. Is something wrong?"

"Wrong?" I bit back a near-hysterical giggle. "Yes. Something's very wrong."

"Is she hurt?"

"No. No, she's . . . Your Grace, Evening was killed last night. She's dead."

Luna's ears flattened against her head. "Dead?" she whispered.

Raysel's sudden laughter cut off any answer I could have given. We all turned to stare at her as she released her husband's arm, sweeping out of the room on the tide of her own merriment.

"What—" I said.

"Connor, go with her," said Luna. It wasn't a request.

Nodding dolefully, Connor shoved his hands into his pockets and trailed after his wife. He caught my eye as he passed, and the look on his face was sad, almost beaten. Raysel's the one with the Kitsune blood, but he was the one who looked like a whipped puppy.

The three of us stood for a moment in uncomfortable silence before Luna glanced to Sylvester and said, "She's still a little unstable from everything that . . . from everything. My family has always been subject to . . . well. We don't recover quickly from the sort of things she was forced to go through. It's just our way." She shifted as she spoke, refusing to meet my eyes.

No one seems to know what "things" Luna and her daughter went through during their absence, but the haunted look in Luna's face told me they might have been worse than I'd ever dreamed. "Of course," I said, feeling somehow embarrassed to have witnessed Raysel's outburst, and turned to Sylvester.

The color had drained from his face, leaving him pale and shaking. He didn't seem to have noticed Raysel's dramatic exit. "Dead?" he said.

"Murdered," I said, looking down, trying to avoid the shock I knew I'd see in his expression. Too late. "They shot her, then slit her throat with an iron blade."

A sharp silence fell over the room. I raised my head, meeting Sylvester's eyes. "Iron?" he said.

"Yes. She died from her wounds." Not from anything more merciful.

"So there's no way it was anything but murder." There was something broken in his tone. The purebloods have to stick together, because they have nowhere else to turn, and so every death hits them hard. Changelings don't work that way. We're too scattered and too different, and it can take us years, sometimes, to find out when someone dies. Death is more of a danger for us, and that makes it seem less impossible. That doesn't make it any better.

"I'm sorry," I said lamely.

"I . . . yes. Yes, of course." His fingers sought Luna's

and gripped them hard. "Oh, Evening. Was there . . . was that all you had to tell?"

"Before she died, she asked me to find her killers," I said, watching him carefully. "I'm here because I wanted you to know. And because I have to ask for help."

"I wish you'd come sooner," said Luna, very quietly. "We've missed you, and no homecoming should be darkened by this sort of news. It's an ill omen."

Sylvester's concerns were more immediate than ill omens. Expression sharpening, he asked, "You said yes?" All I had to do was nod. Sylvester knew my word would bind me, whether or not I wanted it to. I didn't see a reason to tell him about the curse; he was already going to worry enough. "Oh, Toby. Why did you agree?'

"Because I didn't have a choice." I folded my hands behind my back. "If you don't want to help, I'll understand."

"I didn't say that. I . . . damn. Can you give us a few minutes? Please?" His voice was tight with the strain of holding back tears. He didn't want to cry in front of me anymore than I wanted to watch him cry.

"I haven't been here in a while," I said, taking the hint. "I'll go see what Luna's done with the gardens. Send for me?"

Sylvester nodded, mutely. Luna echoed the gesture, ears still pressed flat.

Seized by a strange impulse, I darted forward and hugged them both at once, one with each arm, before I turned to run out of the room, gathering my skirt in both hands. I was lucky; I got out fast enough. No matter what else might happen before I left the knowe, I wouldn't have to see him cry.

TWELVE

I DIDN'T WORRY ABOUT PROPRIETY as I came running out of the audience chamber; I just dropped my skirts and let my forehead rest against the cool stone of the nearest pillar, taking deep breaths as I struggled not to break down and cry. I'd been avoiding the Torquills for six months because I didn't want to face Sylvester, and all I'd been doing was letting him sink further into his own guilt. Had I been doing *anybody* any favors with the way I'd been behaving?

The page was gone when I looked up. Good. It had been a long week—one that kept getting longer—and I didn't trust myself to be polite, especially not after what had just happened with the Torquills. My manners have always been the first thing to go when I get upset, and some people say that they stopped coming back a long time ago.

Slicking a few wayward wisps of hair back from my face, I turned to start down the hall, and nearly tripped over the hem of my dress. Cheeks burning, I picked up my skirt and started again, swearing under my breath. I hate Court attire.

At least the irritation lifted my mood, making it harder to dwell on how wrong I'd been about Sylvester's reaction to my return. I walked around the corner, stepping over a hopscotch grid some kid had finger painted on the marble floor and opened a door at random. The walls of the hall on the other side were papered in a tasteless pattern of yellow mustard and flowering heather, and I nodded, satisfied that I was going the right way. I kept walking.

The first time I came to Shadowed Hills, I was nine years old, and I was awed. Then I was annoyed, and then I was lost. The halls bend back on themselves and loop in long, impossible curves; doors you've seen before lead places you've never been, and doors that weren't there yesterday take you right back where you started. It's like a giant labyrinth with a sense of humor, and it can be really annoying. I learned to find my way around the place by memorizing landmarks, combining practice with sheer good luck, and sometimes I still found myself wishing for a pocketful of bread crumbs.

The yellow-and-purple walls gave way to plain stone, cobblestones replacing the checkerboard marble of the floor. Rose goblins watched me from windowsills and the corners of rooms, replacing the more common cats that tend to lurk in knowes. Sylvester, ironically enough, is allergic. Luckily, his wife's gardens provide plenty of spiny replacements for the standard feline. Rose goblins look like cats, act in a similar fashion, and shed thorns instead of fur. The perfect hypoallergenic pet.

Most of Shadowed Hills borders on tacky, but Luna's gardens make up for it. She has at least a dozen, and she tends them all herself. Kitsune aren't known for their gardening skills. Luna's something special. She's a goose girl in a lady's clothes when she's playing Duchess, but among the flowers, she's a Queen. They do everything but bow when she walks by.

The third hall I turned down dead-ended just past the winter kitchens, ending at a plain wooden door with a stained glass rose set at eye level. Smiling, I pushed the door open and stepped through into the Garden of Glass Roses.

Anything Luna touches grows, but roses have always been her pride and joy. The Garden of Glass Roses is entirely enclosed, filling a circular room with white marble walls that give way about ten feet up to a filigreed silver-and-glass dome. White crushed quartz pathways glitter in the sunlight that filters through the roses, throwing up glints of prismatic color. And everywhere, roses, growing in wild, seemingly unfettered profusion. Their slight transparency seems odd at first glance, until the mind admits what the eye is seeing: every flower, every petal and bud, is living, blossoming glass, stained with washes of flawless color. Best of all, glass roses have no scent. That garden is one of the very few places in Shadowed Hills that *doesn't* smell like roses.

Twitching my skirt away from reaching thorns, I walked down the nearest path to a bench carved from the same unornamented marble as the walls. Gowns are for dancing, not for roving in the roses—not that I do much of either when I can help it. I sat down with a groan, dropping my head into my hands.

This case was like a puzzle box: Every time I pushed a piece aside, there was another one waiting. Human logic has never been able to stand up to fae insanity, and I'd been thinking like a human for too long, because the longer I looked at things, the less sense they seemed to make. Evening was working with Devin, right up until the hope chest she'd somehow been hiding got her killed. Sylvester was surprised by the murder, but

Raysel laughed. The Queen of the Mists wouldn't help me, even though Evening was a pureblood, and she didn't want me looking for answers. What the hell was going on?

Nothing ever makes reliable sense when the fae are involved: the only constant about us is that we force things to change.

Something rustled in the underbrush. I raised my head, but the only motion I saw came from the crystal butterflies flitting dutifully from flower to flower: glass insects to pollinate glass roses. "Hello?" I called, fighting down my natural paranoia. Nothing would attack me in Shadowed Hills. Besides, if something did, I'd just hit them with the local flora until they cut it out.

"Hello!" The cheerful reply originated from inside a thick patch of red and purple love-lies-bleeding. "That you, Toby?"

"Usually," I said, tone wary. "Who's there?"

The flowers rustled, and Connor O'Dell rolled out of them, grinning. He'd managed to lose his coronet somewhere between the throne room and the garden, and there were rose petals in his hair. "Me," he said, standing. At least someone was having a decent day. Maybe it was just getting away from Raysel; that could cheer anyone up. "I didn't think you liked roses."

"I don't like most roses."

"But you like these roses?"

"I like these roses." He walked over to sit down next to me with a jaunty flourish. I bit back a smile. "You have something in your hair."

"Do I?" He shook his head like a dog trying to shed water after a bath, and yellow glass rose petals showered down onto the bench, ringing like crystal as they hit the marble. "Huh. I guess I did. That'll teach me to hide out under the rosebushes."

"No, you'll learn that lesson the first time you roll over on one of these babies and get yourself a cut where it *really* hurts," I said, flicking a petal.

Connor winced. "Are you speaking from experience?"

"Oh, yeah. Those suckers cut *right* through denim."

"Well, what did you expect glass roses to be? Soft?" He grinned, obviously trying to be endearing. It only half worked; I knew him too well to fall for it.

"Not really. Fragile, maybe, or sharp." I picked up a petal, testing the edge with my thumb. It cut deep and clean. I hate the sight of my own blood, but it was blood that started the whole mess, and it would probably be blood that ended it. "They can defend themselves. I respect that."

"So can normal roses. They have thorns."

"So? These roses are nothing *but* thorns. They can't help protecting themselves." I dropped the petal, rubbing my thumb and forefinger together. "Do you hide in the roses often?"

"Only when I want to be left alone. This is a good garden for hiding."

I looked around. "I've never understood why people don't come here more often."

Connor gestured to my bloody fingers, saying, "The roses are too sharp for most people. They want to pick flowers for their lovers and write bad poetry comparing the two—'my love is like a red, red rose,' and all that mess." He leaned back on his hands. "Who wants to compare their lover to a flower that's so sharp it cuts everything it touches?"

"A flower that blooms no matter what the weather or season is like and can actually defend itself when it needs to? I don't see the problem." I shrugged. "If someone wanted to call me a glass rose, I wouldn't complain."

"No, I guess not," he said. The light through the roses

cast shadows across his face, outlining his chin and cheekbones in layers of blue, green, and pale purple. His expression was grave; there was something in his eyes that I recognized, even if I didn't want to admit it. For a moment, I found myself cursing Rayseline Torquill for getting there first. I could've used a man who'd look at me that way now that I was back among the living ... but she *did* get there first, whatever my feelings on the subject might be. I had my chance to take that ship. I refused it for Cliff, and for the joy of playing faerie bride. If I had the chance to do it again, would I have made the same choices? Probably. Did I regret it anyway? Yes. I did.

"We are what we are," I said. "How's Raysel, Connor? Did she settle down?"

Connor turned away, stopping the play of light across his face. I suddenly found it easier to breathe. "She's fine. And yeah, she calmed down."

"Good. I was afraid there might be something wrong with her."

"You mean there isn't?" He sounded bitter and amused at the same time. It was a strange combination.

"Probably not," I said, more slowly.

"You look lovely today. I wanted to remember to tell you." He looked back at me, smiling. "This is the first time I've seen you in a dress where you didn't come off looking like a bear on a leash. It suits you."

I didn't want him smiling at me like that. Not now. I stood and crossed to the nearest stand of love-lies-bleeding, resting my fingertips against a flower. "I like these, too, even though they don't have thorns," I said, hoping he'd take the hint and let me change the subject. "They go beautifully with the glass roses. Do they grow in the mortal world, or are they another of Luna's creations?"

"They're mortal flowers," he said. He was allowing my incredibly transparent change of subject. Clever boy. "I don't know about the bluegrass—it seems too literal—but the purple flowers are a human thing."

"They have such a great name. Love-lies-bleeding. I wonder why they call them that." I left my fingers resting against the edge of the flower, looking down. It was better than trying to look at him.

"Why do the humans do anything?" I heard him stand, feet scuffling on the broken quartz path. "Luna gave me a bunch for my birthday—this huge vase filled with love-lies-bleeding and love-lies-dying and six kinds of love-in-idleness. If she wasn't my mother-in-law, I'd think it was a hint, but since she *is* my mother-in-law, I know it's a hint."

"What does she want?" I asked, not looking up. "Grandchildren?"

"What would Luna do with grandchildren? Plant them?"

I had to chuckle. "True enough. So do you know what she wants?"

"Yes."

"What is it?" I said, finally looking over at him.

Connor brushed the dirt off his pants, looking at anything and everything but me. "You know, now that I think about it, bluegrass isn't usually blue. It's green. It has to be something she came up with."

"Connor—"

He raised his hand. I stopped, just watching him. He looked back at me, seal-dark eyes grave, and said, "She wants me to fall in love with her daughter." Suddenly formal, he bowed. "Have a good afternoon, Toby. Enjoy your roses. I'm sorry about Evening." He turned while I was still gaping, openmouthed, and walked out of the garden, leaving me alone.

THIRTEEN

SILENCE CLOSED AROUND ME, drowning out everything else. I sat heavily back down on the bench, closing my hand around the rose petals Connor had dropped. They left stinging cuts on my palm and fingers, nicks too small to draw blood, but big enough to let me fight my way back out of the stillness Connor's departure had created. I was there to get resources to help me solve the murder of a friend, not to fall for another woman's husband, especially when that other woman was Rayseline Torquill, heir apparent to Shadowed Hills. Fae inheritance is nonlinear, but Sylvester and Luna didn't have any better prospects.

I've never gone out of my way to collect enemies in high places, and I wasn't there to fall in love. I was there because I had a job to do.

I don't know how long I sat there before I heard footsteps approaching. I raised my head, petals slipping through my fingers to shatter on the path. It wasn't Connor. The page who'd come to my apartment stood there, mouth pressed into a thin line. He winced at the sound of breaking glass, but covered the gesture almost before it was made. The purebloods train their courtiers well.

"The Duke requests your presence, if it suits you," he said, keeping his eyes forward, away from me. I was willing to bet he'd received a dressing-down from someone—probably Etienne—for stopping me at the doors. Poor kid.

"Okay," I said, and stood, aware that any chance I had left to make a good impression would go out the window if I tripped on my skirt. "What's your name?"

He met my eyes, looking startled. "Quentin." He paused before asking, "Have I given you some offense?"

"No, you haven't," I said. "You've been more than correct. I just wanted to be able to tell the Duke what a good job you're doing."

Quentin straightened, too surprised to mask the pleased smile that lit his face. "I . . . that is appreciated, milady."

"A word of advice, though, while you're listening. Don't let it go to your head."

"Milady?"

"Don't let any of it go to your head. Not your position, not your nature, not who or what you are. You may be immortal, but you aren't invincible." I thought of Evening, lying broken where Faerie's courtiers could never reach her, and suppressed a shudder. "None of us are."

He frowned, looking bewildered. "Yes, milady." He was agreeing because etiquette demanded it, and we both knew it. Unfortunately, nothing I could say would make him understand, and there was no point in arguing if he wouldn't listen. That never works on anyone. Warn the purebloods to be careful and they'll ignore you; warn the changelings and they'll take notes on the great games you're suggesting. It's a miracle we've lasted this long.

I sighed. "Let's go see the Duke, shall we?"

"Yes, milady," he said. He bowed and turned to lead me out of the garden. I glanced back over my shoulder, watching the light play through the roses, and wondered why it couldn't all be that way. Why can't Faerie be the stuff of dreams, all courtly manners and glass roses, Courts and pageants? Why do we have to include murder and mystery and the stuff of nightmares?

Light glittered off the shattered petals on the path, answering me. It can't all be dreams because a broken dream will kill you as surely as a nightmare will, and with a lot less mercy. At least the nightmares don't smile while they take you down.

Quentin waited for me at the exit, holding the garden door open in the proper courtly fashion as he waited for me to catch up. I nodded in answer to his courtesy, letting him close the door behind me. "How was he?" I asked.

"Milady?"

"The Duke. When he told you to come get me. How was he?"

Looking discomforted again, Quentin shrugged, beginning to walk down the hall. "I didn't see him, milady. Sir Etienne gave me the order to retrieve you."

I smiled a little. "Etienne, huh? How is the old warhorse doing, anyway?"

Not even Quentin's training could hide the smirk that crossed his face, although his words were entirely proper. "I'm fairly sure Sir Etienne would object to being referred to in such terms."

"Which would be why I do it," I said. "Guess that means he's doing okay?"

"Yes, milady."

"Good to know." A few more of the Duchy's inhabitants were in evidence now, emerging as the day wore on toward evening. The place would only get more crowded as night fell and more of the locals woke up. For now, we only had the fae equivalent of night people to deal with—those rare souls who chose a diurnal existence. Shadowed Hills is a good place for the daylight folks. Luna stays awake all day for the sake of her gardens, and Sylvester stays awake for the sake of his wife. I recognized a few of the Hobs who were dusting and tidying the corners, but that was about it. Hobs are strictly domestic spirits, and they tend to attach themselves to single households for generations, often raising their children to join them.

Quentin was looking straight ahead as he walked, paying no more attention to the domestics than he'd pay to the furnishings. Also standard to a courtier's training. A page is supposed to be animate furniture most of the time, and tables don't acknowledge couches.

The silence between us was bothering me, so I did what came naturally: I broke it. "You live here, right?"

"Yes, milady. My . . . my parents gave me in fosterage to the Duke and Duchess Torquill for the sake of my education."

"Where are you from? I can tell it's in Canada, but that's about my limit." A lot of pureblood parents ship their children off to some noble Court as soon as they're old enough to stand up on their own. Too early, if you ask me. Faerie teaches its children to be courtiers before it teaches them to be people.

There was a pause before Quentin shrugged, the not-quite-human lines of his body turning the simple gesture into something elegant. "My parents have requested that my home fief not be named, for fear that the mistakes I make while young may reflect poorly upon their honor."

Ouch. Blind fosterings aren't unheard of, but they've always seemed like a lousy way to get rid of kids who've managed to get old enough to be a nuisance. Normally, it's the changelings that get farmed out that way, not the purebloods. "Well, I'm sure you'll bring nothing but honor to your parents and their house."

"I should hope so, milady." He hesitated before adding, "It's been very strange being away from home."

I was trying to formulate a reply when a group of shrieking children ran past, stealing his attention. They were a motley bunch—fae kids usually are—and almost all changelings, although there were a few precious purebloods running at the center of the pack. "Hey!" Quentin shouted, indignant. "No running in the halls!" I turned away, hiding a smile behind my hand. No matter how elegant and strange he tried to seem, he was still a teenager.

The kid at the head of the pack was a Tylwyth Teg half-blood with muddy hair and clothes that were probably older than he was. He turned without slowing to blow a juicy raspberry at Quentin, and then they were gone, vanishing around a corner with loud cries of "Bang, bang! I got you!" and "No you didn't!"

Quentin watched them go, scowling, before he managed to compose himself. Turning back to me, he said, "I'm sorry, milady. The children get overexcited at times. I promise they'll be spoken to."

"It's okay; let them play," I said. "When's the last time you got the chance to play like that?"

"Milady?"

"Seriously. When's the last time you got the chance to just play, without worrying about honor or manners or what you looked like?" I stopped and leaned against the wall, watching the inhabitants of the knowe as they wandered through their day, but more important, watching Quentin. "When's the last time you didn't need to worry about whether your friends were purebloods or changelings?"

Quentin hesitated, looking almost uncertain as to whether he should answer. I quirked an eyebrow, and he admitted, "A long time, milady."

"Do you miss your folks?"

That was the wrong thing to ask: Quentin stiffened, saying, "I wouldn't distract myself from my duties, milady. If you please, the Duke is waiting for us."

"Of course." I pushed away from the wall, smoothing my skirt with the heels of my hands. "Wouldn't dream of upsetting the Duke, would we?"

Quentin gaped. "Of course we wouldn't dream of upsetting him! He's the Duke!"

I frowned. "Okay, work with me here. You're pureblooded, and unless I'm wrong—and trust me, I'm not—both your parents were Daoine Sidhe. What have you been taught about being pureblooded?" He squirmed, cheeks reddening, and refused to meet my eyes. "Come on, it's okay; I don't bite. What did they tell you?"

"That it's our right and our duty to rule Faerie in the absence of our King and Queens, because the lesser elements need to be kept under control." It had the air of something learned by rote. It also had a certain spark of sincerity. He might not believe it yet, but he would.

"The lesser elements being?"

"The changelings," he said, and cringed, obviously waiting for me to fly off the handle.

This reputation I seemed to have developed was starting to be a real drag. "Okay," I said, keeping my tone calm. "Do I strike you as somebody that needs to be 'kept under control'?"

"No, milady."

"Why not?"

"I—you just don't. That's all." He tugged on his sleeve, still squirming. I'd finally found the person under all that inbred arrogance. Good for me. Now I just had to make him listen.

"How about him?" I pointed to a Coblynau half-blood who was chatting up a donkey-tailed maid in front of one of the hall's many bookshelves. "Does he need to be controlled?"

"No, but . . ."

"Or them?" This time I indicated a pair of Candela walking arm-in-arm down the hall, lost in one another's eyes, with the glowing spheres of their Merry Dancers in attendance. "Do they need to be controlled? Does *anyone* here look like they need to be kept 'under control'?"

"I . . . I don't know."

"Right. Let me tell you something: the only reason I worry about upsetting Sylvester is because he's my friend, and I don't like upsetting my friends." Not that you could tell from my recent behavior—but Quentin didn't know that. "I don't do it because he's better than I am, because he's not. His rank gives him the right to command me, and I recognize that; we're not living in a democracy. I'll give him my attention and my courtesy, but that's because I respect him. I've never feared or honored him just because he was the Duke, and I refuse to start doing it now."

"But . . ."

"Hear me out," I said, shaking my head. "Shadowed Hills is the most egalitarian duchy I've ever visited, and a lot of what makes it like that is the way Sylvester rules. He demands respect for *who* he is, not *what* he is. I refuse to see that change if I can help it. Am I making sense?"

Quentin nodded, eyes wide. "I . . . yes."

"Good. Let's go see Sylvester."

"Yes, milady."

"That's another thing—my name's not milady. It's Toby. I'm not a cartoon dog."

"Yes, Toby," he said, and smiled at me. Maybe I was doing better than I thought. "Will you follow me now?"

"It wouldn't do for me to ditch my escort, would it?" I stepped up beside him, and he grinned, offering his arm with all the gallantry and style one expects from a trained courtier. The difference in our heights made walking somewhat awkward, but no one laughed at us. Never laugh at a changeling in formal dress with a fledgling Daoine Sidhe on her arm. One of them is bound to take offense, and you could wind up with a serious problem on your hands. Besides, there was no way for us to look sillier than some of the other couples in the hall, even if their oddities could be ascribed to things like belonging to radically different species. We'd grow out of it; Quentin was bound to get taller, and I almost never went out in public wearing a dress. They'd still look silly in ten years.

We stopped at the audience chamber doors, Quentin releasing my arm. I gave him a quizzical look, and he shrugged, saying, "I don't have permission to enter with you, milady."

"Gotcha," I said. I might have tried to invite him anyway, but I still needed to tell Sylvester about the Queen's reaction. Smiling, I offered, "I should be around a little more after this. I'll bring a ball or something. We can have a party, just you and me, where nobody cares whether we're dignified or not. Cool?"

"I'd like that," said Quentin. "Cool."

"Good," I said, and went back into the audience chamber.

The room seemed even emptier than it had before, now that it was just Sylvester and Luna waiting for me on the dais. They'd abandoned their chairs; Sylvester was sitting on the steps, and Luna was curled next to him, her head resting on his shoulder. Sylvester looked up when he heard me close the doors, and waved, beckoning me forward.

Luna sat up once I was in conversational distance, offering a wan smile. Her ears were still half flat, telegraphing her distress. I couldn't blame her.

"Toby," said Sylvester wearily. "Are you all right? Really? I . . . it's been so long since you've come to see us, and when you finally do, you come with news of a murder . . . and Evening. She's been here since forever. She was over a thousand years old, did you know that? The only one older living in this state is the Luidaeg."

"I know," I said, moving to sit down on the bottom step, looking up at the pair of them. I laced my fingers around one knee, resisting the urge to fidget. "I have to find the answers to why all this is happening. I don't . . . I owe it to her to find out why she died."

"It's not just that, is it?"

Unwilling to answer him, I turned my face away.

After several seconds of silence, Sylvester sighed. "This isn't the first place you came, is it?" I shook my head, looking back as he smacked the top step of the dais. "Dammit, Toby. You went Home, didn't you? Answer me!"

"Yeah," I said. "I did."

"Oak and ash, *why?* You knew I'd help you if you asked. I've been waiting for you to ask."

"We all have," Luna said. "We've been so worried."

"I didn't think you would," I said, lacing my fingers tighter together. "I'm sorry. I just . . . I didn't think."

"Oh, Toby." Sylvester closed his eyes. "What did you promise him?"

"Bill to be settled later."

"And it's too late to talk you into telling him you won't take his help, I suppose."

I laughed, a little wildly. "Devin could call me on breach of contract if I even tried—and I won't try unless you order me to. I *have* to find the answers to this."

"Was there no one else?" Luna placed her hand on Sylvester's arm, squeezing gently. "Even if you didn't think you could come here, the Queen . . ."

"Sent me away." Sylvester opened his eyes, both of them staring as I continued, "I went to her first. She said no one's allowed to even speak Evening's name, much less try to find out what happened. She ordered me out of her Court. Frankly, she scared me. I'm afraid she may not be entirely stable."

"That's not news, but it's also not encouraging," said Sylvester, his tone as grim as my own. There was a new sharpness in his eyes. It can be easy to forget that Sylvester won the right to hold Shadowed Hills; it wasn't just his heritage that got him his throne. He was a hero once, and he earned everything he has. He changes when there's a threat to be overcome: it's like he pulls on a second skin, one he almost forgets the rest of the time, and becomes a hero again. A tired, old hero, one who wields a pen instead of a sword and rides waves of paperwork rather than a white charger, but still a hero. "I'm not happy that you went to Devin when she threw you out. You should have come here."

"I wasn't sure of my welcome."

"Never doubt your welcome in my halls again—and that, Toby, is an order." The stress on the last word was subtle but firm. He was my liege. He orders, I obey.

"Yes, Your Grace," I said, inclining my head.

"Good. Now, I want you to stay away from the Queen as much as you can; frankly, I don't trust her to react rationally. Come back here tomorrow morning, just so

I know you haven't managed to get yourself in more trouble—do you understand?" I nodded. He continued, "It's clearly too late to stop you from involving yourself with Devin again, but be careful. I don't want to see you getting hurt."

"I'm not sure my safety is really a priority right now," I said, shaking my head before I stood. "I'll do my best."

"That's all I've ever been able to ask from you." Sylvester stood in turn, moving to embrace me. I didn't pull away. "I'll send the knights out, and start sending out inquiries. If there's anything to be learned here, I'll learn it. And if you need help, call us. We'll be there."

"I'll call," I said.

Sylvester let me go, looking at me sternly. "Promise, Toby."

I held up my hands. "I promise! I promise."

That appeared to be enough to satisfy them. Luna rose as well, and hugged me briefly before giving me a nudge toward the doors. "We'd keep you here all day if we could," she said. "That's why you need to go. Finish doing what you're bound to do, and come back to us."

"I'll do what I can," I said, and forced a smile before turning to make my exit.

Quentin was standing by the door in the hall, back to playing the perfect footman. There were several people waiting for an audience, and so he didn't move from his position, but he winked as I brushed by. I spared him a tight, pleased smile. He was a good kid, and he was learning. Maybe there's some hope for us yet.

It was late enough that a steady trickle of people filled the halls, heading toward the audience chamber at a leisurely pace. It's a good thing Faerie isn't big on fire marshals: while the traffic wasn't heavy enough to stop me from making my way to the door, it would have complicated an evacuation. Most of the people I passed gave me odd looks for going against the current, although one fragile-looking Gwragen wedged into a niche on the wall offered me a conspiratorial smile as I passed. I guess she thought she'd found a kindred spirit, someone else who just wanted to get away from the crowd. She was right, in a way, although my urge to get away was born of urgency, and not the natural Gwragen reluctance to get caught up in social niceties. I returned her smile and kept going, rushing down the last stretch of hallway to the knowe's back exit.

The late afternoon light was momentarily blinding as I stepped back into the mortal world. I raised an arm to cover my eyes, waiting for the brightness to fade. When it did, I looked around to find myself at the bottom of the hill, dressed in my own clothes, with a warm buzzing in the air that told me my human disguise was back in place. I reached back to check the tip of one ear, confirming that it was round. It was. I shoved my hands into my pockets, looking up the hill toward the oak that served as the door in, before I sighed and started across the parking lot.

My car was where I'd left it, apparently undisturbed, despite the fact that I'd left it unlocked; no real surprise there. Pleasant Hill isn't a big crime town—the worst they usually get is groups of teenagers pushing each other around and saying "you suck." It's a nice change, especially after San Francisco, where it's perfectly acceptable to give your girlfriend an ear as a courting gift in some of the less reputable neighborhoods.

I opened the door and got in, fastening my seat belt. The radio came on when I turned the key, and I hit the scan button until it found the local eighties channel. I prefer listening to music I can recognize, and that doesn't include most of the stuff that makes the current top forty.

Thoughts about the case and Shadowed Hills kept me occupied until I reached the Bay Bridge and needed to pay attention to the traffic. Even with the other cars to deal with, it wasn't a difficult merge—not unless you counted the two tailgaters and the little old lady who seemed convinced that the speed limit was fifteen miles an hour—and I wasn't in a hurry. I had plenty to think about while I waited to reach the tollgate. I inched forward, following the flow of traffic, and shook my head. I'd just think about it until the puzzle came together and everything made sense. Then I'd find Evening's killers, bring them to justice, and go to bed for a week.

The toll taker at the tollbooth didn't even look at me as he held out his hand, saying blandly, "Four dollars."

Smiling, I reached into my pocket and slipped him four of the mushrooms I'd plucked from the grass under my window. "Miss Suzy had a steamboat, the steamboat had a bell," I said to him. He started to protest, and I finished, "Miss Suzy went to heaven, the steamboat went to New Jersey where it enjoyed a lucrative career in children's programming." The smell of copper and cut grass rose around me, twining around the toll taker's head.

A brief, stabbing pain hit me behind the eyes, and I tightened my grip on the steering wheel. The illusion seemed to have worked, because the toll taker dropped the mushrooms into the fare box, waving me through. I smiled wanly, tipped an imaginary hat, and drove on. Yes, it was mean and petty and something I probably shouldn't do. On the other hand, substituting random pieces of greenery for human money is a long-standing tradition, and the fae are supposed to revere and uphold tradition, right? Besides, I only do it when they're rude to me. And when I don't have exact change.

Traffic on the bridge was light, and I was beginning to think that I was going to make it the rest of the way home without incident. I smiled, anticipating a smooth trip to my apartment, followed by a pause where I could start assembling clues into something that resembled a coherent picture. The temptation to blame it on the Queen was pretty strong, even though it would probably get me executed. Unfortunately, I didn't think that theory would get me very far; something wasn't right there. Oh, well. There was time for me to think about it.

I'm sure it's written somewhere, possibly in Fate's day planner: "October Daye is never to be given enough time to actually think about what she's going to do next." I was exactly halfway over the bridge, surrounded by water, when a deep, rumbling chuckle rolled out of the backseat, and a figure loomed up in the rearview mirror.

There was someone else in the car.

FOURTEEN

MY FINGERS CLENCHED ON THE WHEEL as I stiffened, forcing myself to keep looking straight ahead. This was just great. Positively peachy. Finding an intruder in my car when I was on a bridge, driving over more water than I cared to think about? Exactly what my day *didn't* need. I searched frantically for options and couldn't find any. There was nothing I could do but keep on driving.

After a moment I cleared my throat, and said, "You realize that if I go off the bridge here, we're both going to die."

I don't know what kind of reply I was expecting, but it certainly wasn't what I got: a deep, rolling chuckle, one that was almost closer to a growl. Laughter over the idea of a watery grave is never precisely a sign that you're dealing with a sane individual.

Swallowing, I tried again. "I've got to admit, you've got the advantage. I'm pretty sure you know who I am, or else you wouldn't be here. You mind telling me why you're in my car?"

The only answer was another chuckle. I fought the urge to turn around for a better look. Even if he was unarmed, which I doubted, you should never give up any degree of control over your car when you're on the Bay Bridge. It's a form of Darwinism: if you're dumb enough to take your eyes off the road while crossing part of one of the largest bodies of water in the world, you're too dumb to be allowed to live. Then again, if the guy in the backseat killed me, that would also be a form of Darwinism. This situation seemed less escapable by the moment.

"My patience isn't eternal, you know," I said, calm fading from my voice. I was scared and I was angry, and there was no sense in trying to hide it. "If you're going to threaten me, can you hurry and do it before we crash? I just got this rust bucket paid off, and I *really* don't feel like looking for another car."

This time, he didn't laugh; he just loomed even larger in my rearview mirror, edges blurred by a block-me illusion and his silence telegraphing the fact that one way or another, he didn't expect me to be shopping for a new car anytime soon.

He was in the car. That was a fact. It was something I couldn't change, and that meant I needed to stay calm. It's hard to be rational when you're mad, and it's even harder when you're scared, so I refused to go with either one. Once the bastard was out of the car, I could pull over and have a nice nervous breakdown. Assuming I survived.

The first off-ramp was just ahead. Good. The San Francisco streets aren't necessarily safer than the Bay Bridge, but it's harder to fall to your death if you make a wrong turn. Harder, not impossible; if the world actually has an edge, it's probably hidden down a one-way street somewhere in San Francisco.

I tightened my grip on the wheel, sending a silent "sorry" to my car. I was serious when I said I didn't want to go shopping for a new one. Sure, it was a 1974 VW Bug with enough miles on it that I thought someone might have driven it to Hawaii, but it was still my car. I chose it because I liked it, and I was honestly sorry we weren't going to get more time together. At least it was going to die in the line of duty.

The exit loomed, and I hit the gas, accelerating off the bridge and onto Harrison Street. Most of the traffic stayed behind us, heading toward more acceptably touristy locations. That was dandy. I watched the shadowy man in the mirror as he moved closer to my side of the car, obviously still under the assumption that we were playing by some sensible set of rules. He was wrong.

I like games. I usually win.

As soon as he was fully in motion, I slammed my foot down on the gas, jerking the car into a hard left. He flew across the car, hitting the door with a satisfying thud. Horns blared around us as we went rocketing the wrong way down a one-way street. "What the—?" demanded a voice from the back. I didn't recognize it—good. That meant it wasn't anyone I knew, and there'd be less guilt on my part if I managed to smash the car into a wall and kill him. I can be mercenary, but I'm not heartless.

"It's called reckless driving, asshole!" We were on a direct collision course with a taxi. I swerved at the last moment, swearing. The man in the back did the same, more loudly. I didn't want to hurt anyone but him, and I'd settle for shaking him up enough that he wouldn't chase me when I ran. "I know *I'll* survive if we crash. How about you? Did you remember to buckle up?"

"You're going to kill us both!"

"That's the idea!" It was actually fun, in a fatalistic sort of way. I smiled grimly as we wove in and out of traffic, watching the near misses become less miss and more near. There's nothing like a good high-speed car chase to get the evening started off right, even if there's technically only one car involved.

"Stop this car right now, or I'll—"

"You'll what?" I turned down another one-way street. We were going with the flow of traffic this time, if you ignored the fact that I was doing ninety when everyone else was doing twenty-five. "Hit me? Honey, if you take the wheel away from your Auntie Toby while we're going this fast, we're both going to die—that means you *and* me, not just me. Settle back and enjoy the ride, unless your employer paid you so well that you're willing to die."

The figure in the backseat pulled back, snarling, "Pointy-eared bitch . . ."

"Actually, I'm a pointy-eared slut. Only purebloods get to be bitches." I swerved left, and heard him hit the side panel. "Are you still not wearing your seat belt?"

"I'll kill you!"

"You'll have to get in line." Somehow, we'd wound up driving half on and half off the sidewalk. That was fine by me, as long as the pedestrians kept getting out of our way.

This time he just snarled. Fine. He was getting pissed and I was getting tired, and it was time to stop. I slammed my foot down on the brake, bringing the VW to a screeching halt as I undid my seat belt with one hand. The shocks were definitely going to be a write-off, but it was almost worth it—I hadn't had that much fun in ages.

My unwelcome passenger hit the back of my seat with a resounding thump. I caught a brief glimpse of his angry snarl, thin lips drawn back from oversized yellow teeth, before I was out the door and on my way down the street, not looking back.

Fear and adrenaline are a runner's best friends. I was almost a quarter of a block away when I heard the car door slam, followed by a man's voice shouting for me to stop. That wasn't going to happen. The man was a Redcap, and Redcaps are almost all paid thugs—they don't attack at random. Someone sent him after me. Whoever it was had almost certainly killed Evening, and once they'd tortured me into telling them where to find the hope chest, I'd be the next to die. I kept running, and I never even heard the gun go off.

The bullet hit the back of my left shoulder just above the collarbone. I screamed, staggered, and forced myself to keep going. It took a second for the pain to settle down into a single throbbing ache, one that broadcast, loud and clear, the fact that I had bigger issues than the fact that a hired thug was taking shots at me in the middle of a San Francisco street: The bullet had been made of iron. I could feel the burning its passage left behind, and I focused on that, forcing my legs to keep going. Part of me wanted to give in to the pain and collapse, and that part was just going to have to cope, because there was no way I was going to stop and let a lunatic slaughter me with iron. Simple death I could deal with, maybe. But death by iron . . . nothing hurts more than an iron-dealt wound. I rode Evening's death. I didn't need to experience that kind of pain firsthand. Ever.

The street was almost deserted—just my luck. The one time I actually wanted a crowd, and there wasn't a soul in sight. The front of my shirt was soaked with blood. I could feel myself slowing down, iron working its way farther and farther into my body. It was going to be a race between blood loss and iron poisoning to see which one could take me out faster. If I didn't find a way to at least stop the bleeding soon, I was going to be writing myself out of my own mystery before it even got started; exit October, stage left. All the assassin had to do was follow and wait.

I ran until it felt like the running was going to kill me, eyes half-closed and one hand clamped over the open wound at my shoulder.

Sometimes, it's all about the timing. I half ran, half taggered up to a bus stop just as the bus arrived, and I grabbed the rail, hauling myself aboard without missing a beat. The bastard with the gun was far enough behind that he couldn't get a clean shot, and the chances of him catching the bus before it left were almost nonexistent. Time and the San Francisco bus system wait for no man.

The driver stared at me as I dug for change with my left hand. I did my best to ignore him, focusing on getting my fingers to obey my commands. They were still responding, but it wasn't going to last; the iron was working its way farther into my shoulder, and my entire arm was going slowly numb. I stared back, aware of how I had to look, blood soaking my sweater and matting my hair down against my shoulders. Was I still wearing my disguise? I didn't know, but after the iron bullet, I wouldn't have bet on it. Iron kills magic.

"Is there a problem, ma'am?" asked the driver.

I dropped my coins into the fare box. "Drama student," I said, as glibly as I could manage. "Rehearsal got a little overenthusiastic."

I could tell from his face that he didn't believe me; I could also tell that he didn't really want to know. He nodded curtly and slammed the bus doors, only seconds before the bus lurched away from the curb, brakes squealing. I managed to grab a pole and ease myself into the nearest empty seat before I fell, doing my best to keep my back away from the wall. It's rude to get blood on the seats. After about half a block the movement of the bus stopped being jarring and started to soothe my nerves, inviting me to take a nice, long nap. You deserve it, the motion said, you've earned it. You ran away. Now close your eyes and go to sleep.

Even through my exhaustion, I could tell that wouldn't be a good idea. Napping when you're bleeding like a stuck pig—even if the few shell-shocked travelers on the bus were polite enough to ignore it—is a good way to wake up dead. I braced my elbows against my knees and pressed my right hand harder against the point where the bullet had entered. It wasn't doing any good. No matter how much pressure I applied, I couldn't stop the bleeding from my back. Shuddering, I wiped my left hand across my lips, and froze. They were wet.

Looking at the blood streaking my fingers, I considered the irony of it all. I'd survived Simon Torquill and Oleander de Merelands, I'd survived the siege on the Queen's Court, and here I was bleeding to death on the six-fifteen bus, surrounded by people trying to pretend that I wasn't doing exactly that. People talk about heroes dying "good deaths." You think somebody died well and valiantly, and it was worth it—and then somebody opens fire, and you realize that no matter how good your death is, it's the last thing you'll ever get. That makes it bad enough in my book.

I knew one thing: sitting still wouldn't save me. I forced myself to stand at the next stop, staggering toward the exit. If I was going to bleed to death, I was at least going to do it outside. My head spun with every step. I hadn't realized how much blood I'd really lost until I started moving again.

The bus steps seemed to have gotten higher while I sat. I leaned heavily on the rail, inching down to the bottom, where I froze, head pounding, and tried to get my balance back. Where was I? Had the bus moved at all?

Blood loss and iron poisoning both do interesting things to the brain, and suddenly, I just wasn't sure.

"Hey, lady, are you getting off?" said the bus driver.

"Where am I?" I asked. The words echoed like they'd been shouted down a long tunnel.

The driver didn't seem to notice how distorted my voice had become. Poor man. He must have been half deaf. "We're at the north entrance to Golden Gate Park, lady. Is this your stop?" He paused, and then asked more gently, "Do you need a doctor?"

Shaking my head, I stepped off the last step and onto the curb, leaving my fingerprints scribed on the handrail. It dimly occurred to me that leaving bloody handprints around the city was a bad idea; I just wasn't sure why. The driver looked at me, then at the blood on his bus, and shook his head. I wanted to make some pithy, memorable comment and tell him I'd be fine, but I didn't trust the words not to come out in Cantonese just to spite me. I missed my chance, if I'd ever had it. The doors slammed shut and the bus pulled away, leaving me standing on the sidewalk in front of Golden Gate Park.

Golden Gate Park. I knew people there. I was almost sure I knew people there. Turning, I stumbled past joggers and tourists, starting down the asphalt path that led into the park proper.

The path twisted and curved, and I followed it with dogged determination, not really caring where it went. It was getting harder to think. My shoulder was still bleeding, but it didn't really hurt anymore; I was almost too dizzy to keep walking, and it didn't hurt. That wasn't a good sign. When gunshot wounds stop hurting, it's usually because you're not strong enough for the pain. Your body shuts it off rather than dealing with it. But I was in the park. I'd made it that far. I might have a chance.

Golden Gate Park swears fealty to no Lord. It may

look like one huge holding from outside, but it's not; it's more like a coral reef of tiny fiefdoms, scattered through the landscape like secret stars. Most of the park's power is in the doors it hides. If I could reach one of those doors before my strength gave out, I might be okay. It wasn't likely, but it was possible. And if I didn't make it to one of those doors, and I was lucky, I'd collapse where my body wouldn't be found until the night-haunts had finished with me.

Of course, the odds were better that I'd be handing some mortal fool a corpse with pointed ears, leaving the survivors to handle all questions that came next. Faerie's managed to stay hidden this long on nothing but sheer chance, and chance can't last forever.

The taste of roses was rising in my throat, overwhelming the acrid taste of blood. "Sorry, Evening," I whispered. There are some things even promises can't do. Dimly, I wondered what would happen when the blood stopped. Would it hurt? Or would I just go to sleep? So many questions, so little time before shock and blood loss made them academic.

The tang of incense undercut the taste of blood and roses, catching my attention. I was halfway down the side of a small hill before I realized I'd left the pavement, and my feet went out from under me, losing their purchase on the slick grass. I slid the rest of the way. At least there was no more pain: I was somewhere comfortably past pain, where nothing really mattered anymore. I knew there was something I needed to do, but I was starting to lose track of what it was. The smell of incense was getting stronger, beckoning me forward. I looked up and froze.

I was sprawled in front of a stylized Oriental gateway. It was mostly hidden by leafy trees and climbing ferns, but that didn't matter; I knew it. I could have been dead and still known that gate. It haunted my dreams.

The Japanese Tea Gardens.

After everything that happened there, I would have been happier trusting myself to the hospitality of Blind Michael's Hunt on a full moon night with no candle to guide me home. But even as I pushed myself upright, I knew the choice wasn't mine. You can't afford to be picky when you're bleeding to death, and it would make perfect sense for me to die in the Tea Gardens. I'd failed to do it once before. Might as well get it right this time.

I picked myself unsteadily up and staggered toward the admissions booth. My left arm was dangling uselessly, and I fumbled to keep my balance as I dug my right hand into the pocket of my jeans. There was nothing there but squashed mushrooms and bloody lint. I'd thrown the last of my change in the fare box on the bus, not bothering to check to see how much I was paying. Too late now. It's rude to trick your way into someone else's knowe, but I was out of options and out of time. If I couldn't pay, I'd just have to make my way inside another way.

The woman at the gate blinked, eyes widening at the state of my clothes. She was blonde, with feathered hair and a brain that was probably equally feathered, but I could see traces of faerie blood in the shape of her eyes and the way she held her head. That was probably why she'd been hired, even if the blood wasn't strong enough to make her anything more than mortal. The fae that live in Golden Gate Park look out for their own.

This woman's heritage was a small blessing to me; it would make her more susceptible. Even if I couldn't convince her I wasn't what she thought I was, I should be able to enchant her long enough for me to get into the Tea Gardens. Lily might not be able to help me, but she was the most likely of a very slim set of options. At least I knew that if I got onto her land, I could die in peace.

Biting my tongue, I whispered the first three lines of "The Owl and the Pussycat" under my breath, and stumbled as the iron wound in my shoulder burst from distant numbness into bright new pain. I caught myself on the edge of the booth, taking a deep, unsteady breath, and handed my bloody lint and mushrooms to the woman behind the counter.

It almost wasn't enough. What little power I had was starting to fade as I slipped in and out of full consciousness. She frowned before squinting at the contents of her palm, seeming to see through my hasty illusion.

Coins, I thought, as firmly as I could. *You don't see anything but coins. It's exact change.* Her frown deepened before resolving into a sunny smile. She dropped the mushrooms into her register.

"Welcome to the Japanese Tea Gardens! Have a nice day," she said, radiating that odd brand of insincerity that seems bred into gatekeepers of all types. I forced myself to smile and half walked, half staggered onward. It had been a great day for petty thievery—between the gatekeeper and the toll taker, there were at least two people who'd be coming up with short registers at the end of the day. Of course, I'd been rewarded for my tricks with an iron gunshot wound. Who says there's no such thing as karma?

The paths through the Japanese Tea Gardens are made of narrow, weathered planks. Trees and beds of flowers surround them, occasionally yielding to rock gardens or shallow stretches of water. Bridges punctuate the landscape, some arching up at angles that actually require stairs. It takes a pretty good sense of balance to make it through the Tea Gardens without falling, even if you avoid the bridges. At the moment, balance wasn't something I had a large supply of. The paths were slippery with water and decay, and the lack of traction nearly knocked me over half a dozen times before I managed to get out of sight of the front gate.

At the base of the moon bridge I gave up, sitting down in a patch of ferns. The movement just made me dizzier, throwing the world into a kaleidoscope dance of water, blood, and shadows. I shuddered, falling forward, and caught myself with my good arm before I could pitch face-first into the water. My reflection rippled in front of me, giving me a clear picture of the situation. My illusions were entirely gone—any tourist coming down the path would find themselves looking at more than they had bargained for—and blood caked my lips and hair, soaking my sweater almost to the waist.

I looked into my own eyes, and knew I was going to die.

One of the koi surfaced to stare at me, breaking my reflection into countless ripples. I looked down at it, almost smiling as I reached out to stroke its head with my numb left hand. It didn't shy away from the gesture. "Hey, remember me?" I whispered. "Did you miss me? I think . . . I think I may be staying this time . . ." The fish sank back below the surface, leaving my fingers dangling in the water. Faint rings of red rippled out from where they touched.

I didn't even feel my face hitting the pond. Everything was darkness, glorious darkness and the final, perfect absence of pain. It was done, all of it, the running and the fighting and the pain. After everything that I'd gone through, it was finally over, and this time, the waters would carry me home.

FIFTEEN

"TOBY, DON'T BE DEAD, don't be dead." It sounded almost like Tybalt's voice, too distorted and far away to really tell. Water was soaking through my sweater, plastering my hair down against my cheeks; my eyelids were heavy. Too heavy to bother opening. I leaned into the arms that were holding me up and let myself go limp, falling back down into the darkness.

Time passed. How much, I couldn't say; I only knew that I was rising toward consciousness, and I fought that ascent with everything I had. Waking held pain and duty and too many questions, while sleep held only peace, and the shadows of sunlight on the water. I was done. Sleep was all I wanted now.

You can't always get what you want. The pain hit without warning. I gasped, opening my eyes in surprise, only to squeeze them shut again as my head began throbbing. What little I'd seen told me next to nothing about where I was, only that there was a roof above me, and that the dim light wasn't natural. I was inside; I just didn't know where. Not that it mattered, since I was too weak to move and in too much pain to care. Hopefully, I wasn't slated to be somebody's dinner. At least if I was, it would probably help my headache.

A little experimentation showed that I could move my right hand. The ground beneath me was soft, springy, damp to the touch, and faintly warm. I frowned, becoming curious despite myself. Where *was* I?

Footsteps approached from behind me. I couldn't run; I couldn't even make my eyes open again. All I could do was lie there, frozen, as a hand caressed my temples and a soft voice whispered, "She is not yet ready for you. Sleep."

The blessed dark rose again, reclaiming me.

I dreamed of glass roses and the taste of penny-royal.

Waking came faster the second time, even if I was no more willing; going back to my body meant going back to the pain, and it had gotten worse while I slept, spreading out from my head and shoulder until every breath caught in my chest. But I was alive. The realization hit me, and I opened my eyes, too startled to play dead any longer. I was alive.

I was looking up at a ceiling of woven willow branches, held up by a series of arches that appeared to have grown from the mossy floor. Pixies clustered on every available surface, their shimmering glow lighting the room. The moss beneath me was soaking wet, and as a consequence, so was I. I knew where I was. Lily's knowe.

The only entrance I know of to the knowe required climbing straight up the steepest bridge in the garden. I was pretty sure I hadn't done that before I blacked out. I was honestly surprised I'd reached the Tea Gardens at all. "Hello?" I said. My voice came out in a whisper. "Is anybody there?"

"You're awake." It was the voice I'd heard earlier,

soft, feminine, and faintly worried. "Stay where you are. Do not move. We will fetch her."

"Got it," I said, and closed my eyes. Not moving wouldn't be hard; I doubted my ability to roll over, much less run away. I didn't hear the speaker leave, but after some indefinite amount of time—minutes or hours, I had no idea—soft footsteps approached, accompanied by the rustle of silk. They stopped just beside my head.

"Hello, Lily," I said, not opening my eyes. "Sorry to just drop in like this."

"You are always welcome here," she chided. Her voice was like water over stones, laced with a Japanese accent. "Even when you do not choose to come, you are welcome."

"Sorry," I said, still whispering. I wasn't sure I could raise my voice if I wanted to. "I got a little banged up."

"I noticed. Everyone noticed. What did you do to poor Marcia?" A hand touched my shoulder, testing the edge of the wound. Her fingers were cool, and the pain faded where she touched. "She was very upset, and there were mushrooms in the cash register."

I let out my breath in a hiss, relaxing as the worst of the pain slipped away. "I didn't have any money, and I needed to get inside."

"Silly changeling," she chided. "Does it never occur to you that you could ask?"

"Not my style," I said, managing a faint smile.

Lily made a clucking noise, like she was scolding an unruly child, but continued stroking my shoulder, fingers leaving trails of numbness behind. I opened my eyes, tilting my head back to watch her. "Hush," she said, "be still."

"Yes, ma'am," I said, watching as she reached over me to pluck a sprig of foxglove from the mossy bank. Her hands were slim and covered with delicate sil-

ver scales, the fingers webbed to the first knuckle. Only
her fingernails looked human, and even they were a pale
silver-blue. I could see the shadow of her face if I turned
my head just right, and memory supplied what vision
couldn't: she was impossibly delicate, with jade eyes and
long black hair braided back with willow branches, pale
skin decorated by dainty silver-and-green scales. She
was beautiful, but it wasn't human beauty. Even by fae
standards, Lily was unique.

"Oh, October," she said, waving the flowers above my
face. "You are my favorite type of puzzle, child—the sort
that makes no sense at all. May I help you this time, or
would you rather bleed to death over what has passed
between us?"

"How did you bring me here?" I asked, looking past
the flowers to her face.

"I didn't," she said, and smiled. "Blood in the water,
remember? When you were brought to my doors, I could
let you in, and grant you succor, because of the permission you gave me with that blood. I can do no more unless you grant me your consent."

"Brought to your doors?" I asked.

"You have more friends than you believe, October.
Will you let me help you?"

Undine magic has rules. When I bled in Lily's waters,
I gave her permission to keep me alive; she couldn't do
anything more than that unless I told her she could.

"Of course," I said, closing my eyes again. With Evening's curse hanging over me, I couldn't afford to pass
on anything that might be an offer of help.

"Very well, then. For now, rest. I need nothing more
of you." I felt her bringing the foxgloves down to the
edge of the wound in my shoulder, brushing them over
the worst of the damage. They stung as they touched
skin before a cool, anesthetic numbness began to spread

outward from their petals. Foxglove is poisonous—lovely, deadly, and probably not the best thing to put in an open wound. Then again, I'd been paying my tolls with mushrooms all day, and I'm not a healer. If Lily thought rubbing foxglove into my shoulder would help me, she was probably right, and even if she wasn't, she couldn't do more damage than I already had.

Lily started chanting in Japanese. The anesthetic coolness spread further, dulling the feeling in my arm and neck as the air filled with the scent of water lilies and hibiscus flowers. When the chant was done, she pressed her hand against my cheek, and said, "The world will wait for you, and be here on your return."

That was all the permission I needed. I sighed and stopped fighting to stay awake, letting myself drift away, back into the dark.

Lily's been a part of my life for as long as I can remember; longer than Sylvester, even, and that takes some doing. Mom used to take me to the Tea Gardens when we were still playing human, putting Daddy off with excuses about "girl time." Lily was always there, glad to see us, but watching my mother with a wariness I didn't understand until much, much later. Lily watched her because it's hard to trust a faerie bride: they're building a life on lies, and they'll deny anything that gets in their way.

She was still there when I left the Summerlands. I toyed briefly with going to serve her instead of Devin, but Devin's offer was flashier, more exciting, and I was my mother's daughter; I was looking for excitement. Still, we stayed close, and her doors remained open to me, right up until the day things went wrong . . . for both of us.

I went to Lily a few days after I broke free of the pond, still in shock and half hysterical with grief. I wanted to know why she hadn't saved me. I learned more than I'd bargained for.

"He placed walls around my fiefdom," she said. "I was lonely, October, so lonely, and my magic is for growth and healing, not transformation. I couldn't save you, child. I could only keep you as comfortable as the water would allow. I'm sorry."

Lily was as much Simon's prisoner as I was because for fourteen years, the world forgot she'd ever existed. The residents of her fiefdom scattered, suddenly homeless and not able to understand why. She was closer to dead than I was until the spell broke, because at least they remembered to mourn for me. I couldn't hate her for things that Simon did to both of us. We had something very much in common: someday, we were going to make Simon Torquill pay.

The taste of hibiscus flowers called me out of memory and back to my body. I sighed and opened my eyes, blinking. The pain was gone. So was my shirt, along with the rest of my clothing; I wasn't wearing anything except the strips of moss and willow bark Lily had wrapped around my wounded shoulder. Swell. I'm not body-shy—it's hard to grow up in the Summerlands, where clothes are solidly optional, and stay body-shy—but that doesn't mean I enjoy nudity. Naked people are, by definition, unarmed.

Bracing my right elbow against the ground, I levered myself into a sitting position. The motion made my head spin. At least my headache had faded: it was only half as bad as it had been before. Lily was kneeling a few yards away, dipping something in the water of a small pond. Now that my eyes were focusing, I could tell that the rustling noise came from her heavy silk robes; they were dark green and embroidered in white and silver with a pattern of sinuous dragons. A pair of pixies rested on the ebony chopsticks holding her hair in place, throwing flickering shadows over her face.

"Move slowly," she said, rising and walking over to kneel beside me. "I have done my best, but the human in you protests the intrusion of magic, and the iron blocks me further. I can do no more."

"Sorry; wasn't my idea," I said, moving my arm experimentally backward. The bandages on my shoulder pulled, and I winced. Lily clucked her tongue, starting to dampen the poultice with a silk sponge. The water soothed away most of the soreness, but not all of it. I wasn't surprised she couldn't heal me all the way: she was fighting iron, and I had no right to expect a miracle. If she'd been anything less than an Undine in her own realm she probably wouldn't have been able to do as much as she had. None of that stopped me from being disappointed as I realized how extensive the remaining damage was. It wasn't enough to cripple me—I'd still have use of the arm, even while it was healing—but it was going to make my job an awful lot harder than it had been before.

Guess that'd teach me to be careless. I looked to Lily, and smiled as earnestly as I could while disappointed and hurting. "It's a pretty good job."

She waved one fine-webbed hand, dismissing my words. Anything that smacks of saying "thank you" is unsteady ground in Faerie. "It is no more and no less than hospitality demands. Really, October, there wouldn't be any need for this sort of thing if you would just stop jumping in front of bullets."

"I'll try to remember that."

"Good." The gills under her jaw fluttered, and I felt a sudden pang of concern. She was trying to hide it, but I knew her well enough to see how worn out she was.

Healing spells are tiring, even when you're not fighting against iron.

"Lily, you okay over there?"

"I am tired, October, nothing more. It will pass." She smiled, creasing the scales around her mouth. "Now, tell me, why did you have to be pulled from my pond? You were bleeding all over my fish."

"Because you'd miss me if I died?" I shrugged. "Just a thought."

"You may be right," Lily said, smile fading. "What happened?"

She deserved to know, even if I didn't want to tell her. Forcing myself to look her in the eye, I took a deep breath and started from the beginning.

Telling the whole story took less time than I expected, all of it passing in rapid flurries of words. It was a relief to say some of it aloud, here, where Lily's control meant there was no risk of eavesdroppers. The close urgency of the events was already gone, reducing them to simple facts. Lily listened, expression growing grim as I explained more and more of the last fairy tale that Evening Winterrose would ever be a part of. By the time I reached the end, her lips were pressed into a thin, hard line. "It seems you've had a busy week," she said.

"Not my choice."

"Even so." She rose, inclining her head toward me. "I will return with tea and, I think, a robe for you to wear. You will rest here a while before I allow you to leave. Foolish child."

She stepped onto the water and was gone, leaving only the faint scent of hibiscus and water lilies in her wake.

"Swell," I said, and flopped backward into the moss to wait.

SIXTEEN

THE ROBE LILY BROUGHT fit pretty well, even if it left me feeling more exposed than I'd been before. Nudity is fine—not my favorite thing, but fine. Clinging silk robes meant for someone six inches shorter are less fine. The hem stopped at mid-thigh, and the neckline barely covered my chest. To make matters worse, or at least more mortifying, the whole thing was a rosy shade of cream: taken as a whole, I felt like the star of some demented piece of fantasy porn.

The poultice swaddling my left shoulder would kill that idea pretty quickly. I could move the arm more easily than when I first woke—changelings don't recover as fast as purebloods, though we bounce back faster than humans—but I wasn't sure the improvement would be enough. I couldn't move it fast enough to do anything useful, and heavy lifting was definitely out of the question for a few days. I wouldn't have worried about it before people started shooting at me. Now that they'd started, I had plenty of reason to worry.

Whoever killed Evening and set a Redcap on my trail

wasn't going to back off. If there'd been any chance of that, it died when the man started taking shots at me on a public street. Whatever the game was, I was in it until it was over.

Lily kept moistening the moss around the poultice, refusing to let me move more than I had to in order to reach my tea. The combination of my body's natural defenses and Undine water was helping, but movement wasn't easy. I hadn't even been able to help her wash the blood out of my hair. She'd pulled it into a braid when she was done, tying it off with a strip of fabric torn from my irreparably stained blouse. I still looked like hell, but it was one of the outer circles, and the fact that I didn't seem likely to drop dead any second was a definite improvement.

"Drink this," said Lily, handing me another cup of tea. "It will help."

It smelled like rosehips and hibiscus, just like the last eleven batches. I took it, asking, "Am I going to be done drinking this stuff any time soon?" I understood the logic. The tea was helping me recover the blood I'd lost, and it was forcing Undine water into my system at the same time. That was fine. It didn't make the idea of drowning in syrupy floral tea any more appealing.

Lily gave me a stern look. "You'll be done when I say you are."

"Right." I took a sip, grimacing. There was a good reason for me to drink the tea. Still, I would've killed for a cup of coffee.

More gently, Lily said, "I'm sorry if I'm fussing, October, but I don't wish to see you killed for your hastiness. Not if I can help you by keeping you here."

"I'm not being hasty, Lily. I have a job to do." The Undine take a long, slow view of time. To Lily, a year and a day were very much the same.

"You're not? Does that mean you had to be fished out of the viewing pool over nothing? How curious. I should have realized you'd intended to collapse there from exhaustion and overabuse and insisted you be put back again. I apologize."

I sighed. "Lily, being hasty doesn't usually get you shot."

"I see. So I suppose you paused to think through whatever actions *did* lead to your being shot before you took them?"

"I . . ." Lily narrowed her eyes, and I stopped, reviewing the events of the afternoon in my head. I hadn't been thinking, or even acting: just reacting. I'd been reacting since I heard Evening's voice on my answering machine. Looking away, I said, "No."

"I didn't think so. People have been trying to kill you for as long as I've known you; it seems to be a normal part of your existence, and I've grown resigned to that fact. Even so, I've never seen you giving so little care to evading their efforts. It almost seems like you want them to catch you."

"Lily, I—"

"No," she said, and I stopped, run up against the wall of her implacability. "You forget, how well I knew your mother. Amandine's excuses were always very much like yours. Nothing you say will be new to me."

I raised my eyes, and she met them without flinching. Her lips were curved in a faint, sad smile, creasing the scales that ran across her cheeks. "Maybe not. But you always let her go."

The smile softened, growing sadder and more accepting at the same time. "I always regretted it, as well."

"We do what we have to."

"As, I suppose, we must." She sighed. "Ah, well."

"Now what?" I asked.

"Now you leave me. Even if I could hold you here against your will—even if I would, after what we've been through together—the Winterrose has bound you, and I can't defy the law so directly. The sun will be down soon."

"... down?" I asked, staring at her. "Lily, it was night when I got here." Fleetingly, I wondered how much work I'd managed to miss.

"Time passes, October," she said. I didn't have an answer to that. Lily looked at me levelly and continued, "Once the sun is down, Marcia will summon a taxi for you, and I will have one of my handmaids escort you to the edge of the park. Once you have left my lands, you may do whatever you feel is needed, and I will have done what hospitality demands."

"Okay," I said.

"I am not done." Her tone sharpened, becoming colder. "I wouldn't let you go at all were it not for the binding, and had you not been my unwilling guest once before; understand that. Your mother will not forgive me for your death."

"My mother hasn't left the Summerlands in twenty years," I said, unable to stop myself. "I doubt she's going to come out to yell at you."

"I think you might be surprised by what she would do." I looked at her and couldn't think of a single way to answer that. So we just sat and drank our tea while the silence stretched out between us, until Lily raised her head, acknowledging some unseen sign.

"The sun is down," she said, and stood, moving with fluid grace. "Come, October. It's time to go. I just hope, for your sake, that you've rested well enough."

I pushed myself to my feet and followed her, pausing to take my bloody clothes from a Puca with dragonfly wings and white-blind eyes. She looked familiar, like someone I'd known once, but I didn't ask. The stories you find in the independent knowes usually aren't pretty ones.

Lily stopped, looking at me. "You should dress," she said. "It's cold outside, and you aren't as accustomed to it as I am."

"True," I said. No one is as accustomed to cold as the Undine, unless you count the various breeds of snow fae. Lily could walk naked in subzero temperatures and not be bothered.

Pulling my jeans over the bottom of the too-short robe turned it into a slightly tasteless, expensive-looking silk blouse; pulling my sweater on, bloodstains and all, made me feel a little more like I was in control of the situation, despite the hole through the left shoulder. Not being dressed like an escapee from a faerie whorehouse will do that for me every time. I would have put my bra back on, but that would have required removing the robe; I wadded it into a ball instead, shoving it into the waistband of my jeans. My left arm bent reluctantly, but it bent. I'd have to be satisfied with that. Nodding to myself, I followed Lily through the darkness and back into the world of men.

Night had chased away the tourists, filling the shadows with a different kind of crowd. There are no fireflies in California, but points of light still danced over the surface of the water, darting away from ambitious fish. There are benefits to a pixie infestation; fireflies don't pierce the night with glittering laughter or spin each other through ornate midair ballets. White Christmas lights were strung through the branches of the trees, providing brighter, more constant illumination. Pixies who had tired of aerial acrobatics perched on the cords, and clusters of the more human-sized residents were scattered along the pathways, talking and laughing. The

Tea Gardens are always at their best when no one but the night-side inhabitants are there to see them. That's when no one—and nothing—has to hide.

The conversations quieted as we drew close, and I could feel eyes on my back as we passed. I didn't turn. Some things are better left alone, and that includes questions from the people who lost their home for fourteen years because it had become my prison. I'm sorry, and I'd undo it in a heartbeat, if I could . . . but I was learning more and more each day that looking back never solved anything.

Lily's promised handmaid was sitting balanced on the low wooden fence beside the gate, chatting with a tall, brown-haired man whose eyes were ringed with the characteristic gleam of faerie ointment. I stopped, eyes widening.

"Juliet?" I asked.

The woman turned toward the sound of her name and smiled, revealing oversized canines behind cherry-red lips. Narrow stripes ran up the sides of her face, vanishing into the gold-and-brown streaks of her hair. "Hey, Tobes," she said, sliding down from the fence with hip-shot ease, half smirking at me. "Surprised much?"

"Julie," I said, almost in a whisper. Somehow, we closed the distance between us; somehow, I was hugging her, laughing so hard I was almost crying—or was that crying so hard that I was almost laughing? Julie had her arms around me, and was doing much the same, with the added rumbling undertone of her purr. The man she'd been talking to stood back, out of the way, watching our reunion with a small, puzzled smile.

Finally, I pushed Julie out to arm's length, staring at her. "What are you *doing* here?"

"The usual." Julie shrugged, rolling her eyes to indicate that the usual was nothing of any real importance.

"Uncle Tybalt's in another snit, so I'm here, playing handmaid until it's safe to go home."

"What'd you do?"

She grinned again. "I bit him."

"Good for you." I squeezed her upper arms, returning her grin with one of my own. Julie's a Cait Sidhe changeling, the result of a dalliance between one of Tybalt's courtiers and a mortal woman. Unfortunately for everyone involved, Julie flunked the Changeling's Choice in the most dramatic way possible. There was an accident—I never got the details—and her mortal mother was killed, while Juliet, at the age of six, tapped into her racial talent for shapeshifting. The police who came for the cleanup found a body, but no little girl. Julie was already in the hands of her father's family.

It took them years to lure her back to human form. From what I've heard, Tybalt tried everything, until finally, one day, she just changed. That's been their relationship ever since; as her de facto uncle, he tries to make her follow the laws of the Court of Cats, and she pretty much ignores them, right up to the point where she gets tossed out on her tail. Again. She was a bitter, resentful, maladjusted kid who grew into an equally maladjusted teenager; it was only natural that we'd become friends the day we met. She had a lot of anger in her, and she knew how to express it. As someone who'd always been better at repression than expression, I envied that.

Julie also has the lovely distinction of being the reason Tybalt dislikes me so much. We had quite a few hostile encounters during my time in the Summerlands, most of which ended with him reminding me that he'd be happy to gut me if it weren't for my mother. When we grew up, Julie followed me out of her uncle's Court and all the way to Home—the first Cait Sidhe to pull that kind of stunt. Lucky me, he decided to blame me instead of her, because I was the "smart one." That's me. Making enemies with my brain for as long as I can remember.

"Wanna meet my sweetie?" Julie asked, grabbing the brown-haired man by the arm and pulling him over to be admired. "Ross, this is October Daye. Tobes, this is Ross Hampton."

"Charmed," he said, extending his hand. I took it, shaking firmly as I studied him. He was quarter-blooded at best, and his heritage was subtle; there was something in the shadows of his eyes that should have given me a clue, but I was too tired to quite put my finger on it. "Julie talks about you a lot."

"Now I'm worried," I said, taking my hand back and glancing toward Lily.

"His mother was a servitor of these lands," Lily said. She leaned up onto her toes, ruffling Ross' hair. He took it with good grace, even stooping to make it easier. "In her absence, we act as his home and hearth. He needs aid to see through our more basic illusions, but that isn't enough to rob him of his place."

Thin blood is a social stigma in Faerie. It isn't enough to ban you completely. Some of Faerie's greatest scholars and magical theoreticians were thin-blooded: it gave them the ability to see us for what we were, but at a distance, and that made them stronger than most people could understand. It said something about Lily that she was willing to take in Ross and Marcia the way she had.

"Fair enough," I said, sliding my hands into my pockets. Looking back to Julie, I said, "I guess you know what's up?"

"Lil says you're having problems with idiots with guns, so Ross and me are here to get you through the big bad park and down to your waiting chariot, which happens to be a San Francisco city taxicab," she said, hugging Ross' arm to her chest in a proprietary manner. "It'll be a cakewalk."

"Right," I said and glanced at Lily, who shook her head. This was my choice. She knew that Julie was Cait Sidhe enough to never take threats of physical violence seriously: she thought of herself as the biggest threat on the block, even though her blood was as thin as mine. As for Ross . . . he might mean well, but he was quarter-blooded, which meant his magic would be weak, if it existed at all. She was giving me a quarter-blood who probably couldn't do anything but scream and hide and a Cait Sidhe changeling who thought she could scare just about anything away by shouting and showing her claws. Why?

Because she thought it would convince me not to go. Shaking my head, I started for the gate. If anything attacked us, we could just panic at it until it went away. "Come on. Let's get this traveling freak show on the road."

Lily followed as far as she could. As we passed from her land back into the park proper, she stopped, saying, "October?"

Juliet and Ross were a few feet ahead of me, Julie still holding his arm. I looked back to Lily, silhouetted by the garden gates, and said, "Yeah?"

"Be careful."

"Aren't I always?" I asked. Then I turned, not waiting for an answer, and followed my escort out the gate.

It was almost totally dark outside the Tea Gardens, the shadows broken only by randomly spaced streetlights and the sparkle of passing pixies. Figures both fae and human moved through those shadows, taking whatever trails the night held for them. None of Golden Gate Park's nighttime inhabitants need much in the way of light; all it would do was show them the things they'd rather leave hidden.

Julie led the way once we were clear of Lily's domain. Her Cait Sidhe heritage gave her night vision that put mine to shame, and even mine was probably worlds better than Ross'. Faerie ointment lets humans see through illusions, but it can't change the human eye. He was stuck with what his blood could give him. I did my best to keep pace. The throbbing in my shoulder was constant, but not enough to be more than a mild distraction. Lily did her work well.

"It's a nice night, for December," I said, squinting into the foggy dark. "I can almost pretend to see my hand in front of my face."

"I guess," Julie said. "It's not raining. That's something."

"I like the rain."

Julie threw me a dirty look, eyes glowing a pale, annoyed green. I smirked at her. Most cats don't like water, and despite her pretensions of tigerhood, Julie was no different. Yes, tigers have stripes; so do tabbies. If you want to know the difference, try tossing one of each into your swimming pool. Then I would recommend running.

"I don't," she said, sullenly.

"I do," Ross said. Some of the tension slipped out of Julie's shoulders and she smiled, giving me a "what can you do?" shrug. I grinned back. Cliff taught me a lot about the sort of attitude changes you sometimes have to pull midstream if you want to keep peace in a relationship. I was starting to think this Ross guy was something more than a casual fling.

The Cait Sidhe don't fall in love often; mostly, they get involved in short, torrid affairs that don't mean anything to either side, and they never fall in love with changelings if they can help it. It's easier that way. Falling in love with someone that's going to get old and die while you live forever isn't a survival trait, and so they've learned to keep their distance ... but all that means is that when they finally fall, they fall hard. Julie's only half Cait Sidhe, but I'd never seen her look at anyone the way she was looking at Ross. I studied him with a bit more interest, trying to puzzle out where his fae blood had come from.

He must have been used to those sorts of looks, because he smiled, and said, "My mother's father was one of the Roane."

"Oh, I see," I said. The Roane are gentler cousins to the Selkies. They aren't as inclined to vengeance, and their magic is innate—they're shapeshifters, like the Cait Sidhe, not skinshifters like the Selkies. They're also practically extinct.

Julie flashed another grin my way. "He's my guy."

"That's cool," I said. The light was getting brighter as we approached the street, where my taxi was hopefully waiting. I wanted to go home, drink a gallon of orange juice, and eat something before I started calling people to let them know I was alive. I grimaced. Sylvester had to be in a state of utter panic, and Devin probably wasn't much better.

A branch snapped behind us. I whirled, wincing as the bandage on my shoulder pulled the edges of the still raw gunshot wound together. There was nothing there. I still stood there for a moment before turning back to my bewildered escort, taking the time as much to catch my breath as to scan the darkness for danger.

Julie looked amused, but Ross looked terrified. Trying to be soothing, I said, "I'm just jumpy."

"I don't smell anything," Julie said, "but the wind is blowing away from us. I don't *think* we're being followed." Ross looked at her nervously, and the tiger-striped changeling smiled. "It's okay, sweetie, we're cool. You've got me and Tobes with you. What could happen?"

Never tempt fate. It plays for keeps. I started to turn when I heard the second branch snap—and it was closer now, so much closer—but I already knew that I wouldn't be fast enough. You're never fast enough when the danger is real.

The gunshot sounded like thunder.

Ross screamed. I didn't look back, not even when Julie started snarling like the tiger she pretended to be. There wasn't time to worry about them; there was barely time to react. I already knew what had happened, and I cursed myself for a fool even as I ducked, letting the second shot pass over my head. The Redcap who tried to kill me earlier saw me get on the bus. After that, it was just a matter of following the trail to Lily's door and waiting for me to come out again. We'd walked right into his trap.

He was standing on the open ground between us and the street below, gun drawn, fog swirling thick around his ankles. Six and a half feet of muscle and grinning, shark-toothed malice would have been enough to give me pause even without the gun ... but having it definitely upgraded him from "possible threat" to "probable cause of death."

I was standing frozen, trying to figure out what to do when Julie hurtled over my head with a snarl, turning in midair to hit him feetfirst in the chest. He staggered back, batting her aside like a house cat. She hit the ground still snarling, bouncing back to her feet and glancing to me. I knew my cue when I saw it. Julie and I fought beside each other when we both worked for Devin; we'd even been pretty good at it. I knew how she would move. She knew how I would dodge. And tag-team tactics are your best bet when you're as outgunned as we were.

It's hard to pay attention to more than one person at a time—that's why gangs have such an advantage in most fights. I pulled my arm back as I charged, punching the bastard in the side of the head as hard as I could. The rebound ran all the way along my arm, and I bit back a scream as I felt something rip. Still, it had the desired effect, because he snarled and turned toward me, raising his gun. That gave Julie the opening she needed to hit him again, shrieking and spitting as she clawed at his eyes. It's never good to be a single person fighting off a gang. Unless you take them out as they appear, your opponents will just keep bouncing back and getting in the way.

Unfortunately for us, he was catching on. He swung at Julie, and she ducked out of the way, timing her dodge to match my next blow—but rather than turning his attention toward me, he adjusted his aim so that his gun was pointed directly between her eyes. She froze, eyes going wide and frightened. I don't think anyone had ever pointed a gun at her before, and at that sort of range, he didn't even need to be accurate: all he had to do was pull the trigger.

Wincing, I braced to hit him again. It wouldn't hurt him, but it might get him to look away long enough for Julie to dodge. He was a goon, and goons don't usually get the job because of their brains. If we kept switching off, we might be able to keep either of us from being shot before we had a plan, and that struck me as a good idea. Changelings don't take as much damage from iron as the purebloods, but any sort of bullet can ruin an otherwise good day.

He was still focused on Julie, cocking the hammer slowly back as I hit him from the side. He turned, gun now swinging toward me, and Julie fell back, obviously off balance. Oh, oak and ash. She wasn't going to rush him this time; she was too scared. He wasn't going to get distracted.

"Whoa, big fella," I said, stepping backward. I'd run if

he missed . . . and if he didn't, I was pretty much screwed.
"No need to get violent—" The gun went off half a second before the pain hit. I screamed, clapping my hands
over the new hole in my right thigh. Judging by the pulse
of blood between my fingers, he'd managed to miss the
major artery—and considering how close he was, that
wasn't good. He'd been shooting to wound. He wanted
to take his time.

Forcing myself not to hyperventilate, I raised my
head. If I was going to die, I was going to do it with my
eyes open. He was standing right in front of me, Julie
crumpled on the ground behind him.

"Nice driving, bitch," he growled, and raised his gun.
Evening, I'm sorry, I thought. I kept my eyes on his,
squaring my shoulders, and waited for him to pull the
trigger. This was it: end of game.

Tybalt dropped out of the trees above us, landing solidly on the Redcap's head.

The gun went flying, and I fell backward, barely catching myself. I still don't know why I didn't pass out. I
couldn't move; all I could do was stare, openmouthed.
I'd never seen the King of Cats fight before. He was suddenly everywhere, made of nothing but fangs and claws
and fury, snarling like a chainsaw trying to sing opera.
Our witless assassin never stood a chance.

Julie crawled to her feet, shaking herself before running back into the darkness. My heart sank as I realized that I hadn't heard a sound from Ross since the
fight began. I wanted to follow her, but I couldn't get my
feet to move. Tybalt's hand, claws extended, was coming
down across the Redcap's throat. I managed to turn my
head before the blow fell, and spotted the gun, now easily three feet away. I struggled to my hands and knees,
crawling across the grass to grab it. The wounds in my
thigh and shoulder screamed with every move.

There were still three iron bullets in the gun, enough to kill a dozen changelings. I guess I should've been honored that someone would go to so much trouble to get me out of the way. I just felt sick. The remaining bullets sang to the wounds in my shoulder and thigh, making the pain even worse. Iron knows itself. That's part of what makes it so dangerous.

A faint sniffling started behind me, climbing in pitch and volume to become a sustained wail. I pushed myself to my feet and turned, still looking at the ground. I didn't want to see what I knew was waiting there—but I had to. Even the purebloods mourn their dead.

Julie was cradling Ross in her arms, hair fanned out over both of them like a shroud. There wasn't much blood, just a few streaks splattered down the front of Ross' shirt; it wasn't enough to explain why he wasn't moving until Julie raised her head, the motion pulling her hair aside and revealing the pitted hole that had taken away most of his forehead above the left eye. He must have died almost instantly. Somehow, I doubted telling Julie that would help. Lily sent them to protect me. So why did I feel like I was the one that had failed to protect *them?*

A hand fell on my shoulder. I tried to jump, and staggered as the pain in my leg reasserted itself. Tybalt slung a bloody arm around me, stopping my fall by bracing me against him. He looked down at me, pupils contracted to slits, and I swallowed.

"I . . ." I said. He glanced over at Julie and Ross, then back to me. I nodded. "I didn't mean to."

"I know you didn't mean them any harm; neither did Lily," he said, in a gentler tone than I'd ever heard him use before. "Julie will know that, too, when she can. But she won't understand it now."

"Are you hurt?" I looked over as much of him as I

could, from where I was pulled against his chest: none of the blood seemed to be his. The Redcap lay where he had fallen, not moving, but somehow—thinking of the blankness in Julie's eyes—I couldn't find any pity in my heart. He was hired to kill, and he did his job. Hopefully, whoever it was also paid him well enough to die.

Tybalt blinked, looking startled. "I'm not hurt. You, on the other hand—"

"I've already got iron poisoning. With this much Undine water in me, this isn't going to make it any worse."

"Still . . ."

"I can stand," I said, and pushed myself away. After a moment's hesitation, he let go. Never taking his eyes off me, he lowered his hand to the wound at my thigh, pressed two fingers against it, and raised them to his mouth, tongue flicking out to taste the blood. I suppressed a shudder.

"This isn't dying blood," he said finally. "You'll live."

"Great, that's great reassurance. It makes me feel all better."

"It should. Having you die tonight would be inconvenient."

I pressed my hands tight around my leg, biting back several sharp retorts. The blood was slowing down—Tybalt was right. It wouldn't kill me. "Because you'd be stuck with the damn box?"

"Of course," he said.

Silly me. Why would he rescue me if it wasn't for his debts? Under normal circumstances, he'd probably have brought popcorn. "You fought well. I've never seen you fight before."

He allowed himself a thin smile. "You kept him distracted long enough for me to get up into the trees."

That was as close as Faerie's complex laws of

etiquette would let us get to thanking each other. I nodded instead, asking, "What were you doing here?"

"I've been waiting for you."

I blinked. That wasn't what I'd been expecting to hear. "What?"

"You were . . . injured when you entered the Tea Gardens," he said, glancing briefly away. "I thought you might have trouble getting out again, and I was right. I'm usually right when it comes to you and trouble."

"You . . . why?" I asked, dumbfounded.

He shrugged. "The terms of my promise." I gave him a blank look, and he continued, "I said I'd give . . . it . . . back to you. I can't do that if you die."

"I realize that. I just . . ." I paused. "I guess I didn't think you'd take it quite that seriously."

"I take my promises *very* seriously—all my promises. Now if you don't mind, this wasn't exactly subtle, and the gunshots alone would attract the police. I need to dispose of the evidence."

Evidence? The Redcap's body would need to be moved until the night-haunts came; the same went for Ross. I didn't know if his body was different enough from the human norm to need replacing, or whether he was close enough to immortal for the night-haunts to want him, but it didn't matter. Whatever happened to him now, he'd still be just as dead.

He'd be dead. His blood wouldn't. If there was one thing I'd learned from Evening's death, it was that the dead still had a lot of things to tell me. A hired Redcap wasn't likely to have any nasty blood curses lurking to surprise unwary changelings, either. "Tybalt, the body. I need to—"

"You need to get out of here."

Julie was still wailing, rocking Ross' body back and

forth. I started to step toward her, but the pain in my leg stopped me even before I felt Tybalt's restraining hand.

"Go home, October," he said, voice pitched low. "I'll take care of this."

I turned back to glare at him. "Don't you *care?*" I demanded, gesturing toward them.

"I care more than you'll give me credit for. But dead is dead, and I'm going to keep my word. Go get your leg taken care of, and make sure you're not going to make me a liar by dying. Go *home*."

I shook his hand away from my shoulder, glaring at him, but turned to limp the rest of the way down the hill. If he wanted to pick up the pieces, I'd have to let him, and he was right; there wasn't time to fiddle with the body before the mortal police showed up. I had enough to worry about without getting arrested for hanging around in a public place drinking the blood of a corpse.

The taxi Lily promised was waiting on the street, radio turned up so loudly that the driver probably hadn't even heard the gunshots. I slid into the backseat, snapping out my address. No one would follow me; Tybalt would make sure of that. I had to trust him, because I'd already committed myself to trusting him, and it was do or die.

The driver grunted assent and pulled out, guiding us into the late December fog. Despite the blare of the radio, I thought I could still hear Julie crying. Whoever killed Evening now had more to answer for than the taste of phantom roses; they had a man who loved a Cait Sidhe girl, and who died in the company of friends that couldn't save him. And they were going to pay.

SEVENTEEN

THE DRIVER KEPT HIS EYES on the road, grunting, "You're gonna have to pay for that."

"What?" I looked up from my hasty attempt at turning my previously discarded bra into a tourniquet for my injured leg. It worked pretty well, once I remembered to remove the underwire.

"The seat. I don't care what happened, and if you don't wanna go to the hospital, that's your deal, but you're gonna have to pay for the upholstery."

Oh. Right. "I thought Lily already paid you," I said, lamely.

"For the ride, she paid me. For the cleaning I'm gonna have to do after I drop you off, she didn't pay me." He glanced at me through the rearview mirror. "You don't mind my saying, you should really rethink that hospital idea."

"I'll take it under advisement," I said, sagging back against the seat and closing my eyes. "I don't have my purse with me." I didn't have my purse anywhere, since I'd left it in the car when I turned and ran. "If you'll walk me to my door, I can pay you for the cleaning." If he walked me to my door, I was guaranteed to *get* there.

"Deal," he said.

We made the rest of the drive in silence.

At my apartment complex, he pulled into one of the visitor's spaces in front of the manager's office and stopped the cab, moving to open my door before I could convince my stiffening leg to move. "Come on," he said gruffly, offering his arm. "You ain't gonna make it up there on your own."

I gave him a startled glance, finally noticing the shimmer of the human disguise wrapped around him. He smiled, amused.

"What's the matter? You ain't never seen a cab driver before?"

"It's been a while," I said, using his elbow to pull myself out of the car. I tasted the balance of his blood automatically as I rose, and relaxed. Bridge Troll. They're big, placid, dependable people, and they take their responsibilities—even ones as small as walking a woman to her front door in order to get paid—seriously.

We didn't talk as he helped me up the path toward my apartment. I came to a sudden stop when the door came into view, almost stumbling.

"Hey, lady, careful," he said, big hand going to my shoulder to steady me. He eyed my porch with suspicion. "That guy a friend of yours?"

"Yeah," I said, relief washing over me. "He is."

For the second time in less than a week, there was someone waiting on my doorstep. Devin looked up when he heard our voices, and then jumped to his feet, almost running toward us.

"Toby!" Ignoring the cabbie entirely, he put his hands on my shoulders, yanking me toward him. I hissed as he hit the poultice, world briefly whiting out from the pain.

"Oh, root and branch, Julie said it was bad, but I had no idea . . ."

"Julie?" I said, as the cabbie said, startled, "Toby?"

Devin and I both turned to stare at him. That was all right; he was staring at me.

"Toby?" he repeated. "As in October Daye?"

"Sadly, yeah," I said, blinking as confusion won out over the pain in my thigh and shoulder. "Do I know you?"

"No, but you helped my baby sister outta a tight spot once, about seventeen years ago." He grinned, showing teeth that not even an illusion could make look like anything but chunks of craggy stone. "You forget what I said about the upholstery, you hear? I don't want your money. There's a Bannick I know, he'll do it almost free anyhow. You need a cab, you just call and ask for Danny. 'S the least I can do." He paused before adding, almost shyly, " 'S good to see you're back in business. This Kingdom needs more folks like you." Then he was gone, heading rapidly back down the path, leaving me to lean on Devin and stare bemusedly after him.

"That was weird," I said finally.

"I don't really care about weird." Devin's tone was sharp. "I care about getting you inside and taking a look at those wounds. What did you *do,* Toby?"

"Oh, the usual," I said, letting him lead me toward my front door. "Wrecked my car. Got shot. Twice, actually. With iron bullets. Lost a lot of blood. Lily managed to give a lot of it back to me, but that was before I got shot the second time . . ." The world was spinning. I leaned on Devin's hands. That was a familiar feeling: being dizzy with blood loss and leaning on Devin.

"When you decide to go back to work, you don't screw around, do you?"

I didn't have an answer for that. Instead, I stumbled, and Devin picked me up, carrying me into my apartment. That seemed wrong somehow. Frowning, I asked, "Didn't I lock the door?"

"Hush. You locked it, but I'm the one who taught you how to *pick* locks, remember?" He put me down on the couch. "Get your pants off."

"Always the romantic, aren't you?" I pulled the gun out of my waistband, leaning over to put it on the coffee table. The last thing I needed to do was shoot myself.

"After Julie called, I thought heroic measures might be required." Devin picked up a large black box, shaking it in my direction. "I brought the first aid kit."

Devin's line of work wasn't exactly gentle, and it didn't attract healers. Consequentially, he had a lot of experience with healing potions, charms, salves, and anything else that could patch a body back together faster than nature could manage on its own. Healing potions take their toll, but when you're hard up enough to need them, it always seems like a fair trade.

Normally, I would've been eyeing the box with unalloyed delight. This time, however, there was a little problem. "Iron bullets, Devin," I said, closing my eyes. "You're not gonna have a charm that can handle iron poisoning."

"Maybe not, but I can at least take care of the blood loss and the flesh wounds," he said. I felt his fingers unsnapping the buckle of my jeans as he knelt. "You won't do anyone any good if you're dead."

"That's debatable," I said, and went limp, letting him work.

Devin hissed as he peeled my jeans back. "What were you planning to do about this? Wish it away?"

"I dunno. Think it would work?"

"Not unless you've got a Djinn hiding in your closet."

I smelled the sharp, antiseptic tang of disinfectant, and felt him starting to wipe the blood off.

"Not last time I checked." Opening my eyes, I looked down.

It wasn't all that bad at first glance. The bullet had passed cleanly through, leaving a small, almost tidy hole on the front of my thigh. The damage was worse around the exit wound; I couldn't see it, but I could feel the ragged edges of the muscles there scraping against each other. As Devin wiped away the blood, thin red-and-white lines became visible, radiating out from the wound like the heralds of infection. That was the real danger. Not the blood loss, not the injury; the iron.

"Have you tried to spin an illusion since you were shot?" Devin asked, head still bent as he worked at my leg.

"I cast a confusion spell on the girl working the gate," I offered, starting to feel faintly nauseated by the sight of so much blood. How much blood is in a body, anyway? And how much of that could I afford to lose?

"And after the second time?"

I hesitated. Tybalt had pushed me toward the cab, and my hair was down, covering my ears . . . "No," I confessed, eyes going wide. "Maeve's teeth, Devin, I just took a taxi without an illusion on! What if the driver had been human?"

"He would've thought you were a comic book geek on your way home from a convention," Devin said, briskly. "People ignore more than you give them credit for. Can you try weaving an illusion? Just a little one? I want to see if you can do it."

"Sure," I said, and raked the fingers of my left hand through the air, intending to gather a handful of shadows to work with. I caught nothing. My magic, always reluctant to answer my commands, didn't even stir.

I went cold.

"Devin . . ."

"Iron poisoning. You're lucky it passed straight through; you'd be dead by now if it hadn't," he said, reaching into the first aid kit and coming up with a bottle of something green. "Drink this. It should help with the dizziness."

"Do I want to know where you bought this?" I asked, taking the bottle. The liquid inside smelled like wasabi and pineapple.

"Probably not," he said, beginning to rub a thick purple cream around the wound in my thigh. I gritted my teeth against the stinging. The cream sank into my skin, leaving a cool numbness in its wake. "Try not to get shot again. You can only have one dose this month."

I looked at the bottle with new respect. "Or what?"

"You melt."

"Got it." The liquid tasted like it smelled and tingled all the way down. I handed the bottle back to Devin, not terribly surprised when I realized that my dizziness was gone. "So, iron poisoning. How long am I going to be reduced to living by my wits alone?"

"A few days. You'll need to guard against infection, but it won't kill you." He gave my thigh a critical look. "This needs stitches. I can do it, or you can. Whichever makes you more comfortable."

"Go ahead," I said, closing my eyes again. "You've had more practice."

"You should've stuck around, instead of running off to play with the purebloods," he said, chiding lightly to distract me from the feeling of the needle biting through my flesh. "I told you you'd get soft."

"I wanted to see what getting soft was like," I said, digging my fingers into the cushions and forbidding myself to move. It wasn't easy.

"And the verdict?"

"It was nice. You should try it sometime."

"I'll keep that in mind." He pressed on the edges of the wound, forcing them closer together as he worked. After five stitches, he pulled his hand away. "I need you to lie down on your stomach so I can take care of the back."

"Am I going to get a lollipop when you're done?" I asked, scooting over so that I could lie down on the couch, eyes still closed. "I like the grape ones."

"Hush," he said again, going back to work. First the cream; then the sharp bite of the needle, and the feeling of thread pulling flesh back together. "Is being the one to find Evening's killer really worth all this, Toby?"

"She was your friend, too."

"She was a noble. Isn't that what we have a queen for?" A hint of bitterness crept into his tone as he tied off the last of the stitches. "Let the nobility take care of their own, and get your ass out of the line of fire."

"Not an option."

He sighed. "You always were a stubborn little fool."

Lifting my head, I twisted around and smiled at him. "I learned from the best."

"I suppose you did," he said, reaching out to cup my chin in the palm of his hand. "I wasn't a very good teacher."

"You were good enough," I said. He moved to let me push myself upright, hand still cupping my chin. "I'm still alive, aren't I?"

"Yes, but at this rate, for how long?" Devin was kneeling, the first aid kit still open beside him. "I want you out of this."

"That's not an option," I said softly.

It wasn't often that I got the chance to see Devin outside the carefully constructed confines of his office.

His hair was mussed, hanging to half cover one eye. I reached out to brush it aside, and he caught my hand, expression grim.

"Don't make me beg, Toby. Please. Walk away from this. Let the Queen's Court deal with it." He squeezed my hand. "You just came back to me. I'm not ready to let you go again."

"I never said . . ."

"You didn't have to. You came Home." Hand still cupping my chin, Devin leaned forward and kissed me.

I worked for Devin for years; he'd had his hands over every inch of my body for reasons both sexual and practical, from pulling my clothes off to bandaging a wound. In all those years, he'd never kissed me with so much urgency or such a feeling of need. I found myself responding despite my injuries, first returning the kiss, then sliding down off the couch to kneel beside him. His stitches were good. They didn't even pull as I knelt.

Devin was the one to break away, releasing the hand he was holding as he said, "I need to look at your shoulder."

"Wow," I said, dizzy now for reasons that had nothing to do with blood loss. "Way to kill the mood."

He smirked. "No, darling. The amount of blood you've decided to accessorize with could do that quite admirably without my help."

I glanced down at myself as I slid back onto the couch. The robe I'd borrowed from Lily wasn't pink anymore. Dried blood had turned it a mottled shade of brown, with a brighter streak of red over my left shoulder where exertion had reopened the gunshot wound.

"I need a shower," I said.

"We'll get to that in a minute," Devin said, reaching up to peel away my robe.

Lily's carefully constructed poultice had pulled away

during the fight and was dangling loose against my collarbone. Devin tugged the last of the bindings away, dropping the whole bundle onto the floor. "She does good work," he admitted, almost grudgingly. "It looks like she even managed to wash most of the iron out before it could really work its way into your body. That probably explains why you're still conscious."

"You really are a happy little ray of sunshine today, aren't you?" I was looking at the exit wound, and the visible damage still looked about half as bad as my thigh, despite having been made with the same caliber bullet. "Does it need stitches?"

"To be on the safe side? Yes." Devin picked up the cloth he'd used to clean the blood off my leg. "I don't think I need to worry about disinfecting this." More quietly, he added, "It's going to scar, you know."

"Iron always does." I watched him wash the blood away, considering the severity of the damage. Lily really did an amazing job. My arm wouldn't be up to my normal standards for a while—probably several weeks, if ever—but it wouldn't be useless, as long as I could take things easy.

As if that's ever been an option.

Devin closed the front with three stitches, and the back with only two. "There." He returned the needle and surgical thread to the first aid kit before standing, offering me his hands. I raised my eyebrows, and he nodded toward the bathroom. "Didn't you want a shower?"

"Yes," I admitted. "But I'm a little naked here."

A smile tugged at the corners of his mouth. "Isn't that the best state in which to *take* a shower? Nudity is, I believe, a prerequisite."

"If you insist." Taking his hands, I let him pull me off the couch. I stumbled slightly as I put my weight on my injured leg, relieved when it didn't buckle. I probably couldn't run, but I could walk, at least for now. Depending on the infection, well, we'd see how long that lasted.

Devin didn't comment on the way I leaned on him as we walked to the bathroom. I appreciated that, almost as much as I appreciated his steadying arm around my waist. "You still like your showers hot, don't you?" he asked, letting go at the bathroom door.

"The hotter, the better," I said, before the mirror caught my attention. "Oh."

"Yes," said Devin grimly. Sitting down on the edge of the tub, he turned on the taps. Hot steam began to fill the room. "You see why I was a trifle concerned."

"Uh, yeah. I do." Muck had plastered my hair almost flat against my head, and there was a distinct gray undertone to my complexion. I've seen corpses that looked like they had more life left in them. Considering the way I looked, I shouldn't have been doing anything but calling Danny and requesting a ride to the nearest emergency room—do not pass Go, do not collect two hundred dollars.

"You look better than you did."

"This is *better?*"

Devin looked up, saying simply, "Yes."

That was a sobering thought. I was still standing there contemplating it, when he walked over, put his hands around my waist, and lifted me off the floor. "Hey!" I protested.

"Shower now," he said. "And then, I'll put you to bed with a nice hot drink to make you feel better."

"Is that all you'll put me to bed with?" I asked.

Devin smiled and lowered me into the bathtub.

Hot water on fresh wounds may be medicinally helpful, but it hurts like hell. I gasped as the spray from the showerhead hit me, fighting the urge to scream. Devin watched, holding the shower curtain open, before he asked, "Will you be all right?"

Iron poisoning, two gunshot wounds, and he was asking if I'd be all right? I forced a smile, reaching for the curtain. "If I can't take a shower by myself, you can go ahead and bury me," I said, and pulled it closed.

He laughed, saying, "Have it your way," as he left the bathroom. I waited for the sound of the door closing, and turned myself to the serious business of getting clean.

You never realize how wonderful it is to be clean until you've been dirty for days. I stayed in the shower for almost half an hour, glorying in the hot water and the fact that no one was trying to kill me. When the water started to cool I turned it off, wringing as much as I could out of my hair before grabbing a towel off the rack and stepping gingerly out of the stall.

Devin was waiting for me in the hall. He pressed a mug of thick yellow liquid into my hands. "Drink this."

I sniffed. It was warm and smelled like gingerbread. "This is . . . ?"

"Good for you."

"Right," I said, and sipped. It was bitter. I grimaced. "How good for me are we talking? Because this tastes—"

"Good enough."

"Right," I repeated. Devin watched intently as I finished the mug.

When I was done, he took it away from me, setting it on the hallway table. "There's another cup in your coffeepot," he said. "Drink it in the morning. You'll feel better."

"Promise?" I asked, with a small smile.

Devin put his arms around my waist again, nearly dislodging my towel. "Would I lie to you?" he asked, bending toward me.

"All the time," I said, and leaned in to meet him.

His first kiss was careful, all too aware of my recent injuries. I pressed closer, putting my arms around his neck, lacing my fingers into his hair. That seemed to be the signal he'd been waiting for; his second kiss was more assertive, more the Devin I knew, the one who took my virginity on the roof of Home, with the fog blocking out everything else in the world.

When my bad leg buckled, he picked me up and carried me into the bedroom, kissing me all the way.

We left the towel behind.

EIGHTEEN

DEVIN'S VOICE IN MY EAR, as I was drifting toward a safe, comfortable slumber: "Let this go, October. Just . . . just let her go."

"I can't," I mumbled.

He sighed. The bedsprings creaked as he stood. "My kids will be here in the morning," he said, and that was the last thing I knew before the sun slanting through my bedroom window hit my face and brought me slowly back to consciousness.

I peeled my eyes open, staring at the ceiling. Not dead. That was a start. The inside of my mouth tasted terrible, and my head felt like it had been the ball in the all-Summerlands soccer finals. Adding this to the pain in my shoulder and thigh, I figured I should just stay asleep until sometime in, say, March. I'd already managed to sleep through dawn, thus proving that iron poisoning and blood loss are the best knockout drugs known to man.

At least I wasn't bleeding, thanks to Devin and Lily. If I could get through a few hours without someone deciding the world would be a better place without me in it, I might actually start feeling like a normal person again.

Levering myself into a sitting position, I fumbled for my robe on the bedroom floor, and frowned as I realized the cats weren't demanding to be fed. "That's weird." Cagney and Lacey *always* demanded breakfast when they saw signs that I might be awake. "Girls?"

There was no reply.

Frowning, I pulled on my robe and left the room, scanning for signs of my feline roommates. "Girls? Kitty-kitty? Hey, not funny, you two . . ." They still didn't answer. At least my leg was holding up my weight without much of a complaint.

Devin was gone, as I'd expected; he hadn't even bothered to leave a note. Only the mug on my hallway table, sides caked with thick yellow gunk, proved that he'd actually been there. I picked it up and paused, throat tightening. The light on my answering machine was blinking.

"Please, not again," I said, and pressed the button. The machine beeped.

"October, this is Pete." My manager sounded deeply unhappy to be talking to my answering machine. Considering how difficult it was to get decent help on the night shift, I couldn't blame him.

"Oh, crap," I said, leaning against the wall. I knew what came next. I'd been hearing it a lot since I got out of the pond.

"I covered for you as best I could, but you've been a no-call, no-show for two nights now. I'm afraid we're going to have to let you go. Your last paycheck will be mailed to the address we have on file." He hesitated, adding, "Whatever this is . . . I just hope you're all right."

The message ended.

"Gunshot wounds, iron poisoning, missing cats, dead friend, and now I need to find a new job," I muttered, pushing away from the wall and swallowing my relief at the fact that it hadn't been something worse. No one else was dead. After the things that had been happening lately, that was a mercy in and of itself. "Damn it, Evening. Couldn't you have found yourself a flunky who didn't have to pay the rent?"

I walked into the living room, wincing when I saw the gun on the coffee table. Someone was really trying to have me killed, and the gun in my living room suddenly looked like a symbol of the entire damn mess. I kicked the coffee table with my good leg, sending the gun sliding across the floor to vanish behind the curtains.

"Screw you, Evening!" I shouted. "Screw your duty and your dying and . . . and your going off and leaving me to deal with this alone!" I stopped, fury spent as quickly as it had come. It wasn't doing anyone any good. Not even me.

The silence that followed my outburst was followed by a familiar, if muffled sound: Siamese voices, raised in angry protest at their mistreatment by the world. "Girls?" The yowls led me to the front door. I opened it, and the cats came racing inside, ears flat against their heads, eyes wide and wild. I stared at them. "Jeez, girls. Were you out there all night? You know there's a reason you're not allowed to go outside!"

Cagney looked up at me, ears still flat, and yowled again. I sighed. "Right. You got out when Devin brought me inside." Lacey added her voice to the choir, both of them beginning to twine around my ankles. I don't normally mind them being friendly. I also don't normally have a hole in my thigh and a case of iron poisoning threatening to dump me on my ass. "Yes, I know," I said, stepping over them on my way to the kitchen. "You nearly froze to death out there, you haven't been fed since the fall of Rome, and I'm evil. How about you let me get to the kitchen without breaking my neck?"

The cats seemed unimpressed by this offer and complained all the way into the kitchen, stopping only after their bowl was full of mashed-up artificial fish. The last of Devin's yellow gunk was caked on the inside of my coffeepot. I scraped it thickly into my mug and shoved the mug into the microwave, asking, "You two need anything else?" The cats didn't answer.

I rinsed the coffeepot and filled it with water, studying my reflection in the toaster. I looked like hell. My skin was pale, the skin around my eyes looked bruised, my neck was livid with scrapes and bruises from its encounter with the seat belt, and somehow I *still* looked better than I had the night before. Sleep and a hefty dose of several healing potions will do that for a girl.

Sleep, healing potions, and a little company. I half smiled as I filled the coffee machine, setting it to percolate. Maybe it was wrong of me to go looking for a silver lining in the current stupid mess, but if there was one, it was in the bridges I was starting to rebuild. Sylvester had missed me. Shadowed Hills was willing to welcome me. And Devin . . .

I touched the side of my neck, remembering the touch of Devin's lips. Devin still cared. In his own screwed-up way, he'd never stopped.

The ding of the microwave snapped me back to the present. Withdrawing the mug, I sipped the gingerbread-scented goo and waited for the coffee to finish. The iron in my blood still had me weak and befuddled, but time and not getting myself killed would take care of that. In the meantime, at least the stuff Devin had left me was helping to keep me on my feet.

The taste of roses tried to rise in my throat, seeming

thinner and weaker than before. I wasn't the only one being slowed down by the iron poisoning. I shoved it down as hard as I could and took another large gulp of Devin's gingerbread slime before topping off my mug with coffee. No matter how much I wanted to stand around and dwell on things, the fact remained that I was on a very real deadline, and the trail to Evening's killers was having more and more time to get cold.

The gingerbread slime was substantially easier to stomach when mixed with coffee. I topped the mug off again, adding six spoonfuls of sugar before heading for the hall. The day looked pretty simple, really. I'd call Sylvester and let him know that I was still alive. Then, when Devin's kids showed up, I'd head for Home, and I'd tell him everything. The hope chest, the key, the curse Evening slapped on me before she died, everything. He had the pieces I was missing about the way things had changed in the years I missed, and between the two of us, we might just have enough to end this whole damn mess.

The mixture of coffee and healing potion was sweet and sharp on my tongue, and it tasted like surviving to see tomorrow. I was reaching for the telephone when the doorbell rang.

I tensed, turning to stare at the door before slowly, grudgingly relaxing. Devin told me he'd be sending his kids in the morning. It was past noon; I should've been expecting them. Tightening the knot on my robe, I walked over and opened the door.

Gillian was standing on the doorstep.

I hadn't seen my little girl up close since she was two years old. She was just a shape through a telephoto lens, a figure that I took clandestine pictures of whenever I got to really feeling sorry for myself and used my old job skills to catch up with the daughter I'd lost. That didn't matter. There are some people you know no matter how far apart you are.

She was taller than I was—just by a few inches, but still—with the coltish build of a girl who wasn't quite done growing. She had her father's thick, dark hair, with the slight curl I'd always loved, and his Italian complexion. Even her eyes were his. She didn't look a thing like me, and I loved her all the more for that.

I must have made some sound of surprise, because she looked up and smiled. I would have given everything I had, and more, for that smile.

"Gilly?" I whispered.

Her smile grew. "Hi, Mom."

"Gilly," I repeated, like I was trying to convince myself. "You're here."

"I hope you don't mind?" She bit her lip, smile dying as quickly as it came. "I got your address off one of the letters you sent to Dad. I thought maybe you wouldn't mind if I stopped by for a little while. Just to say Merry Christmas, and everything."

"Mind? Why would I—no! I mean, no, I don't mind a bit. You can stay just as long as you want." The words were coming too fast, getting tangled around each other. I forced myself to slow down. "I mean, of course. Please, come in. Come in."

Still smiling, she stepped past me into the living room. I closed the door, wanting to scream and laugh and cry and jump around. I settled for folding my hands behind my back, watching her avidly.

Gilly looked around the room, and frowned. "Mom? Are you okay?"

"What?" I followed her gaze to the couch and winced as I saw the mud and blood caked on the cushions. "Oh, that. Yeah, Gilly, I'm fine. I just got a little bit banged up at work and haven't had a chance to call the dry cleaner, that's all." I hesitated. "Is it still Gilly? I mean, you're a lot older now. Do you like Gillian better?"

She ignored my question, still studying the room. "At work? I thought you worked at a grocery store."

"It can get pretty physical when you're shifting crates in the stockroom."

"Have you seen a doctor? Are you sure you're okay?"

"Yeah, honey, I'm sure." I nonchalantly pulled my robe a little tighter, hiding the bruises around my neck. "It was just a little scrape that bled a lot."

"Oh, okay," she said, craning her neck to peer down the hallway. For a moment, I thought she sounded almost disappointed. "So, you live alone, right? Big place for just one person."

"I got a good deal, and it's rent-controlled. It's just me and the cats. I like it that way. It's peaceful." I was lying, but I was hoping she couldn't tell. I didn't want to scare her away.

"Any close neighbors?"

"A few. I don't really know them very well." My shoulder was starting to throb. I tried massaging it with the palm of my hand. It didn't help. "Can I get you anything? Milk? Coffee?" Do human teenagers even drink coffee? I didn't know.

She shook her head, smile turning secretive. "That's okay. I'll eat soon. Can I see the rest of the apartment?"

"Sure, honey." I started toward the hall, trying not to limp, and paused. Something wasn't right. As much as I wanted this to be real, it wasn't ringing true. "Gilly? Does your father know you're here?"

"Oh, totally," she said, looking toward to the kitchen. The cats had vanished, leaving their breakfast half eaten. That wasn't a good sign. "He said I could come."

"So he doesn't mind spending Christmas without

you?" Why was I finding that hard to believe? Oh, yeah. Because I'm not completely stupid.

"He'll find something to do. He always does."

Her tone was dismissive, and I frowned. There was something she wasn't saying. "Gillian, what's going on here? I'm flattered that you came to me, I honestly am, but are you in some sort of trouble?"

"Trouble?" She leaned against the couch, suddenly moving with a bizarre predatory grace. "What makes you think I'm in trouble?"

"It's just strange to see you here like this." I reached up to push the hair out my eyes, and froze. I wasn't wearing a human disguise. I was still too dizzied by iron poisoning to spin one, and my hair wasn't covering my ears. She could see me for what I was, really and truly see me . . . and she hadn't batted an eye. Combined with the way she was moving . . .

My nerves started screaming "danger, Will Robinson, danger." Mixed with the iron poisoning and the sudden feeling that something had gone terribly wrong, it wasn't making for a pleasant emotional cocktail. I took a step backward, stopping when my shoulders hit the wall.

Gilly smiled, displaying far too many sharp white teeth.

"Gilly?" I whispered.

"Guess again," she said, still smiling, and lunged.

She caught me without really trying, slamming me against the wall as she wrapped her hands around my upper arms. I felt a stitch give way in my shoulder, and fought back a scream. All the humanity had leeched out of her eyes, bleaching them to a flat, pale yellow.

"Doppelganger," I spat, forcing myself to meet those alien yellow eyes.

"Good guess, mongrel," she said. "Want to make a guess at what happens next?" Her face was still mostly

Gillian's. She still looked like my little girl. I shook my head, not answering her, and she tightened her grip, nails scraping the surface of my skin through the bathrobe. "Come on, Daye. Guess."

"You're going to get out of here and leave me alone?"

She laughed. "Oh, come on. You can't *really* be that stupid, can you?"

"Actually, most people seem to think I can." That's right, October, mouth off to the monster. That's a good idea. No, really.

The Doppelganger snarled, face twisting into something a little less human. Good. The less she looked like my daughter, the easier this became. "I'm going to kill you. You know that, right?" She dug her nails into my shoulders, and I moaned, fighting a scream. I didn't need to alert my neighbors: they'd just rush in and get slaughtered by something they didn't even know existed. "You're a brave, stupid little thief. Tell me where you put the box, and I won't make you suffer; I'll just tear your throat out, and you'll die quick, you'll die merciful. Come on, thief. Tell me."

So that was what this was about. I should have known. I closed my eyes, trying to focus past the pain, and said, "I don't know what you're talking about. Sorry."

She let go of my right shoulder. I barely had time to stiffen before she struck me, nails slicing four shallow, parallel lines down the side of my cheek. I kept my eyes closed, feeling the blood run down the curve of my jaw.

"Do you bleed sweet, little thief?" she asked, running her tongue along the cuts. Her saliva burned like acid. I whimpered, trying to pull away. She put her hand back on my shoulder, holding me in place, and said crossly, "You should have screamed by now. It doesn't taste as good when you don't scream. Why won't you scream for me?"

"Sorry, but we only serve diet agony here," I whispered through gritted teeth. "No artificial colors or flavors." This time, she let go of both shoulders. I tensed, waiting for a blow that didn't come, and heard her step away.

After a long moment of silence, I opened my eyes.

The Doppelganger had lost most of its resemblance to Gilly, thank Maeve. It was taller, wider and sexless, the angles of its body becoming inexplicably wrong. Its skin was mottled in shapeless patches of gray and green that shifted as I watched, picking up faint tinges of the colors around it. It was probably chameleonic, blending into the scenery until it was ready to strike. Not really something you want to invite to Christmas dinner.

"Run," it said in a deep, grating voice before it smiled again. "Run now."

I raised a hand to my bleeding cheek. "Run?" I echoed.

"Run. Don't worry—you can't run fast enough. I'm going to catch you. It's still more fun for me if you try."

I've never been very concerned with how much fun people have when they're trying to kill me. That didn't mean I could stand there and wait to die. The couch was between me and the Redcap's gun, while the Doppelganger was between me and the front door. That left only one direction I could take, and I took it.

Ignoring the pain in my leg, I turned and bolted for the back of the apartment, slamming the hallway door as every late-night horror movie I'd ever seen flashed through my mind. The windows in the bedrooms were too high and narrow to climb through, and there were no windows in the bathroom. Unfortunately, when I rented the place, I wasn't exactly thinking in terms of how quickly could I escape a homicidal shapeshifter without using the front door.

Lacking any other options, I ran into the bedroom, locked the door, and shoved a chair under the knob. I heard the hall door slam open, hitting the wall with a crash that almost certainly took care of my security deposit. I didn't have time to worry about that: I was too busy scrambling to get the baseball bat out from under my bed. It was more for comfort than anything else—I wasn't dumb enough to think I could take the thing down with a piece of dime-store sports equipment—but it gave me something to hold onto and made me feel a little less naked. I spared a moment's longing thought for the gun in my living room. There's nothing like heavy weaponry to cure a little spiritual nudity.

The Doppelganger's slow, patient steps echoed down the hall. It was in no hurry. The damn thing was probably having a good time. Glad somebody was.

The taste of roses was starting to rise in the back of my throat, taking advantage of my distraction, and I could feel the wounds in my shoulder and thigh beginning to bleed again. Blood loss was going to become an issue. Of course, with no way out of the apartment and a homicidal Doppelganger on my trail, that just might be the kinder way to die.

The footsteps stopped outside the door, and the Doppelganger whispered, "Found you, little thief. And you're scared now, even if you won't scream. You're so scared I can taste it from here." I took a step back, holding the bat in front of me like a sword. I didn't bother trying to run. Why would I? There was nowhere left to go.

It hit the door hard, bowing it inward. The cheap plywood door started to give way on the second hit. It was never meant to stand up to this sort of abuse. This was it: this was the end. I was going to die wearing nothing but a bathrobe, at the hands of a Doppelganger I'd been stupid enough to invite into my home. I was never going to find the answers I was looking for. Evening and Ross would never be avenged.

The doorbell rang.

Silence reigned as the Doppelganger ceased its assault on the door. There was a long pause, both of us sorting out what to do next.

And then I heard my own voice call, cheerfully, "Coming!"

Footsteps moved away, down the hall, too light for a creature the size of the Doppelganger . . . but just right to be believably mine.

I stayed where it was until the footsteps faded. Then I undid the lock and pushed the chair out of the way, opening the half-shattered door. The hall was empty. The Doppelganger had actually gone to answer the doorbell. Oh, that was smart. Why didn't it just hang a sign on its back that said kick me?

The carpet crunched underfoot as I inched along, despite my best efforts to be quiet. Considering the beating I'd taken—and the amount of blood I was losing—I thought I was doing pretty well just by not falling down. Not that it would do me any good if the Doppelganger caught me out in the open. I might be walking into a trap, but that was a chance I had to take.

I was halfway down the hall when I heard the voices arguing from my living room. "You don't understand!" Dare, the combination of anxiety and desperation making her voice impossible to miss, even without the affected accent. "When Devin says to come here, we come here. You can't tell us to go. We can't listen. He won't let us."

"She's right, ma'am." Oh, root and branch, Manuel was with her. I shuddered, unable to stop myself from imagining what the Doppelganger would do to them, and forced myself another few feet down the hall.

"Devin said we had to come and help you with anything you needed."

"I'm sorry, kids," my voice replied. The Doppelganger was using a painfully cheerful tone that would have been a clue that something was wrong all by itself, if Manuel and Dare had known me better. I never sound that happy before sundown. "I just don't think it's a good idea for you to visit right now. Maybe you can come back later? I'll bake you some cookies . . ."

Okay, that was *it*. I hadn't had a chance to use the kitchen for anything more elaborate than coffee and fried eggs, and I'd be damned if some invading monster was going to beat me to it. I stepped into the living room, bat still held in front of me like a poor man's broadsword. "You are *not* using my kitchen."

It wasn't the best comeback ever, but considering how much blood I'd lost, I didn't think I was doing too badly. My double turned to face me, stolen eyes narrowing. "I thought I sent you to your room."

Manuel and Dare gaped as they looked between us. It wasn't hard to tell us apart: the Doppelganger was fully clothed, and I was wearing nothing but a bathrobe. Also, I was the one doing all the bleeding. "You did. Unfortunately, I'm a little old to be grounded."

"Uh . . . ma'am?" said Manuel, wide-eyed.

The Doppelganger lashed out with one hand, fingers morphing into talons, and shoved Manuel away from the door. He shrieked in pain and surprise as he fell backward, tumbling out of sight.

"Manny!" Dare shouted.

The Doppelganger turned and stalked toward me, growing taller as it abandoned the pretense of my form. "Bad girl," it chided, grinning. "Bad, *bad* girl. Time to be punished."

It was moving slowly, certain of its own strength. That

was the only opening I was likely to get, and so I took it, swinging my bat as hard toward its midsection as I could. Something in my shoulder ripped free, and the world was suddenly bathed in a fresh veil of pain.

The Doppelganger reached out and caught the bat midswing, careless as a child gathering daisies. It tightened its hand, and the wood shattered into splinters, leaving me holding nothing but the bottom third of what used to be a bat.

"Oh, crap . . ." I said, starting to back away. Aluminum. Next time, I was going to buy aluminum. Or maybe a tire iron.

Moving too fast to dodge, the Doppelganger reached out and grabbed my chin, talons cutting into my cheek. "You're a stupid thief, but you're scared enough now," it said, still smiling. "You're going to tell me everything I need to know." Dropping the splinters of my bat, it dug its fingers under my armpit and lifted me off the ground. My heart was pounding so hard that it hurt almost as badly as my injuries. I'd seen death before, even recently, but it had never been that close.

That might have been the end, if the Doppelganger hadn't made one small, fatal mistake: it turned its back on Dare. I didn't know her very well, and I still could have told it that turning its back on her wasn't a good idea. The young changeling had been given time to process all her possible responses to someone smacking her brother aside like a stray dog, and she'd settled on the one that came most naturally. Rage.

"Hey, *ugly!*" she shouted. The Doppelganger didn't turn around. That's probably why it was so surprised when the knives started slamming into its back. It bellowed, dropping me. Miraculously, I landed on the one part of my body that hadn't previously been in pain: my ass.

Snarling, it turned toward Dare. I had to give the girl this much: she might have been an arrogant little brat, but she looked into the face of death and was sincerely unimpressed. "I've seen scarier things than you on blind dates," she said. She still needed a dialogue coach, but I wasn't in any position to judge. "You wanna piece of me?"

Apparently it did, because it stalked toward her, still snarling. She didn't flinch, but flung another knife, this time aiming for the throat. The creature batted it aside without a pause. I think that's when Dare realized that maybe insulting something that large when it's close enough to catch you isn't a good idea, because she started backing away, eyes wide.

My shoulder wasn't just bleeding anymore, it was gushing, blood soaking my robe and running freely down my arm. I forced myself to stand, squinting past the pain that threatened to knock me down again. Four of Dare's knives were embedded in the thing's back. Two were stuck in the lower back, and one in the side of its arm, but the fourth was at an angle that might put it through the rib cage if somebody grabbed hold of the hilt and shoved upward.

I've always made a pretty good somebody. Moving as fast as I could still manage, I wrapped my hands around the knife's hilt, slippery with almost black blood. My left hand didn't want to close, but I forced it, gritting my teeth as the Doppelganger's blood started burning my skin. Dare was whimpering somewhere in front of me, blocked from sight by the bulk of the thing's body.

That did it. My hand finally caught a good grip, and I shoved the knife up as hard as I could. The Doppelganger bellowed, whipping halfway around, but I managed to keep hold of the knife, twisting it and driving it deeper in. One clawed fist hit my right arm as the creature tried to rip me off its back, slashing through the muscle of my bicep. It didn't matter anymore. I was committed: I couldn't have let go of that knife if I'd wanted to.

"Dare, the front!" I shouted.

She didn't say anything, but I heard her high heels hitting the floor as she launched herself at the thing. The Doppelganger kept bellowing, lashing out in all directions as it tried to get away. I twisted the knife harder, not letting the pain of the blood washing over my hands force me to let go. It felt like the skin was being eaten off my bones. At least if that happened, it would probably stop hurting. I heard Dare strike again, screaming and cursing, and the Doppelganger fell. It landed unmoving, with me still clinging to its back.

When I was certain it had thrashed its last, I pried my unwilling hands away from the hilt of Dare's knife, forcing myself to my feet. Dare's last strike had opened its throat in a ghoulish parody of Evening's death, bathing her in a veil of acidic gore. She was clutching her last knife in one hand, eyes wide and glassy with shock.

Manuel stumbled back into the doorway, apparently having just gotten up; combats never last as long as they feel from the inside. Four parallel slashes ran down his chest, marking where the Doppelganger hit him. Congrats, kid. You've got your first scars. "What . . ."

The Doppelganger's edges were starting to smoke and blur. I stepped away from it. "This is the part where it melts." And it was doing just that, dissolving into a pool of sticky slime that was never going to come out of the carpet.

"Ms. Daye?" Dare said, in a surprisingly meek voice. Was this her first kill? Oberon's blood, had I just watched her lose the last of her innocence? "Ms. Daye, are you okay?"

I turned to look at her, part of my brain noting idly

that her eyes were even greener when I was dizzy with iron poisoning and blood loss. "No," I said, almost smiling as I felt the pain finally start to fade. Shock will do that for you. "I'm pretty sure I'm not okay. But it was nice of you to ask." Then I collapsed. This losing consciousness thing was becoming a habit.

NINETEEN

VOICES DRIFTED THROUGH the haze. I tried not to react, waiting for the things they were saying to come clear before I took the irrevocable step of opening my eyes. Once you've admitted you're alive, you usually aren't allowed to go back to playing dead.

"I thought I told you two to take care of her!" shouted Devin. His voice sounded like it was coming from just a few feet away—and it sounded like he was pretty pissed. If it was possible for a changeling to die of high blood pressure, he'd probably manage it one day. When did Devin come back to the apartment? I sorted through my recollections of the day and couldn't remember letting him in.

The air smelled like cigarettes. I've never been a smoker, and that thought introduced the revolutionary idea that maybe we weren't in my apartment. I tensed, then relaxed, waiting. If Devin was there, I wasn't in danger. Well, not much danger, anyway.

"We got there in time!" Dare protested, voice desperate. Poor kid. She was a brat, but she'd done her best. If nothing else, she'd saved my ass, and I appreciated it.

"In time for what? In time to watch her get slaughtered? What a great idea! Why didn't you bring a camera? You could have taken pictures!"

"She's not dead!" Dare yelled, sounding like she was on the verge of tears. Devin never taught his kids to defend themselves from him; instead, he taught them that submission was a virtue. If you wanted to keep him off your back, you learned how to do it on your own time and without any outside help. That was the first lesson you needed to learn before you could leave him.

"No thanks to the two of you!"

The two of them? I'd only heard Dare speak—where was Manuel? Frowning, I opened one eye, treating myself to a blurry view of Devin's office. I bet the neighbors enjoyed watching a pair of blood-spattered teenagers carry me out down the walkway. It was probably the most entertaining thing they'd seen all week.

Opening the other eye, I blinked until the room came into focus. Dare and Manuel were sitting on folding chairs in front of Devin's desk, watching as he stalked back and forth. The kids looked almost sick, and Dare was clinging to Manuel's arm like it was some kind of lifeline.

"But we—" she said.

Devin lunged, shoving her shoulders against the back of the chair. It rocked up onto its rear legs. She whimpered, and he yelled, "Be quiet! You were stupid! You should have been there hours before you were!"

"Manuel said we had time—" she protested weakly.

That was enough. Maybe I loved the man and maybe I didn't, but no matter how scared he was, there was no reason for him to go taking it out on Dare. Using my right arm as a brace, I pushed myself upright. "Be nice to them, Devin. They did their job." It felt like I was talking through a mouthful of cotton, but nothing hurt—at least not yet. I was sure the pain would be catching up with me soon.

"Toby!" Devin let go of Dare and rushed to kneel beside me, anxiously scanning my face. "Toby, what happened? Why did that thing attack you? Are you all right? What did it want? You're awake!"

"Talking usually indicates consciousness," I said, reaching out to gingerly pat his shoulder. "I'm okay. For meanings of the word that include 'just got the crap kicked out of me by a Doppelganger,' that is."

Manuel turned toward us, smiling wanly. "Hello, ma'am." Dare just kept clinging to his arm, shivering. She looked terrified, and I couldn't blame her. Devin could be pretty scary when he put his mind to it.

"Hey, guys," I said, matching Manuel's smile with one of my own. Looking back to Devin, I added, "Those two saved my life, so knock it off. Stop yelling at them."

His expression twisted, turning dark. "They were the ones that let your life be put in danger in the first place. If they'd been there when they were supposed to be . . ."

"I would have still been in bed," I said, and shook my head. "It used my daughter's face to get into the apartment, Devin. *It was Gillian.* I'd have let it in whether or not they were there. Hell, if they'd been there when it showed up, I would've thrown them out. If they'd been there when you wanted them to be, I'd be dead now."

He froze, expression faltering as my words sunk in. I was right and he knew it: it wasn't fair to blame them for my stupidity. He settled for folding his arms and glaring, saying, "You should be more careful."

"How?" I asked. "Stop talking to people? Don't leave the house—or what, better yet, just stay here forever? I can't find out what happened to Evening if I do that, and if I don't find out who killed her, you don't get paid." *If*

I don't find out what happened, paying you is going to be the least of my worries.

Devin sighed, reaching out to lay the back of his hand against my cheek. "I'd rather have you alive than get paid, Toby. There's still time to walk away. If you don't want this in the hands of the Courts, just tell me what you have so far, and I'll make it someone else's problem. You can let it be, and know that you did what you could."

"I can't," I said, shaking my head. "I gave her my word."

That was a lie: I didn't give my word, Evening took it. Devin didn't know that. There's nothing shameful or embarrassing about getting caught in a binding, especially one thrown by someone as powerful as Evening, and I'd been planning to come Home to tell him everything. I opened my mouth to tell him and stopped. Something wasn't right. The idea of telling him just seemed wrong.

"Toby . . ." he sighed.

"I know."

We sat there looking at each other for a few minutes, Dare and Manuel watching from their seats. The poor kids must have felt like they were sitting on a nuclear testing site. Which of us was scarier—him or me?

I was almost ready to start apologizing for being dumb enough to get myself cursed when Devin shook his head, turning his face away. "If anything happens to you . . ."

"We'll just run on past experience and assume I'll be back in fourteen years. You can yell at me then."

He didn't look at me. Apparently, this was one of those situations that humor couldn't defuse. I've never been very good at spotting those. "That's not funny."

The pain hadn't returned; except for the couch springs poking me in the small of the back, I felt fine. That worried me. It might mean I was finally too broken to fix. "Can I walk?"

Turning back to me, Devin smiled, eyes still sad. "Would I be trying to keep you here if you couldn't walk?" he asked, and offered his hands. "Get up. There's a mirror in the bathroom."

Getting up was easier said than done, even with his help. Once I was upright, I kept hold of his hands, waiting for the world to stop swimming in and out of focus. At least my legs were doing what I told them to.

"I got it," I said, letting go and turning to stumble toward the door.

Going from the well-lit office to the dark hall was disorienting. My toes caught on the doorframe, and I tripped, catching myself against the wall with my left arm. I froze, staring at my outflung arm. Nothing hurt. Not my leg, not my shoulder, nothing.

Another unpleasant thought hit me as I pushed myself away from the wall as slowly as I could manage without overbalancing. What time was it? I'd promised Sylvester that I'd call if I needed help, and that was *before* I went and got myself shot. He had to be frantic with worry.

I could call once I knew how bad the damage was. Opening the door to the women's bathroom, I stepped inside.

The only difference between the bathrooms at Home is that the men's room gets better graffiti and the women's room is quieter. The men's room also has a working urinal—the one in the women's room was spray-painted purple and filled with cement before I came to live there. I don't know why, but I'm sure that there was a lot of beer involved. A Gwragen half-blood was slouching against the sink, a cigarette dangling from her candy-apple red lips. The color was definitely not lipstick. She straightened as I entered, dropping her cigarette to the tile floor and making a hasty exit. I watched her go, blinking. Root and branch, was I *that* frightening?

Steeling myself, I turned to risk a glance in the mirror. I was ready for anything, except what I actually saw.

"What the . . . ?"

The change Toby's clothes while she's asleep trend had continued: my bloody bathrobe was gone, replaced by a gauzy purple nightgown probably purchased from the sort of catalog that came wrapped in brown paper. It was ankle-length, but left my shoulders—more than just my shoulders—bare. That might have bothered me, but I was too busy taking in the view to care.

My hair was tied in a ponytail, uncovering my face and neck. The dark circles under my eyes were gone, and my skin was smooth, not even bruised. I still looked like death warmed over, but it wasn't an immediate death anymore; more like something found in a ditch.

A knot of scar tissue marked my left shoulder, exactly where I expected the gunshot wound to be. There was no pain. Slowly, I pulled up the nightgown and bared my right leg to the hip. The bullet hole through my thigh had been healed the same way. No wonder I could walk: as far as my legs knew, they were fine. Devin somehow managed to patch me up all the way while I was out.

Of course there were scars. There's no magic in the world that can heal iron without leaving a scar.

I paused, registering the other thing that had changed. My head was clear. Whatever healed the gunshot wounds also managed to cure my iron poisoning. I didn't think that was possible. How could that be possible?

The taste of roses tickled the back of my throat. I stiffened. "Oh, no, not now . . ."

That was all the time I had. Evening's binding flowed over me like a wave, strengthened by my return to health and anxious after my enforced idleness. Memories of her death slammed down on me, smothering the room in a veil of red, and my blood rose to meet the memories headlong, not giving me time to brace myself. Silly me, thinking I could act like I was Daoine Sidhe without paying the cost. There are always costs. The pixie, the key, the gunshots and the blood and the screaming—they were in the roses, waiting for me and dragging me down. They were all the same, as they had always been the same and always would be. Death doesn't change. Death never changes.

Breaking free before the memory pulled me all the way into Evening's grave was even harder this time. My blood had been in contact with iron, and recently. It didn't just remember what it felt like to die by iron—it *knew*.

Let me go, I thought. *If I die here, you lose, too. Let me go . . .*

I slammed back into my body to find myself clinging to the edge of the sink, dry-heaving over the floor. I didn't remember dropping to my knees or anything else after the roses hit. The world was spinning, making my chest and stomach ache.

Moaning, I let my head drop against the sink. I knew the binding would keep me moving; that sort of thing never lets you hold still for long. I just hadn't realized how far it would go to motivate me.

It was at least partially my fault. The memories I took from Evening's blood strengthened the binding, wrapping it around me until there was no way out. It would have goaded me on and made me miserable if I hadn't ridden her blood, it would even have killed me, but it wouldn't have used her death against me. And it was getting stronger. Eventually it would be strong enough that I wouldn't be able to fight it, and it would force me to ride the memories of Evening's dying moments until my heart gave out.

She probably didn't mean for it to be that way, but unfortunately for the both of us, she thought like what she was: she thought like a pureblood. A pureblood could have ridden the blood without complications, gathering the information they wanted and shrugging the rest of it away. Evening thought in terms of what she knew, but I was just a changeling, and my magic wasn't that strong. Her binding was too much for me to hold off forever. And it was getting stronger.

I was in serious trouble.

The door opened behind me. I didn't move, keeping my eyes closed and trying to steady my breathing. Anything that wanted to kill me would have to come through Devin and his kids, and if they'd done that already, there was no point in trying to run. Leaving my head against the sink seemed like a much better idea. At least that way there was a chance I'd die without throwing up again.

Hesitant footsteps crossed the floor, stopping about a yard away. "Yes?" I said, still not taking my head off the sink. It was a nice sink. Well, actually, it was a filthy, disgusting sink, and I didn't want to think about the things caked around the drain, but it was giving me something to prop my head against, and that was what counted.

"Ms. Daye?" Dare, sounding uneasy and a little scared. For once, I couldn't blame her. I'd made it pretty clear that I didn't like her, and Devin was probably threatening to do all sorts of nasty things to her if she didn't get along with me, or at least keep me alive. The two have never been mutually exclusive. That was a good thing; Evening and I would never have been able to handle it if we were required to get along.

"Yes, Dare?"

She took a step forward, feet scuffling against the linoleum. I lifted my head to watch her progress, not bothering to try and stand. I'm not that stupid.

"Are you feeling okay, Ms. Daye?"

"Of course," I said, putting my head back down. "I always snuggle up with the bathroom fixtures."

"You don't look like you feel okay," she said, coming a few steps closer. Brave girl. "Should I get Devin?" That showed a certain unexpected courage on her part—Devin's kids never called him by name where anyone could hear them.

"I'd rather you didn't." I abandoned the comforting stability of the sink and climbed back onto my feet, bracing one hand against the mirror. I was ready to catch myself if I fell, but that didn't mean I was looking forward to the possibility. "I'm fine."

Dare eyed me dubiously, saying, "You don't *look* fine . . ."

"Okay, let's try I'm better now than you're going to be if you call Devin." I leaned against the mirror, trying to look fierce. There are better conditions under which to look intimidating—any conditions that don't involve me being dressed in a low-cut purple nightgown, for a start. "I think he's worried enough, don't you?"

The implied threat actually seemed to relax her. You take comfort in the things you know, and what she knew was the chaotic and sometimes violent world of Home. "You want me to give you a few minutes to get back together?"

"That's probably a good idea, yeah." I swallowed, trying to clear the taste of roses from my mouth. It wasn't working very well. I hadn't really expected it to.

Dare hesitated, rocking back and forth on her heels before turning wide eyes toward me again. I was grateful for the reprieve in the rocking—watching her do that in high heels had been making me dizzy. "Can I ask you a question, Ms. Daye?"

"Sure," I said, with a shrug. It wasn't like she couldn't learn my darkest, deepest secrets just by breaking into Devin's files. I expected her to ask something vulgar or pointless and be finished.

She surprised me. "How did you meet Devin?"

"Devin?" I straightened, really seeing at her for the first time since she entered the room. She looked anxious, almost strained, like she was breaking some sort of vast, unwritten law. I didn't understand it. "It was a long time ago," I said slowly.

"Do you remember?"

Of course I remember, I thought. *The question is why you care.* "I met him a long time ago, when I ran away from ... never mind what I was running away from. I was trying to avoid places where people might know me, and I managed to get myself pretty messed up. One day I just turned around and he was there. Said a friend told him where to find me. He asked if I might want to try something new." I shrugged. "I came Home with him." And that was the end of that. By the time I realized what I was getting myself into, it was too late.

"Were you ..." Dare paused.

"Were we what? Friends? Yeah, after we established that me working for him didn't mean belonging to him." Those first few years had been nothing short of chaos, filled with power plays and tiny battles that never quite escalated into war. "Lovers? Yeah, that, too. At first it was because I needed to pay my debts, and then it was because he cared about me. Or seemed to, anyway." Our relationship—if you wanted to call it that—ended the night I came into the room we sometimes shared and found him fucking Julie like it was an Olympic sport. Sex for payment was one thing. Sex with my friends was another. I took Connor up on his offer of dinner the very next day. "He bought me, the same way he probably bought you. I needed a place to go, and Home was that place, at least for a while."

Dare's cheeks reddened, embarrassment betraying her age. "Oh."

The sex. People always focused on the sex. "You know the rules," I said, more gruffly than I intended. Memory does that to me: that's part of why I don't like it very much.

But Dare didn't deserve that. Softening my tone, I said, "If you don't like the way it works here, get off the street. Find yourself someplace else to go."

"I'm trying," she said, so softly that I almost missed it. Then she looked up again, eyes pleading as she asked, "How did you get away?"

I blinked at her. "He's not holding you captive."

"If you think that, you got stupid." She shook her head. "We came here because no place else would take us when our momma died. They all said go away, come back when you're older, when you know better, when you've learned. Only no one wants to teach us how to be older, or how to know better—not even Devin. They just teach us how to be broken."

"Dare . . ."

"Devin's not so bad. He knows the deal, but—it's like you said. There're always costs."

"What are you asking me for?"

"You got out." Dare looked at me. "We all know about you, because he talks about you all the time. Even when he thought you were dead, he kept talking about you. We've heard about everything you've ever done, because you're the one that got away—you're the one that was his, and stopped belonging to him. And I want to know how you did it. Because we're gonna do it, too."

She was serious. I stared at her. Damn. Finally, quietly, I said, "I'll do what I can to help you. If there's anything I can do. Believe me. There's no right way to do it . . . but it can be done, and if I can help you, I will."

The look she gave me was radiant, full of gratitude and awe. I winced, trying to keep my dismay from showing on my face. The lingering taste of roses helped—it gave me something that I could focus on other than the look in her eyes. I've never liked being looked at like I was a hero. I always wind up letting someone down. Sometimes I get lucky. Sometimes the only person who gets hurt is me.

TWENTY

DEVIN LOOKED UP WHEN his door opened and smiled. He was alone—Manuel had vanished on some unknown errand—and his expression was somewhere between smug and exhausted. Smug was winning. It probably had seniority. "I see Dare found you."

"I hadn't gone far," I said. "I got sort of distracted by my reflection." Dare slipped in behind me, finding a place along the wall.

"Surprise."

"Yeah. Big surprise." I shook my head. "What did you do?"

"It was bad, Toby." He walked over to me, expression grave. There were shadows lurking in his eyes, making it plain that the past few days had used him almost as hard as they'd used me. "We didn't think you were going to make it. *I* didn't think you were going to make it."

"So what did you do?"

"I fixed it."

"Devin, half those wounds were made with iron. You

don't have any charms that strong." I didn't think there were charms that strong anywhere in the world.

He shrugged, trying to look unconcerned as he reached for my hands. I pulled them away. "I called in some favors. That's all."

"Who could possibly have owed you enough that they'd cure iron poisoning just because you asked them to?" And who could possibly have had that much *power?* I was intruding on his personal matters. That was unforgivably rude of me, but it had to be done, because I had to know what his actions were going to cost. I had to know if it was more than I could pay.

Devin reached for my hands again. This time I let him take them. "The Luidaeg."

Dare gasped.

"What?" I stared at him. I'd been expecting him to say something I didn't want to hear, but this went beyond my worst imaginings. "You went to *her?*"

"She owed me for past favors. I collected on the debt."

"Devin, that's insane! You—she's a monster, she's practically a demon! She's—"

"Not in my debt anymore," he finished. "That was worth a lot more to her than your life. She doesn't like debts. She was so relieved when I said we were square that I'm surprised she didn't make you ten years younger and give you a dinette set when she finished healing you."

"So you ransomed my life from the *Luidaeg?*" I still couldn't believe it. Maybe I didn't want to.

Devin looked past me, seeming to see Dare for the first time. "You're excused. Wait in the front until I call with new orders."

Dare looked surprised, then nodded, replying, "Yes,

sir," before she turned and skittered out of the room. I turned to watch her go.

"Toby."

Devin released my hands when I looked back toward him, taking hold of the sides of my face instead, and kissing me deeply. I caught hold of his wrists, returning the kiss for a few seconds before I pulled his hands away. Heart pounding and breath short, I managed, "You shouldn't have done that. You shouldn't have gone to her."

"I had to."

"What's it going to cost me?"

"It's a gift."

"A gift."

Hearing the disbelief in my tone, Devin frowned. "Yes, a gift. Is that so hard to believe?"

This time, when he kissed me, I resisted less, letting him pull me close before I broke away and said, "You've never given away anything in your life. Everything goes on someone's bill."

"Things change." He kissed the side of my jaw. "People change. I've changed."

"That much?"

"Maybe," he said, and pulled back enough to look at me. There was something in his eyes I couldn't identify, some weird blend of love and fear and gnawing need. "I thought you were dead, Toby. Do you understand that? Have you fully grasped how close you came? I don't think you have."

"Devin . . ."

"You'd almost stopped bleeding by the time they brought you here, because you had no blood left to lose. You were leaving me. You were leaving me again, and this time, you weren't coming back. There was no way

I was letting that happen, Toby. Not if there was something I could do to stop it." He almost smiled, stroking his fingers down the sides of my face. "I couldn't let you leave me yet. You just came Home."

If I'd actually lost that much blood, he was probably right. Nothing short of divine intervention could have saved me. "So you went to the Luidaeg," I said, again. If I said it enough times, maybe his reply would change.

"I did. And I'd do it again."

"Devin, I . . ."

"Don't." We'd been careful before, both of us aware of my injuries and how poor my condition really was. There was no caution now, as he abandoned all efforts at gentleness, pulled me close, and kissed me hard. When he broke away, he whispered, "Just don't. You can't thank me and I wouldn't let you if you tried, so let's leave it at this: I won't let you die. I'm not finished with you. You have something I need too much for that."

His hands were sliding lower and lower on my sides, now cupping the curve of my hips. I put my own hands over them, and shook my head. "There isn't time for this, Devin," I said, regret coloring my voice. "I have to call Sylvester and let him know that I'm all right, and then I need to go. It's not finished."

"You don't need to call Sylvester," said Devin, with a little smile. "I'm not entirely thoughtless. I called him while you were still recovering."

I blinked. "You did?"

"Yes. Which he promptly rewarded by accusing me of being the one who got you injured in the first place." Devin's smile turned wry. "He doesn't care for me much, does he?"

That sounded like Sylvester. I relaxed, shrugging. "He thinks you'll lure me away from him."

Devin raised an eyebrow. "And will I?"

"The possibility exists. For now . . . where, exactly, are my clothes?"

"Your closet? That seems like a reasonable location."

"You brought me here without bringing anything for me to wear?"

"The kids were a little too busy keeping you alive to stop for dainties, Toby. Besides, that nightgown looks good on you."

"It makes me look like an underpaid hooker."

Smirking, Devin said, "Well, as I was saying . . ."

"Devin!" I stepped backward, out of his hands, and shook my head. "Is there anything *else* I can wear? I'm not going out dressed like this."

"As I've failed to convince you not to go out at all, I suppose I'll have to provide assistance." Devin walked over to his desk, pressing the button for the intercom. "Dare, get Ms. Daye's things and bring them to my office." He looked back to me as he released the button. "I'm afraid that puts an end to our privacy. She'll be here quickly. Kids are always in such a hurry."

"Well, you do teach us that we should never slow down if we can help it."

"Can you blame me? Changeling years are short ones." He spread his hands. "We have to use them wisely, while we still can."

"I guess." I paused, looking at him. "I always thought it was a lot of time. I mean, we can live for centuries. If we don't go around getting shot at, anyway."

"It may be a lot of time, but it's short time." He leaned back against his desk, offering me his arm. I walked over, leaning up against him, letting him wrap that arm around my waist. "It's very short time. It runs out."

I tilted my head back, still watching him. "So you teach us how to use it up?"

"Better than watching it dwindle. We have to burn brightly. We can't burn forever."

I frowned. "Now you're starting to worry me."

"Don't be worried; there's nothing to worry about." He pressed a kiss to my forehead. "You have a job to do, don't you? Have you found any leads?"

"Rayseline Torquill. She laughed."

"What?"

"It's not important." I shook my head. "It wasn't Simon, or Oleander, convenient as that would be; I'd know their work anywhere, and this wasn't it. The Queen didn't react rationally to the news, so it could have been someone at her Court." I paused. "And it *wasn't* Blind Michael."

"How do you know that?"

"There was a body."

Devin grimaced. "Where are you going to go next?"

The taste of roses clung to my tongue like sugar, giving me all the direction I needed. "Goldengreen."

He blinked. "Evening's knowe?"

"There may be answers there."

"Isn't that dangerous?"

"At this point anything I do is going to be dangerous. Whoever started this has already tried to kill me twice. I can't exactly stop now." I paused. "They killed a man. One of Lily's. He was just a kid, and now he's dead, and I couldn't save him."

"I know about Ross," he said. There was an odd blankness in his eyes. Before I could really consider what it meant, he continued, "You're taking Manuel and Dare."

That was enough to shock me into protest, forgetting about the look on his face. "What? No way! They'd just be in the way. No."

"You came to me for help, and that's what I'm giving you. They're going with you."

"Devin, this is—"

"You're paying me to help you, remember?" There was a sudden, brittle edge to his voice. I froze, eyes going wide.

"Devin . . ."

"Answer the question."

"You know I am."

"Then let me do my job. They're going with you." He pulled his arm away from my waist. "I'm not letting you out of here alone. Not after what's happened already."

"I'm not responsible if they get hurt."

"Of course not."

"I don't like this."

"I didn't expect you to."

"You're being an idiot," I said flatly.

"Maybe so, but it stands a chance of keeping you alive." He flashed a grin, which faded as quickly as it came. "This isn't for everyone, Toby. This world . . . maybe you shouldn't have come back. I'm glad you did. But maybe it was wrong."

This time, I was the one to lean in, kissing him as gently as I could. When I pulled away he was staring at me, surprised. "I chose this. Maybe I shouldn't have come. But I did."

"Once one of my . . ." He chuckled. "You never really left me, did you?"

The door creaked open before I could think of an answer, admitting an anxious Dare. She was clutching a plastic bag to her chest like a shield. "Sir?"

I pulled away from Devin, straightening. "You can toss that over here, kid." She darted a glance to Devin, who nodded, before pulling back and tossing me the bag. She had a good arm. Of course, considering the way she'd been flinging knives at my apartment, that wasn't really a surprise.

Opening the bag, I found a pair of jeans, my running shoes, and a wine-red cotton blouse, which was probably a good choice, considering all the bleeding I'd been doing. A smaller bag held underclothes, athletic bandages, and another cell phone. I gave Devin a curious look.

He shrugged. "You're creative and accident-prone. You'll find a use for them."

"I didn't mean the bandages."

"That's the trouble with miniaturizing technology. It gets easier and easier to lose. Of course, losing it gets easier when you lose the entire car."

"Where did all this *come* from, Devin?"

A pained expression crossed his face. "You were out for quite a while. I had plenty of time to send a few of the kids to your apartment for supplies. And no, they didn't break anything the Doppelganger hadn't already destroyed, although they did manage to convince the police to go away." He smirked. "It seems someone called in a noise complaint on you."

"Right," I said. "I'll go get dressed."

"Pity."

"Jerk."

"Accurate."

Grinning, feeling better than I had in months, I left the office and walked back to the bathroom.

Changing clothes in a public restroom is an acquired skill, one that becomes an art when the bathroom floor hasn't been washed in a decade or more. I recognized some of those stains. Still, it wasn't hard to shimmy out of the nightgown and into my jeans, and I felt much better once I was wearing real clothes. They weren't much as armor goes, but they were all I had.

Shoving my hands into the pockets of my jeans to tug them into place, I paused, my fingers striking metal. I grabbed hold and pulled out the key I'd taken from the rose goblin, frowning in confusion. Hadn't it been in my other jeans? The ones I'd ruined by almost bleeding out on them?

It glittered in my hand, briefly taking on a hint of its prior luminescence. Evening's last memories told me it was the key to Goldengreen; it needed to be kept safe. A brief flicker of blood-memory rose up, whispering that "safe" meant "secret." I shoved the key back into my pocket, checking to be sure it was hidden before stuffing my borrowed nightgown into the plastic bag. It was a magic key. Maybe there was still something I needed to unlock.

When I returned to the office, Manuel and Dare were there, waiting. Dare had managed to find a heavy denim jacket that clanked when she moved; considering how many knives she'd been able to conceal without the coat, I decided I didn't want to ask. Between that, the miniskirt and high heels, and the midriff-baring shirt that read PORN STAR IN TRAINING, she wasn't exactly in the running for Miss Subtle USA.

Manuel was more sedately dressed. He'd tossed a windbreaker over his jersey and sweatpants, letting it hang loosely enough to imply that there might be something beneath it without shouting "Hey, I'm armed." It wasn't much better than his sister, but you work with what you have.

I walked past them, dropping the bag on Devin's desk. "Good job with the clothes."

"Not a problem. Here." He tossed me a set of keys.

I caught them automatically, and frowned. "What's this?"

"Were you planning to walk to Goldengreen?"

"Oh, no," I said, realization dawning. "My car's back at the bridge."

"No, your car has been towed, stolen, or both. You're taking one of mine."

"Devin, I can't—"

"You're paying for it, remember?" He winked. "Don't worry. I'm always open to a fair trade."

"Good." Not caring if the kids saw, I leaned over to kiss him again before heading for the door. "Come on, guys. We're taking the car."

"If you haven't called by nightfall, I'll send help," Devin said, behind me now.

"Good idea," I said, and left the office. The kids followed.

I paused at the front door, saying, "Disguises up." The air filled with our magic, the sharpness of my copper blurring into Dare's apples and Manuel's cinnamon. Soon enough, the spells were cast, and three normal-looking people stepped out into the late December afternoon.

Manuel was silent until we were outside. Then he asked quietly, "Where are we going?"

Trust Devin's kids not to ask until there was no turning back. He really did teach them—teach us—not to worry about consequences. "Goldengreen."

"The knowe of the Winterrose?" asked Manuel, looking faintly horrified.

Dare, in contrast, just frowned. "Why are we going there?"

"Because if I knew her as well as I thought I did, there'll be answers there."

"And if there aren't?"

I paused. "If there aren't, we'll find another way." If they weren't there, I was screwed, but there was no reason to tell them that. Devin was right: I was running on changeling time, and the progression of Evening's curse meant that time was running out. Dead people don't solve mysteries or pay their dues. If Goldengreen didn't have what I needed, it was about to get a lot harder for me to pay my debts.

TWENTY-ONE

THE MORTAL-SIDE ENTRANCE TO Goldengreen is tucked behind the San Francisco Art Museum, right at the edge of the cliff that overlooks the sea. That always struck me as an ideal place for Evening's knowe: isolated and urban at the same time, a thing of borders, like the city itself. It's beautiful there. I'd wondered whether Evening personally oversaw the construction of the museum—after all, the doors connecting Goldengreen to the mortal world were probably older than the city. If she didn't plan the construction, she at least influenced it. That woman had strings all over the city, tied in places so old that no one realized they were there. The mortal world was going to miss her. But not as much as I was.

Devin's car was a battered Ford Taurus that handled better than my poor VW ever had. We pulled down the winding driveway to the employee parking lot, stopping behind a clump of eucalyptus trees. The museum was closed for the holidays, and there were no other cars.

I glanced in the rearview mirror. Manuel was looking

out the window, hands folded in his lap, while Dare was filing her nails. They were ready and eager to help—after all, being ready and eager was better than facing Devin's temper. With Evening's curse pressing down more and more heavily, I was slowing down. They were probably exactly what I needed. And I really didn't want to deal with them.

I cleared my throat. They looked up, fixing me with twin sets of apple-green eyes. The longer I spent around them, the more I understood why people complain about fae giving them the evil eye. I kept wanting to buy them each a pair of sunglasses.

"We're here." Dare started to unbuckle her belt, and I raised my hand to stop her. "No. You're staying with the car."

"What?" she demanded. Manuel stared. "The boss said we're supposed to keep you safe while you do stuff. How're we supposed to do that from the car?"

"I don't know how you're going to keep me safe from the car, and I don't care. I'm not taking you inside with me."

Manuel frowned. "Why not?"

"Because Goldengreen isn't just a place; it's a knowe. That means it's a little bit alive. With Evening gone, it's going to be pissed. I don't know what it'll be like inside, but I'm hoping it'll remember me well enough not to eat me."

Manuel nodded slowly, saying, "That's bad."

I sighed. "Yeah. Right now, I don't need any distractions. I need you to stay here, or I'll wind up so busy trying to protect you that I'll miss something."

"But, Ms. Daye—"

"I mean it, Dare. I need you to stay here. Both of you." I glared at them. Dare made a show of glaring back, but finally they both looked away, giving in.

"I'll be right back," I said lamely, taking the keys from the ignition and climbing out of the car. "You guys keep yourself amused. I don't care what you do, as long as you don't get arrested or hurt the car. I'll be back as soon as I can."

As I closed the door, Manuel said, "Ma'am?"

"Yeah?"

"How will we know if you need us?" He looked at me seriously. "The boss is gonna be really, really mad if you get hurt again."

That was true. I didn't want to get the kids in trouble. I just wanted them out of my way while I went in and used a key they didn't know I had to unlock a door I wasn't sure existed. "If I get in trouble, I'll scream," I said. "You can come running."

"Will we hear you?"

"The way I scream, people in China will hear me. Just stay here, okay?"

"Ms. Daye?"

"Yes, Dare?" It was like trying to leave kindergartners with a babysitter. If I was lucky, they'd run out of questions before the sun went down. Maybe.

"Here." She pulled a knife out of her sleeve, offering it to me. I didn't recognize the style of the blade, but if it was street legal, I'm a Kelpie. "In case you don't scream fast enough."

"Good idea," I said. She looked almost disappointed by my reaction—she was still young enough for the rules against saying thank you to seem pointless. I winked, sliding the knife into my belt with the edge facing outward to keep me from cutting myself. She brightened, reading the unspoken gratitude in my eyes. She was pretty smart when she let herself be.

The taste of roses was rising in my throat again; the curse was going to backhand me soon, and they didn't need to see that. I nodded a quick good-bye and turned, walking toward the museum. I heard the car doors slam behind me. Fine. As long as they didn't wander too far or follow me, I didn't care what they did. Maybe Manuel would pick the locks on the museum doors and show his sister something more culturally enriching than the latest shows on MTV.

To an onlooker, I would have looked like I was losing my mind as I walked down the path and through the motions to let me into Goldengreen. I circled a sundial three times, touching it at six, nine, and three o'clock, before kneeling, picking up a rock, and throwing it hard off the cliff. I waited for a moment after that, listening for the splash. The waves are a hundred feet down, and somehow I still expect to hear a splash. I never have.

The tall grass parted around me as I stepped off the path, brambles brushing my jeans without snagging hold. If that wasn't proof of magic, nothing is. Unseen sprites whispered in my ears, daring me to turn, but I kept looking straight ahead. If I broke the pattern, I wouldn't be able to find it for a month; the wards were too well constructed. The main route into the knowe ran through the middle of the museum, and the only other road I knew took at least an hour to finish. I didn't have the time to waste.

Knowes are hidden because they have to be, and not just from mortal eyes. The fae are territorial by nature; we move around, but what's ours is ours, and we're willing to hold it against whatever comes. Most of Faerie's civil wars have been fought over land. Evening was a Countess in name only, with title and lands but no subjects; there was no one to protect her knowe for her. She used her magic instead, wrapping her Court in layers of illusion, tucking the doors in shadows and the walls in the whisper of wind on the water. Which was all well and good, but it made getting inside difficult.

I waded through twenty feet of underbrush before a path appeared, unspooling through the weeds to end at the door of the battered supply shed shadowed by two enormous oak trees. Evening told me she'd planted those trees herself, a hundred years before I was born. She'd been coming this way for a long, long time.

The whispering faded as I walked toward the shed. Its job was done. There were more accessible entrances, but this was the way you took when you didn't want anyone to see you coming. This was the hidden road. I put my hand on the doorknob, fingers tightening as a jolt of static grazed my skin. That was my last warning. If I went any farther, I was committed.

I opened the door.

It swung open on hinges that might as well have been greased, despite the rust caking them. Evening was never a world-class showman as the purebloods go, but these were her lands, and they worked by her rules . . . at least for now. The spells she'd woven so carefully would fade away until the doorway into Goldengreen lost its moorings and the shed became just another abandoned storage spot. Faerie would lose another foothold in the mortal world—but not yet. For the moment, the path could still lead me out of one reality and into another. Closing my eyes, I released the knob, and stepped through.

The door slammed behind me, already out of reach as distance rippled and distorted. The air was hot and cold at the same time, hard to breathe. This wasn't a smooth and well-crafted door like the entrance to Shadowed Hills; this was a hole ripped between worlds, existing in both and neither at the same time.

A single step took me to the path's end, and the human world dropped away like a bad dream. I opened my eyes, taking a deep breath of cleaner, preindustrial air as I squinted down the dimly lit hall. It was never totally dark in Goldengreen, but this was closer than I'd ever seen it. Evening must have turned off the lights when she left, and since she hadn't come back, they hadn't been turned back on. That was exactly what I *didn't* need. Goldengreen's illusions were almost legendary. In the darkness, those illusions would be harder to avoid, and that could be bad for both my sanity and my health. Knowes need to be cared for, and Goldengreen had just lost its keeper, which meant I couldn't expect it to be in a good mood. Some people say it's silly to personify the hills; I say I'd rather overpersonify than be wrong. I figure they're less likely to kill me if they're flattered.

Holding my hands out in front of me, I started walking down the hall. My hip hit the edge of a low marble table after only a few steps, and something crashed to the floor. I winced. Well, that was one less vase to break the next time I came. I kept walking, and the sound of my footsteps abruptly broadened, announcing my arrival in the knowe's central courtyard. I allowed myself a small smile. There would probably be a way to turn the lights on from here, and once I could see, I could start looking for the door that fit my key.

I took three steps into the open, and froze.

Someone was breathing behind me.

Dropping a hand to the knife at my belt, I squinted into the shadows. Whoever it was had better attack quick, or they were going to find out just what a bad week I'd been having. My friends were getting shot at, there were bits of Doppelganger mashed into my living room carpet, and my former boss and maybe-lover had been forced to barter with the Luidaeg to keep me breathing. I was not in the mood to screw around.

The breathing changed after about five minutes of

stillness, suddenly accompanied by a new sound: footsteps. I stayed where I was, and was rewarded by a figure coming slowly clear through the darkness. Whoever it was, it was male, and not much taller than I was.

Grabbing the knife from my belt, I lunged. It was a calculated risk: I was guessing that if the man on the other end of my impromptu tackle had a gun, I would have already been dead. Anyone wanting to shoot me passed up a flawless target when they ignored my entrance. If he didn't have a gun, the odds were shifted in my favor. He might still be better armed, but people expecting to maintain the element of surprise aren't usually ready for you to fight back. I've always preferred being the jumper.

I hit him sideways, elbow impacting with his solar plexus. Something in my shoulder ripped as I put pressure on the fresh scar, flaring into angry, throbbing pain. Even magical healing only compensates for so much; the scar looked old, but it wasn't.

Gravity pulled us both to the floor. I grabbed his wrist with my right hand and planted my knee in his stomach, knocking the air out of him. He tried to squirm free, making the sort of hurt, startled barking sound a seal would make if you hit it with a stick. He wasn't going for a weapon. I paused. Who did I know that would start barking like a seal if you hurt him?

"Connor?"

"Yeah," he gasped. Most of the nobility are wimps—they don't get hurt often enough to take it in stride. I wish I could be a wimp. "Nice to see you, too."

"Why the hell are you sneaking around in here?" I let go of him and stood. A spreading dampness was covering my shoulder; I was fairly sure I'd managed to reopen something. "That's not a smart thing to do. I've had a lousy week."

Connor levered himself into a sitting position, making little huffing noises. He'd obviously expected some sort of help getting up, even if it was just my hand. "I heard," he said. The darkness kept me from seeing his face. I found myself perversely grateful for that. "Lily told me about what happened to Ross. You're lucky you're still alive."

"When did you see Lily?" I asked, narrowing my eyes. Last time I'd checked, Lily hadn't been speaking to any of the local nobles. Like most of Golden Gate Park's landholders, she liked to keep to herself.

"Sylvester sent me. He was looking for you."

"What? Devin called him. He knew where I was."

Connor paused. "Toby, no one called. I came here because Lily said she thought you might have ended up here. The whole Duchy's up in arms. Sylvester's terrified."

I felt myself going cold. "That can't be right."

"Believe it." He stood, still breathing a little unevenly. "You hit pretty hard for a girl."

"And you fall down pretty easy for a boy. Connor, are you serious? Sylvester really doesn't know where I am?"

"He has no idea." Connor's feet scuffled against the floor, sending echoes through the room. "Do you mind if I turn on the lights? Having this discussion in the dark is starting to creep me out."

"If you know how to do it, be my guest."

"Right." Footsteps moved away from me, followed by a scraping sound before the room filled with warm, colorless light that seemed to emanate from the walls. Connor was about five feet away, hand pressed flat against one of the decorative sconces. I must have been staring, because he shrugged.

"Evening showed me," he said. "She thought it was a good idea for someone else to know."

"How long ago?"

"A few months."

That implied one of two things. Either Evening had been expecting to die . . . or this wasn't Connor. "Here." I offered him the knife I'd borrowed from Dare, hilt first. "Take this."

He blinked. "What? Why?"

"Because I need you to cut yourself." He looked blank, and I sighed. "I just got attacked by a Doppel-ganger, Connor. I don't really think whoever wants me dead is going to spring for another one when the first one failed, but a girl can't be too careful."

"You're serious."

"Usually, yes."

Glowering, he took the knife and nicked his index finger, holding it up to show me. "See? Perfectly normal blood."

Doppelgangers can fake a lot of things. They can't fake bleeding. "Excellent. My knife, if you would?" I held out my hand, and, still glowering, he pressed the hilt back into my palm.

Sliding the knife back into my belt, I turned to look around the room. It seemed smaller with the lights on. A simple silver throne sat in the center, and doors were scattered almost at random around the perimeter, lead-ing to who knew where. I'd never seen half of them used, and I was probably going to need to try them all before the day was out. Evening's coat of arms hung on the wall, alone; there was another set of arms there once, but Dawn had been dead for almost twenty years. It just took her sister a while to catch up.

"It's odd that she showed you how to work the lights," I said. "She never showed me."

"Would you have trusted her if she tried?"

That stopped me. Even before the pond, I was never

the most trusting of people; afterward, I'd stopped pay-
ing attention to anything but my own paranoia. Would
I have trusted Evening if she'd offered? Probably not.
Was I hurt that she hadn't asked? Unfortunately, yes.

"No," I said, finally. "I wouldn't have."

"That's probably why she didn't."

I shook my head, keeping my eyes on the wall. "I
didn't come here to talk about my personal problems."

"So why are you here?"

"Because I have a job to do."

"And that job is in Goldengreen? You should be calling Sylvester before he freaks out completely."

"Like I said, I thought someone had already called
him." I looked back toward Connor, sighing. "My job is
wherever Evening's killers are. I don't know where that
is, so I'm starting here."

"Are you sure you're up for this?"

"Does it matter?" I asked. "What can they do at this
point? Kill me? They're already trying. It doesn't matter
whether I'm up for this: I'm involved, and I get unin-
volved when this ends or I die. No sooner."

Connor frowned. "You're bleeding." He sounded
surprised.

"I know." I took a look at the blood soaking my shirt,
and sighed. "That's the third shirt this week. I swear, I
should just go topless."

"What happened?" His surprise had shifted, becoming hurt irritation. Jeez. It wasn't like I needed someone
to protect me—and if I had, there were people in line
ahead of him.

"Do you mean over the last week, or just now?" I
deadpanned.

"Just now. I already know most of the last week."

"Remember that Doppelganger attack I mentioned?"
He nodded. "That happened. Look, you can come when

I grovel at Sylvester's feet about the fact that no one called him."

"You're still bleeding." He put his hand on my shoulder, and my heartbeat doubled. Moving with what I hoped was casual slowness, I stepped out from under it. I didn't need this. Not now. Probably not ever.

Get a grip, dummy, I thought. *What, Devin's not enough for you?* "I reopened the wound when I tackled you. Don't worry. I heal fast."

Connor took a deep breath and asked, "Will you let me help you?"

He just kept coming up with the stumpers. Next he'd probably ask how I got in without using the front door. I turned back to the wall, saying, "Connor, I can't involve you in this."

"You think Raysel did it, don't you?" It wasn't a question.

"I think she might have." I shoved my hands into my pockets. "Does that bother you?" I looked over my shoulder, waiting for him to flinch or betray some sign of guilt—anything to get my hormone levels down.

He didn't oblige. His expression was neutral as he said, "I don't think she did it; it's not her style. But I can see why you'd suspect her. Does *that* bother *you?*"

"Yes," I admitted. "It bothers me." There was no point in lying.

"Why?"

"Because I can't figure out why you went and married someone like her." There: I'd said it. Maybe he'd give me an answer I could believe.

"It was political." It was his turn to look away. "Saltmist needed a truce, Raysel needed a husband. She liked my looks, her parents approved, Duchess Lorden told me to go, I went."

"It was an arranged marriage?" My opinion of his

taste went up about twenty points, but I was still horrified. Being a feudal society doesn't mean we have to be *that* feudal. "We still *have* those?"

"My wife certainly thinks so."

"That's just not right."

"That's how things are. My home Duchy needs the alliance, and I'll do whatever it takes to protect my home." He squared his shoulders, and my heart did a stuttering box step.

"I'm sorry," I said, voice unintentionally soft.

He stepped toward me. "So am I."

For a moment, we just stared into one another's eyes. His were brown from edge to edge, darkening at the center rather than resolving into a defined pupil. You could drown in those eyes. I wanted to. It would have been safer than whatever I was doing with Devin, and a lot less likely to get me killed ... and it wasn't an option. If I was looking for sex, I already had it, and if I was looking for love, I was probably out of luck—and either way, this wasn't my road to take. Bracing my hands against his chest, I pushed him backward.

"We can't do this," I said. My voice was hollow. It wasn't so much that I wanted him as it was that I wanted the idea of him; the idea of someone who would hold me and tell me things were going to be okay, without having to go back Home.

Connor gave me a hurt look, reaching out to put his hand on my shoulder. "Why not? I want to. So do you. Why can't we?"

"Let's start with the easy stuff," I said, stepping out from under his hand. "You're married, and I don't want to be banished. Is that a good answer?"

"Raysel won't care; you know that. As long as we stay married, she stays heir, and that makes her happy. It's not a marriage. It's a treaty."

"I care. I won't step on her toes." I took another step back, shaking my head. "It's not worth it, Connor."

"I don't think you mean that," he said, voice pitched low. The tone sent a thrumming down my spine. My central nervous system voted to abdicate. No, no, no. This was *not* going to happen. Not with him.

"Look, Connor, maybe it would be worth it. I don't know. Ask me again when we know who killed Evening, and maybe I'll have a good answer." I shoved my hands into my pockets. "For right now, can we just try to figure out who did this before they decide to try it again?"

He nodded, somewhat reluctantly, and let his hand fall to his side. I felt a surge of relief mixed with remorse, and took a deep, slow breath. Oberon's bones, what had I been thinking?

I cast a sidelong glance his way. He was studying one of the carvings on the wall, carefully not looking at me. The answer was simple: I hadn't been thinking at all. I'd just been reacting. I didn't love him, but there was a time when I might have, and that was enough to move me forward. I needed to be needed. This wasn't the right way.

"Toby?"

"Yeah?"

"What are you looking for?"

His tone told me he wanted to move on. I seized the opening. "I don't know—something useful. Answers, maybe."

"Are answers usually that easy to find?"

"After the week I've had, the world owes me some easy answers."

"Are you finding any?"

That ranked high on the stupid questions list. "Not yet. Just some empty halls and you." I turned in a circle, scanning the room. There were shadows in the corners, even with the lights on. There were no bodies, and the ghost of Hamlet's father didn't seem likely to show up, but it was bad enough. I almost thought I could hear faint noises drifting down the center hall.

"Welcome to the haunted halls of Elsinore," I muttered.

Connor glanced at me. "What was that?"

"Shakespeare."

"Why?"

I paused, and in the silence of that moment, I heard the sounds from the hall again. They were real, and they were getting louder. "Did you come alone?"

"What?" He blinked. "Of course. Who would I have brought with me? Sylvester has people checking every place you might've gone."

"Right." I stepped backward. Whoever was coming down the hall was too quiet to be Manuel or Dare. "Not to be alarmist or anything, but there are people trying to kill me right now, which means staying here might not be the best plan."

"What?"

There was a clean snapping noise from the direction of the hall. It's hard to mistake the sound of a bullet being chambered, especially when people have recently decided shooting you is great fun. I grabbed Connor's hand and bolted for the nearest door, hissing, "Run!"

There was a muffled snarl from the hall, followed by the sound of running footsteps. Sometimes I hate being right.

The door didn't want to open. I yanked the key out of my pocket and shoved it against the lock, shouting, "Open, dammit! In Evening's name!" Nothing happened. The steps were getting closer. Not letting myself look backward, I shouted, "In Oberon's name! In *somebody's* name! *In my mother's name, open up, damn you!*"

The lock released and the door slammed open, sending Connor and me tumbling into a narrow hallway. I paused long enough to kick the door shut and throw the lock before taking off down the hall. I didn't know where it would take us, but I knew what would happen if we stayed where we were, and in this case, I preferred the unknown. Connor stumbled, and I caught his hand as I ran, hauling him behind me.

Connor was already starting to strain to keep up— Selkies are built for endurance in water, not on land. "Where are we going?" he gasped.

"Away!" I heard the door smash behind us, and the sound of running feet. I didn't know how much of a lead we had, and I wasn't sure I wanted to. We'd escape, or we'd die. Even odds.

"We don't know they want to hurt us! We don't even know who they are!"

"Pardon me if I don't wait around to find out!" The strain of dragging Connor was making my shoulder throb in earnest, but I didn't let go. He'd die if I did.

"But—"

"They have guns! Now shut up and run!"

A dim light was starting to fill the hall, illuminating rough stone walls. The floor shifted under our feet, going from raised cobblestones to hard-packed sand. Connor stumbled again, but I kept dragging him, picking up speed as we went. "Come on, we're almost there!" I had no idea where "there" was, although I was betting against popping out of a magic wardrobe. The sand made me think of beaches: that was fine. There are plenty of beaches in San Francisco—there was even one right next to the museum.

In retrospect, I shouldn't have been surprised when the ground dropped out from under our feet and we ran out into the open air.

There was time to glimpse the face of the cliff behind us, and the narrow mouth of the cave we'd just run out of. Then we were falling, and there was no more time for anything but screaming. Being dropped a hundred feet above the Pacific has a tendency to bring out the worst in me. Connor's hand slipped out of mine as we fell. I strained to catch it. Then it was too late: I hit the water feetfirst, knocking the air out of my lungs. The waves closed over me like a fist, and the world went dark.

TWENTY-TWO

I DRIFTED, EYES CLOSED, head down, until the pressure in my chest snapped me awake and I started to thrash, looking for the surface. I hadn't panicked, but it was only a matter of time, and if I didn't hit the air before I lost control, I was going to be another red mark on the Coast Guard's already checkered record. Everyone has something they can't handle. For some people it's tight spaces or heights. For me, it's water. I can't take baths anymore, much less go swimming: it's showers and polite excuses all the way. It's too much like going back to the pond.

The sea around me was getting darker. It was light when Connor and I hit the water; the sun should have been visible. Unless I was swimming the wrong way.

I flipped myself around, pushing as hard as I could in the opposite direction. The waves weren't helping—but then, oceans aren't known for helping stranded swimmers, especially not ones foolish enough to dive from great heights while fully clothed. I was amazed that I hadn't broken my neck.

It was getting harder to keep swimming: exhaustion, oxygen deprivation, and my wounded shoulder were conspiring with terror to slow me down. Just to make matters worse, the taste of roses was tickling the back of my throat. I was weak, and the curse was getting stronger; I couldn't defend myself. If it grabbed me before I reached the air, the threat it represented was going to become a self-fulfilling prophecy, because there was no way I'd survive.

Something hit me from below. I kicked down, suddenly fueled by a new brand of panic, and was rewarded when my heels hit something soft. That would teach the local wildlife not to mess with a drowning changeling. I continued to flail upward until it hit me again. My answering kick was weaker this time. I was running out of energy; I couldn't tell which way I was going, and the lack of oxygen was starting to blur my vision. The something hit me a third time, and I went limp, giving up. The sharks could have me.

Whatever it was grabbed the back of my shirt and started swimming upward, towing me easily to the surface. I gasped for air, and it held me up until I started treading water. The waves were fairly mild; once I could breathe again, I started looking for shore. If I could reach it before—well, there were a lot of "befores" to worry about. Before the curse hit, before I panicked completely, before I drowned . . .

Something barked behind me, and I turned, coming face-to-muzzle with a harbor seal. I was startled enough that I dipped below the surface for a moment before bobbing back up again, coughing. The seal barked merrily, seeming amused by my surprise.

Selkie. I'd fallen off a cliff into the ocean with a Selkie, and I'd been worried about drowning. I would've been embarrassed if I hadn't been so tired. The curse was burning like it was going to hit at any second; I didn't have much time.

"Connor?" I said, voice shaking. "Will you take me to shore?" He nodded, swimming closer and letting me loop my arms around his neck. His body was almost as long as mine, strong and healthy as real seals so seldom are.

We were only about a hundred yards from shore, but when you're traveling by seal-back, that's more than far enough to be decidedly unpleasant. I kept my eyes closed, trying to ignore the waves slapping my face. It's rude to get seasick on your escort, however tempting it may be.

The tide tossed us onto the sand just as I thought I couldn't stand anymore. I staggered to my feet, stumbling away from the water. I almost made it to the dry sand before the curse hit me like a rose-tinted anvil, dropping me to my knees. There wasn't time to fight; there wasn't even time to scream. The real world dropped away, and I was lost.

Maybe it was the result of my barely restrained panic; maybe the curse was getting better at hurting me. Either way, it wasn't just Evening's death this time. It rifled my memory with casual ease, pulling up the gut-wrenching moment when my lungs forgot what air was and handing it back to me in a tidy package of blood magic and iron. The sand shuddered, first becoming bloody carpet, then the damp, sun-warmed wood of the Tea Garden path. If I screamed, the sound was buried under the memories. There was no present. There was only the past, and I was drowning in it.

Someone was shaking me. Neither of the loops of memory that had ensnared me included shaking—thrashing, bleeding, and dying, but no shaking. I tried to rise toward it and was slapped back by a branch of phantom roses, shoving me down. Dimly, far away, I heard screaming. I couldn't tell if it was mine or not, and it didn't matter. This time there was no tourist to help me into the water. The pulse of my heart was like a drumbeat, slowing down under the weight of blood and iron and tangled memory.

I wondered if I was ever going to stop hurting.

Connor slapped me.

The new pain was physical and sharp, letting me reclaim just a little ground. My heartbeat sped up as Connor slapped me again and again, the pain spiking each time to let me climb another step closer to the real world.

He was pulling back his hand to slap me again when I opened my eyes. "Hey," I said, voice harsh, "you can stop now. Please."

"I thought you were going to die," he said, eyes wide.

"Join the club," I said, trying to be flippant. I wasn't succeeding. I tried to sit up, and he put an arm behind me, letting me lean against his side.

"What happened?"

"I inhaled too much water."

"Try again," Connor said, voice cold. "I'm a Selkie, remember? We drown people semiprofessionally: I know what drowning looks like. If you think I'm going to believe you inhaled too much water, you must think I'm either blind or stupid. I don't know which is worse."

I blinked at him, flushing. I hadn't meant to offend him; I just didn't realize my lie would be that obvious. Of course, most drowning victims don't go fetal in the sand and scream their throats raw. The water in their lungs sort of prevents that. "I . . ."

"What happened, Toby? The truth."

You have to trust someone eventually. That's just how it works. Maybe Connor O'Dell wouldn't have been my first choice, but it looked like he was my last one. "Evening happened," I said, closing my eyes. "When she died, she made sure that I'd do what she asked. She wanted to be avenged, and so she—"

"Dare! She's over here!" I opened my eyes to see Manuel and Dare running toward us, Dare stumbling in her high heels. "Ma'am! Ms. Daye!" Spotting Connor, they sped up, sudden murder in their expressions.

Connor tensed, and I smiled weakly, lifting one hand to wave. "They're with me." More loudly, I called, "Hey, guys. He's with me, too."

The pair staggered to a stop. Uncertainly, Manuel asked, "Are you all right, Ms. Daye?"

"I'm fine, Manuel; just a little damp. Connor was kind enough to fish me out of the water." The ease of the lie astounded me. I guess battered, aching, and cursed had become status quo. "What are you two doing down here?"

"We saw these men go inside, only they were wearing don't-look-heres so we couldn't really look right at them, and Manny thought that maybe meant we should follow them, only we couldn't find a way in, and—" I held up my hand, stopping Dare's breathless tirade.

"Let's try it this way," I said. "Manuel? What happened?"

"We followed some men to the museum; they had a key, we didn't. We circled the building and reached the cliff just in time to see you fall," he said, tone brisk and formal.

"So you followed me after I told you not to, and saw us come out of the cliff?"

"Yes."

"Manuel?"

"Yes?"

"That was dumb."

"Yes, ma'am."

Turning to Connor, I asked, "Can you help me up? I need to get these two Home." He shook his head, and scooped me into his arms as he stood. I yelped. "Hey!"

"What?"

"Put me down!" He started to walk down the beach, Manuel and Dare trailing along behind us. "Aren't you listening? Put me down!"

"No. I am taking you—all of you—back to Shadowed Hills. You can leave when I'm sure you'll survive."

Considering recent events, that would probably be sometime in June. I sighed, settling back in his arms. My shoulder was starting to throb, providing a handy reminder that we weren't safe where we were. Shadowed Hills? All right, that would do.

"This isn't gonna calm Sylvester's nerves," I mumbled.

"Tough."

"Shouldn't we call Home first? To say where we're going?" Manuel sounded unaccountably nervous, like he was afraid Devin would blame him for my impromptu swim. Maybe he would.

Digging into my pocket, I produced the waterlogged cell phone and tossed it onto the beach. "With what? My phone's ruined. Have you got one?"

"No . . ."

"There you go, then. Connor, how are we getting to Shadowed Hills?"

"You have a car."

"I can drive!" Dare said.

Connor and I exchanged a look, and he declared, "*I'll* drive." Dare pouted. Connor shook his head. "Sorry, kid. Not this time."

Confident that Connor had matters in hand, I closed my eyes, letting myself relax. Shadowed Hills is safer than almost anywhere I know; most people have better things to do than bother Sylvester, who has a history of permanent solutions to temporary annoyances. He used to be a hero, after all, and some habits die hard. Besides, how often do you get to watch a Selkie try to drive?

Not that often, it turns out, even when the opportunity actually bothers to arise. Connor put me into the passenger seat, I closed my eyes, and we were there, exhaustion blanking out all the miles in between. I woke up when Connor stopped the car. Dare and Manuel cast worried glances my way as Connor scooped me out of the passenger seat, but I didn't fight; I just let him carry me up the hill and into the knowe. I wasn't entirely certain I could have made the walk.

Luna was waiting in the entry hall. There were no footmen in evidence; they had all apparently figured out that the safest place to be was far away from their worried Duchess. Her hair was uncombed, and her tails were knotting themselves behind her, winding and unwinding around each other in agitation.

"Are you all right?" she demanded, turning toward our sandy, water-stained party. The fact that I was curled in Connor's arms probably made things look even worse, but I didn't really have the strength to do much else. Manuel and Dare were trying to vanish behind us. Like most of Devin's kids, they were fine when they were following orders, but they didn't ad lib well. He never taught them how to be flexible. "Sylvester's gone to challenge Devin for proof that you're not dead. I hope you're pleased with yourself."

"Hi, Luna," I said, smiling tiredly.

She studied me, frowning, before she said, "You look terrible. What happened?"

"We sort of fell out of a cliff and into the ocean."

"We?"

Connor winced. "It wasn't exactly intentional . . ." he began.

Luna ignored him. "What were you doing?"

"Running," I said.

"From what?"

"I don't quite know," I said. "Mostly from the noises in the hall."

"You fell off a cliff because you were running from noises?"

"In Goldengreen," Connor said, apparently deciding he needed to contribute. Bad idea. Luna turned on him, glaring, and he cringed. I would've expected him to know better.

"Were you hurt?" she asked, turning back to me.

"Not badly." I gestured to my bleeding shoulder. "I got shot a few days ago, but that's mostly been healed."

"Shot and injured enough that you couldn't manage to make a phone call. Oh, that's not bad at all." Looking around us to Manuel and Dare, who were trying not to be noticed, she added, "And you brought guests."

Dare stared at her feet, ears turning a deep red. Manuel bobbed a quick bow and mumbled, "Nice to meet you, ma'am."

Luna's icy demeanor melted fractionally as she smiled. She's never been good at staying mad, and she usually gets that way because she's worried about someone—frequently me. I have a talent for panicking her. "It's good to meet you, too."

I poked Connor in the shoulder. "Put me down." He gave me a dirty look, but wasn't going to argue in front of Luna. I staggered as he lowered me to my feet, and Dare stepped forward, offering me her arm. I took it gratefully. "Hey, kid."

Leaning toward me, she whispered, "She has three tails."

"Yes," I said, in a normal tone of voice. Whispering is rude, especially when you're dealing with someone whose ears are sensitive enough to hear mice rustling in a field. "Her Grace is one of the Kitsune." Luna smiled, and I smiled back.

"Kitsune?" Manuel said. "Fox fairy?"

"Exactly," Luna agreed. "October, while introductions are all well and good, I hope you don't think this is going to distract me from finding out what happened. My husband's been unbearable with worry over you."

I sighed. "All right, Luna. Is there a place where Manuel and Dare can go clean up, and maybe get something to eat?" The kids stared at me, but didn't protest. Never question the boss in public.

Luna snapped her fingers. A mote of light appeared in front of her. "Follow this, and it will lead you to the kitchens," she said. "Quentin will meet you there; he can help with anything you need."

"But . . ." Dare said, glancing at me.

"Don't worry, Dare; it's safe here," I said. "Safe is what Shadowed Hills does best." That was true, as long as we didn't mention the nasty, still-unsolved matter of Luna and Raysel disappearing for a decade. "Now shoo—it's not nice to keep people waiting, and Quentin's a friend of mine." Dare started to protest, but Manuel shushed her and took her hand, pulling her along as he followed Luna's guide.

Luna turned to me once they'd vanished around the corner, asking, "Devin's?"

"Yes."

"For how long?"

"Long enough." I shook my head. "They're good kids. Manuel—the boy—has more common sense, but I think his sister's close to breaking. They need to get out."

"Were you perhaps thinking of bringing them here?"

I smiled sheepishly. "You do have a tradition of taking in strays."

"Yes, I do," she said, glancing at Connor. He stiffened, but said nothing. Luna dismissed him with a glance, turning back to me. "Is this an exchange?"

"I don't know what you mean."

She sighed. "Do you really think I can't smell him on you? But no matter. What happened?"

The question meant I could avoid the subject of Devin for a little while—but not, I knew, forever. If Luna was asking now, Sylvester would be asking later. "Look, can we go somewhere? This isn't the most private place in the knowe."

"Of course. Connor, bring her." Luna turned, starting for a pale blue door that I hadn't noticed before. Probably because it hadn't been there. Knowes are like that.

Before I could say anything, Connor had scooped me off my feet again. "Hey!"

He grinned. "Just following orders."

I sighed, deciding struggling would be more trouble than it was worth, and let him carry me through the door. There was an indoor garden on the other side, looking like nothing so much as the yard of an old English country house. Cobblestone paths wound around boulders draped with moss, while rioting roses and honeysuckle did their best to obscure delicate marble statuary. Luna led us to a space between two hedges, where the ground was carpeted with clover and buttercups. "Put her down, please."

Connor lowered me gently into a seated position. I leaned back on my hands, digging my fingers into the clover. Luna knelt beside me.

"I've never seen this garden before," I said.

"I planted it while you were away, as a memorial to my internment and your death. It has happier connotations now that we've both come home." She fixed me with a stern eye. "You're bleeding."

"I tore my scar." I pulled the fabric of my shirt aside to show the narrow fissure through the middle of the scar on my shoulder.

Luna frowned, reaching out to touch it with delicate fingers. "This is newer than it looks. And the wound was made with iron."

"You're right on both counts."

"Whose idea was it to take you to the Luidaeg?"

I froze. "How can you . . . ?"

"I've seen her work a time or two. This was her, wasn't it?"

"Yes." Luna knew the Luidaeg? I suppose I should have known—they've both lived in the Bay Area for centuries —but somehow the idea was jarring. I couldn't imagine what sort of a situation would have brought those two together.

"Of course." She produced a roll of gauze from a pocket in her skirt, passing it to me. "Wrap yourself." Seeing my expression, she added, "You learn to carry bandages when you work with roses as much as I do."

"Right," I said, and started clumsily binding my shoulder.

Luna made no move to help, but waited until I tied off the gauze before saying, "Now. Tell me what's happened—tell me everything. No lies. I'll know."

I looked at her, then nodded and began from the beginning. This time I told the whole story, or as much of it as I felt was safe. There were still a few things I wasn't ready to share: I left out the hope chest and my suspicions about Raysel, preferring to wait until I had more answers. I told them everything else. The phone calls, the gunshots, the Doppelganger, even the binding that Evening had buried in my bones. Everything.

Luna's lips were pulled back in a silent snarl by the time I finished, displaying the vulpine teeth she usually kept politely concealed. "Why didn't you tell us this to begin with?" Even Connor was just staring at me, stunned. I wasn't sure which was worse: the fury in Luna's eyes, or the bleak despair in his. Skinshifters sit on a strange edge, not changelings, but not quite purebloods. They're weaker than most fae because their blood is so confused. He knew what the curse meant as well as I did because his blood was as thin as mine.

"What good would it have done, Luna?" The bitterness in my tone surprised even me. "It was too late as soon as I heard her message. I finish this, or I die."

"You know what you have to do," she said. "It's obvious."

I frowned. "Actually, no, it's not. What are you talking about?"

"You have to visit the Luidaeg." She said it like it was a perfectly reasonable idea.

Like hell. Raising the dead would have seemed like a reasonable idea compared to visiting the Luidaeg. I stared. "I have to what?"

"Visit the Luidaeg."

"This is sudden. And sort of insane."

"I know. But it's what you have to do."

Connor turned toward her, eyes wide. Good for him. It's not every day your mother-in-law tries to send your friends to visit a demon. "Luna—"

"Connor, be quiet. This is October's road to follow, not yours."

"And why, exactly, do you think this is a good idea? Are you trying to get me killed?"

"No. I'm trying to save you." Luna narrowed her eyes. "When the Luidaeg healed your wounds, she became a part of this story. She tasted your blood, Evening's with it. She knows that binding now, how it's built, what went into making it and catching you with it. If there's anyone who can tell you how to get out of this, it's the sea witch. She's the only person strong enough, and fair enough, to do it."

"Fair?"

"She follows the rules. Whether she wants to or not, she follows them. If you go through her, there's a chance you'll come out alive on the other side." Luna sighed. "You're too much like your mother. It's difficult to believe that you've managed to live this long."

"Luck," I said, voice flat. I didn't like her bringing my mother into this. It felt like dirty pool.

Luna shook her head. "I don't think this is a good idea, or a wise one, but it's the only one I have. She may be able to help you. I can't."

I looked at her for a moment, and then slowly rose, bracing myself against the hedge. "I understand, Your Grace."

"Do you?"

"I think so." I sighed. "I should've told you sooner."

"Yes, you should have," she said, standing. "It's too late for that now. You have to get help, Toby. Please."

"Do you really think the Luidaeg will help me?"

Connor had fallen silent, staring at us in dismay.

"I don't think you have any other options," Luna said.

"Right." I raked my hair back with one hand. "Can . . . I hate to ask this, but can Manuel and Dare stay here until I get back?" The question was bigger than it seemed. I wasn't just asking if they could wait for me; I was asking, if the Luidaeg didn't let me come back, whether Luna would take care of them. Dare asked me to get them out. I couldn't get them far, but I could get them to Shadowed Hills, and Sylvester wouldn't let Devin take them if they didn't want to go. They could be safe here, if they were willing to be.

Luna nodded. "Of course. They're eating and harassing Quentin now; I'll speak to them after you've gone." She cocked her head to the side, listening to something. "It sounds like they've decided to teach him a new form of poker. Poor dear."

"That's my kids for you." I grinned.

"Quite. Your kids, indeed. Do you know how to find the Luidaeg?"

I paused. "No. I never needed to."

"I didn't think so." She snapped her fingers. A thorny face appeared in the bushes. "Hello, dear. Toby needs an escort." The rose goblin rattled its thorns as it padded out to sit in front of her, turning vivid yellow eyes toward me.

"Hey, you," I said, pleased. "It's nice to see you again." It opened its mouth and chirped, apparently pleased as well. It's always nice to be remembered.

"It will lead you where you need to go," Luna said, stepping back. "Trust it, but don't let it out of your sight until you've reached your destination."

"What if I do?"

"You'll regret it." She smiled, sadly. "Just come back, all right? We mourned you once. I'd rather not do it again."

"It's not on my list of goals either, Your Grace." I straightened, getting my balance back, and looked to the rose goblin. "Any time."

It sneezed and took off at a run, heading for the garden's edge. There wasn't time for pauses or good-byes: I launched myself after it, somehow finding the strength to run. Behind me, Luna called, "Trust the goblin!" just as it leaped and vanished through the stone of the wall.

Luna had never led me astray. She could be imperious

and vague at the same time, but she'd never lied to me, and so I kept running, jumping after it without pause.

The wall parted like mist, opening on a long tunnel. The goblin was a slash of moving green in the dark ten feet ahead. I kept my eyes on its back, ignoring the stitch in my side as I pounded after it. It leaped for another wall, vanishing again, and I followed, landing on a swaying theater catwalk. The goblin paused, looking back over its shoulder to see that I was still behind it. Then it stepped to the edge of the catwalk, and launched itself into the darkness.

In for a penny, in for a pound. I jumped after it, managing not to stumble when my feet hit solid ground. The goblin kept running, and I followed, into the dark.

TWENTY-THREE

THE LAST LEAP LEFT US STANDING at the mouth of an alley in a part of town I'd never seen before. Seagulls shrieked overhead, and the air stank of garbage mixed with the windblown smell of rotten fish and motor oil. We had to be near the docks, and not in one of the nicer areas. It was water-hag territory . . . and whatever else the Luidaeg may be, she's definitely a water-hag.

Every child in Faerie grows up knowing about the Luidaeg. She is more of a bogey than Oleander, whose stories are only a few centuries old; the Luidaeg has been one of Faerie's childhood terrors since Faerie *began*. My conviction that this was a bad idea just kept growing.

The rose goblin sat down, yawning. I eyed it. "Is this it? Are we there?" It rattled its thorns in satisfaction. Apparently so. Frowning, I turned to study the alley.

Piles of trash were shoved up against the walls, and puddles of stagnant water had formed wherever the asphalt was cracked or pitted. A single door was set into the right-hand wall a few feet from where we stood, the wood stained with salt, the hinges caked with rust. I looked at it, stomach sinking. Someday I'll figure out why everything in Faerie seems to end up in San Francisco. Rumor said the Luidaeg had been in the city for almost seventy years. They said she could give you anything you wanted, for a price. There were things I wanted, sure, but the cost always seemed like it would just be too high for me to pay.

If Luna didn't know what she was doing, I was in trouble.

The rose goblin had moved to sit on my foot, grooming the space between its toes. "Are you sure this is where we're supposed to be?" It looked up, offering a rusty purr. I sighed. "Right, great. Nice neighborhood."

"Thanks," said a voice behind me. "Personally, I think it sucks. But it's home, and the rent's lower than the property values."

I whirled, dislodging the goblin. The woman behind me smiled sardonically, tucking her groceries up under one arm. I hadn't heard her approaching. The rose goblin flattened its thorns and hissed: not the best sign. "Uh. Hi."

"Hi, yourself. Nice vermin." She gave the goblin a thoughtful look. I frowned.

"Don't I know you?"

"Maybe," she said, and smirked. "You never did give me my receipt, *honey*." She looked human, with curly, ponytailed black hair and freckles sprinkled over darkly tanned cheeks, where they almost hid her fading acne scars. She was wearing greasy overalls, heavy work boots, and a faded flannel shirt, placing her squarely in the category of local.

I blinked. "Oh. You." She'd seen the rose goblin. A human couldn't have done that. "I tried, but you were gone too fast. Look, I'm looking for someone. Do you live around here?"

"Guess so." She shifted the bag to her other arm, the contents rattling. "Don't you know where you're going?"

"Like I said, I'm looking for someone."

"Right. Nice ears, by the way. Oberon's bastards always did breed like rats." She knelt to chuck the rose goblin under the chin. It hissed again and darted behind my legs. Smirking, she looked up, pupils narrowing to slits. "I think you're looking for me."

I was expecting something like that, and managed not to jump. Barely. "Are you . . . ?"

"The Luidaeg, yes. You're a good guesser. Of course, you're standing on my doorstep, so maybe it's not such a guess. How'd you find me, anyway?" She sniffed the air, still crouching, and gave me a thoughtful look. "You stink of the Rose Roads. Not just one strain of roses, either—I can smell the Winterrose on you, and Luna's line, as well as your own. Old roses and new roses . . ." She paused. "Maybe you'd better come inside."

"I . . ."

"Look, if you're not here to see me, you can stay out here. Whatever stupid quest you think you're on can go unfulfilled; you haven't made it my problem yet." She straightened and dug a key out of her pocket. "But I'm going in before my ice cream melts." Pushing open the door, she stepped into the darkness.

I stared after her until she stuck her head back out, asking, "Well? Are you coming?"

What was I supposed to say to the sea witch, terror of faerie children everywhere? No?

The apartment was dark, furnished with rejects from a hundred different thrift stores. Things moved in the shadows. I didn't want to know what they were, anymore than I wanted to know the nature of the things crunching under my feet as I walked down the cluttered hallway. The rose goblin crept behind me, staying pressed against my ankles. I glanced down. It whined.

The Luidaeg pushed past, heading for the kitchen. "By the root and fucking branch, pick that thing up. It'll start squalling like a baby if you don't."

I knelt, scooping the goblin into my arms. It made a cheeping noise and subsided, clinging. "How did you . . . ?"

"I've dealt with the little bastards before. They were an accident on the part of a niece of mine." She reappeared in the kitchen door, a Diet Coke in one hand. "They're all predictable—goblins *and* Oberon's bastards. What do you want?"

"What?" I wasn't keeping up. This whole thing had me off my guard.

"Want. What do you want? I mean, I've been expecting you, I just didn't expect to see you so soon." She popped the can open and took a swig. "It's cool if you don't want to say. I just hope you like my company, since we're stuck here until you spill it."

"How do you know I want something? Maybe I'm here because I'm grateful for the way you saved my life." That was dangerously close to saying thank you—but she'd thanked me earlier. Maybe she was old enough that the restrictions didn't apply.

Her laugh was bitter. "Like hell. The last time one of you thin-blooded bastards was grateful, I wound up getting chased halfway across the Summerlands by jerks with torches who said I'd enchanted the kid to make him serve me. I don't need that shit. I don't look for gratitude, and I don't get it. If you're here, you want something. What is it?"

The goblin in my arms whined. I resisted the urge to

do the same. She laughed again. "Let me guess. I'm not what you were expecting, am I?"

"You're a little more normal than I thought you'd be," I admitted. I don't lie to the Queen. Somehow, I thought the Luidaeg deserved the same courtesy.

"Of course I am." She walked toward me until we were nearly nose-to-nose. "You came here looking for a monster, right? Well, I hate to disappoint. You're Amandine's daughter, aren't you?" I nodded, and she smirked. "You're more like your mama than she wanted you to be, and I bet you can roll the balance of the blood on your tongue like wine. Well, go ahead, baby doll. Give me a taste."

Her eyes widened to fill the world, pupils expanding into endless darkness. Almost against my will I did as she commanded, looking deep to see what she was and what roads her blood had traveled. Deep, so deep . . .

. . . *water and fire, blood and burning. She and her sisters were goddesses then, she and Black Annis and Gentle Annie, tending the younger children, roaming the bogs and rivers of the world. Maeve's Firstborn, pulled from her in blood and screaming while Oberon walked far, far away. But they died one by one at the hands of men and fae, by iron and ash and rowan and fire they died, until the Luidaeg was the last, running, always running, called monster and demon because her blood was so much older and wilder than their own . . .*

I ripped myself free of her eyes with a gasp, staggering backward. A final thought lashed across my vision, burning: . . . *did we lose it all for the roses? Oh, Mother, you* fool . . .

My grip tightened on the goblin, and it hissed, raising its thorns just enough to prick my skin. Shuddering, I forced myself to calm down and relax my hold, still staring at the Luidaeg.

She looked at me, one brow arched. "Well?" she asked. "Know what I am yet?"

"I . . . you . . ." The answer was there, written in blood and ashes and Maeve's despairing cries as she knelt on the graves of her daughters. The legends said the Luidaeg was a monster. They hadn't warned me about why.

"Oberon was nowhere to be seen when my sisters and I were born. The year had turned; he was off trysting with his pretty Summer Queen. And neither of them raised a hand when their children, their perfect, pretty children, started hunting us down like dogs. We were my mother's daughters, not Titania's. They couldn't be bothered." Her smile was thin and bitter. "His law came down too late for us."

"You're Maeve's daughter." She was one of the Firstborn, the oldest denizens of Faerie, our foundations and beginnings. They're all supposed to be dead or in hiding, not drinking Diet Coke in low-rent apartments in my hometown.

The Luidaeg smiled thinly. "And you're Amandine's. I was wondering how long it would take for a member of *that* line to bother tracking me down—although I'll admit, your blood's a bit thinner than I expected. Tried to fix matters on her own, did she? She always was brainless. Runs in the family." She sipped her soda again. "Now you know what I am."

"You're no monster."

"I was close enough for fairy tales." The Luidaeg shook her head, and I realized I'd looked more deeply than she expected. Interesting. "I'm tired of this. What do you want? Tell me or get out."

"You healed me."

"And?"

"I know it wasn't out of the goodness of your heart."

"I hate debts."

"Did you taste the curse?"

"Curse?" She grinned. "You mean that nasty binding the Winterrose slapped on you? Oh, yeah, I tasted it. That's one of the meaner pieces of work I've seen this century. She really pulled out the stops on *that* one. Always was a nasty bitch, that one."

"Is there a way out of it?"

"Sure. Fulfill it."

"Is there any other way?"

"What, it wasn't clear enough for you?" She cleared her throat. When she spoke again her voice was Evening's, clipped and cruel: "Find the answers, October Daye, find the reasons and find the one who caused this, or find only your own death." She paused, and her voice was her own again. "The Winterrose is good at what she does. There's no loophole."

That was exactly what I hadn't wanted to hear. "So I'm trapped."

"Yep." She sat down on a rickety chair, crossing her legs. "I just can't figure out how she got you to drink her blood. It wouldn't be nearly this strong if you hadn't done that."

I winced. No point in lying now. "I did that on my own, actually."

The Luidaeg blinked. "You were that stupid by *yourself*? Wonderful. Amandine's line is going to die out all on its own. I won't have to lift a finger."

"I didn't know," I protested, filing her comment away for later examination.

"That you were cursed? Yeah, because that's not something *I* would have noticed."

"No, that drinking her blood would make the curse stronger."

"They don't teach kids anything anymore." She took a long drink of her Diet Coke. "In my day, you'd never have lived this long without knowing how to make your enemies rot from the inside out."

"There's a pleasant image."

"I thought so. What do you want from me? I can't break a curse spun by the Winterrose. It's against the rules."

"I want information."

That sparked her interest. She straightened, pushing her hair back with a hand that seemed to glisten. Her entire body was starting to gleam, like it was covered by a thin patina of oil. The changes were subtle, but they were happening steadily, her human disguise being shucked away. I was almost afraid to see what was underneath. "Information, huh? You should know I don't work cheap."

"That isn't a problem."

"What can you give me?"

I shifted the rose goblin to one arm as I dug into the pocket of my jeans, coming up with Evening's key. The metal burst into sudden, rosy luminescence. I fought the urge to flinch. "This is . . ."

The Luidaeg stood, cutting me off mid-word. "A key to the summer roads. An old one." She held out one hand, demanding, "Give it to me."

"Tell me what I need to know."

"How much?"

"Everything."

She eyed me. "Three questions, three true answers, and you give me the key."

"Four. All true, and you don't count a question unless I say it's part of the game."

"Four, and you answer one for me."

"Done."

"I'll even give you a freebie before you start: I don't . know who decided to prune the Winterrose. Now ask away." The Luidaeg settled in her chair again.

That took out my first question, and any chance of an easy answer. Crap. I've never been very good at guessing games. "First question: what exactly is a hope chest?"

She blinked at me, surprised. "A hope chest?" she echoed. When I nodded she asked, "A real one or an imitation?"

"Is that your question?"

"No, that's me getting the information I need to answer you," she said, sourly. "Clarification is in the rules, remember? Now, is it a real hope chest?"

"I think so."

"The four sacred woods interlocked, carved with knives of water and air? Did it burn your fingers when you touched it?"

"How did you know I'd—"

"Come off it. You really think I can't see the signs, once I look for them? What is it? What can it do? Well, first off, the stories are true—some of them, anyway. The first hope chest was a gift from Oberon to Titania, to allow her to adjust her Court to her desire. She passed it along to the first of her half-blood children, and somewhere along the line, there were more of them. No one knows who made the later ones. *I* don't know, so don't ask.

"A hope chest can shift the balance of the blood. So, yes, it can make you human, if that's what you were thinking; it can also take you the other way." Her smile was sharp. "I don't recommend that road, Amandine's daughter. You're not ready for the consequences yet."

"Oh," I whispered. I'd touched it: I'd held the power to choose one world over the other. Why did that scare me? "Next question: why did you heal me?"

"Devin paid me." The Luidaeg shrugged, tossing her empty can aside. "They were going to burn me at the stake about sixty years ago, and he managed to stave it off. I've owed him since them. He gave me a chance to pay that debt, and I took it."

"Iron wounds?"

"I won't even charge you for that one, half-blood. I wanted my freedom pretty bad." She shook her head. "When you've lived as long as I have, any kind of captivity is chafing."

"Did he tell you why?" It was a shot in the dark: there were only so many roads this could go down, and none of them looked good. At least I was probably safe on this one.

The Luidaeg smiled. "Oh. Finally, a good question."

"What?" I didn't like that smile.

"Why did he ask me to heal you? Why did he let a demon out of his debt for something so small? He said," she continued in Devin's voice, "I'm not done with her yet. She hasn't found it. Now heal her, or I'll see you burn!" She chuckled, returning to her own voice. "Like he could. Jerk."

The bottom dropped out of the world. "What?"

"Don't like that answer? Sorry; I promised you the truth. How you take it is up to you. Last question."

I stared at her. She smiled. Then I swallowed, hard. I knew what came next, but that didn't stop me from wishing I could ask her for just one more thing: just one bit of proof that my sudden suspicion was wrong. "No," I said, and tossed her the key.

She caught it, blinking. "No? What do you mean *no*?"

"No, I won't ask now. Later." An image was coming together in my mind, sickeningly obvious now that I was letting myself consider it. Blood was where this started: Evening's blood on the carpet, my blood on the concrete, the blood of an assassin and an innocent man drying on the grass at Golden Gate Park. Everything looped back to the beginning of everything else, like the metalwork on Evening's key. It all came back to blood and roses.

Sometimes I think everything in Faerie boils down to one of those two.

"What?" she demanded, half-standing. "You can't do that!"

"I can. I owe you a question, too, you know. You can ask it now." I smiled, trying to hide the sickening thud of my heart. She could kill me without thinking twice. It would almost have been kinder than what I was about to do. At least then I wouldn't be a traitor—just dead. "I have to tell the truth."

"What's to stop me from gutting you where you stand?" she snarled, hands twisting into claws. "Answer *that!*"

"Simple," I said, keeping my arms wrapped tight around the rose goblin. "If you kill me, I'll die with you in my debt. You won't stand for that. You said so yourself."

She backed off a half step, glaring at me. "You'll ask that question someday."

"Maybe."

"I'll have the right to kill you when you do."

"Maybe; maybe not. We aren't there yet." Besides, there was no guarantee I'd live that long.

The Luidaeg paused, and then actually, grudgingly, smiled. "You're pretty smart, considering your mother. Maybe the brains skipped a generation."

"I'll take that in the spirit in which it was given." I half bowed. The rose goblin squirmed out of my arms, perching on my shoulder.

"What are you going to do now?"

If it hadn't been for the attack in the park, I could have gotten out of it, because what I was thinking wouldn't have been a viable option without blood. My blood wasn't good enough, and neither was Evening's. I needed the blood of someone who was involved, blood that would hold at least a trace of the truth. Without the attack, I could have let it go. But the attack happened, and we had the blood—Tybalt had been covered in the stuff. It would be dry by now, but it was worth trying. There was a chance, and I had to know.

"The only thing I can do," I said, sighing. "I'm going to ask the dead."

TWENTY-FOUR

FINDING A TAXI NEAR the docks after dark is something I never want to do again. I would have called Danny; unfortunately, I couldn't find a phone, and I was reduced to waving my arms whenever a likely car passed by, hoping someone would take pity and stop. Eventually, someone did.

The rose goblin had never been in a car before. It kept peering out the windows, making interested mewling noises until I had to fight not to laugh. The last thing I needed to do was convince the driver the woman he'd picked up in one of the worst parts of town was crazy. Besides, I was afraid the laughter would be more hysterical than anything else. I'd left the Luidaeg's apartment in a daze, fumbling for a line of reasoning that didn't lead back to blood. There wasn't one. The entire case was bound in blood magic and chains of broken lives; it made sense to solve it the same way. So what if I didn't want to? That never stopped me before.

It was past midnight when we reached my apartment. I paid the cabbie with the last of my cash, wincing as I did it. If I didn't find a new job soon, I was going to be re-placing fae problems with more mundane ones. Maybe I could learn to be a bartender. They work nights, don't they?

The rose goblin rode my shoulder as I walked up the path to my door. The wards hadn't been reset the last time I left, mainly because I'd been carried out by Man-uel and Dare. I hesitated, contemplating what might be inside, then unlocked the door and opened it, flipping on the living room light. Waiting rarely solves the question of what's under the couch.

There was barely time to take in the carnage left by the Doppelganger's attack before two angry brown-and-cream shapes darted out from under the coffee table, yowling. The rose goblin rallied, leaping to the floor and rattling its thorns. The cats backed off a few feet, bemused, and glared at me. Not only had I gone away, but I'd come back with a . . . well, with a something, and it was threatening them.

I laughed, closing the door behind me. "Cagney, Lacey, back off. This is . . ." I paused, trying to think of a suitable name. "This is Spike. He's visiting." The rose goblin looked up at me and rattled its thorns, chirping.

The cats weren't as easy to mollify. They yowled again, now circling us both. Spike turned in circles to match them, rattling whenever they got too close. "Spike, guys, stop it. You can fight later." All three stopped, turning to look at me. I'd just gotten cats to obey. Wonders never cease.

I crouched to look at them, and they looked back, oddly calm. Sometimes, when they do things like that, I wonder if they're actually Cait Sidhe planted to keep an eye on me—but that way lies madness. They're just cats, and all cats know the same strange roads, in the end.

"I need to speak to your King," I said. They blinked

luminous blue eyes, looking blank as only cats can. I sighed. "I need to see Tybalt. I know you can find him."

They gave no evidence of understanding; Lacey started to wash Cagney's ear, ignoring me. Spike looked between them and rattled its thorns, confused. I stayed where I was, waiting. "Guys, don't make me force the issue," I said. "You know you have to take me to him if I demand it. You can find the Court of Cats. I can order you. I'd rather ask."

The cats exchanged a look, Lacey abandoning her bathing efforts. Cats aren't the smartest creatures alive, but they recognize a demand, even from a changeling. Cats and faeries have a special relationship, one that's pulled them at least partially into our world, and they know a plea when they hear one. Stretching to show their unconcern, they started for the door.

I let out a breath I hadn't known I was holding. They were going to take me. Cagney paused at the door, letting out a decisive yowl. The tone was easy to read: an obvious "come on or shut up." I started to follow, and then turned back, retrieving the gun from beneath the edge of the curtains. It was heavy in my hand, and the closeness of the iron burned, but any protection was better than none. If iron bullets weren't enough, this was already over.

Spike rattled. I looked back at it, shaking my head. "Stay?" It rattled again. "Stay. Guard." That seemed to get through: it settled into a watching posture, eyes on the window. Great. A week of death, iron, and demons, and now my house was being guarded by a mobile rosebush.

The cats were waiting outside. I slid the gun into my pocket, and nodded. "Lead the way."

They walked down the path to the common walkway connecting my apartment to the mail and laundry rooms. I followed a few feet behind, keeping them in sight, concentrating so hard on their bobbing tails that I didn't even notice when the path diverged from the ones I knew. The sound of hissing broke my concentration, and I looked up.

"Oh, boy."

We were standing in a narrow alley I almost recognized from the area near Golden Gate Park—almost, but not quite. Space had twisted to form arched curves and folded angles, becoming subtly wrong. Every available space was covered with cats, from pampered house pets to grizzled back fence warriors. Something that looked like a lynx crouched toward the back of the mob, hissing with the rest. It was enough to remind me, graphically, that size doesn't mean much when you're outnumbered.

"October."

I turned, leaving my hands in my pockets as I said, "Hello, Tybalt."

The King of Cats was sprawled atop a stack of mattresses blocking the alley's mouth, flanked on either side by large, angry-looking calicos. About a dozen human-form Cait Sidhe lounged on the walls and ground around him, dressed in tatters and rags. Most of them didn't look like they went on two legs very often. Cagney and Lacey melted into the throng, vanishing; they brought me, their disappearance said. That was all the help I'd get.

"You're here," Tybalt said, sounding more amused than surprised. The height of his "throne" put him above me, allowing him to look down on me without quite straining either of our necks. He'd changed his clothes, trading them for skintight jeans and a black silk shirt. Good. If I was lucky, they hadn't done the laundry yet. The courtiers around him watched me with predatory eyes. You're a predator or you're prey, their expressions said, and we'll kill you either way. "Why are you here? This isn't your Court."

"This is the Cat's Court; I have business with their King. That means truce."

"Business?"

"Yes, business," I said. Offending him on his own turf might be the last thing I ever did. "The attack in the park—"

He frowned. "What about it?"

"It wasn't random; someone paid for it, and I need to know who."

"Do you think *I* know?" he asked. A ripple ran through the crowd, low and dangerous.

"No. I think *he* knew."

That made him pause. He sat up a little, attention focusing on me. "He's dead, October."

"And I'm Amandine's daughter. You know what she could do." I squared my shoulders, standing a bit straighter. It helped hide my terror. "I told you when the attack happened that I needed his blood. I can follow it to answers."

"You'd do that?" Tybalt frowned, something like respect creeping into the expression.

"I've done it before." I carefully didn't mention when. Half the Kingdom seemed to know about Evening's curse: I didn't need him joining their ranks.

"Is it safe?"

"Does it matter?"

"No. I suppose not." He rose, walking toward the back of the alley. The cats parted to let him pass, closing ranks again behind him. "I'll be back in a moment. Wait for me." When he reached the deepest part of the shadows he spread his hands and they opened like a curtain, letting him step through and disappear.

I was still watching the shadows when something

slammed into my back. The impact had me on the ground before I could react, slamming the gun in my pocket up against my thigh hard enough that I knew it was going to leave a bruise. "What the—" I yelped, as I went down.

The only answer was an incoherent snarl. I tried to lift my head and it was shoved down again, knocking my cheek against the pavement so hard that it left my ears ringing. The cats around me were yowling at the top of their lungs. Well, it was nice to know they'd noticed. I went limp, letting whoever was above me think that I'd given up, and then pushed myself into a roll, ignoring the renewed pain as the gun dug farther into my leg. I was rewarded with an earsplitting shriek, and found myself pinning Julie to the alley floor. She howled, bucking against my hands, and managed to flip me over. At least I'd gone from my stomach to my back; she was straddling me now, face bestial with fury.

"What are you doing?" I demanded, just before she grabbed my throat with both hands. Conversation didn't seem to be high on her list of priorities: banging my head against the ground was. I screamed, scrabbling for the purchase I needed to shove her away.

I was still screaming when hands grabbed her from behind and Tybalt threw her against the nearest wall. She rebounded and bounced back to her feet, hands crooked to expose her claws. He roared at her, full-throated, and she paused in apparent chagrin before opening her mouth and roaring back. Her tone didn't even begin to approach his in strength or primal fury. Stalking forward, he smacked her across the face, knocking her to the ground. Julie hissed, more kitten than tiger, and he roared again.

That was the end of it. She whimpered and flattened herself against the pavement, rolling over to expose her neck. Tybalt knelt and ran one clawed finger down the length of her jugular vein before pulling her off the ground into a rough hug. The message was clear: she could have died, and he had spared her. Now she would obey.

I pushed myself to my feet, watching them despite the pain in my head. I'd never seen that sort of fight before, but I understood it. Julie's attack was unexpected, but it wasn't just an attack on me: when Tybalt involved himself, it became a dominance challenge. Unsurprisingly, the changeling lost.

"Kill her," Julie hissed, pulling away from him. "Kill her or let me."

Tybalt frowned, lowering his arms. The shirt that he'd been wearing in the park was draped over one shoulder, pale cloth mottled with dried blood. "No," he said, voice rough. There were undertones of the jungle there, dark and alien. "I will not. She's here under truce."

"Then I'll follow her, and kill her when she's not under truce," Julie said, glaring.

"Why do you want to kill me?" I demanded.

The look she shot me was so full of hate that I stepped back, surprised. "You killed Ross," she hissed.

"I did not!" I protested. I might have led him to his death, but I didn't kill him. Sometimes semantics matter. "It wasn't my fault!"

"Yes, it was, you stupid bitch!" She started to rush me again. Tybalt raised one arm to block her.

"I'd leave now if I were you, October. This Court is closed." He took the shirt from his shoulder and threw it to me. I caught it one-handed, crumpling it in my fist. The bloodstains covered half the fabric: it would be enough.

Actually, it was too much: some of the blood had to be Tybalt's. He was handing me the key to his own memories, and that's not something any faerie gives lightly. "Tybalt . . ."

"Go." He shook his head. "This isn't the time or the place." Julie shrieked, and he pulled her back again. The other human-form Cait Sidhe were standing now, their eyes glowing through the darkness. It was starting to feel like a scene from a Hitchcock film. I nodded, clutching the shirt, and managed a clumsy bow before I turned and walked toward the mouth of the alley. The cats parted to let me pass, their voices fading behind me as I stepped over the discarded mattresses and pillows of Tybalt's throne.

When I had reached the sidewalk outside to find myself facing Golden Gate Park's east gate I turned, looking back into the now empty alleyway. The Court of Cats never stayed in one place for long; as soon as I had stepped outside, it had probably moved on, leaving me and Tybalt's bloodstained shirt behind.

I lowered the shirt, studying it. The blood was clotted in dark patches, staining the front and arms. I scraped at one of the larger stains with a fingernail. It wouldn't flake off. All right: I'd try the direct method. I stepped back into the alley, out of view of the street, and raised the shirt in order to run my tongue across the stain. The taste was foul—blood, sweat, and dirt—but it was just a taste; there was no magic in it. I frowned. The blood had been dry for too long: if I wanted to ride it, I'd have to wake it up first. Maybe riding the blood wasn't my best idea ever, but it was the only lead I had.

I turned to look at the park, just on the other side of the road. Lily was an Undine: water was her purview and the focus of her fiefdom, and if anyone could wake the blood, it was her. She might not like the idea, but she'd probably do it if I asked. She might even forgive me later.

TWENTY-FIVE

MARCIA WAS BEHIND THE TICKET booth, chin in her hand. I paused, trying to figure out what she was doing there before dawn, before shaking my head and continuing to walk. I didn't have any money on me; hopefully, she'd let me in anyway.

She lifted her head and smiled as I approached, chirping, "Good morning! Lily said you'd be coming, and I should go ahead and let you right in."

I paused. "Lily's expecting me?"

"Of course!" she said, still smiling. I half expected her face to crack. "She was sure you'd be here. We were all told to watch for you." She leaned forward conspiratorially, and I caught the gleam of faerie ointment around her eyes. Maybe her blood wasn't as thin as I'd guessed. "To tell the truth, I'm surprised you weren't here sooner."

"Right," I said, slowly. "So should I just . . ."

"You can just go on in. Lily's waiting." Her smile faded, message delivered, and she looked at me with an odd coldness in her bland blue eyes.

"Right." I know a brush-off when I see one. I walked

on into the Tea Gardens, keeping my eyes off the water as I headed for the highest of the curved moon bridges. Its apex was almost hidden by a jigsaw-mesh of cherry branches, making it look like it ascended forever. That little optical illusion is more accurate than most people realize; it's just that mortal eyes can't see all the way up. Gripping the handrail, I began my climb.

The branches of the surrounding trees knit closer and closer together as I climbed, hiding me entirely as I stepped onto the air above the visible top of the bridge. I continued to climb, and they continued to twist together, becoming a solid ceiling of green. My final step brought me from clear air to solid, marshy ground. Lily was kneeling by a low table not far away, facing me.

Two teacups sat on the table, and the matching pot was in her hands. All three were painted with curved black lines suggesting the arch of cherry branches or of bones. "October. Please, come sit."

"Hey, Lily," I said, walking over to kneel on the other side of the table. The gun in my pocket pressed against my skin. I felt the iron through my clothes, like the beginnings of frostbite. "I'm sorry to barge in on you like this, but I need—"

"I know what you want." She leaned across the table, filling the first cup. "I knew it would come to this when I heard that Ross had died in shepherding you, that the King of Cats killed a man outside my fiefdom's bawn, that Juliet would no more claim my charities." A pained expression crossed her face, flickered, and was gone.

I winced, looking away. "Lily, I'm so sorry. I . . ."

"You are more like your mother than you seem ever willing to believe," she said, and sighed. "Are you sure there is no other way?"

"I'm sure," I said, turning back to her. I hate it when I'm the last one to figure things out—but I'm getting used to it, at least where Lily's concerned. "I have to know."

"You may be your mother's daughter, October, but you are not Amandine. This is not safe for you as it would be for her. Find another way."

"There isn't another way," I said, biting back a bitter laugh. She had no idea how dangerous this was. "I'm running out of time. I need to know."

"Why?"

I just looked at her. We held that tableau for a long moment before she put the teapot down, one webbed hand still wrapped around the handle.

Voice soft, Lily said, "Please don't do this. For the sake of your survival, and your sanity, please. Can't I make you change your mind?"

"I'm sorry, Lily. I don't have any other options left."

"Give it to me," she said, holding out her hand. I handed her the shirt, and she took it, removing the lid from the teapot. It was empty. Still serene, she stuffed the shirt inside, replacing the lid before giving the teapot an experimental shake. It made a splashing noise, and she nodded, apparently satisfied. "Your cup, if you please."

I picked up the still empty cup, and she tipped the pot over it. The liquid that poured out was thick and red, steaming in the cool air. If there was water in it, I couldn't tell; it looked like blood, pure and simple.

"October . . ." Lily said. "It's not too late. Put down the cup and find another way."

"There isn't one," I said, and raised the cup to my lips.

The blood was hot and coppery on my tongue. I almost gagged, but then the taste of it was gone, replaced by the crimson haze of someone else's memories.

The first memories that came were flavored with

the sweet, sharp taste of pennyroyal filtered through a screen of gold. An alleyway, just before dawn; my own face as seen through someone else's eyes, my hair blown wild with running, my expression tired and all but permanently wounded. *So she's back again,* said Tybalt's voice, soft in my mind's ears. *Lost and gone for so long, and now she's come back to us, now she's come back to me . . .*

That wasn't the memory I needed. I forced myself back into my body and took another gulp of Lily's "tea," riding the blood down, past those half-golden memories and into something darker, and far less familiar.

The memories that rose this time were bitter gray beneath the red, and they tasted like hawthorn and ashes. Rowan and thorn preserve me, but I'd found what I was looking for.

. . . it would be an easy job, very easy, not much to do: follow the changeling, catch her, learn everything she knows, and kill her, and the pay would be more than worth it. Maybe I could even keep her alive for just a little longer than I have to, have a little fun . . .

Swallowing bile, I took another mouthful. The mix of blood and Undine water burned my lips, but I didn't care; I needed to go deeper, to what was waiting underneath. One way or another, I needed to know. The blood almost masked the taste of roses as I held my breath, clinging to the memory of my own body to keep myself from going completely under.

The air was smoky, filled with the blare of music. Stupid junk the kids were listening to these days . . . "Hey, I do this, you pay me, right? No matter what gets broke in the process."

Devin turned. Slimy bastard. No honor among thieves; I know better'n to trust him, but the money's so *good.* "Just bring me the box and proof she's dead for real this *time, not just lost in some pond somewhere," he said. His smile was bitter; his eyes were empty.*

Behind my own growing horror, I saw those eyes and understood that this was really happening. I worked for Devin. I was his flunky and his lover, and I knew what that look meant. When he looked like that, somebody was getting written off as a loss; somebody was already dead. And this time, it was me.

Devin was still speaking, voice getting more distant as my grasp on the spell faltered: *"The Winterrose has managed to trick me before. Toby's a little fool, but she's Amandine's daughter. I can't trust her not to ruin this for me."*

Denial ceased to be an option—and so did breathing as Evening's curse slammed down without warning, knocking me deeper into the memories of the assassin Devin set on my trail. The memory of Evening's death and my transformation became tangled in the curse, along with the sudden bitter addition of the night I followed my mother's people into Faerie. The weight of that memory alone was enough to force me farther down until I was drowning in a rosy mist.

There were three deaths waiting for me: I could have my choice of suffocation, iron, or gunfire, and any of them could carry me home, stop my heart, and end the pain. All I had to do was stop fighting. I could write myself out of the play, just like Ophelia before me; it could be over. Maybe I could've kept fighting temptation if the curse hadn't decided to start playing dirty . . . but like the Luidaeg said, it was a beautiful piece of work, and it had been strengthened past its original purpose by my own foolishness.

Wouldn't it be nice to get what you were looking for? it whispered. *I can give you peace. I can be your flight of angels. Just give up and let me in.*

The taste of roses filled the world. Maybe it was right; maybe I was done. I'd done what I was bound to do. I found the killers, or at least the one who hired them. The hope chest was safe with Tybalt. There was nothing left for me to do, and I had no Home to go to. Blood and betrayal: who needs anything else? Devin was my mentor, my friend, and my lover, and he'd tried to kill me. He'd ordered the deaths of at least two people, and he'd lied about it without blinking. Nothing was the way I'd left it; my world was dead. Why did I bother fighting?

I went limp beneath the weight of memory, letting the phantom roses wrap around me. I was ready to die, to sleep, to dream no more. No more dreams. No more deaths. No more anything. The world started to slip away.

Something that burned hot and cold at the same time hit me in the middle of my chest. The roses lost their grip as I was jerked, gasping, back into my body. The pain didn't stop. I opened my eyes, and Lily was standing over me, one hand clutching the other, the skin looking cracked and seared.

The gun I'd stolen was on top of me, the chamber open to let the iron bullets spill out. They were bitterly cold, even through my shirt. My cup was shattered on the ground beside me, the moss around it dark with blood.

I sat up, scooping the bullets into my hand and shoving them back into the chamber before snapping it closed. I didn't turn back toward Lily until they were all out of sight.

"You left," she whispered. "I told you it was dangerous, but you did it anyway . . . and you left. Your body was here, and there was no one inside it."

I glanced at her burned hand. Iron hurts purebloods worse than it hurts changelings, and as an Undine, Lily was more susceptible than most; she was only flesh because she wanted to be. To an Undine, iron is like acid, and the fact that she was willing to touch it at all showed something more than friendship. I set the thought regretfully aside. There would be time to think about what she'd done for me later . . . and time to wonder whether I could ever repay it.

Her expression was slowly returning to its normal serenity, although her eyes were pained. "Did you find what you needed?"

What I needed? I looked at the gun I was holding and nodded, slowly.

"Yeah, I did," I said.

"And?" There was a waiting, worried edge to her voice. She knew what came next as well as I did, even if she didn't know why.

I sighed. "Can you call me a taxi?"

TWENTY-SIX

IN THE END, LILY DIDN'T CALL the taxi; I did. Danny said he could be there in fifteen minutes, and that was good enough, because it also gave me time to call Shadowed Hills and leave a terse, angry message with the Hob who answered the phone. "Tell Sylvester I'm going Home," I said. "I'll try not to die before I get there."

"Wait for him," Lily said, watching me drop the phone back into its cradle. "You don't have to do this alone."

"Time's too short, and the stakes are too high." If Devin was willing to kill me to get his hands on the hope chest, how long would it be before he started trying to find its hiding place? How long before there were assassins in the bushes at Shadowed Hills, hired killers watching the Court of Cats for targets? "This ends now."

"Yes," she said, anxiously. "It very well may."

I paused. "Can you send a messenger to Tybalt?" She nodded. "Tell him it was Devin; tell him he knows why, if he thinks about it. And tell him I'm sorry I got him involved in this."

"Toby . . ."

"Just tell him." I kissed her forehead and left the Tea Gardens as quickly as I could, heading for the parking lot where Danny would be meeting me.

I didn't look back.

Danny picked up pretty quickly on my desire to make the drive in silence. Maybe it was the fact that I cried the whole way. The street in front of Home was deserted when we pulled up; he took the money Lily had given me for cab fare, looking at me with worry in his eyes. "You gonna be okay in there? You need some muscle?"

I patted his elbow. "I'll be fine, Danny."

"You sure?"

"I'm sure."

"All right. You need me, you call." Then he was gone, tires squealing as he blazed off down the street. I watched until I was sure that he was gone before pulling the gun out of my pocket and turning to walk up to the door.

It was time to go Home.

Home's door was often closed but never locked; all you had to do to get inside is want to be there. Kids were posted in the front room twenty-four hours a day, making sure trouble didn't start unless they started it. But when I turned the doorknob, nothing happened. The door was locked against me. Devin knew I was coming.

"This is October Daye!" I shouted, pounding my hand against the door. "Let me in!"

Footsteps, and the sound of locks being undone. The door opened, revealing a drawn-looking Manuel with gauze taped above one eye, not quite concealing the swelling. I caught my breath, letting it out in a slow hiss as Dare peeked around him, frighteningly pale, bruises standing out in sharp relief on her cheek and neck. Manuel saw the gun, and his eyes widened.

"What are you doing here?" I asked, voice pitched low. "I told Luna to have you wait."

"Devin called us," Manuel said. "We always come when he calls." Dare was shaking her head in small, sharp motions, making go away gestures with her hands. Devin was angry that I'd left them at Shadowed Hills and gone on without them. Knowing what I knew now, he was angry they hadn't been able to keep watching me for him.

Dare wanted me out of harm's way, but that wasn't an option. Not with the taste of roses lingering in my mouth. "If you go now, I'll come for you when this is done," I said, still quietly.

Manuel looked at me solemnly, opening the door wider in invitation. Dare whimpered and he shushed her, not looking away from my face. They were staying. This was their Home, whether they wanted it or not, and they were staying until the end.

I stepped into the room, scanning for potential trouble. I didn't see any; we were alone. From where I stood, the building didn't hold anyone but two green-eyed kids, a cursed changeling, and a killer. The room was smaller without its smattering of teenagers, and the scars on the walls seemed older. For the first time, it looked like what it really was: a flophouse with a fancy name, where kids who didn't know any better let themselves be abused by someone who should have known better.

Crossing the room, I smashed the glass over the call button for Devin's office with the butt of my gun. Shards flew in all directions, and Dare gasped, eyes wide with a mixture of awe and terror. When did I become the hero? When did she start looking at me like that?

"What are you doing?" she asked.

"I'm finishing things," I said, trying to project a calm I didn't feel. Silently I told myself we'd get out of there alive; I was going to live up to the unspoken expectations in her eyes. It was the only promise I could make. "It's about to get messy. I'd go now, if I were you." I knew they wouldn't go—I wouldn't have, when I belonged there—but I had to give them the chance.

"He'll kill you if you don't leave now," Manuel said.

"Since he's planning to kill me anyway, I don't see where that changes things." I hit the button, ignoring the broken glass. It was too late for a little more blood to make a difference. "I know you're there, Devin. It's time for you to be out here." Stepping back, I waited.

I didn't have to wait long. Devin's voice crackled over the intercom, saying "Toby? What's going on? Where did you go?" There was fear there. Not much, but if I'd needed any further confirmation, that would have been enough to give it to me.

I pushed the button down again. "I know, Devin."

"You know what?"

"I know everything. I know who you hired, and when, and how." I was extemporizing wildly, but he had no way of knowing that. "I know about the men you sent to kill me. I know you seduced me because you thought it might get you what you wanted. I know my shoulder will never be the same and I may never sleep again and you'd better get your ass out here *right now*." The last words were practically a hiss, my fury boiling over. He betrayed Evening, and he betrayed *me*. There was no way I was forgiving that.

The intercom was silent. I turned to point the gun in my hand toward the door to the back hall. After several endless minutes it swung open and Devin stepped out, holding up empty hands in surrender.

"It didn't have to be like this, Toby," he said, voice weary in defeat. The brightness of his eyes had faded, turning slate gray, like a storm had come to his private sky. It had to happen eventually; October always brings rain, even in California.

"You killed her."

"You have no proof of that."

I kept the gun aimed squarely at his chest. "Pretty sure the Queen wouldn't see things that way."

"Pretty sure you're not planning to take me to her Court to find out." He shook his head. "I never wanted to lie to you, October. Why wouldn't you just . . . let it go? We could have been happy. Finally happy. I really do love you. I always have."

"Why, Devin? Root and branch, why did you do this?"

"Because I'm going to live forever." There was a challenge in his eyes. "Maybe you're willing to settle for changeling time, but I'm not. The purebloods could give us all immortality, but they refuse, because we're 'not good enough.' If they won't give me what's mine, I'll take it. That's all I've been doing. Taking what belongs to me."

"That's sick."

"That's the way the world works. What, are you happy that you're going to die? Do you *enjoy* waking up every morning and realizing your body got a little bit closer to breaking in the night? Because I don't. We could have lived forever, together, if you'd just let it go."

"You had Evening killed because you wanted to be immortal?"

"No," he said. A small knot of pain let go in my shoulders, only to snarl tighter than ever before when he continued, "that's why I killed her myself."

That was the one thing I hadn't allowed myself to consider: that he could have held the knife. "You bastard," I whispered.

"I paid three Redcaps to hold her down while I slit

her throat. She screamed, Toby. You should have heard her. It was like music . . . but it was too late. The key was gone, and it wasn't over yet. Everything after that could have been avoided if she'd just listened to me."

"Devin . . ."

"You always had so many illusions—sort of funny for someone as inept with them as you are. I tried so hard to beat them out of you." His smile was proprietary. "I could've managed it if you'd given me a few more years. You could be standing beside me now, on the right side. You could understand."

"I don't want to understand," I said. "You make me sick."

"Human morality, October. Get over it. It's not going to get you very far." He stepped toward me, stopping when I raised the gun. "She's still dead. No matter what you do, she stays dead. Can you really stand to lose us both?"

"I can't stand not to." Questions were whirled through my head faster than I could ask them. How did he edit Evening's blood memory? That's supposed to be impossible, but he did it. How many more assassins were there? The ones in Goldengreen—I had to assume they were real, but I'd never seen them.

And in the end, it didn't matter. Those were the questions I could answer later; what mattered now was ending this, here, tonight, before any other innocents got hurt.

Devin's tone changed, becoming wheedling. "I never wanted you involved, Toby. I didn't think she'd call you—I really didn't. If you'd just stopped when I asked . . ."

"You'd have killed me anyway, eventually." I stepped forward, eyes narrowed. "I haven't belonged to you in a long time, and honor doesn't protect me anymore. I'm not stupid, Devin. You know better."

"You won't shoot me," he said, and smiled. "You can't."

"I can't?"

"No. You still love me. You're still too human. You can't kill someone you love." He sounded completely sure of himself. "I know you. You can't fool me."

"No, Devin, you know a girl who didn't know enough to get away from you." My hands were shaking, aim wavering as my focus slipped. Anger makes everything personal. As if this wasn't already personal enough. "Love you? *Love* you? You killed Evening, and you killed Ross, and you tried to kill me. You put your kids in harm's way, and now you have the . . . the *audacity* to say that I love you? Oberon's blood, Devin, will you just grow up already?"

"Yes. You love me." He lowered his hands. "You always have, and you always will, no matter what I do to you. All changelings are crazy, Toby. You know that. Your madness is your loyalty."

"Screw you," I said, and steadied my aim.

I shouldn't have waited so long. Dare shouted, "Manny, no!" and I whirled, letting Devin out of my sight. That wasn't my first mistake; it stood a good chance of being my last.

Manuel—sweet, innocent Manuel—was holding a revolver, feet braced at shoulder width, the barrel of the gun aimed at my chest. He was trembling. I froze. I was willing to bet that he'd never shot anyone, that he didn't want to shoot me, but I wasn't going to test it. Smart people don't gamble with guns.

"He said . . . he said we wouldn't have to . . . hurt you . . . if you'd just stop getting in the way. You could come back here. You could be family like you used to. But you wouldn't *listen!*" Manny was almost crying, face slick with sweat. "Put down the gun, Ms. Daye."

"Manny?"

"Just put it down."

"I thought Evening was your friend, Manny. What are you—"

He gestured violently with the gun, looking upset enough that I didn't trust him not to fire without meaning to. "She didn't listen! You won't listen! You want to stay alive around here, when the boss talks, you *listen!*"

I knelt, careful to move slowly as I placed my gun on the floor. "Where'd you get the gun, Manny?" I asked, not rising. "Did Devin give it to you? He did, didn't he?"

"Be quiet, Toby," Devin said. His voice was flat. Maeve's bones, had I really let him touch me? Had I really touched *him?* What kind of a fool was I? "Manuel, shoot her. Don't kill her, just hurt her. The leg, I think."

Manny was crying now, and his hands were clutching the gun so tightly that his knuckles had gone white. I cleared my throat, pulling his attention back to my face. "Do the bullets burn, Manny?" I asked, in as conversational a tone as I could manage. "Do they make your skin crawl? That's iron, Manny. He wants you to shoot me with iron bullets."

"Manuel, shoot her *now.*"

I stood carefully, holding my hands up at shoulder level. "Can you do it? Can you torture me with iron, for him?"

"Manuel, are you listening to me?" Devin snapped. "Don't make me take that gun away from you."

"He won't do it himself." I kept my hands raised. "Don't you wonder why?"

"Be quiet, bitch." Devin stormed over to me, grabbing my arm and twisting it behind my back, just like I'd done to Dare on the day we met. His fingers dug into my elbow. I winced, gritting my teeth against the pain. "Don't confuse him."

"Why not, Devin? Don't you want him to understand? You always told me that knowledge was power."

"October . . ." For a second—just a second—I thought I saw the man I knew behind the blankness in his eyes. "Don't make this harder than it has to be."

"Don't you want him to grow up just like you?" I could see Dare out of the corner of my eye, creeping toward Manuel. *Be careful, little girl,* I thought, *please, be careful . . .*

His hand tightened. I could almost feel the bruises forming. "I didn't want to kill Evening. I worked with her, for you. I let her pretend you were still alive, and so she helped us. She never did it for us. Just for you. I never wanted her dead. But she wouldn't give me the hope chest, and I needed it, Toby, more than you can dream. You played at being a pureblood, but you know you'll never be one. You know why I needed it. Changeling time runs out so fast." He sighed. "She had to die."

"Why are you telling me this?" I needed to keep him talking, if only for Dare's sake. That girl was still doing her damnedest to turn me into a hero. "Scooby and the gang aren't here yet."

Devin released my arm, stepping away. "I want you to understand that it wasn't personal. I missed you. I wasn't lying when I told you that."

By moving, Devin had given Manuel a clear shot at my entire body. Dare was too far away to reach him in time, and in a way, I was grateful. She wouldn't get hurt trying to save me.

"You changed." I turned to look at him, resisting the urge to rub the circulation back into my arm. If I was going to die, I was going to do it with something resembling dignity.

"So did you." He sounded almost sorry. Then his eyes hardened, the moment passing, and he turned to Manuel. "Take your time, make it hurt. She'll tell us where she hid it."

Manuel raised the gun, whispering a prayer. I closed my eyes, hoping his aim was bad and the first bullet would do the job. That it would end quickly.

I didn't see what came next. I opened my eyes to see Dare leaping onto her brother's back, momentum sending them both crashing to the floor. The gun went off when it hit the floor, bullet punching through the ceiling. I dove for my own gun an instant too late, shying back as Devin grabbed it from under my hands.

"Toby, get the gun!" Dare shrieked, trying to keep Manuel pinned. He had fifty pounds and six inches on her: there was no way she'd keep him down for long. I pushed myself to my feet, keeping my eyes on Devin. His attention was entirely on Dare, face twisted into an expression that went past rage or sanity. He was gone.

He'd been gone for a long time.

"No one disobeys me!" he snarled.

Dare looked up, eyes going wide, and screamed as the first bullet hit her in the side. Blood sprayed over the wall behind her, hitting Manuel across the face. The terror in her eyes turned to pleading as she glanced toward me, like she was hoping I could take it back. Even then, she thought I'd be her hero.

She finished her scream and jerked back, trying to curl into a ball. It was too late. The next two bullets were close behind the first, and by the time I'd recovered enough to lunge for Devin, her screams had stopped. Manuel was doing the screaming for her. My shoulder caught Devin in the ribs, bowling him over and sending the gun sliding across the floor. I had an instant to wonder where it landed before his foot caught me in the stomach, flinging me back.

I curled around myself, retching, as he climbed back

to his feet; his second kick caught me in the chest, sending stabbing pains through my ribs and sternum. "Look what you did! You killed her." There was no sanity left in his voice: he believed what he was saying. He pulled the trigger, and he still blamed me. Not that it mattered. I'd blame myself enough for both of us.

"Devin . . ." I gasped.

"Shut up!" The scope of the world had narrowed, becoming nothing but Devin, pain, and the growing taste of roses. I think his world had become just as small. He'd abandoned his sanity in the twisting maze of changeling time, and the balance of his blood had thrown him to the point from which there was no coming back. Sitting on the fence isn't easy. Sometimes the fence breaks, and you fall.

Neither of us expected the gunshot. Devin raised a hand to his chest, touching the stain blooming there before looking back to me, eyes gone terribly wide. Mouth moving with words he never managed to finish, he folded and fell.

Behind him, still crying, Manuel lowered the gun.

The taste of roses rose and burst in the back of my throat, choking me as it dissipated. I hadn't realized how constant it had become until it was gone. I stood with agonizing slowness; every breath hurt, but at least I was alive. Manuel didn't move as I walked over and pried the gun from his fingers, dropping it to the floor.

He lifted his head when it hit the ground, expression bleak. "He . . . he . . ."

"Shhh. I know."

And I put my arms around him, and held him.

TWENTY-SEVEN

WE STOOD THERE FOR almost fifteen minutes before I pulled back, looking at Manuel. "Is there anyone else here?" He gazed at me, eyes gone wide and glassy with shock. I shook his shoulders, as gently as I could manage. "Manuel, is there anyone else here? Anyone at all?"

"He . . . sent them all away," he said. "He knew you were coming. He didn't want anyone else to be here when you came."

He sent away everyone but the two kids I cared about. I closed my eyes. Until today, I'd never known that he could be evil. "Come on, Manuel. Let's go get your things."

"I don't want to leave her."

I looked back to his face, forcing myself to smile. "You have to, Manny. It's time for the night-haunts to come, and they won't do it while we're here."

"But . . ."

"Come on."

The room Dare and Manuel shared with half a dozen

more of Devin's kids was dark and cluttered, hammocks hanging from the middle of the ceiling to keep the mattresses from using up all the available floor space. It was familiar enough to hurt like hell. I used to share a room just like it with Mitch and Julie and a rotating group of others, all of us fighting for our little corners and the pretense of dignity that having "a little privacy" could create.

I leaned against the wall, watching as Manuel packed up their meager store of possessions. The hollow echo of the night-haunts' wings whispered down the hall from the front of the building, warning the living to stay away; their only business was with the dead. The night-haunts work fast. By the time Manuel came back to the doorway, clutching a duffel bag in one hand and a tattered red suitcase in the other, the sound of wings was gone.

Eyes still glassy, he looked at me, and asked, "Where are we going?"

"I don't know."

The bodies in the front weren't any easier to look at now that they seemed human. I forced myself to keep my eyes on the door, tugging Manuel along in my wake. He went silent again at the first sight of his sister's manikin, retreating back into shock. I couldn't blame him. He'd lost his sister and his teacher in the same night. Who was going to take care of him now?

"Wait here," I said. Manuel didn't respond; just stood there, staring dully at the wall. "I'm going to go to the office. Can you wait here for me?" I paused, giving him time to answer. He didn't. "All right. Just scream if anything comes." I left him there, standing silent in the company of the artificial dead, as I turned to enter Devin's office for the very last time.

The lights were off, casting the whole room into shadow. I paused at the doorway, just looking at the darkness. No one ever went into Devin's office without him, and he was never in the office with the lights off. He was really gone.

We'd have to come back later and search the place, tear it brick from brick to find out who might have known what he was planning, who he'd hired, what he'd paid them. For right now, that could wait; the dead weren't coming back, no matter what we did. The first aid kit was underneath the desk. I picked it up, wincing as the movement put pressure on my ribs, and turned toward the door. Then I paused, looking back toward the bulletin board on the wall. All those pictures . . .

Finding my picture was easy. Mitch towered above Julie and me, making us both look very small, and even younger than we were, in our brand-new street clothes and our nervous attempts at looking dangerous. I took out the tack, continuing to scan the board.

In the end, I found their picture by the eyes. That shade of glaring green even photographed too bright to overlook. I pulled the shot of Dare and Manuel off the wall, tucking it, and the picture of my little gang, into the back pocket of my jeans. Then I turned, leaving the ghosts behind me as I walked back out to where Manuel was waiting.

He wasn't waiting alone. I stopped in the doorway, blinking.

Help arrived while I was in the office, in the form of Sylvester Torquill and all the knights he'd been able to recall in the time it took for Lily's message to reach him. The knights were arrayed around the room, looking uncertain—what were they supposed to be fighting? There was nothing left standing—while Sylvester stood beside Manuel, sheathed sword hanging by his side.

"Hey, Your Grace," I said wearily. I walked toward him, putting the first aid kit down at his feet. "Please tell me you brought a car. I am so not taking another taxi."

"Are you hurt?" Sylvester reached out, wiping a smear of blood off my cheek. "Tell me this isn't yours."

"It's Devin's," I said. I could feel myself starting to cry. "Or Dare's, maybe. I don't know. I'm hurt, but I'll probably live."

Sylvester winced. "I'm so sorry. I called back the knights as soon as Lily told me where you were going, but the warding spells on the building were stronger than I expected them to be. We couldn't find our way in."

"There's a Coblynau charm above the door outside," I said, and frowned. "If you didn't find the sign, how did you . . . ?"

"We followed the night-haunts."

"Oh, oak and ash." I took a step forward, leaning my head against Sylvester's chest. "It was Devin. It was Devin all along. You were right. I should never . . . I should never have . . ."

"Shhh," he said, putting his arms around me. I made a pained noise, and he pulled back, eyes gone wide. "October?"

"Sorry." I forced a smile. "It's my ribs. I think they're broken."

"How?"

"Devin decided I needed some kicking." I indicated the first aid kit. "Think we can have somebody patch me up?"

"I'm taking you home with me. Both of you." Sylvester's tone left no room for argument. "You need to see Jin before I'll willingly let you out of my sight."

"Yes, Your Grace," I agreed.

Picking up the first aid kit, I put an arm around Manuel's shoulders and pulled him with me as we followed Sylvester out into the cleansing dark of the night outside.

Sylvester and his knights had come in three large white

vans that wouldn't have looked out of place in the parking lot of a dry cleaning service. Sylvester guided us to the middle van, taking the seat beside me. I flinched as I fastened my seat belt, trying to avoid putting pressure on my ribs. Then I closed my eyes, leaning back against the seat, and let myself relax. Sylvester could take care of things for a little while. That's what liege lords—and friends—are for.

We were swarmed by anxious faces when we reached Shadowed Hills, with Luna and Connor at the head of the pack. Rayseline was nowhere to be seen. Sylvester commanded me into the hands of Jin, the knowe's resident healer, and I went willingly, too exhausted to fight. She patched my ribs, shouted at me for reopening the wound in my shoulder, shouted at me more for failing to eat anything substantial for several days, and put me to bed with a stack of sandwiches and orders not to move without her permission. I was exhausted enough that I actually listened. Good thing, too; the sixteen hours I spent asleep in Shadowed Hills were the last moments of true relaxation I'd have for several weeks.

It took me a week to recover from everything that happened. When the magic-burn caught up with me after being delayed by Evening's curse and my brief contact with the hope chest, it caught up hard. Jin nursed me through the worst of it, and when I could walk again, she handed me over to Mitch and Stacy, who were all too happy to take me. I stayed with them for ten days, while the kids exploited me for every bit of spoiling they could get, and Mitch made regular runs to my place to pacify the landlord. He made sure my carpet got replaced. I almost thanked him for that.

Sylvester took charge of Manuel and of organizing a wake for Dare. She had no family but Manuel; no one in the mortal world would mourn for her. We buried the body the night-haunts left in the Summerlands, in the forest outside the walls of the ducal knowe, and Sylvester stood beside me, and held me when I cried. I was her hero, and I failed her. In the end, I was just like everyone else.

I visit her grave as often as I can. I leave bouquets of rosemary and rue, and I tell her that I'm sorry, and I promise her that next time, I'll do better. Next time someone makes me a hero, I'll save them.

It took three weeks to clear Devin's things out of Home. All the records he'd kept, all the things he'd stolen. Half his kids were never found; their things are in a storeroom at Shadowed Hills, waiting until their owners come to claim them. Somehow, I doubt that's ever going to happen. I wish things had been different. I'd give almost anything to have Evening insult me one more time, or to see Dare looking at me with hero worship in her eyes. But sometimes the pieces fall together the way they want to, and you can't change the story; all you can do is try to ride it out.

The last time we went Home, after everything worth saving had been removed, we went with torches, and with three fat salamanders in crystal jars. Sylvester put his hand on my shoulder, asking, "Are you sure you want to do this? I can, if you'd prefer."

"It's all right." I took the lid off the first of the jars, shaking the salamander out onto the sidewalk. It sat there, blinking opalescent eyes in dull reptilian confusion, until Sylvester tossed a lit torch through the open door of Home. It turned, suddenly interested, and raced swiftly forward to pursue the flame. Its siblings followed close behind it.

We managed to catch the salamanders before the fire trucks arrived, luring them back out of the flames with sticks of cinnamon wood and myrrh. The source of the fire was never determined.

Manuel has a place at Shadowed Hills for as long as he wants it. He's recovering from the loss of his sister, and he seems happy enough, most of the time. He doesn't have the fire in him that Dare had. Maybe that's for the best. He avoids me when I come to Shadowed Hills, and I let him. Someday he'll be able to look at me again. I can wait.

I've been at Shadowed Hills a lot more since Devin died. Luna's helping me get my P.I. license reinstated; walking away didn't work, so I may as well try going back willingly. Maybe if I'd done that in the first place, none of this would have happened. Connor and I pass each other in the halls; he tries to get me alone, and I try to avoid him. I'm just starting to get my life back. I won't trade it away that cheaply.

The hope chest was in my possession for two days after Tybalt returned it to me, and I never opened it. I never even touched it after the night I found it. That doesn't mean it didn't have the chance to change me. My headaches aren't as bad as they used to be. My night vision is sharper—still within the range of changeling-normal, but enough of a change that I can tell. If I'd touched the chest again . . .

The balance of my blood can hurt, but it's mine. I'd like to keep it that way. I gave the hope chest to the Queen. I still don't know why she wouldn't help me; I'm still afraid she's losing her mind, even though I don't know what I can do about it. There's not much that one changeling can do to challenge the highest-ranked noble in the Kingdom. For now, I'll watch and wait to see what happens.

I owe Tybalt for helping me, and the Queen owes me for returning the hope chest to the purebloods. She hates that debt more than I hate mine. She'll have to pay me someday—love makes the world go round, but favors keep Faerie standing. Sometimes I wonder how much of an enemy I made in the Queen by being involved in all this. I didn't have a choice, but I don't think that matters to her. There's something very wrong there. Meanwhile, the Luidaeg owes me, and that may be the most dangerous debt of them all. The day she pays it off, well, we'll cross that bridge when we come to it.

We never found the rest of Devin's assassins, but that doesn't matter; it's been long enough now that I need to stop jumping at shadows. I can't spend the rest of my life waiting for some underpaid goon to step out of the bushes and take me down: living that way isn't living at all. The mastermind died. The curse was fulfilled. At this point . . . everything else is just a matter of details.

I'm picking up the pieces of my old life, a few at a time; I'm catching up. It'll be a long process, and I'll never get back everything I've lost, but at least I've started trying. Someday, I'll find Simon and Oleander, and I'll make them pay for what they did. Someday, my daughter will let me be a part of her life again. There's plenty of time. Devin lost sight of that. I won't. As long as you're alive, there's time.

My name is October Christine Daye; I live in a city by the sea where the fog paints the early morning, parking is more precious than gold, and Kelpies wait for the unwary on street corners. Neither of the worlds I live in is quite mine, but no one can take them away from me. I did what had to be done, and I think I may finally be starting to understand what's important. It's all about finding the way home, wherever that is. I plan on finding out.

I have time.

Coming in March 2010
The second October Daye novel from

SEANAN McGUIRE
A LOCAL HABITATION

Read on for a sneak preview.

WAKING UP was complicated by the fact that I had absolutely no idea where I was. I opened my eyes, blinking at the ceiling. The air tasted like ashes. It wasn't long past dawn; that was probably what woke me.

The ceiling looked familiar. There was a water stain roughly the shape of Iowa in one corner, and that was enough to convince me that I was at home, in my own bedroom and—I glanced down at myself—still dressed for clubbing, in skimpy lace-trimmed tank top and miniskirt. Only the battered brown leather jacket seemed out of place. Maybe if I'd been trying out as the ingénue in an Indiana Jones movie . . .

I groaned, dropping my head back onto the pillow with a thump. "Oh, oak and *ash*." My memories of the previous night were fuzzy, but not fuzzy enough. As drunken mistakes go, letting Tybalt carry me home ranked high on the list. And he was never, ever going to let me forget it.

Pushing myself into a sitting position, I swung my feet around to the floor, kicking one of the shoes I'd been wearing the night before in the process. The remaining shoe was sitting atop my purse with my house key tucked into the heel.

"At least he's a considerate source of aggravation," I muttered, and stood, walking gingerly toward the kitchen.

Three heads of roughly the same size and shape poked over the back of the couch as I approached. Two were brown and cream, belonging to my half-Siamese cats, Cagney and Lacey. The third was gray-green and thorny, and belonged to Spike, the resident rose goblin.

"Morning," I said. The cats withdrew while Spike scrabbled fully into view, rattling its thorns in enthusiastic greeting. Adorable, if weird.

The concept of "name it and it's yours" has always been part of Faerie. Unfortunately, I didn't think about that until after I gave Spike a name, effectively binding it to me. Luna was too busy being glad I wasn't dead to mind my taking her rose goblin—she has more—and the cats stopped sulking as soon as they realized it didn't eat cat food. I don't mind having it around. It's pretty easy to take care of; all it really needs is mulch, potting soil, and sunlight.

My illusions had faded when the sun rose, leaving me looking like nothing but my half-Daoine Sidhe, half-human self, pointy ears and all. I'm no more suited to the human world than Spike is, thanks to some genetic gifts from my darling, clinically-insane mother. At least I can fake it when I need to, which makes grocery shopping a lot easier.

Most breeds of fae are nocturnal, and that includes the Daoine Sidhe. Circumstance arranges for me to be awake in the morning more often than I like, and that's why coffee has always been an important part of my balanced breakfast. After three cups, I wasn't feeling quite ready to face Tybalt again, but it was enough of a start to leave me willing to face the day. Mug in hand, I walked out of the kitchen and back toward my room. The first order of business: getting out of my club clothes, which smelled like alcohol and sweat. The second order of business: shower. After that, the day could start.

There was a note taped to the bedroom door.

I stopped, blinking. It didn't surprise me that I'd missed it in my pre-coffee stagger toward the kitchen; it surprised me that it existed at all. Wary of further surprises, I tugged it loose of the masking tape and unfolded it.

"October—

You were sleeping so peacefully that I was loath to wake you. Duke Torquill, after demanding to know what I was doing in your apartment, has requested that I inform you of his intent to visit after 'tending to some business at the Queen's Court.' I recommend wearing something clingy, as that may distract him from whatever he wishes to lecture you about this time. Hopefully, it's your manners.

You are truly endearing when you sleep. I attribute this to the exotic nature of seeing you in a state of silence.

—Tybalt"

The thought of Sylvester calling my apartment only to find himself talking to Tybalt was strangely fascinating. I stood there for a moment, contemplating its sheer unlikelihood. The idea that Tybalt had stayed in my apartment long enough to take a message was more worrisome, but since I didn't think he'd want to steal my silver—if I had any silver worth stealing—I decided to let it go.

Letting go of the thought didn't do anything to resolve my more immediate problem: Sylvester was coming to visit. I scanned the front of the apartment, taking note of the dishes on the table, the unfolded laundry piled on the couch and the heaps of junk mail threatening to cascade off the coffee table and conquer the floor. I'm not the world's best housekeeper. Combine that with the fact that I'd been regularly pulling eighteen-hour days since getting my PI license reinstated, and it was no wonder my apartment was a disaster zone. I just wasn't sure I wanted my liege to see it that way.

Unfortunately, I couldn't say "sorry, come back later." For all that my fourteen-year absence means that I'm currently somewhat outside the social order at Shadowed Hills, I'm still a knight errant in Sylvester's service. If he wants to drop by my apartment, he has every right to do so. Of course, his impending visit almost certainly meant he had a job for me. Swell. Nothing says "hangover recovery" like being called to active duty.

Spike was twining around my ankles. I knelt to pick it up, wincing as it settled to the serious business of kneading my forearms with needle-sharp claws.

"Come on, Spike. Let's get dressed." It kept purring as I carried it to the bedroom, calling over my shoulder, "Cagney, Lacey, watch the door." The cats ignored me. Cats are like that.

One advantage to being a changeling: my hangovers

are a lot milder than they should be. Thanks to the coffee, my head was almost clear by the time I finished my dramatically shortened shower. I got dressed at double speed, choosing practical clothing for what was bound to be a long day. I had just finished tying my shoelaces when someone knocked on the front door, the sound punctuated by the rattle of Spike's thorns.

"At least I'm not naked," I muttered, and rose.

Sylvester had his hand raised to knock again when I swept the door open in front of him. He stood there for a moment, looking almost comically startled. Then he smiled, offering me his hands. "October. Did Tybalt give you my message?"

"Hey, your Grace," I said, taking his hands for a second before allowing him to pull me into a hug. A human disguise covered his true features with the dogwood flower and daffodil smell of his magic. I've learned to find that particular combination of scents soothing. It means safety. "Yeah, he did. I'm sorry I missed your call."

"Oh, don't be. You don't sleep enough," he said, letting me go and stepping past me into the apartment. "I had no idea you and the King of Cats were getting on so well."

I reddened. "We're not. He followed me home."

Sylvester raised an eyebrow, saying more with a gesture than words could have expressed. I shut the door, resisting the urge to hunch my shoulders like a scolded teenager. There are some conversations I never wanted to have with my liege. "Why was the King of Cats answering your phone?" was the start of one of them.

Clearing his throat, he said, "I would have called sooner, but I only recently learned that I was needed at the Queen's Court."

"Do I even want to ask why?"

A shadow crossed his face, there and gone in an instant. "No."

"Right." We fell quiet, with me looking at him and him looking at my apartment. There was an aura of bewildered disapproval from his side of things, like he couldn't understand why I'd choose to live in a place like this when I had all the Summerlands to choose from. For all that Sylvester's one of the most tolerant nobles I've ever known, I knew that confusion was sincere. He really *didn't* understand, and there was no way I could possibly explain.

Sylvester's one of the Daoine Sidhe, the first nobility of Faerie. His hair is signal-flare red, and his eyes are a warm gold that would look more natural on one of the Cait Sidhe. There's nothing conventionally pretty about him, but when he smiles, he's breathtaking. Even dressed in a human disguise that blunted the points of his ears and layered a veneer of humanity over his otherwise too-perfect features, his essential nature came shining through.

All the Daoine Sidhe are like that. I swear, if they hadn't raised me, I'd hate them all on general principle.

"October, about your living conditions—"

I clapped my hands together. "Who wants coffee?"

"Please. But really, October, you know you're always welcome at—"

"Cream and sugar?"

"Both. But . . ." He paused, eyeing me. "We're still not having this conversation, are we?"

"Nope," I replied cheerfully, turning to step back into the apartment's tiny kitchen. "When I'm ready to come home for keeps, I'll let you know. For right now? It's hard to run a business when your mailing address is 'third oak tree at the top of the big hill.'"

"You wouldn't have to run a business if you lived in Shadowed Hills," he pointed out.

"No, but I *like* running a business, your Grace. It makes me feel useful. And it's helping me get reconnected with everything I missed. I'm not ready to give that up yet." I leaned out of the kitchen, passing him a mug of coffee. "Careful, it's hot. And besides, Raysel would kill me in my sleep."

He took the mug with a small moue of distaste, agreeing mournfully, "There is that, yes."

Rayseline Torquill is Sylvester's only daughter and currently, his only heir. There's just one problem. Thanks to Sylvester's brother, Simon—an evil bastard if there ever was one—she grew up in a magical prison, and the experience drove her largely insane. No one knows for sure what happened to her there, but from the look on her mother's face when I've asked about it, Simon was actually merciful when he turned me into a fish. There's something I never thought I'd say . . . but whatever happened to Raysel and her mother, it was worse.

Unfortunately, feeling sorry for Raysel doesn't change the fact that she's a sadistic nutcase. I would have been happy to keep my distance, but in addition to being the daughter of my liege, Raysel is convinced that her husband Connor—my sort-of-ex, and her spouse for purely diplomatic reasons—still has the hots for me. Even more unfortunately, she isn't wrong. It wasn't that we had an untrusting relationship; I simply trusted her to kill me if she got the chance.

I leaned up against the wall next to the kitchen doorway. "So what brings you here today? Beyond the urge to critique my housekeeping, I mean."

"I have a job for you."

"Figured on that part," I said, sipping my coffee. "What's the deal?"

"I need you to go to Fremont."

"What?" That wasn't what I'd been expecting him to

say. I wasn't entirely sure what I'd expected, but it wasn't Fremont.

Sylvester raised an eyebrow. "Fremont. It's a city, near San Jose?"

"I know." In addition to being a city near San Jose, Fremont was at the leading edge of the tech industry and one of the most boring places in California. Last time I'd checked it had a fae population that could be counted on both hands, because boring or not, it wasn't safe. It was sandwiched between two Duchies—Shadowed Hills and Dreamer's Glass—and had been declared an independent County three years after I vanished, partially on its own merits, but partially to delay the inevitable supernatural turf war.

The fae are territorial by nature. We like to fight, especially when we know we'll win. One of those Duchies was eventually going to decide it needed a new sunroom, and that little "independent County" was going to find itself right in the middle. The formation of Tamed Lightning may have been a good political move, but in the short-term, it guaranteed that living in Fremont wasn't for the faint of heart.

I couldn't think of many reasons to go to Fremont. Most of them involved diplomatic duty. I hate diplomatic duty. I'm not very good at it, largely because I'm not very diplomatic.

"Good. That makes this easier."

Diplomatic duty. It had to be. "Easier?"

"It's about my niece."

"Your niece?" Talking to Sylvester is sometimes an adventure in and of itself. "I didn't know you had a niece."

"Yes." He at least had the grace to look sheepish as he continued, saying, "Her name's January. She's my sister's daughter. We ... weren't advertising the relationship until recently, for political reasons. She's a lovely girl—a bit strange, but sweet—and I need you to go check on her." Sylvester was calling someone "a bit strange"? That didn't bode well. It was like the Luidaeg calling someone "a bit temperamental."

"So what's going on?"

"She can't visit often—political reasons, again—but she calls weekly to keep me updated. She hasn't called or answered her phone for three weeks. Before that, she seemed . . . distracted. I'm afraid there may be something wrong."

"You're sending me instead of going yourself or sending Etienne because . . . ?" Etienne became the head of Sylvester's guards before I was born. Better yet, he's purebred Tuatha de Dannan. He would have been a much better choice.

"If I go myself, Duchess Riordan could view it as an act of war." He sipped his coffee. "Etienne is known to be fully in my service, while you, my dear, currently possess a small amount of potential objectivity."

"That's what I get for not living at home," I grumbled. Dear, sweet Duchess Riordan, ruler of Dreamer's Glass and living proof that scum rises to the top. "So that's my assignment? Babysitting your niece?"

"Not babysitting. She's a grown woman. I just want you to check in and make sure she's all right. It shouldn't take more than two or three days."

That got my attention. *"Days?"*

"Just long enough to make sure that everything's all right. We're sending Quentin along to assist you, and Luna's made your hotel reservations."

Now it was my turn to raise an eyebrow. "You think I'm going to need assistance?"

"To be quite honest, I haven't the faintest idea." He looked down into his coffee cup, shoulders slumping. "Something's going on down there. I just don't know what it is, and I'm worried about her. She's always been one to bite off more than she can chew."

"Hey. Don't worry. I'll find out."

"Things may not be as . . . simple as they sound at first. There are other complications."

"Like what?"

"January is my niece, yes. She's also the Countess of Tamed Lightning."

My eyes widened. That put a whole new spin on the situation. January being Countess explained why Tamed Lightning had been able to become a full County in the first place; Dreamer's Glass might be willing to challenge one small County, but they wouldn't want to challenge the neighboring Duchy at the same time. Even if the relationship had been kept quiet, the people at or above the Ducal level would have known. Gossip spreads too fast in Faerie for something that juicy to be kept quiet. "I see."

"Then you must see how it makes this politically awkward."

"Dreamer's Glass could view it as the start of something bigger than family concern." I may not like politics, but I have a rudimentary understanding of the way they work.

"Exactly." He looked up. "No matter what's going on, Toby, I can't guarantee that I'll be able to send help."

"But you're sure this is an easy job."

"I wouldn't send Quentin if I didn't think you'd both be safe."

I sighed. "Right. I'll call regularly to keep you posted."

"And you'll be careful?"

"I'll take every precaution." How many precautions did I need? Political issues aside, it was a babysitting assignment. Those don't usually rank too high on the "danger" scale.

"Good. January's the only blood family I have left

in this country, except for Rayseline. Now, January's an adult, but I've considered her my responsibility since her mother passed away. Please, take care of her."

"What about—"

"I have no brother." His expression was grim.

"I understand, your Grace." The last time Sylvester asked me to take care of his family, my failure cost us both: he lost Luna, and I lost fourteen years. His twin brother, Simon, was the cause of both those losses. "I'm going to try."

"I appreciate it." He put his cup down on a clear patch of coffee table, pulling a folder out of his coat. "This contains directions, a copy of your hotel reservations, a local parking pass, and a map of the local fiefdoms. I'll reimburse any expenses, of course."

"Of course." I took the folder, flipping through it. "I can't think of anything else I'm likely to need." I looked up. "Why are you sending Quentin with me, exactly?"

"We're responsible for his education." A smile ghosted across his face. "Seeing how you handle things will be nothing if not educational."

I sighed. "Great. Where am I picking him up?"

"He's waiting by your car."

"He's what?" I groaned. "Oh, oak and *ash*, Sylvester, it's too damn early in the morning for this."

"Is it?" he asked, feigning innocence. Sylvester's wife, Luna, is one of the few truly diurnal fae I've ever met. After a few hundred years of marriage, he's learned to adjust. The rest of us are just expected to cope.

"I hate you."

"Of course you do." He chuckled as he stood. "I'll get out of your way and let you prepare. I'd appreciate it if you could leave immediately."

"Certainly, your Grace," I said, and moved to hug him before showing him to the door.

"Open roads and kind fires, Toby," he said, returning the hug.

"Open roads," I replied, and closed the door behind him before downing the rest of my coffee in one convulsive gulp.

Sending Quentin with me? What the hell were they thinking? This was already going to be half-babysitting assignment, half-diplomatic mission—the fact that I was coming from one of the Duchies flanking Tamed Lightning made the politics unavoidable. Now they were adding *literal* babysitting to the job. That didn't make me happy. After all, if Sylvester thought I was the best one to handle things, it was probably also going to be at least half natural disaster.

How nice.